THE VINYL DETECTIVE

UNDERSCORE

ANDREW CARTMEL

TITAN BOOKS

The Vinyl Detective: Underscore
Print edition ISBN: 9781803367989
E-book edition ISBN: 9781803367996

Published by Titan Books
A division of Titan Publishing Group Ltd
144 Southwark Street, London SE1 0UP
www.titanbooks.com

First edition: April 2025
10 9 8 7 6 5 4 3 2 1

EU RP
eucomply OÜ Pärnu mnt 139b-14 11317
Talinn, Estonia
hello@eucompliancepartner.com
+3375690241

Printed and bound by CPI Group (UK) Ltd, Croydon CR0 4YY.

Also by Andrew Cartmel
and available from Titan Books

The Vinyl Detective series

Written in Dead Wax
The Run-Out Groove
Victory Disc
Flip Back
Low Action
Attack and Decay
Noise Floor

The Paperback Sleuth series

Death in Fine Condition
Ashram Assassin
Like a Bullet

For Joe Kraemer, who writes music for the movies.

1: MENTION OF MURDER

Nevada was busy washing the dishes, which was fair enough since I'd cooked dinner.

But I don't want to downgrade her multi-tasking skills. My darling was also assiduously micromanaging my assignment of feeding the cats. "Put Fanny's bowl up on the counter, so Turk doesn't eat hers as well."

"How many years have I been doing this?" I asked. The answer was, since before I'd met Nevada, and since Fanny and Turk were kittens.

"I know, I know," said Nevada contritely. "But it's the bavette beef and you know how they go nuts over that."

I was indeed aware of our little carnivores' enthusiasm for this particular cut, also known less pretentiously as "skirt".

I put one bowl with the carefully diced bavette, or skirt, on the floor for the impatiently waiting Turk and then set the other one up on the counter, safely out of Turk's immediate reach. She looked at me with her disquieting turquoise eyes and made a noise of sour reprimand. Turk clearly disagreed with Nevada about the whole policy of keeping her sibling's dinner safe.

"It's only fair, little one," said Nevada at the sink. "Your sister has to have her good food, too."

Turk made a noise that could only be interpreted as indecorous contradiction and then settled down to the serious business of devouring beef. "I hope Fanny comes home soon," said Nevada. "I worry about her when she's out."

The doorbell rang. "Perhaps that's her now," I said.

"Ha ha, very funny," said Nevada, somewhat insincerely. She leaned over the sink and craned her head to look out the window and see who our visitor might actually be. I took the more direct approach of just going to the front door and opening it. I fully expected to be confronted with Tinkler, our ever-present and only occasionally irritating friend, here to cadge a meal, smoke weed with my sweetheart and listen to music with me, while sharing with us both his hopeless lust and devotion for a mutual pal.

But I couldn't have been more wrong.

Instead of chubby, affable and only intermittently annoying Tinkler I was confronted with a very slender and very nervous young woman.

She had long, straight blonde hair which looked like a blatant dye job to me, though I'd have to run it past Nevada for an expert opinion. Framed by that hair, her face was potentially pretty. Indeed she possessed something of the bloodless beauty of a girl in a high tower in a fairy tale, though at the moment she was robbed of any such quality by a very evident tension. She had blue-green eyes and it's probably wrong of me to have found them all the more appealing because they reminded me of those of my cat, currently greedily eating her dinner on the kitchen floor.

Our guest also had a small gold ring through one of her nostrils, which matched another one in her navel, which was on display along with a band of very flat, very pale belly in the gap between the snug black tube top she wore and her baggy grey trousers, which were made of some kind of corduroy with fat thick cords. (Nevada would subsequently tell me this was called elephant corduroy; and confirm the dye job.) The girl's dazzling white trainers matched the white Puffa jacket whose notional role in keeping out the unseasonal biting chill of this midsummer evening was largely checkmated by being worn wide open, along with bare midriff, etc.

But being cold seemed like the very least of her concerns as our visitor gave me an intense stare.

"I'm Desdemona Higgins," she said.

"Okay…" I said, somewhat relieved to sense the sudden and comforting presence of Nevada at my back. And not just because this was rather an odd name.

"We have to talk," said Desdemona Higgins.

"In that case," said Nevada over my shoulder, "you'd better come inside."

The women went into the living room and sat down while I went into the kitchen to make coffee. Turk had finished her dinner, leaving an exemplary clean bowl on the floor, and obviously had designs on her sister's portion, its careful placement up on the counter being no serious impediment to a cat who could jump up the way Turk could. Indeed she was standing tall and alert on her hind legs now, sussing out Fanny's bowl and evidently preparing to make just such a jump.

She sank down on her haunches again as I came in, clearly disappointed that her fiendish scheme had been derailed. When it became obvious that I would be in the kitchen for some while, she gave up in disgust, making a small contemptuous sound as she strode out.

I kept my ears open as I made the coffee but what I heard from the living room was mostly silence. And when I carried the three mugs through—our best instant, but a long way from our best coffee; this is the most that mysterious, uninvited visitors could expect on a summer's eve—both women looked up at me in relief. It had clearly been a rather tense silence.

We made brief and sporadic small talk, with Desdemona Higgins thanking me and saying it was good coffee. But I could have told her that. Finally Nevada decided to cut the crap and ask why she was there.

Desdemona looked at us over her mug. She hesitated as though summoning courage, then all at once blurted out, "We know she's been here to talk to you."

I noticed the plural pronoun and I saw that Nevada had registered it, too. There was something a little disturbing in our mystery visitor being only one member of a shadowy group described as "we". Beyond that, this was a baffling statement since I had no idea who "she" might be—more mystery pronoun fun. Nor I imagine did Nevada.

Our friend Agatha—the mutual chum upon whom Tinkler lavished his hopeless devotion and lust—would normally be the most plausible pronoun candidate, being a regular visitor. But Agatha hadn't been a regular visitor lately because she was away on an extended holiday touring the Blue Coast. So that seemed to exclude her as a possibility.

I glanced at Nevada. The look she gave me said to give nothing away. She seemed content to wait and see if our visitor would give anything away herself. Which Desdemona did soon enough, setting her coffee aside and wrapping her Puffa jacket more tightly around her, as if she was cold in our nice, warm living room. She peered out at us, a small face nestled inside the bulky garment, and said, "Everybody knows what her grandfather did to our grandmother."

This sounded dispiritingly like a family feud being pointlessly perpetuated over generations and something I would be only too glad to stay out of. But Nevada was in charge of negotiations here and she was still playing her cards close to the chest.

"Everybody knows, you say?" she said.

"All right, it's an obscure case now," allowed Desdemona, leaning forward and letting her jacket fall open again. "After all these years. But back in the day it was a *cause célèbre*." I saw a flicker of surprise from Nevada at this correct use of a French phrase and I could tell she was a little impressed despite herself. "And we know the truth," said Desdemona. "We know her grandfather did it."

She looked at me and then at Nevada.

"He killed her."

At this statement Nevada and I, who had been staying carefully silent, became even more silent and even more careful.

"He's a murderer," said Desdemona. "It's as simple as that."

Nevada and I looked at each other, wondering what we were getting drawn into here.

Nothing at all, if I had any say in it.

"All this business about clearing his name," said Desdemona. "It's delusional."

"Delusional?" said Nevada. "That's rather a strong word." She was doing a masterful job of holding her own in a conversation that was like driving through thick fog.

And now, with the mention of murder, I was beginning to wonder if it might be just as dangerous...

"He was never sentenced for the crime," said Desdemona, looking from Nevada to me and back again. She seemed to have concluded that Nevada was the one who made the decisions here, and she wasn't necessarily wrong. "But everybody knew he did it," she said. "They knew he was guilty as hell." Desdemona had now locked eyes with Nevada. "So you see, it's pointless you taking the job."

"Pointless, you say?" said Nevada politely.

"We already know the outcome. We already know the truth. So there's nothing for you to find out." Desdemona suddenly slithered out of her white Puffa jacket, like a serpent shedding a very swollen skin. Apparently she'd finally had enough of sweating inside it in our nice, warm house. Or maybe she only now felt sufficiently comfortable to take it off, as though it had been some kind of protective armour she couldn't remove until she was sure she was safe.

But a third possibility was that it was some kind of sexual challenge. Desdemona was considerably less skinny than she'd looked shrouded in her thick jacket. In fact she had a rather voluptuous body which she now seemed intent on displaying for us. She and Nevada looked at each other, fixedly and steadily, as if each was daring the other to blink.

"Or maybe you know all that, and you decided to take the job anyway." Desdemona's voice had taken on a satirical, sing-song quality, as though she was mocking us. "Despite knowing it's pointless, despite knowing it's cruel to give Chloë false hope."

Needless to say, we had no idea who Chloë might be.

Desdemona was smiling a humourless little smile. "But perhaps you don't care about that. Because all you care about is the money."

Nevada considered this for a moment and then said, "So, you don't want us to take the job?"

"That's right."

"Perhaps you'd like to *pay* us not to take the job."

Even knowing Nevada as well as I did, I was impressed at how swiftly and coolly my honeypie was transforming this cryptic encounter into a potential salaried gig.

Desdemona blinked with surprise. "Pay you?"

Nevada shrugged, exuding her coolest cool. "Didn't you just say that all we care about is the money? In that case, since you also say you want us to stay out of things, wouldn't it make perfect sense to take advantage of our shallowness and greed by *paying* us to stay out of those things? Anyway, it's certainly one possibility."

It certainly was. And judging by the thoughtful expression that now settled on Desdemona's face, it was one she didn't seem averse to considering. For the first time since her arrival, she lost her worried, hunted look and began to seem genuinely at ease. Nevada glanced at me. There was a flash of mischief in my beloved's eyes, as much as to say, *We might be about to get paid for doing nothing at all.*

Any chance of this, admittedly pleasant, prospect vanished with the sudden sound of a peremptory knocking on our front door. We were all startled, but it was interesting to note that this startlement didn't translate for Desdemona—the most nervous member of our group—into any kind of anxiety.

Instead, she looked distinctly annoyed.

I went to the door and opened it. A young man was standing there. He was very tall and very thin, and doing a remarkably fine job of wearing a hooded jacket made of various kinds of mismatched tartan without looking ridiculous. After the spectacle of that jacket, his jeans and trainers were disappointingly ordinary. He had fair, wavy hair and bright, watchful eyes in a narrow face with a sharp nose. It was intriguing how he managed to look simultaneously weaselly and handsome.

"Sorry to trouble you," he said in an aristocratic drawl, "but I think my sister…"

Even before he said the word *sister*, I had realised that there was a family resemblance between this young man in his tartan hoodie and our visitor in her elephant cords. It was chiefly in the distinctive, close-set eyes, which were now looking past me, down the hall, to where Desdemona had appeared from the sitting room, followed by Nevada who looked both amused and intrigued. Desdemona on the other hand seemed rather angry.

"This is my brother," she sighed. It was an elaborately disgusted sigh.

"Cass," said the young man. This was apparently his name. "Pleased to meet you." He then set about busily shaking my hand and Nevada's.

He was inside the house now, good and proper, so I surrendered to the inevitable and shut the door behind him, repressing the urge to make some disgusted sighs of my own. This was supposed to be a quiet evening at home for Nevada and I and the cats. With, at most, Tinkler in the way of uninvited guests. And Tinkler at least was a known quantity.

"My brother, who was supposed to be waiting in the car," added Desdemona.

"I got worried," said Cass. "I was concerned for your safety. You've been in here for ages."

"No I haven't. And you are not concerned for my safety. You just couldn't resist sticking your nose in."

They were siblings all right. We led them into the living room, where Cass and Desdemona settled in the armchairs and Nevada and I sat on the sofa, as though we'd rehearsed these moves.

Desdemona was saying, "Oh well, since you're here, since you insist on being here, you might as well be part of this discussion."

"What discussion?" Cass looked suddenly alert. I decided that, despite his taste in jackets, he wasn't entirely a fool after all.

"I was just suggesting," said Nevada smoothly, "that you could pay us for staying out of it."

We didn't even know what "it" was, yet it looked like she was ready, willing and able to begin haggling over an exact figure for our remuneration.

"Stay out of it?" said Cass.

"Yes."

"You want us to pay you?" said Cass.

"Just a suggestion," said Nevada, all silky charm.

"You shouldn't need to be paid," said Cass decisively. "You should just be glad to do the decent thing."

"When was the last time anyone did the decent thing?" said his sister.

So cynical for one so young, I thought.

"When was the last time *you* did the decent thing?" she added. Now it was her brother Desdemona was locking eyes with. She really was quite combative.

Nevada let the sibling hostility simmer for a moment or two and then said, "But if you're asking us to forego work, to forfeit potential income…" she was warming to her theme here, "then surely you should be willing to compensate us."

"It's not in the budget," snapped Cass.

He had a knack for making decisive declarations. Without, I thought, possessing all the facts. Not that Nevada and I could be said to possess all the facts here either. Or indeed any of them.

"Why not?" said Desdemona.

"Why not what?" said Cass.

"Why isn't it in the budget?" said Desdemona. "We haven't even finalised the budget. How can you know it isn't in the budget?"

Cass made a sound which was a posh, drawling version of his sister's disgusted sigh. "Because I know that Jasper won't buy it," he said.

At this point warning bells began to sound in my head.

How many people called Jasper could there be?

Even allowing for the fact that Cass was a posh buffoon and would inevitably know other posh buffoons and that Jasper was a posh buffoon sort of name… I looked over at Nevada, who met my gaze. You didn't have to be a registered telepath to know she was thinking the same thing.

But I was the one who took the plunge. "Jasper McClew?" I said.

The brother and sister looked at me, surprised and impressed. I was a little embarrassed to realise how pleased I was about the impressed bit. But that look faded swiftly and my pleased glow along with it.

"That's right," said Desdemona. "Jasper said you knew him."

"He said you'd interfered with his investigative journalism before," said Cass.

There was so much to get angry—indeed furious—about here that it was hard to know where to start. But Nevada beat me to it. "Investigative journalism?" she said.

"Yes," said Cass.

"He's calling himself an investigative journalist now?" said Nevada.

"Well, what else is he?" said Desdemona.

"A guy with an internet connection," I said.

They stared at me blankly, so Nevada enlarged on the theme. "He is, at best, a guy with an internet connection," she said. "Although I suppose anyone can call themselves a journalist or an investigator these days."

"Jasper told us you'd be hostile," said Desdemona.

"We're not hostile," said Nevada. "We're just realistic. Would you like some coffee, Cass?"

This sudden piece of left-field politeness seemed to surprise and wrongfoot our guests. It certainly surprised and wrongfooted me, since I was the chump who'd have to make and fetch said coffee, which I proceeded to do when Cass accepted the offer with reciprocal politeness and a certain amount of aristocratic aplomb. As I boiled the kettle and spooned the instant, making enough for all of us, I realised what Nevada was up to.

By taking the emotional temperature down in the room and putting things on a courteous social footing she was setting the scene for a further valiant attempt to fleece our guests. She was good at this, and was liable to try anything short of turning them upside down and shaking them to see if money came out of their pockets.

As I served the coffee, Desdemona said, "So what did she tell you about us?"

Not at all deterred by being presented with a question she had no answer to, Nevada gave me a bright smile as I handed her a mug. She was positively enjoying herself. She was really in her element here. "I'm sure you'll understand," she said, "that if we are working for someone, we have to maintain client confidentiality."

This was a lovely sally because it was entirely true while confirming nothing and giving away nothing at all, yet also maintaining the illusion that we were totally on top of what the hell was going on here. When in fact we knew effectively nothing.

"Of course," said Cass, giving his sister a look which suggested she was a peasant and an oaf to have even asked such a question.

"Do you know where she's staying?" said Desdemona abruptly.

"Chloë?" said Nevada. It was the obvious inference, but still, full marks to her for remembering the name.

"Yes," said Desdemona.

Her brother was staring at her, aghast, but she went on. "Do you happen to know where she might be staying?"

For her part, Desdemona's expression was suddenly one of beseeching need. To my surprise, I found my heart going out to her. Brother Cass, however, definitely didn't feel the same way. "Listen, Des…" he said, in a low threatening voice.

Desdemona ignored him and kept looking at Nevada. Her big eyes, so reminiscent of our cat's, were pleading silently. And, as if this wasn't enough, she began pleading aloud. "Perhaps if I could talk to her directly…" she said.

"*Des*," snarled Cass.

Everyone ignored him, which he didn't like much.

Nevada met Desdemona's piteous gaze and said, "I'm not sure that's such a good idea." A handy phrase which, when you think about it, could be applied to just about any situation.

"She does *not* want to know where that woman is," said Cass.

"Yes I fucking do," said Desdemona. It was impressive how quickly they'd got to the stage of swearing at each other, in front of total strangers. That's families for you. Although I suppose it could be argued that she hadn't sworn directly at him. "You are not going to tell me what I'm going to do," she added.

"Somebody has to," said Cass. "When clearly you don't know what's good for you."

"What's good for me? And I suppose you know what's good for me?"

"Better than you do."

"I just want to talk to Chloë."

"All I'm saying," said Cass, "is that you're not exactly disinterested where she's concerned."

"Oh, go fuck yourself," said Desdemona.

Well, she'd definitely sworn directly at him this time.

He turned to look at us for sympathy or support, and he might even have received some of the former, but just then the doorbell rang.

Suddenly the hostility between the siblings evaporated and they assumed identical looks of furtive fear, like two little kids caught doing something they shouldn't. "Is that her?" they said in perfect unison.

I looked at Nevada. There was only one way to find out.

Nevada turned to them and smiled and said, "And what if it is?"

I didn't hear what their response, if any, might be to this rather brilliant quip from my honey because I went to the front door and opened it. I must confess I was a little disappointed to find that instead of the second mystery woman of the evening it was merely Tinkler come to call.

He grinned his trademark cockeyed grin at me and said, "What's happening?"

"I could hardly begin to tell you," I said, and led him inside.

In the living room Cass and Desdemona were both on their feet, ready and tense, though for what and why I couldn't guess. As soon as they saw Tinkler they both relaxed—sagged, actually—and assumed identical expressions of relief. Although it only took an instant for Desdemona's expression to change to something more like disappointment.

I introduced Tinkler. Cass, who evidently liked shaking hands, shook his hand energetically while Desdemona sank back into her chair and continued to look disappointed. I'm sure Tinkler wasn't offended. He would have been used to his arrival engendering this kind of reaction by now.

"I'm Cass and this is Des," said Cass.

"Nice to meet you," said Desdemona from the armchair in which she was slumped. Her expression of profound disappointment didn't alter, but I was impressed by the bright friendliness of her voice which apparently was something she could conjure up entirely on autopilot.

"Well, we'd better be going," said Cass, also in a bright

and friendly voice. He was every bit as convincing as his sister. We might have just spent a convivial evening together and he was reluctantly tearing himself away from our company. "Come on, Des," he said. And Desdemona, whom I didn't see as being big on obedience, on this occasion rose obediently from her armchair and accompanied him to the door. We saw them out. Tinkler didn't join us. He was already nosing around my record collection, knowing all too well where I kept the new vinyl arrivals.

We watched Desdemona and Cass disappear into the darkening summer evening, made quite sure that they were gone and then returned to the living room.

"What was that all about?" said Tinkler.

"We have no idea," I said.

"We have some idea," said Nevada. "And it could involve money."

"And murder," I said.

"Just a typical day at *chez* Vinyl Detective," said Tinkler.

"You can't say 'at chez'," said Nevada, making no attempt to hide her scorn. "Chez already means 'at'."

"Consider my education ongoing," said Tinkler. "I haven't missed supper, have I?"

2: CHLOË

Tinkler got his meal, salmon and butterbean salad with marinated red onion, capers and fresh mint. He tucked into it with a level of enthusiasm which matched the way our cats attacked their diced bavette. Tinkler hoovered up the salad and asked for seconds, despite his complaints about being given leftovers. "Leftover by about twenty minutes," said Nevada.

He might even be said to have earned this supper because, after eating and listening to details—what few we had—of our encounter with Cass and Desdemona and hearing the mention of our old friend Jasper McClew, he went online and after a little adroit searching found a page stylishly designed in black and white with bright red highlights that featured a moody monochrome photograph of Mr McClew himself.

"The photographer who took that picture is a genius," said Nevada.

"Because they made him look good?" said Tinkler.

"Because they made him look human."

"A bit harsh," said Tinkler. He then proceeded to chortle over the text, which was headlined *McClew's Clues*.

"I wonder how long it took them to dream up that zinger?" said Tinkler.

Beneath this title, slightly smaller lettering boasted *A True Crime Podcast Solving the Coldest of Cold Cases…*

The surprising level of professionalism and general slickness on show in the design was somewhat undermined by the banner at the bottom which read *Website Under Construction*, and the fact there weren't actually any podcasts available yet.

"So Desdemona and what's-his-name…" said Tinkler.

"Cass," said Nevada. "I wonder if that's short for Cassio?"

"Why?" said Tinkler.

"Because they're both names from *Othello*, you lout."

"No need to get personal. We can't all be Shakespeare scholars."

"Full marks for knowing it's Shakespeare, though," said Nevada.

"I know more than that."

"Really?"

"I know it's not a great play to name your children after." Tinkler took out a small, flat, pink tin from his pocket and removed cigarette papers and a tiny plastic bag of vegetable matter from it. "Tragic ending and all that."

"Desdemona and Cassio are the two most blameless characters in it," said Nevada.

"Being…?"

"Being Othello's wife and his best friend."

"Both of whom came to a sticky end, right?"

"Well done, Tinkler," I said. "You're showing a surprising depth of knowledge."

He grinned and held up the small plastic bag. "Once I've smoked some of this, I'll probably be able to recite the whole play from memory."

"Please don't," said Nevada.

"Anyway, see my earlier comment about being lousy names for your kids."

"Cassio gets out of it okay," said Nevada. "He ends up as governor of Cyprus."

"Yay Cassio," said Tinkler. "Governor of Cyprus. Impressive."

"But Desdemona…" Nevada trailed off and Tinkler looked up at her with sudden and atypical alertness.

"Murdered, right?" he said.

Nevada nodded. "Strangled," she said thoughtfully.

"Bummer," said Tinkler.

There was silence for a moment in our little house and then Nevada said, "Why are we even talking about them?"

"Desdemona and Cassio?" said Tinkler.

"Desdemona and Cass, who *might* be called Cassio," said Nevada.

"Count on it." Tinkler was studiously assembling a joint. He showed impressive skill and dexterity in this enterprise, but then he was highly motivated. "We're talking about them because they're apparently assisting Jasper McClew with his true crime podcast." He paused in joint-assembly to make air quotes with his fingers for both "true crime" and "podcast". "In some capacity or other."

"Presumably they're providing the true crime," I said.

"Which is their grandfather murdering what's-her-name's grandmother?"

"Chloë," said Nevada. "And it's the other way around."

"Their grandmother murdering her grandfather?"

"No," said Nevada. "Stop it. Now you're making me confused."

I stepped in at this point. "They said Chloë's grandfather murdered their grandmother."

"Thank you for the clarification. Whichever way round it is, it all sounds like it happened a long, long time ago." Tinkler licked the cigarette paper, sealing the weed inside.

"Cold case," I said.

"The coldest of cold cases," quoted Nevada.

"Website under construction," quoted Tinkler. He held up his creation, an admirably neat, thin white cylinder and waggled it invitingly at her. "Going to help me smoke this?"

Nevada shook her head. "No thanks."

"What?"

"Sorry, after what happened earlier, I'm not in the mood."

"You're going to let unexpected visitors turning up in the middle of the night and talking about murder, ancient murder at that, put you off smoking *drugs*? Tut-tut. Shows a distinct lack of moral fibre."

Nevada smiled. "I just want to keep a clear head."

"Oh foolish child."

"At least for the time being."

"That's more like it," said Tinkler. "Meanwhile I shall go outside and smoke this one in the garden."

"Thank you, Tinkler. That's very considerate of you."

"I'm Mr Considerate." Tinkler waved the neat little spliff at us. "And, remember, there's plenty more where this came from." He opened the back door. "Now, Fanny are you going to join me in the garden? Wait a minute, this is Turk."

Nevada sighed. "And you're not even stoned yet."

"I corrected myself, didn't I? Come on, Turk."

Duly accompanied by the cat, he went out into the back garden, taking care to shut the door behind him so as not to catch her tail in it. Nevada and I exchanged a look. Whatever we might have been about to say to one another, we never got around to it.

Because at that point the doorbell rang. Again.

We stared at each other.

I got up to go and answer it, experiencing a brief, swooning swoop of déjà vu. I walked down the hallway with Nevada at my side, and opened the front door. It was night now, and the creamy smell of our lilac came riding into the house on a flow of cool air.

Standing there looking at us was a petite young woman. She had a sweetly appealing elfin face, haloed by an impressive mass of black curly hair. She was wearing a baggy T-shirt, tie-dyed in trippy shades of pink and green, and long denim shorts which looked like a skirt until you noticed it was split in the middle into separate legs. Her feet were shod in what looked like serious hiking boots, low cut in sturdy chocolate brown leather with pale blue laces and pale blue trim. The boots went with the large and serious rucksack on her back.

She looked for all the world like she might be in search of a youth hostel to spend the night in. But this impression was immediately dispelled when she smiled at us and said, "Hello, I'm sorry it's so late." She fixed her gaze on me. "Are you the Vinyl Detective?"

"Yes," I said. I'd given up prevaricating on this point.

"And I'm Nevada," said Nevada.

"My name is Chloë Loconsole."

Nevada smiled back at her. "You'd better come in, Chloë."

More, though milder, déjà vu buzzed through my brain as I went back into the kitchen to make some coffee.

This time I used the good stuff. It seemed called for. And I was glad I did. The smell coming from the mugs stirred something deep in my nervous system and caused my spirits to lift and my energy reserves to rally as I carried the tray of refreshments towards the living room, walking down the hallway past Chloë's backpack which was standing alertly against the wall, parked there like a patient pet, or a small and exceptionally well-behaved child.

Nevada gave me a dazzling smile as I joined her and Chloë. In striking contrast to the earlier interlude with Desdemona, there had been a steady flow of animated conversation coming from the living room all the while I was gone. This paused momentarily as I handed out the mugs.

I have to admit that Chloë won my heart by the way she sniffed the coffee and her face lit up with pleased surprise. She knew quality when she smelled it.

She didn't say anything, but she didn't have to. I could tell by the appreciative way she sipped it that here was a woman who wouldn't have been satisfied with the instant.

Nevada said, "I've just been filling Chloë in on our usual terms and conditions, darling."

"We have terms and conditions now, do we?" I said. I sipped my own coffee and felt the unique combination of stimulation and relaxation which the magic elixir provided flowing through me. Both the women smiled at me.

"Chloë has a record for you to find," said Nevada.

"I'm pleased to hear it," I said. This wasn't entirely true. After Cass and Desdemona's hit-and-run visit, I didn't particularly want any part of what sounded like a potentially very messy affair. And Jasper McClew being in the mix certainly didn't make it sound any more inviting. But at least I was on familiar, or anyway recognisable, terrain if someone wanted me to look for a record.

And, I have to admit, I was instantly intrigued.

"What record?" I asked.

Chloë set aside her mug—reluctantly, I was pleased to note—and said, "It's a film soundtrack. The music underscore. And I'm really hoping you might be able to locate a copy for me."

Her English was perfect but, as she spoke at greater length, I began to detect the faint echo of an accent. And in the lights of the living room I could see that her skin was darker than it had first appeared. A sort of golden-bronze shade which contrasted sharply in my mind, for some reason, with the very pale skin of Desdemona Higgins.

Anyway, all in all, Chloë had a continental look which went naturally with the backpacker vibe. My guess was that she was Spanish or Italian. "It's an LP that was only released in England," she said. "In 1969."

"It's very rare," said Nevada. "And hard to find." She said this happily because rare and hard to find equated to a commensurately large payday for us.

"It's part of the Lansdowne Series," said Chloë.

This instantly got my attention. Lansdowne was a sublabel of EMI/Columbia and it had featured some of the best, and most desirable, British jazz albums of the 1960s, which changed hands for insane sums of money. Mind you, it had also featured the Hawaiian guitar music of Wout Steenhuis. Which didn't.

"What's the record called?" I said.

"*Murder in London.*" Chloë picked up her coffee and took a sip. "It's by Loretto Loconsole."

"He's the musician?" I said.

"The composer, yes. He was my *nonno*."

"*Nonno*," said Nevada, all scholarly linguistic interest. "That's Italian for grandfather?"

"Yes. My grandpa."

With the coffee buzzing in my brain, all my senses were now on high alert.

We know her grandfather did it.

Chloë looked at me. "You have some of his music here.

My *nonno*'s music." She gestured towards the racks of LPs on the far side of the room.

I bit back my immediate impulse to contradict her. It seemed rude to do so. But I was pretty sure I was right and she was wrong, and I didn't have anything by her grandfather. After all, it was my record collection.

As if reading my thoughts—or perhaps my face, Nevada always said I had a lousy poker face—Chloë smiled at me, rose to her feet and crossed the room to the record shelf. She reached into the section where Various Artists were meticulously, some might say obsessively, filed under "V", and carefully slid out a double album in a gatefold sleeve.

It was one of Rocco Pandiani's lavish compilations of 1960s Italian film music on the Easy Tempo label. Nevada watched with interest as Chloë opened it and handed it to me. She pointed at the text printed inside the cover, listing the tracks by the various artists. Sure enough, there on side two was one called 'Raspberry Shrapnel' from a film called *The Daughter of Autumn*.

And it was by Loretto Loconsole.

It seemed the least I could do, having been proved so decisively wrong about my own record collection, to now play this for our guest. I went over to the hi-fi system and crouched down on the floor to turn on the Audio Note monoblocks. As I clicked the switches, the big 300B valves began to quietly glow in a way which would gladden the heart of any audiophile. Chloë came over to see what I was doing.

"These really should have been warming up earlier," I

said, glancing up at her. "Sorry." I didn't add that, if not for the unforeseen intrusion of good old Cass and Desdemona, the amplifiers would indeed have been on and warming up, quite some while ago.

"What fantastic tube amps," said Chloë, looking down over my shoulder. She scored numerous points with me just for knowing what these big constructions of metal and glass were called, let alone admiring them. Though I was interested to note she used American terminology.

I rose from the floor again, having finished kneeling at the shrine of hi-fi, so to speak, and switched on the pre-amp. This was more tube—or, if you were English, valve—equipment, also courtesy of Audio Note. But it lived above floor level, supported on an attractive cherrywood shelf unit that also housed the turntable, plus the phono stage and, much less importantly of course, the CD player.

Chloë was still looking appreciatively at the power amps, not something one can often say about an attractive young woman. Or, in this case, two attractive young women because Nevada, never one to be left out, had now joined her. "He built them himself," she said, proudly, her hand on my shoulder.

This was true enough, though I'd actually assembled the amplifiers from a kit. Admittedly, this in itself had been fairly challenging, involving as it did deciphering circuit diagrams which might have baffled a large team at Bletchley Park and performing meticulous soldering (using silver solder, naturally) at the cost of at least one permanent burn mark on a knuckle. Every man should have a few scars.

But the way Nevada had described it sounded like I'd

personally mined and smelted the ore for the transformers. Maybe that's what a true audiophile would have done.

I took the record out of the sleeve, lifted the Perspex lid on the Garrard, and settled the gleaming black LP on the spindle. Behind me, Chloë was examining the Quads. I turned to see her running her hand across the top of one, as though caressing a big, friendly beast. "And these are speakers?"

"Yup."

"They're electrostatics," said Nevada, with an air of casual expertise which hid the fact that this was about all she could have told you about them.

"They're very elegant," said Chloë.

"Thank you," said Nevada, as if she'd built them.

I clicked the switch to set the platter turning at as close to exactly thirty-three-and-a-third RPM as fine British precision engineering could achieve back in 1958, released the fiddly lock on the SME arm and lowered the needle onto the now-rotating record at exactly the point where Chloë's *nonno*'s tune began. Music filled the room.

It had a jazzy bossa nova feel, featuring Hammond organ, some very adroit tenor sax and as much groovy wordless female vocals as anyone could ask for.

Recorded, I'd noted, in 1967, it was an altogether warm, trippy, infectious sound. A lot of Italian music from this period had a similar vibe, and it sounded as great now as it had back then. Timeless rather than dated. This vast treasure trove of tunes had been rediscovered and embraced by twenty-first-century hipsters under the rubric of lounge music. The original pressings were hopelessly hard to find and commensurately expensive, so discriminating connoisseurs and savvy entrepreneurs—and our friend Rocco Pandiani was both—had set about reissuing the cream of the music on newly founded and very hip record labels. Hence Easy Tempo, which did an exemplary job expertly curating these painstaking and invaluable reissues of such rare material.

You might think you've never heard anything in this vein, but the odds are you have…

For a start there is the crazily infectious song (again, wordless) 'Mah Nà Mah Nà', immortalised in a cover version by the Muppets and played millions of time all over the world. Deriving from the soundtrack of an obscure Italian skin flick, it's a work of genius by Piero Umiliani, one of the giants of the genre, and of course a favourite of mine. Another favourite would be 'Richmond Bridge' by another Piero—Piero Piccioni—a piece I particularly love and not just because we live near the handsome old eponymous bridge.

It was one of the unusual characteristics of the Quad electrostatics that, although they possess a central sweet spot, they sound great everywhere in the room, even behind the speakers. Which was where I was now standing, happily watching the turntable while I listened. I turned around to see that the infectious music had had its effect. Chloë was shamelessly bopping around the room in time to it, and Nevada had shamelessly joined her. I watched the women dance. Nevada was pretty good and, though I'd never admit as much aloud, Chloë was even better—although both of them would have been effortlessly outclassed if Agatha had been here.

It was a pleasure to be presented with this spectacle and I wondered how many young men in London were lucky enough to be enjoying such a show.

Two, was suddenly the answer as the back door abruptly opened.

The women paused in their bopping and looked around.

"Don't stop on my account, for heaven's sake," said Tinkler.

"The music has ended anyway," said Chloë.

It had, now. Chloë casually sank back into an armchair, but she kept her face towards Tinkler in a manner which might have been merely friendly, or might have been cautiously watchful. I noticed also she'd changed armchairs, this time sitting in the one nearest the front door, as if getting ready in case she needed to make a dash, grab her rucksack and escape.

I hoped she wouldn't do any of these things. I was enjoying our musical excursion. Not to mention those fine dance floor moves in my living room. I went to the turntable. Chloë's *nonno*'s tune had been the last track on that side of the LP and the needle was now riding hissing in the run-out groove. I lifted the arm up and away, ending the hiss, and took the record off the platter.

Tinkler was saying, "I heard the music and I had to come in. I'm Jordon, by the way."

"Hello, Jordon." Chloë remained friendly but watchful as Tinkler settled into the other armchair.

"I'm their lovable reprobate chum," he said. "I was out in the garden doing some weeding."

Chloë elevated her eyebrows decoratively. "In the dark?"

It wasn't actually fully dark outside, but it was admittedly a bit late to be gardening.

"Actually," said Tinkler, "in the interest of strict factual accuracy, I wasn't doing some weeding. I was doing some weed."

Now Chloë relaxed and smiled at him, a proper smile. "That makes you the best kind of reprobate chum."

"I'd like to think so," said Tinkler modestly.

I listened to them continue to chat as I put away the Easy Tempo compilation and pulled another album off the shelf.

"By the way," said our guest, "I'm Chloë."

I turned to watch Tinkler, concerned that the look on his face would give the game away. He'd been briefed sufficiently by us earlier to recognise the name of our visitor. But even stoned Tinkler could retain a surprising degree of discretion, especially when there had been recent talk of murder. He turned his head away from Chloë so that his startled expression was directed solely and harmlessly towards me. "That's a nice name," was all he said.

"Thank you," said Chloë.

Tinkler turned back to her and took out another expertly rolled spliff which he must have assembled in the garden. "Would you care to partake of this, Chloë?"

"Maybe later."

Tinkler glanced at Nevada. "Have you girls colluded on your stories? Your boring stories of deferred gratification?"

"We're still busy talking business, Tinkler," said Nevada.

"Then heaven forbid that me and my weed should interfere. Or do I mean my weed and I?"

The record I had selected was a towering classic of Italian film music, Piccioni's *Fumo di Londra*, with its mod livery of Union Jack cover art. On the Black Cat label—great name for a record label, but unfortunately it signified that this was a reissue. An original 1966 Italian copy, on the Parade label, would have cost me hundreds of pounds.

Tinkler recognised the sleeve from across the room and acknowledged my choice with an approving thumbs up. But his real interest was elsewhere. "What was that fantastic music you were listening to before?" he said.

"That was something by my grandpa," said Chloë. Her undisguised pride was rather touching.

"Well, big thanks to your grandad for providing the perfect soundtrack for this space-age bachelor pad." Tinkler gestured around at our humble abode. "Or wait, does it still qualify as a bachelor pad if he has a live-in girlfriend? I suspect it doesn't." He shrugged, looking over at me, standing by the turntable. "Never mind, old friend," he said.

"I'll try and roll with the punches," I said.

I lowered the Ortofon SPU, beautiful and retro with its bulbous black-and-gold headshell, onto the rotating playing surface of the record. As the music filled the room, Chloë was instantly all smiling alert attention. "This is Piero Piccioni?"

"Yes."

"My *nonno* used to call him Peter Pigeon," she said.

"Why? Did he have a sexual thing about pigeons?" said Tinkler.

"You must forgive our friend here," I said. I sat down on the sofa with Nevada. "I don't know why, but you must."

"Peter Pigeon," said Nevada, her sharp mind at work. "Piero is the Italian equivalent of Peter…"

"Yes," said Chloë, watching her expectantly.

"So, does Piccioni mean 'pigeons'?"

"That's right," Chloë grinned happily. "Exactly," she said. "But *nonno* thought Peter Pigeon, singular, sounded better. Funnier."

"It does," said Nevada.

"They were rivals. Friendly rivals. *Nonno* and Peter Pigeon." She snuggled down in the chair, her head bobbing to the music. "This is lovely."

"It's an altogether lovely evening," said Tinkler lazily. He was tapping his foot to the music and smiling his characteristic, stoned, cockeyed smile. He directed this at Chloë. "You don't have a brother waiting outside in a car who's about to barge in, do you?"

The emotional temperature in the room suddenly dropped to subzero. So much for retaining a surprising degree of discretion.

"A brother?" said Chloë. She turned to look at Nevada and me, a sharp frown incised on her forehead. "Cass and Desdemona… Were they here?" She was anything but slow.

Nevada gave Tinkler a look that could have broken his nose and said, "They left shortly before you arrived."

Chloë was leaning forward in her chair. A look of deep concentration had clouded her eyes. But only for a moment. It vanished as she sat back in the chair, apparently having taken this unwelcome news in her stride. "That was quick of them," she said, a hint of a sardonic smile curving her lips. Then she lifted her chin defiantly. "What did they want?"

Nevada and I exchanged a look. The truth was best in these situations, if only because it was easiest to keep track of. "They thought you'd already been to see us," I said.

"Like I said," said Chloë, "that was quick of them."

"They wanted us to not take the case," added Nevada.

Chloë smiled. "My case, you mean?"

"Yes."

"What did they tell you?"

"They said…" I hesitated. Chloë's grandfather had gone from being a remote anonymous abstraction to a sort of living entity, thanks to his music playing in this room and thanks to Chloë's presence here. And her obvious love for him. Which all made it a bit hard to say, but I said it anyway.

"They said your grandfather killed their grandmother."

Chloë nodded in a businesslike way.

"I'd better tell you all about it, then."

3: MURDER IN LONDON

Before Chloë embarked on her tale, I made us some more coffee. It seemed called for.

After I served it, we all sat there, oddly becalmed and quiet. For a moment it seemed Chloë didn't quite know where to begin. This hesitation reminded me strangely of Desdemona just before she had launched into her own cryptic tirade which had really got this fun evening underway.

But Chloë was made of sterner stuff. She gave a little nod as if confirming something to herself, then she lifted her chin, again rather defiantly, and said, "My grandpa died a few years ago…"

"Sorry to hear that," I said.

"You aren't really, though, are you?" Suddenly her dark eyes—which up to now I would have described with words like warm and friendly—had gone cold and hard, and were gazing unblinking into mine. I realised, a little belatedly it's true, that this was not a woman to be messed with. Her voice was smooth and calm but also quite ruthless and unyielding. "You aren't sorry at all."

"Why do you say that?" said Nevada.

Chloë turned those hard dark eyes on her. "Because you think he's a murderer, don't you? Cass and Desdemona told you as much. They said my *nonno* was a killer. And you believe them. And so you're quite glad he's dead—one less murderer in the world. That's what you think. Because you believe them."

"We're not sure what to believe," said Nevada. Which was true enough.

"But I really am sorry to hear that he's dead," I said.

Chloë turned back to me. It wasn't easy meeting that implacable gaze. But I did.

"Why?" she said.

"Because I love his music," I said.

For a moment there was complete silence in the room. As if I had broken some kind of spell by speaking the truth— and unquestionably it was the truth; already some part of my mind was scheming to scoop up any records I encountered in the future by the redoubtable Loretto Loconsole, even if I hadn't been hired to do so.

And, to be frank, whether or not he was a murderer…

The silence was broken by the rattle of the cat-flap in the back door and Turk came nosing in. Eyes wide and alert, she skirted the room cautiously in a broad arc, scoping out the stranger in our midst. Suddenly Chloë bent forward and made a little whispering, kissing noise, rubbing her fingers together, clearly hoping to entice our little intruder.

I could have told her she was wasting her time.

But I would have been wrong.

Because Turk came to her at a run and flung herself on the floor at Chloë's feet. She then rolled over on her back, legs shamelessly akimbo, and proceeded to allow Chloë to rub the thick white fur of her belly, while Nevada and I looked at each other in astonishment.

Chloë began to speak. Her voice was so low and soft that at first I thought she was addressing the cat she was so busy caressing.

She wasn't.

"*Nonno* came here in 1969," she said. "He came because they were shooting a film on location in London and he'd been hired to write the score for it." She looked up at us, forsaking her cat stroking. "That wasn't standard practice, of course. Usually the poor soundtrack composer has nothing at all to do with the making of the film, no connection with the process. They'd only call him in at the last minute, after it's all been shot and edited. And then they'd want him to add his music to enhance the impact of the film, or sometimes to save it from disaster. *Nonno* did that more than once. His brilliant music turned terrible movies into… well, I won't say masterpieces, but at least movies that *worked*. And ones that went on to earn money at the box office."

Turk gave a sour, scandalised yowl. Chloë had stopped stroking her, and she didn't like being ignored. Chloë immediately resumed rubbing the cat's tummy. I was pleased to see that our guest knew her correct place in the evolutionary pecking order.

"Sometimes," she said, "when a composer had a very

good relationship with a director, like Ennio Morricone with Sergio Leone, they would get a chance to read the script at an early stage and write music *before* shooting began. Morricone did that for *Once Upon a Time in the West*, and Leone played his music on the set to get the actors in the mood, before they filmed a sequence."

Chloë slid off the armchair, and sat down on the floor beside Turk, so as to more comfortably continue the high-priority work of feline petting. She looked up at us from this position, which for anyone else might have seemed silly and undignified, but for her was merely rather cool and stylish. "My *nonno* did that once or twice," she said. "But for *Murder in London*, it was something entirely different. You see, he'd worked with the director, Beniamino Rosso, a number of times before. Including on that movie we played the music from."

"*The Daughter of Autumn*," I said.

"Yes, and that film had been a considerable success. So, by the time they collaborated on *Murder in London*, *nonno* and Ben Rosso were quite good friends and had an excellent working relationship. So much so that Ben Rosso decided to do something rather special. He not only gave my grandpa the script to read as soon as it was written, but he even invited him to accompany the crew to London and to watch the film being shot. To get ideas and inspiration and write the music as they went along." She looked at us, her eyes showing a gleam of excitement as she related this tale of a lost world and another time. "You see, they'd also agreed to record the music here in London."

"At Olympic Studios, in fact," I said. "In Barnes."

I'd managed to do some research online concerning this record I was being hired to find, while I'd been preparing the new batch of coffee. Well, relatively new. I calculated that there was still enough of this precious fluid left to provide refills for everyone, so I went around pouring them.

"And Barnes is very near here," said Nevada.

"Really?" said Chloë, accepting the refill gratefully, holding up her cup with one hand while resourcefully stroking our cat with the other.

"Just up the road," said Nevada.

"But don't get too excited," said Tinkler. "They knocked down the studios a few years ago and turned the place into a restaurant."

"Oh." Chloë showed what I thought was appropriate disappointment at this dismaying news: where once the Rolling Stones had recorded 'Sympathy for the Devil' you could now order a grilled chicken and shaved fennel sandwich. Admittedly, with tarragon mayo.

"They've got a plaque on the wall commemorating its former glory, though," said Tinkler. "With a list of all the greats who recorded there."

"I wonder if *nonno* is on it?"

"I don't know, but if not he may have dodged a bullet."

"Why?"

"Because they managed to spell Quincy Jones's name wrong. Who knows what would have happened if they'd had to deal with someone who was Italian?"

"It isn't just a restaurant," said Nevada. "There's also a cinema in there."

"And at least it isn't luxury flats," said Tinkler.

"Anyway," I said, doing my best to get the conversation back on track and addressing Chloë directly, "your grandfather came over to watch the shooting of the film and to record the music."

"Yes." She seemed grateful to resume her story. "He was very excited about the project. He wanted to hire the finest British musicians for the soundtrack, and he proceeded to do so."

She wasn't kidding. My research had also revealed that the score for *Murder in London* featured the cream of the British jazz and session players of the time. Among the luminaries featured on the record was none other than Michael Garrick on piano. "He was very proud of it," said Chloë. "He believed it was some of his best work. Which made what happened all the more tragic."

"So…" said Nevada. "What did happen?"

"Well, to understand that," said Chloë, "you have to know a little more about the film." She suddenly rose from the floor and walked purposefully towards the front door. Judging by the startled looks on the faces of my beloved and my bosom chum, I wasn't the only one who thought that her last statement had been an odd form of farewell. Even Turk let out a small, outraged cry at apparently being abandoned.

But Chloë only went as far as the hallway, where she crouched beside her rucksack, unzipped it and delved inside. A moment later she came back clutching a Blu-ray. She showed it to us. To describe the cover art as lurid would have been something of an understatement. Suffice to say that it was an appropriate accompaniment for the name of the film.

"*Bikini of Blood*?" said Nevada.

"Great title," said Tinkler without hesitation.

"Like a lot of Italian movies of this period," explained Chloë, "the film was released under a number of different titles. *Murder in London* was just one. *Bikini of Blood* was another." She looked at the cover, with disfavour. "And that was the one they chose when they decided to release this Blu-ray. Sadly." She sighed and handed it to Nevada. "Still, they did an excellent job of restoring the print, and it's a high-resolution transfer. And they also provide a lot of informative extras."

"I do like me some extras on a Blu-ray," said Nevada, ever the cineaste, as she scrutinised the fine print on the back of the cover.

"There was some talk of including a documentary about my grandpa and his music," said Chloë. "Unfortunately that didn't happen, though. At least not this time around. But since the Blu-ray was a limited edition and proved quite popular, they're talking about doing another release, and I'm hoping next time *nonno* will get his due."

Nevada tried to hand *Bikini of Blood* back to Chloë, but she wouldn't take it. "No, you keep it."

"But it's a limited edition," said Nevada.

"I have several copies. And I'd like you to keep this one. If you get a chance to watch it, you'll understand more about the film and the circumstances of making it. Which might be helpful." Chloë sank down on the floor beside Turk again and resumed what was rapidly becoming her life's work—rubbing a cat's abdomen. The cat in question purred approval and Chloë smiled indulgently at her. "The story of the film—the story *within* the film, that is—is a bit hard to summarise…"

"Is it about a murder in London?" said Tinkler helpfully.

"Yes, and not just one. But it's about much else besides…"

"Bikinis of blood?"

"I'm afraid not. But there are other interesting aspects to its narrative. Do you know what mudlarking is?"

"Searching the banks of the river for little treasures," said Nevada. The river in question was of course the mighty Thames, that same famed waterway which wove under Richmond Bridge.

"And not always so little," said Chloë. "In the movie, the McGuffin—do you know this expression?"

"Yes," said Nevada, who could have written a dissertation on the contribution of Alfred Hitchcock to the cinema of suspense.

"Okay, so the McGuffin in the story of *Murder in London* is an extremely valuable shipment of drugs which has washed ashore on the banks of the Thames."

"What kind of drugs?" said Tinkler instantly. We had touched on his special subject.

"Well it was the 1960s, so it was LSD," said Chloë. "It had to be, I guess, didn't it?"

"You wouldn't want your LSD to get wet," said Tinkler knowledgably.

"Which is why it was sealed in a waterproof silver container shaped like a mermaid," said Chloë.

"A mermaid?" said Nevada.

"Yes, *The Mermaid Trip* is another one of the many titles of this movie," said Nevada.

"*The Trippy Mermaid*," suggested Tinkler.

"That certainly wouldn't be any worse," said Chloë. "Anyway, this boat is smuggling the LSD into London and they are pursued by the police, so they unexpectedly have to throw the LSD overboard."

"Unexpectedly, in its purpose-built waterproof container," I said.

Chloë grinned at me. "Right," she said.

"Is that a plot point?" said Nevada. "That they were actually expecting the police to pursue them and to have to throw it overboard?"

"In a silver mermaid," I said.

"In a silver mermaid," said Nevada.

Chloë shook her head. "Of course not. This isn't a movie which is strong on what you refer to as plot points. They just happened to be smuggling the LSD into the country in a container that just happened, by pure coincidence, to be waterproof and mermaid shaped. This is the kind of logic, or lack of it, that you can expect in Italian movies of this period. In particular in the kind of movies called *gialli*." She looked at Nevada expectantly. "You know what those are?"

My girl had clearly scored some points by taking the term McGuffin in her stride.

Nevada nodded. "*Gialli* plural for *giallo*, meaning yellow. Referring to an iconic series of crime novels with yellow covers. The term came to mean any kind of sensational thriller."

"That's certainly what these movies were," said Chloë. "Sensational, lurid, prurient thrillers. And not necessarily entirely rational. In fact the whole genre is pretty much batshit crazy."

Kudos for the correct idiomatic use of batshit crazy by a native Italian speaker, I thought.

"So, for no reason at all," summarised Tinkler, "but very luckily, this stash of LSD just happens to be in a waterproof silver mermaid that the smugglers can throw overboard when the police close in on them?"

"Correct," said Chloë. "Which means that when the police finally catch up with them, they have nothing on the criminals, no evidence to arrest them and have to let them go."

"But the smugglers then have the problem of retrieving their drugs," said Nevada.

Chloë nodded at her. "That's right."

"Plot complication," said Tinkler.

"Hence mudlarking," I said.

Chloë looked up from our cat and grinned at me, eyes bright. "Yes," she said. "They have to search the banks of the river for this mermaid. Which of course didn't sink because not only did it just coincidentally happen to be waterproof, it also was designed to float."

"Lucky," said Nevada.

"Of course it floated," said Tinkler. "It was a mermaid."

"We'll have less of your stoned logic," said Nevada.

"We'll have more of it if only you weak-kneed fops would join me in smoking this spliff," said Tinkler, holding it up again. Still no takers, though.

"So the smugglers are searching the riverbanks for the silver mermaid full of LSD," I said.

"Yes," said Chloë. "There's just one problem… Actually, that's not accurate. There's a lot more than one problem. For the smugglers. And not just the smugglers. For all the characters in the movie. Not to mention the people watching it. Because, like I said, coherence is not the strong point of this film."

"Or any *giallo*," said Nevada.

"Exactly," said Chloë. "But there is one major, immediate problem for the smugglers…"

"A silver mermaid isn't exactly inconspicuous," I said.

She chuckled. "Exactly. And, before they can find it, the mermaid is discovered by a beautiful young woman who is not only a mudlark, she's also in the habit of swimming every morning at dawn in the river, in the nude…"

"Yahoo," said Tinkler.

"It was, after all, the 1960s," said Chloë. "And nudity was obligatory in any *giallo*."

"I hope she didn't really swim in the river in the nude. The actress I mean," said Nevada. "Or even not in the nude. I hope she didn't swim in it at all. The Thames is desperately polluted even now. And then…"

"It was, after all, the 1960s," I quoted.

Chloë flashed me an amused look. "Those particular sequences were actually filmed elsewhere, on the Serpentine River in Hyde Park," she said. "Which led to some difficulty matching shots. But then, as I've indicated, shaky narrative continuity is another feature of a *giallo*. But incidentally there *was* quite a lot of swimming done by the film crew in the Thames. In proper diving suits. But we'll get to that later. Where was I?"

"Nude girl," said Tinkler, the ever-reliable.

"Yes, so the mermaid is found by this girl—"

"Who is effectively a mermaid herself," said Nevada.

Chloë paused, impressed. "Yes, that's right. The flesh-and-blood mermaid…"

"Flesh," said Tinkler happily.

"She finds the silver mermaid and takes it back to her houseboat. She lives on a houseboat, of course."

"Of course," I said.

"With a dog who will feature heavily in the story," said Chloë. She glanced at Tinkler. "But not sexually."

"Oh boy, have you got his number," said Nevada.

"I make one little joke about carnal congress with parrots…" said Tinkler.

"Pigeons," said Nevada.

"Anyway," I said.

"Anyway," said Chloë, "the dog features heavily later in the story when the smugglers try to come and take the drugs, and it defends its mistress, attacking them. The whole sequence of the dog attack is quite extraordinary because it is seen from the point of view of someone tripping on LSD."

"The smugglers took LSD before they came to rob the houseboat?" said Tinkler.

"No, the girl on the houseboat did. Anyway, these are some of the most memorable images in the film. Which is why it's also sometimes known as *The Black Dog Murders*."

"How many titles does this freaking movie have?"

"Well, it's additionally known at *The Mermaid Murder Trip* and *The Doberman Murders*. Because the dog the girl has on her houseboat is a Doberman. Not that it would have stopped them using that title even if it was a completely different breed. In addition to the dog, this girl has an unreliable boyfriend…"

"Are there such creatures?" said Tinkler.

"And he's a musician," said Chloë.

"Oh well, there you go."

"He plays electric guitar in a rock band." She looked at me. "Which incidentally explains why the soundtrack, which is mostly jazz, also features some wonderful psychedelic rock guitar."

"Nobody's perfect," I said.

She shook her head quickly. "I think you'll find the way my *nonno* integrated the rock elements into the jazz quite tasteful, and quite impressive. Anyway, the girl on the houseboat has this unreliable musician boyfriend and, when they open the silver mermaid and find the LSD inside, he starts to spread it around and sell it to his musician friends, and word gets out on the London music scene about this amazing, high-quality acid…"

"And the smugglers get wind of it," I said.

"Correct. Because of the careless behaviour of her boyfriend, these ruthless criminals soon track her down and come to attack her and retrieve the drugs. She's alone on the houseboat at night, with music playing, my *nonno*'s music, of course. And she's dancing to the music…"

"With no clothes on?" said Tinkler.

"Of course. It's a *giallo*. It's the 1960s. And not only is she nude and vulnerable, she's taken some LSD. Or rather, her unreliable boyfriend had dosed her with LSD without her knowledge or her consent."

"Could happen to anyone," said Tinkler. An offhand comment which perhaps was not so offhand if you knew what had happened to us in Canterbury some years ago. (An incident which had resulted in, among other things, Tinkler getting some T-shirts printed which read, *I went to Canterbury and all I got was this lousy murder attempt*.)

"So the smugglers are closing in on this poor girl all alone on her houseboat…"

"Where's the boyfriend?" said Nevada.

"In another part of London, being unfaithful to her."

"That's what I call unreliable," said Nevada.

"And so she's high on LSD…"

"With no clothes on," said Tinkler.

"And her assailants are closing in on her on the houseboat, intent on theft and murder. But, of course once they see her, as you say, with no clothes on, they're also intent on sexual assault. But, luckily for her and unluckily for the smugglers, as soon as they step on the houseboat, she's saved by the dog, who savagely attacks the intruders."

"Go, dog," said Tinkler.

"And as I said, the whole thing is shot in this LSD trip style. Did I mention that the dog also helps her find items on her mudlarking expeditions? Earlier in the film, I mean?"

"No," said Nevada.

"Anyway, it is a complicated story."

"So it seems."

"But as you will have gathered," said Chloë, "there's a lot of action along the river. So the movie involved filming in the water, and under it."

"Under it?" said Nevada.

"I mentioned that they had divers. Beniamino Rosso, the director, was a stickler for realism and he wanted to film everything for real, on location. So he had underwater cameras and scuba divers."

"Frogmen," said Tinkler.

"Actually, frogwomen," said Chloë. "The two underwater stunt coordinators, as they were called, were both women."

"Frogwomen," said Tinkler. "Were they *beautiful* frogwomen?"

"One of them certainly was," said Chloë. "The one my grandpa had an affair with." She sipped at her coffee and set it aside. "And the one he's supposed to have murdered."

4: FROGWOMAN

"Let me get this straight," said Tinkler. "Your grandfather had an affair with a beautiful frogwoman?"

"Yes," said Chloë. "He was a very charismatic, talented man and a wonderful musician, and women threw themselves at him."

"Including frogwomen."

"Yes."

"I wish I was a very charismatic, talented man and a wonderful musician. And that I had a wetsuit."

"Shut up, Tinkler. Go on, Chloë."

"I mean, my *nonno* loved my grandmother, of course... But he was still a man. And an Italian man at that. And it was the 1960s..."

"So he was unfaithful," said Nevada laconically.

"Quite a lot, yes."

"Didn't your grandmother mind?"

"Well of course she did. But I suppose she became accustomed to it. If it's possible to become accustomed to that sort of thing. And in this particular case she was over a thousand kilometres away, back at home in Rome."

"At home in Rome," said Tinkler, savouring the rhyme.

"Shut up, Tinkler," said Nevada.

"No, it's fine," said Chloë. "I like your stoned reprobate friend."

"You see, she likes me."

"Nevertheless, shut up and let her get on with the story."

"Well, I'm not sure how much more there is to tell," said Chloë.

As if sensing things were wrapping up, or maybe just because she'd had enough of sycophantic stomach rubbing, Turk rose to her feet and padded off. So Chloë in turn got up off the floor and sat back in her chair again like a respectable human being. "Essentially that's all there is to it," she said. "My *nonno* had an affair with this stunt coordinator, the frogwoman. And she was killed. And he was blamed for the killing."

"What happened?" said Nevada. "How did she die?"

"She was beaten to death. With a prop from the film."

"A prop?" said Nevada.

Chloë was looking at us expectantly. "A very significant prop," she said.

"It wasn't the frigging silver mermaid, was it?" said Tinkler.

Chloë nodded with grim satisfaction, as if we'd passed a test she'd set for us. "It was one of them. One of the silver mermaids. They had a number of replicas made for the film. Some to use in the water, some to use at the river edge for mudlarking, some to use on dry land. Some of them opened up, some didn't. Some floated, some didn't. This particular one was the most heavy and solid of them all. It served as quite a lethal weapon. Someone hit poor Jackie on the head with it. More than once. And they crushed her skull. Poor Jackie."

"Jackie was the frogwoman," said Nevada.

"Yes. Jackie Higgins."

"As in Desdemona Higgins," I said.

"Yes. As in Cass and Desdemona Higgins. Their grandmother." Chloë looked at us and declared fiercely, "But my grandpa didn't do it."

"So why did anyone think he did?" said Nevada. "Just because they'd been having an affair?"

"For that reason. And also because of where the murder took place. Jackie Higgins and my father had been using the houseboat for their assignations. It was handy for her, because she was working nearby on the river. And, unless there was actually filming taking place on the boat, it was deserted. And isolated and private. A perfect place for them to meet. Only people working on the film had access to it, and my grandpa and Jackie made sure they had it to themselves. Apparently, it was comfortable and rather chic."

"Chic?" said Nevada.

Chloë smiled. "You'll see when you watch the film. The houseboat is a masterpiece of interior design. Of 1960s psychedelic interior design. With a big feather bed, silk sheets and cushions, and brightly coloured pop art tapestries. That sort of thing."

"They actually filmed on the houseboat?" said Nevada.

"Yes, as I said, Ben Rosso was a fanatic about shooting everything as realistically as possible."

"It must have been very cramped."

"Indeed. It would have been much easier to shoot the houseboat sequences on a set, in a studio, and there was a lot of pressure on Ben Rosso to do so. But he was stubborn and, in his own way, he was also a genuine artist. He used small, lightweight cameras—small and lightweight for the time, anyway. They're amusingly gigantic when you compare them to, say, a smartphone now. And so they had to build some removable sections in the houseboat walls to allow them to film more easily. Altogether they managed quite well, as you'll see in the movie. In any case, this houseboat was a convenient and private place for my grandpa and Jackie to meet, and to conduct their affair."

Chloë sounded remarkably matter of fact about this arrangement. Almost as if she approved of its practicality and cleverness.

"And so Jackie was killed there?" said Nevada.

"Yes. They found her early in the morning when the second unit camera crew went to the houseboat to do some pick-up shots. Apparently, the script girl became hysterical. She was the one who stumbled on the body. The first hint that something was wrong was when she found this silver mermaid lying on the floor outside the door of the bedroom. It had been carefully cleaned, so the script girl just thought someone had misplaced one of the props. But then she opened the door… I don't want to be ghoulish, but there was apparently a great deal of blood. In the bedroom. Where

Jackie had been waiting, in bed, for my grandpa. Supposedly she'd had a rendezvous with him there the previous night."

"Supposedly?" said Nevada.

"He always denied it."

He would, I thought. Again my lack of a poker face must have betrayed me because Chloë gave me a sharp look and said, "My grandpa was absolutely not meeting her there that night. They were always very meticulous about planning their encounters, and this time there had been no prior arrangement. But during the course of that day someone else pretended to be him, and they left a message for Jackie telling her to be there, making an impromptu last-minute assignation. And then this other person attacked her there on the houseboat. Apparently, they were waiting nearby and watching the houseboat. And, when Jackie arrived, it seems they followed her on board and killed her."

"And who could have done that?" said Nevada.

"Well, that's the million-dollar question," said Chloë. She looked at me with a pleading quality in her expression that reminded me of something. Of someone.

Desdemona Higgins, sitting in the same armchair, not an hour earlier.

"Not that I have a million dollars to answer it," said Chloë.

I felt a cold quiver go through me. "You're hiring me to look for a record," I said. "Not to find a killer." I was rather alarmed to find that, despite my intention that this should sound like a firm statement, it came out more like a tentative question.

"Of course, I want you to find the record," said Chloë.

"And this isn't just a case of me sentimentally wishing to acquire some memento of my *nonno*'s work. In fact, I very badly need you to find that record."

"Why?" I said. "What's so special about it, and why do you need it now?"

"Because I'm now in the middle of supervising reissues of my grandpa's music. There's a growing demand for it, at last, as people have finally begun to realise how wonderful it is."

"It really is wonderful," said Nevada. She was at her most charming and emollient because she sensed the possibility of an argument brewing up. An argument originating in my desire not to get involved in looking for a murderer when I was supposed to be looking for a record.

"Thank you," said Chloë. "My *nonno* was a genius but, for a long time, it's been a battle getting people to recognise that. All this nonsense about him being a killer has clouded his reputation and stopped people from appreciating his work. From seeing his music for what it is. Or, rather, for hearing it for what it is."

She was burning with a fierce pride which, in spite of everything, I found rather impressive. Not to mention attractive. She said, "Piero Piccioni was also suspected of involvement in a murder, you know? Yes, Peter Pigeon. Back in the early 1950s. The body of a young woman was found on a beach near Rome. Piccioni was supposedly implicated. But somehow that scandal never seemed to follow him around for years afterwards or permanently stain his reputation the way this killing in London did for my grandpa. Maybe because

Piccioni had powerful political connections." Chloë looked at us. "Not like my *nonno*," she added bitterly.

"Even my parents remain a little ashamed of him," she said. "They pretend not to be, but I know they are. Because deep down they also think *nonno* did it. That he killed this poor woman. They don't admit as much. But I can tell they believe it. Or half-believe it. But, myself, I've never believed it. Not for an instant." She looked at me, defiantly. "I know what you're going to say," she said.

"What am I going to say?" I said.

"You'll say that I'm blinded by love for him. That my grandpa might really be a killer and I'd never admit it, no matter how much evidence is staring me in the face."

"How much evidence is staring you in the face?" I said.

"Not enough," she said.

Or, snarled, actually.

There was a tense silence. Which was eventually broken by Nevada, the peace broker. "So you're looking after your grandfather's music catalogue now?"

"That's right," said Chloë. "Are you going to say I'm not suitable for the job because I'm too young, or because I'm a woman?"

Nevada smiled at her. "Do you think I'm likely to say that?"

After a moment, Chloë smiled back. "No. I don't think you are. I'm sorry if I'm overly sensitive on the subject, but a lot of people have been saying things like that, ever since I set up the company. They either think I'm unsuitable for the job, or they think the job is unsuitable for me. Because they believe

THE VINYL DETECTIVE

this music is the work of a killer and so it should be forgotten. Buried. Erased from history. Well, I'm not about to let it be forgotten, or buried, or erased. I've been searching through dusty attics and sheds and basements and garages for tapes of my *nonno*'s work. I've been struggling to get clearances and permissions, and to trace ownership and rights deals. I've been auditioning sound engineers and commissioning artwork and advertising and building a website." She looked at us. "By the time I'm finished, I'll have brought all of his music back into print. It'll all be available on download and CD and vinyl."

She looked at me as she pronounced that last word, as if it held special significance for me, which of course it did. "And the world will be able to hear it again," she said.

"And you'll get paid for it," said Nevada, who always maintained a businesslike frame of mind in these matters.

"That's almost a secondary consideration," said Chloë.

"Almost," said Nevada, with a little smile of approval.

"And it won't just be me getting paid for it," said Chloë. "Money will go to my *nonna*, too."

"Your grandmother's still alive?" said Nevada.

"Very much so." Chloë grinned. "She's on the phone to me all the time, checking up on me. Making sure I'm eating properly, threatening to fly out to London to look after me if I don't look after myself. She's a classic Italian grandmother, I guess. And she's wonderful and I love her. But I'm very angry on her behalf. Because she should be quite wealthy now, very wealthy indeed, with all the royalties from my grandpa's music. I'm not denying she's very comfortably off as it is. But she should be much more than that. She should be in the

62

position of someone like Ennio Morricone's widow. And she would be. But my *nonno*'s royalties dried up years ago."

"Because of the reputational damage," said Nevada.

"Because of these lies about my grandpa, yes. When they heard these evil rumours, all this horrid slander, people stopped hiring him. They stopped working with him. They stopped listening to his music. They stopped licensing it. They stopped buying his records. It was terrible." She looked at me. "But I imagine you'd say it was terrible for Jackie Higgins, too."

Again, she'd read me accurately. "Worse, I imagine," I said.

"Is it worse, though?" said Chloë. "I wonder. Maybe it's better to be peacefully dead rather than remain alive and perpetually accused of a murder you didn't commit. To live the rest of your life in that shadow."

"At least you're alive," I said. "And then there's the matter of her family…"

Chloë blinked and looked away from me. "That's true. It would have been very painful for her family. And for Juno."

"Who's Juno?" said Nevada.

"Juno Brunner. I mentioned there were two female divers on the film, working as stunt coordinators. She was the other one."

"And she was a friend of Jackie?"

"Rather more than a friend," said Chloë. "Much more, in fact." She let this sink in. It took Tinkler longest to get the implication, which was unusual given the unremittingly salacious bent of his imagination.

"Holy cow," he said. "Lesbian frogwomen?"

Fortunately Chloë was amused by this. "Well, one of them was a lesbian. And one of them was bisexual."

"So, Jackie and this Juno…" said Tinkler, his mind evidently fizzing with possibilities. Possibly involving underwater orgies complete with snorkels and flippers. And presumably bubbles. A lot of bubbles…

"Juno was her mentor," said Chloë. "Jackie was always a good swimmer. A natural swimmer. She loved being in the water and she won gold medals at school for her swimming. Juno saw her in action and recognised her potential. She trained her to be a scuba diver. In some ways she regarded herself as Jackie's creator."

"Creator?" said Nevada.

"It's an odd word, true. But there were very few women who were pursuing that profession at the time. Juno had been trained as a scuba diver in the military. But she had been forced to leave under unpleasant circumstances…"

"I'll bet," said Tinkler. "Lesbians wouldn't have been too popular in the navy then."

"Or now," said Chloë. "It was and still is enormously tough for any woman to be in the military, and even tougher for one who happens to be gay. So Juno's military career ended in disgrace, but at least she'd learned sufficient skills to enable her to set up in business in civilian life."

"And not just set up in business," said Nevada. "But to get movie work."

"Yes," said Chloë. "Juno was very good at what she did. And soon she was getting so much work that she needed to train up someone else to help her. An apprentice. So she kept her eyes open for someone who showed promise. And she found a suitable candidate."

"Jackie."

"That's right."

"And she and Jackie…"

"Were lovers, yes. Until my grandpa came along. And Jackie fell for him. So although she continued working with Juno on the film, she ceased to be part of Juno's private life."

"And I assume Juno wasn't entirely pleased about that," I said.

Chloë smiled at me. "You assume correctly. She was most unhappy about the affair. So, there you are."

"There I am?" I said.

"You see, there are indeed other suspects aren't there? Other people with motives who might have killed Jackie Higgins."

"Like I said," I said. "I'm not looking to find a killer."

She smiled at me. "Are you sure? It seems to me you have good instincts."

"He does have good instincts," said Nevada instantly, eager to bond us and butter me up, and, not so incidentally, make sure I took the job.

"It doesn't exactly take a genius to work out that Juno would have been pissed off," I said. "And that she might have had a motive for murder."

"Not might have," said Chloë. "Definitely had a motive for murder."

"But if she was going to kill someone," I said, "isn't it more likely she'd kill your grandfather rather than Jackie?"

Chloë shrugged. "Maybe she wanted to kill both of them. And she only managed one."

"Anyway," I said, "it was all a long time ago and she's probably dead now. Juno, I mean."

"No," said Chloë. "I believe Juno Brunner is very much still alive."

"Nevertheless, like I said, I'm only looking for a record."

Chloë and Nevada exchanged a look. "Well," said Chloë as though soothing a fractious child, "it is a very important record."

"Because you want to reissue it?" I said. I was glad to get us back onto the firm ground of vinyl and record-hunting.

"That's right. And I have no other option than to find a vinyl copy because the master tapes have been destroyed."

"Seriously?" I was startled by how much this news stung me. If only based on the roster of musicians who'd played on the sessions, those tapes were priceless. At least to anyone who loved jazz. Or film music. Or any kind of music, for that matter.

"Lost or destroyed," said Chloë. "I believe the latter. I think someone deliberately threw them away or erased them, because of the scandal."

5: NEEDLE DROP

"So they just erased the tapes?" I said.

Chloë shrugged. "Or threw them away. Discarded them."

"That's…" I searched for the right word.

"Blasphemy?" suggested Chloë.

"That's just plain nuts," I said. But she wasn't far wrong. Destroying music of that calibre was distinctly blasphemous.

"Anyway," said Chloë, "with the master tapes gone, you see my predicament?"

"I certainly do," I said. "And I understand why you don't just want to find this record for sentimental reasons."

"That's right. I need it as the audio source for the reissue. The only possible audio source now."

Nevada looked at me. "Can they do that? Make a new record from an old one?"

"Certainly," I said. "If we can find a copy on vinyl, it can be used as the master for a reissue."

"It won't be as good as a master tape, though, will it?" said Nevada.

"It might even be better," said Tinkler.

"You're just high," said Nevada.

"Maybe he is…" I said.

"I certainly am," said Tinkler.

"But that doesn't mean he's wrong," I said. "An LP can be a better source than a master tape. If tapes aren't properly stored, or even if they are, they can deteriorate in ways that vinyl doesn't. Tape stretches. It sheds oxide. It becomes brittle. It prints through. None of these things happen with vinyl."

Chloë was looking at me with approval. She turned to Nevada. "He doesn't just have good instincts," she said. "He knows his stuff."

"Of course he does," said Nevada with a certain proprietary pride.

"The bottom line," I said, "is that if the master tape isn't available, then a pristine vinyl copy is your best bet. In fact, even if you have access to a second- or third-generation master tape then the vinyl is still a better bet."

"Amen to that," said Tinkler. "Give me a needle drop over a bad master tape any day."

"And in this case," said Chloë, "it's not even a matter of a bad master tape. It's a matter of no master tape at all."

"A decent vinyl copy could be used to very good effect," I said. "There was a record label in Spain in the 1980s called Fresh Sound run by a guy called Jordi Pujol. They released rare jazz and their stuff sounded fantastic. And my guess is that it was all needle drops."

"Needle drops," said Chloë. "I like that term."

"I said it first," said Tinkler.

"Music is a matter of microseconds," I said. "If the timing of a recording is off by even the tiniest fraction, then it will sound subtly wrong. It can go from infectious and exciting to plodding and boring. It loses all sense of being a real performance. And tapes are terribly vulnerable to timing errors. Like I said, they can be stretched. Or they can be recorded or copied or transferred on machines that aren't operating perfectly, so there you are, left with a version which is permanently at the wrong speed.

"On the other hand, once you get music down accurately on vinyl, all those problems go away. All you need is a turntable which rotates at thirty-three-and-a-third RPM, and the music will come off that record as fresh and as lifelike as the day it was first played. So all that's required for Chloë to produce a great reissue of her grandfather's music is to find a vinyl original. Preferably undamaged."

"The mastering engineer I have in mind is a very talented guy," said Chloë. "So a little damage won't matter. When he does the transfer, he can do an amazing job of removing the clicks and pops and scratches."

"I'm sure he can," I said, "but any attempt to correct errors is going to further compromise sound quality. So what we want is a pristine copy."

"Or copies," said Tinkler.

Nevada frowned. "What do you mean? Why would we need more than one?"

But I instantly saw what Tinkler was getting at. "Because realistically we have to accept we're not likely to find a copy on which every track is perfect." I looked at Chloë. "How many tracks are there on the album."

"Ten."

"So you might need as many as ten copies," said Tinkler. "One for each track. You only need one track in perfect condition on any given LP. Just so long as you can find pristine examples of all ten tunes."

"Good luck to us finding ten," said Chloë. "The problem will be finding any copies at all."

"Because there were so few pressed in the first place?" I said.

She shook her head. "No, in fact they made tens of thousands of copies of this record. Everyone expected it to sell in big quantities. There was initially a great deal of optimism and excitement about it, and all the omens were good. A very positive article appeared in one of the English music magazines about the recording sessions, which attracted a lot of attention. And my grandpa had finished the recording remarkably quickly. He said he'd been inspired by observing the filming, and the superb British musicians. And, just between you and me, I think Jackie was a big part of that inspiration."

She paused. "I genuinely think he was in love with her. And that shows in the music." She watched us, eyes hot and fierce, as if daring us to contradict her. She was clearly very ready to take offence. "That's another reason I know my grandpa couldn't have killed her. Because he loved her so much."

"Unfortunately," said Nevada, "loving someone intensely doesn't necessarily preclude killing them."

Chloë gave her a sharp look, but Nevada didn't back down. "In fact, in some ways it can make it more likely." She glanced at me, and it wasn't hard to know who she was thinking of.

Othello. And his beloved, blameless, but ultimately murdered wife...

Desdemona.

Chloë shrugged. "Anyway, whatever the reason for his speed and his creative energy, my *nonno* was on fire. He completed the recording sessions while the film was still being shot. And, when they heard the results, people loved what he had done. There was a lot of excitement about the soundtrack and there was a general feeling that the record would be a substantial bestseller. The people at the record company were patting themselves on the back. And patting my grandpa on the back. They smelled a hit. You have to remember there was a lot of interest in Italian film music at this time, thanks to Morricone and his spaghetti westerns, and also to Riz Ortolani for his song 'More' which was nominated for an Oscar and was a big international chart success a few years earlier. So, my *nonno*'s LP was rushed into production and copies were already manufactured by the time that the movie was completed... and by the time..."

"That Jackie was murdered," I said. Somebody had to say it.

Chloë nodded. "She was killed in the last days of filming. Just as the record was being prepared for release. And just when this was about to go into the shops..."

She held up her phone. On it was a photo of the front

cover of the album, which I'd seen. She flipped past it to an image of the back cover, which I hadn't.

It was in black and white. There was a list of the tracks on the record, and the musicians. But most of the back cover was taken up with a photo of a sharply dressed handsome young man with ironic dark eyes. He wore a check jacket and a black polo neck and a natty little hat. And he was smoking a cigarette. Of course. It was the 1960s.

He exuded Italian style and 1960s elan, and casual *dolce vita* cool, all of which was somewhat in contrast to the grumpy stone lions of the fountain he was posing beside—the photo had been taken in Trafalgar Square.

"That's *nonno*," said Chloë. "Can you imagine what the record company thought, after the accusations started?"

I could see what she meant. The young and dashing Loretto Loconsole was smiling a particularly self-satisfied smile, as though he had an amusing little secret he didn't intend to share with the world. And right above the photo, in a giant font, were the words *Murder in London*.

"Jesus," said Nevada, looking over my shoulder.

"Exactly," said Chloë. "You see? When Jackie's body was found and the scandal broke and *nonno* was accused—of murder, of murder in London—there was no way the record company had any intention of releasing the LP. Not with that picture on the cover, with those words over it. As a matter of fact, they had no intention of releasing the LP at all, in any form. It was scrapped, aborted. The whole project was cancelled, while my *nonno* fought to clear his name."

"And succeeded, I assume," I said.

She stared at me. "Why would you assume that?"

"Because he didn't end his days in prison. At least I get the impression that he didn't. From everything you've said, it sounds like he went back to Italy a free man."

Chloë nodded thoughtfully. "I suppose you could say that. 'A free man.' Though in one sense he was never to be free again. Never to be free of suspicion or allegations or whispers behind his back. He certainly never, as you put it, cleared his name."

"So why did they let him go?"

She shrugged. "The English police? They didn't want to let him go. They were very reluctant indeed to release him. But in the end they were compelled to do so. They simply didn't have enough evidence. All they really had to implicate him was the fact of his affair with Jackie."

"I assumed it must have been common knowledge, then," said Nevada.

"Quite the opposite," said Chloë. "Their liaison had been a very well-kept secret. It's not easy hiding something like that from a film crew. But my *nonno* and Jackie had been remarkably successful in doing so. They had been very careful and very discreet. But none of that mattered, because Juno Brunner knew about it. Jackie had told her."

"When they split up," said Nevada.

"Yes," said Chloë. "When she told Juno she was leaving her to be with my grandpa. Juno demanded to know who her rival was, and Jackie told her. So Juno knew about the affair. And she made sure that the police knew about it, after Jackie was killed."

"Well she had to tell them, didn't she?" I said. "She could hardly keep something like that secret in those circumstances."

She gave me a sardonic little smile. "You're assuming it wasn't Juno herself who killed Jackie. And then told the police about my *nonno* so as to implicate him and throw suspicion off herself. To muddy the waters, to use a very appropriate phrase."

"Because she was a diver," said Tinkler.

"No one can sneak anything past you," said Nevada.

"No need to be nasty now."

"Was she ever under suspicion?" said Nevada. "Juno Brunner?"

"I doubt it," said Chloë. "Unlike Jackie's affair with my grandpa, which was dragged out into the light of day and became sensational material for the tabloid newspapers, Juno's relationship with Jackie—which when you think about it would have been even more sensational and scandalous, especially at that time—was allowed to remain secret. The police were apparently blissfully unaware that Juno and Jackie had any connection beyond the purely professional."

"Do you really believe that?" I said.

"Why not?"

"Would the police have really been that naïve?"

Chloë shrugged. "Wasn't it your Queen Victoria who refused to believe that a sexual relationship could exist between two women?"

"This wasn't the reign of Queen Victoria anymore," I said.

"It wasn't so long after it."

"Over sixty years," I said.

"Attitudes hadn't changed so much," said Chloë stubbornly. "Anyway, for whatever reason, the police weren't interested in looking for anyone else as a possible murderer. They certainly weren't interested in looking at Juno. They were convinced they had the guilty party and that it was my grandpa."

"Why did they let him go, then?" I said.

"As I've said, they didn't have any direct evidence. They certainly didn't have any witnesses. My grandpa's fingerprints were at the crime scene, true, but so were the fingerprints of dozens of other people who worked on the film." She gave me a significant look. "Including Juno's. Of course, there was no such thing as DNA analysis at the time. But it would have presumably have just shown the same thing. That many people had been there on the houseboat, all of them part of the film crew. And it was impossible to know which one of them was the killer."

"Or if it was someone else entirely," I said.

"Someone who didn't leave any fingerprints?" said Chloë.

"Someone who wore gloves," I said. "Things were a lot simpler for killers back then. Like you said, no DNA analysis."

"Well, in any case," said Chloë, "the police weren't interested in any further investigations because they were convinced they had their man."

"But I still don't see why they let him go," said Nevada.

"I told you. Insufficient evidence."

"They may not have had sufficient evidence. But we're talking about the 1960s. Insufficient evidence wouldn't have stopped them doing anything. That was an era when the police wouldn't hesitate to manufacture whatever evidence they needed."

"You mean falsify it?" said Chloë.

"Exactly," said Nevada.

"Scotland Yard would have done that?" The note of disappointment in Chloë's voice would have been amusing if it wasn't so heartrending.

"Sure," said Nevada. "The police were corrupt as hell. They wouldn't have scrupled to fabricate evidence if they thought they had the guilty man. Or even if they thought they didn't. They just wanted someone who could be made to take the rap. And your grandfather was a foreigner, so there would have been no hesitation about framing him."

I was a little taken aback by my darling's utter cynicism. But I couldn't have said that she was wrong about any of this.

"Well, luckily for my *nonno*, there was a witness," said Chloë.

"I thought you just said there weren't any," said Tinkler.

"Not to the crime itself. But there was a witness who swore my grandpa was in his hotel on the other side of London at the time when the murder took place."

"So he had an alibi?" said Nevada.

"Yes, an alibi. The concierge at his hotel was willing to swear that *nonno* was there during the crucial hours."

"Well, then that should have been the end of the matter," said Nevada.

"Yes, you'd think so, wouldn't you?" Chloë sighed. "But the concierge had a criminal record. And there were rumours that my *nonno* had simply bribed him."

Nevada nodded. "So his alibi was good enough to let your grandfather escape being charged…"

"And to fly back to Rome, which he did immediately, yes."

"But it wasn't good enough to put an end to the rumours that he'd actually done it."

"Exactly," said Chloë. "He was a free man. But in the eyes of the world he was guilty. And his being free and escaping criminal charges simply made it worse. Certainly the record company thought he was guilty. Because they scrapped his record and cancelled his contract. And although the LPs had already been manufactured, most of them were destroyed."

"What a waste," I said.

Chloë gave me a grateful look. "Yes, wasn't it? Of course, some review copies had already made their way out into the world. And the attempts to destroy all the other copies of the record weren't completely successful. There are some out there." Chloë gestured towards the dark windows of our living room and the city beyond, and the wider world beyond that. "But they won't be easy to find."

I nodded. "As I said, it will be a challenge."

"I like it that you said 'will be'," said Nevada. She looked at Chloë. "It sounds like he's happy to take the job." She turned to me and smiled, "And I always want you to be happy."

77

"I'm not sure happy is exactly the word I'd choose," I said. "I want to make it clear that I'm being hired to find a record, not to expose the true identity of a killer."

Chloë leaned forward. "And I would like to make it clear that I would be very happy indeed if you happened to do both."

"Oh, Christ," I said.

"It's happened before, hasn't it?" said Chloë.

"And we've also nearly got killed before," I said.

6: NO PICNIC

So, that was that.

Chloë went and picked up her rucksack in the hall.

Despite the complications she'd brought into our lives tonight, I was rather sorry to see her go.

She stood in the open doorway as we said our goodbyes, with the smell of lilac once more flowing in on the night air. The unseasonably bitter north wind had ceased to blow and it was now a still night, and feeling warmer. Actually feeling like summer for a change.

Chloë paused and looked at us and, with elaborate casualness, said, "By the way. What exactly did Cass and Desdemona say? I mean, did they tell you about me?"

"Not in any great detail," said Nevada. Then, impelled by her natural sense of mischief, she added, "But there was some discussion about them paying us not to take the case."

I was impressed at how my darling managed to remain strictly truthful while simultaneously giving the false impression that the brother and sister had actually offered us money.

"Well, I hope any such discussion has now been rendered irrelevant."

"It certainly has," said Nevada. She'd hammered out the financial terms of our arrangement with Chloë in some considerable detail. And very much to our advantage. It seemed Ms Loconsole, in spite of her backpacker vibe, was anything but short of money.

"I suppose you're wondering how we came to know each other," Chloë said, out of nowhere. "Myself and Desdemona… And Cass." She added the name of the brother as if it was very much an afterthought.

I, at least, hadn't been wondering. But now the subject had been broached, I must admit I was somewhat intrigued.

"It was through my grandpa, of course," said Chloë. "And their grandmother."

The reality of this suddenly hit home to me, and quite powerfully…

Jackie Higgins, the bisexual young scuba diver was actually the grandmother of the nefarious brother-and-sister team of Cass and Des. I'd casually accepted the fact of this, of course, but the emotional implications of it hadn't really registered with me. But now it did.

"Was Jackie married, then?" I said. She must have had a child, in any case.

Chloë shook her head. "No, she was never married. But that, of course, didn't prevent her becoming pregnant. And she had a baby, a boy, when she was a teenager. It was this that spoiled her chances of becoming a professional athlete. She won some local swimming championships but went no further. Which must have been terrible for her. Because at one time there had even been talk of her qualifying for the Olympics and competing for her country. But instead of gold medals…"

"She got knocked up," said Tinkler succinctly.

Chloë nodded. "Interesting, isn't it, how the destruction of all a young woman's dreams and aspirations can be summed up in just that one short vulgar phrase?"

"Well, I didn't mean to be vulgar," said Tinkler, a little defensively.

Nevada tactfully closed the front door; this was obviously going to be a longer conversation than we'd envisaged. Also, it was starting to get a little chilly standing here, summer or not. Chloë shot her a grateful look.

"No, its vulgarity is quite appropriate," said Chloë to Tinkler. "All too appropriate. The bluntness is highly suitable. And the brevity. Like the act itself, from what I understand."

She must have realised that she was revealing an oddly detailed knowledge of the personal life of one Jackie Higgins because she gave an embarrassed little shrug.

"My *nonno* used to talk to me. We always had long talks together, sitting out in his garden, at his little house near Rome, on summer evenings. We could say anything to each other. There were never any boundaries between us. So one night I asked him about what had happened in London. Of course I'd been aware of it, the way you're aware of such rumours when you're young. Always at the edge of things, like something you see out of the corner of your eye. People falling silent when you come into a room. The family secret. The subject that no one ever talks about out loud, in the open, but everyone is all too eager to whisper about behind closed doors." She looked at us. "This thing that had cast a shadow over his life ever since I'd known him."

Chloë paused and shifted the backpack on her shoulders, as if preparing to begin a difficult climb. "So I took a deep breath, so to speak, and I asked my *nonno* what had really happened. And since I asked him, he told me all about it, very truthfully and candidly. Sitting there in the darkness together in his little garden in Trastevere"—she pronounced the name *trass-tay-vay-ray*. "He told me all about Jackie. And it very rapidly became clear to me that this hadn't been just some kind of casual affair. It wasn't just about the sex. I think they really were in love. And they must have spent hours together, Jackie and my *nonno*, just talking. She had told him so much about herself, and he remembered it all. And now he told it to me, out there in the little garden, in the dark, under the orange trees, that summer, in the night. We talked and talked. Until my *nonna*, Raffaella, came out. And then he fell instantly silent. And I realised from that sudden and very awkward silence and the way she looked at us that she must have guessed what we were talking about. And I felt so ashamed. It's the first time I remember ever feeling shame in connection with them. Those two old people I loved so much. It felt so strange to be caught in the middle, caught up in this shameful secret between them. The idea that there were certain things that couldn't be said in front of both of them…"

She shrugged her shoulders and then, apparently annoyed at the weight of the backpack, took it off again and leaned it against the wall. I considered suggesting that we all move back into the living room, but Chloë seemed somehow more at ease out here, on the point of departure. Maybe it freed her up to say things which might be difficult otherwise.

"Anyway," she said, "that's why I know so much about these things. Because Jackie told my *nonno* and then, many years later, he told me. All about how she had this one-night stand when she was a teenager and became pregnant and then, of course, the father of the child made himself scarce. Left town to never return."

"Of course," said Nevada. "What with him being a man and all."

"Hey," said Tinkler. "Standing right here. Not to mention your boyfriend."

"So Jackie was left with the child," said Chloë. "Fortunately for her, her parents took him off Jackie's hands. They took responsibility for the little boy and raised him. And thus Jackie was free to go ahead and live her life."

"Still," said Nevada. "Having a kid out of wedlock… Back then, in the 1960s, it must have been no picnic."

"No picnic," said Chloë. "I like that idiom. Yes, it was apparently quite tough on her. But, as I said, her parents took responsibility for the kid and looked after him. And he grew up to be quite a successful businessman by all accounts… Cass and Desdemona's dad."

"And you were telling us how you met them," I said. "Cass and Desdemona."

"Yes."

"Presumably it was because of the…" I hesitated over the word *murder*.

"The case," said Nevada, helpfully.

"That's right," said Chloë. "They came to Rome to film a documentary about the case, for Italian television. Someone had the bright idea to bring us together. The grandson and granddaughter of the victim, and the granddaughter of the alleged killer. So that was how I met Desdemona."

After a moment she added, "And Cass."

She paused again, lost in her memories. "I almost refused to do it, the interview… But in the end I agreed." It sounded like she still wasn't sure she'd made the right decision.

"By the way," said Nevada. She was watching Chloë rather carefully, it seemed to me. "She asked if she could have your contact details."

The effect of this casual comment on Chloë was quite remarkable. She actually stiffened physically. "Who?" she said. "Desmona?"

"Yes."

"That fucking bitch?" snarled Chloë. "After she just tried to sabotage me clearing *nonno*'s name? After coming around here tonight to see you guys and trying to stop me hiring you?" She glared at me as if I was personally responsible for this—for trying to prevent her from hiring myself.

Which in some ways wasn't such a bad idea. Not least since she'd let slip that her primary interest was in proving that her grandfather wasn't a killer. Did she even really want me to find the record, I wondered?

I suddenly had the uncomfortable realisation that Chloë was still looking at me. But now with wary interest rather than hostility. "What are you thinking?" she said.

Oh well, at least it made a change from her telling me she already knew what I was thinking.

"I was just speculating whether you really wanted me to find the record…"

"Of course I want you to find it."

She virtually spat these words out, but nonetheless I forced myself to complete my sentence. "…Or whether it's just a smokescreen and you really just want me to find some kind of proof of your grandfather's innocence." It turned out to be a rather long sentence. And a cumbersome one at that.

"I want you to do both," said Chloë. "I do need that record. Unless you can find me a copy on vinyl, I can't reissue it. And it's one of the most important and prestigious works in my grandpa's back catalogue. I must reissue it. And now I learn that Desdemona—" she pronounced the name with venomous care "—was around here earlier trying to not just prevent you from helping clear my *nonno*'s name, but also to destroy my budding business venture by hampering my attempts to release his music. Offering you money so you wouldn't work with me."

"Well, they didn't actually get around to offering us money," said Nevada hastily. "Not as such." The startling transformation of Chloë into a pint-sized pugnacious fury seemed to have effected a reciprocal and equally startling transformation of my darling into someone uncharacteristically contrite and apologetic. It wasn't often one saw Nevada on the back foot, but she clearly now felt she might have played this wrong. "So I'm not sure we could actually say she tried to *sabotage*…"

But Chloë wasn't listening. She was absorbed in some vivid inner landscape, shaking her head balefully and smiling a savage little smile. "She wants my contact details, does she? And she thinks I'll give them to her, does she? No way. Oh, no. No. Fucking. Way."

Chloë scooped up her rucksack and shrugged it back onto her shoulders. She paused, apparently recovering her self-control, then she gave me a probing look.

"You will find my *nonno*'s record?"

"I'll certainly do my best."

"Okay, thank you." She kissed me on the cheek, then kissed Nevada on the cheek and even, much to his undeserving delight, kissed Tinkler on the cheek.

She turned to go, opened the door, then stopped dead.

Chloë stood there motionless for so long that we all wondered what was going on.

Then she turned back and looked at us, eyes dark and large.

"You can tell her I'm staying at the NoMad hotel, in Covent Garden…" she said. "Desdemona, I mean. If you see her again, I mean."

7: THE NEVADA EFFECT

"So, what's the plan?" said Tinkler, after Chloë had left.

"To find the record," I said.

"Good luck with that."

"Thank you."

"I was being sarcastic."

"No kidding," I said.

"Admit it, you have absolutely no idea of how to find the record for the gorgeous Chloë. My god, she is gorgeous, isn't she?" Tinkler paused reminiscently, staring in the general direction which Chloë had departed. "You don't suppose she's a lesbian, do you?" He gave Nevada an imploring look. "My lesbian sense is tingling," he said mournfully. Then he added, "It's a Spider-Man joke."

"There aren't any lesbians anymore," said Nevada.

"What?" said Tinkler. He sounded genuinely stricken.

"It's out of date terminology. All those categories are breaking down. Behaviour doesn't need to be restricted and codified and defined in that way. There's just people who sleep with people."

"Just so long as some of them sleep with me," said Tinkler. "But never mind your woke nonsense. Answer my question. Do you think Chloë's a lesbian?"

"Hmm," said Nevada. "Well, there definitely does seem to be something going on between her and Desdemona…"

"Why are all the good ones taken? Or lesbian?" said Tinkler. Then, hopefully, "Maybe Chloë's bi."

"In your case," said Nevada, "I suspect she's bye-bye. As in wave her farewell."

"Yes, yes," said Tinkler tetchily. "You don't have to spell out your sexual insults. Anyway, that's all just further distraction from the real subject here."

"Which is?"

"The fact that you've agreed to take money, a large sum of money, from poor bisexual Chloë for a rare record that the Vinyl Detective here has no idea how to find." He looked at me. "You don't have any idea of how to find it, do you?"

"No, but what else is new?" I said. "By which I mean…"

"By which he means," said Nevada firmly, "that at this early stage of a case…"

"I love that you call it a case," said Tinkler.

"That, at this early stage of a case, we never know exactly how we're going to find a particular record."

"I love that you say 'we'," said Tinkler.

"So do I," I said.

"So what's the plan?"

I shrugged. "Well I've already checked all the usual sources—"

"Discogs and eBay," said Tinkler impatiently.

"And MusicStack and CD & LP dot com," I said.

"Right, I knew about those," said Tinkler.

"And Dusty Groove and Craig Moerer and Euclid and Jet Set and Recordphile and Paris Jazz Corner," I said.

"Right, I knew about some of those," said Tinkler.

"And, of course, none of them have got a copy," I said.

"So what next?"

"We roll up our sleeves and start looking in earnest," said Nevada.

"What sleeves? And looking where?"

"Well," I said, "it's Barnes Fair this Saturday."

"Barnes Fair?" Tinkler laughed heartily and at some length. "When's the last time anyone found any rare vinyl there?"

"Why don't you join us in the search?" I said. "Early start Saturday morning. Be here just after sunrise. I'll cook breakfast for you."

"Sounds tempting, but I've got to work on Saturday," said Tinkler.

"You wouldn't say that if Agatha was joining us," said Nevada.

"Is she joining us?" said Tinkler eagerly.

"No, she's still sunning her lithe body on the beaches of the Riviera."

"Stop tormenting me with these visions," said Tinkler. "And count me out of Barnes Fair."

* * *

Barnes Fair was an annual ritual. On the second Saturday of July the village green in this affluent suburb of southwest London was given over to what has been called a posh car-boot sale. A very posh car-boot sale. Tinkler wasn't entirely wrong; it had been some years since any real treasures had turned up there vinyl-wise. Indeed, any kind of secondhand goods were increasingly scarce—unless you counted vintage bric-à-brac or clothing, which were always in ample supply. And the latter of which exerted a certain allure for my beloved.

So she was ready, eager and willing to get up early, feed the cats, drink some coffee—despite my offer of breakfast to Tinkler, I preferred to go hunting on an empty stomach—and head out shortly after seven thirty. It was a beautiful, fresh summer morning and, with few pedestrians about and traffic as yet light on the roads, it felt as if we had London to ourselves. The walk to Barnes was a pleasure, and at this hour we didn't even hit any trains at the diabolical double level crossing on Vine Road.

So in no time at all we were walking down the narrow wisteria-lined alley which nestled between an open stretch of Barnes Common on one side and a row of high walled multi-million-pound mansions on the other.

We paused on the little bridge to watch Beverley Brook flowing past with a pair of swans riding sedately on the water, phenomenally and preposterously white, and then entered the village green, where early preparations for the fair were already well advanced. The bouncy castle, for instance, was being inflated with the assistance of a diesel generator whose clamour thoroughly and permanently destroyed the early morning peace. "Oh well," said Nevada, having to shout over the noise of it, "at least the annoying woman hasn't started talking over the PA yet."

All around us small stall holders were setting up their small stalls. People were unloading goods from the eponymous car boots, or from trailers or the interior of cars, and spreading them out on blankets or arranging them carefully on folding tables. Despite trying to maintain an appropriately cynical detachment, I began to feel a stir of excitement. If there was anything really sensational to be found, now was the time to find it, before the fair was officially up and running, and the hordes of civilians had arrived. Of course, even at this time of day, there was the annoying hazard of early-bird dealers scooping things up.

Come to think of it, that was exactly what I was, and exactly what I was here to do.

Nevada and I split up, her to go off in search of stylish but under-priced secondhand clothing and myself to hunt for records. Which were, as I had expected, in short supply. True, there were a couple of established dealers who came every year with a stock of vintage vinyl, but their wares were all-too predictable.

It wasn't that they never had anything good. It was just that, if they did, it would be fully priced. Or more than fully priced. And anything really valuable—such as *Murder in London*—wouldn't even put in an appearance. They'd auction it online for as much as they could get. I don't suppose I could blame them for that.

But I did.

I prowled around the village green, exploring every stall— a process which had a slight feeling of endless circularity about it because, as I proceeded, new stalls sprang up around me, requiring further investigation, and while I investigated those, still more sprang up…

Nonetheless, I eventually reached a point at which the law of diminishing returns began to make itself felt, and I was just about to throw in the towel and rejoin Nevada—she would probably have found something to supplement my wardrobe by now and would want me to try it on—when I noticed an elderly couple unloading the trailer attached to their car.

The car itself was a rather cool and sporty 1960s Sunbeam Alpine in mint green. I only knew what it was called because the name was clearly spelled out across the front of the vehicle, and on its side. The couple also looked like they dated back to the 1960s, but were rather less cool and sporty. They were haggard, grey-haired and combative. They wore matching outfits of shapeless jeans, olive green waxed cotton jackets and inappropriately jolly little tweed caps, as if they were out for a jaunt in the countryside. I suppose they were, depending on where they came from.

The woman was thin and slow-moving, the man corpulent and hyperactive, but between them they were getting their wares arrayed on a waterproof groundsheet with admirable speed and efficiency, despite arguing about every imaginable detail.

Including the pricing of the records.

"Those vinyls are worth something," I heard the man say.

"I know they are," said the woman.

"So why haven't you priced them?"

"I have priced them."

"I don't see any prices on them."

"I've priced them in my head," said the woman. "In my head."

"What good is that?" said the man.

"What do you mean what good is it? If someone asks me how much something is, I can tell them."

"No one's going to ask," said the man. "They won't bother to ask. They need to know the price up front. It encourages them to buy. They'll be too shy to ask. Psychology."

"We'll put some price stickers on them, then."

"We don't have the price stickers," declared the man with satisfaction. "Because someone forgot to bring them."

"All right, just write the price on the covers then."

The initial mention of vinyl, I insist on the singular, had attracted my attention—from about twenty-five metres away; it's amazing how the acuity of your hearing can be enhanced when it's something you really care about. And I'd immediately started towards the couple and their groundsheet at a brisk walk.

When they started talking about price stickers, I sharply increased my pace. Nothing could destroy an immaculate album cover like a price sticker applied by an amateur seller. Or, for that matter, a lot of professional sellers.

And when they commenced a discussion about actually writing the prices on the cover, I would have broken into a full-speed run.

But by then I was already here.

Spread on the groundsheet was a large and baffling assortment of tools, most of them apparently devoted to the art of automobile maintenance. Agatha could probably have told you what they were for. Personally, I had no idea and couldn't have cared less. There was also a stack of mouldering automobile manuals, a vintage lawnmower, an assortment of particularly vile-looking garden gnomes intermingled with porcelain shepherdesses who looked like they were badly in want of chaperones to protect them from said gnomes, a number of abominable and spooky-looking children's dolls, old boardgames in mildewed boxes…

And the records.

These were in four large cardboard cartons which had once contained avocados. This seemed a little odd since the waxed cotton jacketed duo didn't look like they consumed industrial quantities of avocadoes. But no matter. One of the boxes was all singles. Not my department, unless I'd been specifically hired to look for something. Another consisted of 78s on shellac. Ditto.

But the other two were full of LPs. And, by the look of them, at first glance, in surprisingly good shape.

"Good morning," I said to the couple, who gave me a suspicious look as if the last thing they expected, or wanted, having travelled here in their car with its trailer full of their goods and painstakingly unpacked these and put them out on display on this early Saturday morning, was a customer who might actually buy some of their stuff.

I crouched down, grateful as always for having worn my low-cut, crate-digging shoes, and started looking through the LPs.

"Those vinyls are worth something," said the man to me, as if challenging me to deny it.

"I've got all the prices in my head," said the woman. "So if you find something you want, just ask."

"Thank you," I said. "I will."

You can tell almost immediately whether a box of records is worth looking through. If they had belonged to someone who kept them in a damp garage, for instance, you could see that instantly. But these had been kept indoors and, apparently, had been well cared for. Or perhaps never played. Because not only were the covers crisp and undamaged, the first record I slid out of its sleeve gleamed, black and lovely, the beautiful microgrooves on the vinyl entirely pristine.

The only problem was what the records were.

Easy listening. This one was Percy Faith. The others represented the likes of Bert Kaempfert, Andy Williams and Herb Alpert. I might have been interested in some early albums by the latter, but only if they were original American pressings. These were all British.

But then, the record I was looking for was British.

And from exactly this period…

I slipped Percy back into his sleeve and went quickly through the others. Digging deeper into the box, I found that they were all similar music, but you never knew… and the occasional rock album encouraged me to keep looking. The rock ones were all compilations, so not worth anything, but nevertheless…

And then I found some nice blues LPs on the Marble Arch label. These weren't worth much, but they were good music, nicely packaged with classy graphics for their cover designs and their presence here indicated whoever had once owned this collection had possessed some taste.

There was even some jazz, but all traditional stuff. Including Mr Acker Bilk. But this too was a good sign, because Acker Bilk had released a lot of records in the Lansdowne series on Columbia/EMI, just the same as *Murder in London*.

What's more, I noticed that several of these had stickers indicating that they were promotional copies, not for sale. Such records were intended as samples for testing, or to be given to DJs or shops. They were often the best-sounding pressings, because they were the first off the stamper in the factory.

And, importantly, they indicated whoever had owned this collection must have had some kind of insider connection with the record label to have got hold of them. Which might mean they'd have access to a record which wasn't officially released. Like *Murder in London*…

It was a long shot, but nevertheless I was happily daydreaming along these lines when I turned over a copy of Acker Bilk's *The Seven Ages of Acker*, featuring photos of the titular clarinettist dressed as a caveman, a cowboy and a knight in shining armour…

And there it was.

The next record in the avocado box was *Murder in London*.

It would be banal to say I didn't believe it, but it would also be true. I crouched there for a moment, peering into the box, listening to the sounds of the bouncy castle generator, of the grumbling engines of cars as they made their laborious way along narrow paths to the stall holders' pitches, the random rise and fall of voices, the barking of a dog.

And smelling the distant aroma of grilling sausages and frying onions as the breakfast wagon got underway for the day.

I absorbed and noted all these sensory impressions, weighing them carefully just to prove to myself that I truly was awake, that this was real, that I wasn't dreaming.

I wasn't dreaming.

There it was in front of me.

I reached down to pick it up. I wanted to turn the cover over and see Loretto Loconsole smiling at me in Trafalgar Square under that incriminating headline of a title.

But as soon as I touched it, I knew something was wrong.

The cover was there, all right. And it was real and it was original and it was in perfect condition.

But it was also empty.

I lifted it up, flopping comically in my hand without the stiffening presence of the record inside it. I carefully set it to one side, my heart pounding, and told myself to take it easy. How likely was it that the record cover had come all this way, after all these years, to this exact time and place without the record itself somewhere nearby? Surely it was here somewhere?

I began to look through the box with a growing sense of desperation.

"Found something?" said the man.

"I've got all the prices in my head," said the woman. "What have you found?"

"An empty cover," I said. I tried to keep the note of despair out of my voice. I showed the cover to them, hoping it would evoke a glad cry of recognition followed by a flow of useful information leading to the discovery of the errant piece of vinyl.

But they just stared at it blankly.

"What, there's no record inside?" said the man.

"It'll be there somewhere," said the woman.

"I hope so," I said, somewhat hoarsely, crouching on the ground, flipping through the box, looking for a record without a sleeve. A shadow fell across me and I looked up to see Nevada standing there. She sank down to crouch beside me. "Found something?" she said quietly.

The man and the woman were staring at us. Nevada's arrival, and her clear association with me had instantly altered their perception of me; I'd risen substantially in their estimation. I was used to this. The Nevada effect.

I showed Nevada the cover of *Murder in London*. "Holy shit," she said. But she said it very quietly without even moving her lips. She was much better at the whole poker face thing than me.

"Don't get too excited," I said. "There's no record inside."

"*Fuck*. It's just the cover?"

"Yes."

"But if the cover is here…"

"That's what I'm hoping," I said, keeping my voice down.

"Do you want me to help you look?"

"You can if you want," I said. "But I'm okay doing this on my own."

"Okay, well if you're sure…"

"What's up?" I said, because something clearly was.

"I ran into Cass and Desdemona," she said.

"Seriously? Here?"

"Yes. With Jasper McClew."

"Oh, great," I said. "What are they doing here?"

"That's what I intend to find out," said Nevada. "So I'm going to have a coffee with them at Gail's. Come and join us when you're finished here?"

"Okay," I said.

"Good luck."

"Thanks." I suspected I would need it.

She gave me a quick kiss, rose up from her haunches and set off across the green. As she left, the man gave me a glance of reluctant admiration. I was used to that, too.

I went back to my search.

The record wasn't there.

It wasn't there without its cover. There were no records without covers. That left the possibility that it was actually in one of the *other* covers, disguised as Andy Williams, Bert Kaempfert, Acker Bilk et al. So I had to look through every one of these.

I did. It wasn't there.

I also looked through the box of singles and the box of 78s.

The record wasn't there, either.

By the time I'd finished, the couple running the stall looked like they were thoroughly sick of my presence. The Nevada effect was clearly wearing off.

I looked at the empty cover, so mockingly pristine, and reached in my pocket where I kept the cash for such occasions as this.

"You want to buy that?" said the man. "Without the record in it?"

"Yes please."

He looked at his wife, who had the prices in her head. But she clearly didn't have the prices for covers without records in her head, because she was completely thrown. Finally she said, "One pound?" as if rather alarmed at her own temerity. I took out a twenty pound note and handed it to her.

"I don't have change," she said bad temperedly. "Not for this."

"I don't want change," I said.

The couple looked at me rather oddly, as well they might.

"You're giving us twenty pounds?" said the man.

"Yes."

"For an empty cover?" said the woman.

"I'm hoping I'll find the record from inside it."

"Not here you won't," she said. "You've already looked through everything."

"I'm hoping that you guys could have a look when you get home."

"That's fair enough," said the man quickly. "Isn't it, Valerie?" He obviously wanted the twenty quid, and was a lot more eager than his wife to separate a fool from his money.

"I suppose so," she said, and folded the bill and put it into the capacious pocket of her jacket. I was relieved that she did so. Twenty pounds didn't seem much to spend to buy some goodwill and the possibility of actually getting my hands on the record.

"Thank you," I said.

"No worries." The man was positively jovial. "I'll have a look as soon we get home."

"No you won't," said the woman. She turned to me. "No he won't. He'll be knackered when he gets home."

"Understandably," I said. "There's no hurry."

"I'll make sure he looks first thing tomorrow."

"There's no hurry," I repeated. And then I took the plunge. "I realise it's a lot of hassle, to look for one record which might be in another cover, which could be in any cover…"

"Or no cover at all," said Valerie.

"Or no cover at all," I agreed, trying not to wince at the possibility. A piece of vinyl without any paper to protect it was a piece of vinyl that was going to end up scratched to hell. "Anyway, it's a lot of hassle to look for it…"

"No worries," said the man.

"So I wanted to offer to help."

"Help?" said Valerie.

"Maybe I could come and have a look. Myself."

"What, come to our place, you mean?"

"If you wouldn't mind," I said.

Valerie and her husband looked at each other.

"Possibly," he said. He didn't sound very enthusiastic. And she looked even less enthusiastic. So I backpedalled hastily.

"Anyway, perhaps we could discuss it on the phone. At some point."

"Perhaps we could," said Valerie. "At some point."

I desperately wanted their phone number but I knew better than to push for it. So instead I gave them mine, on a business card. Unlike my Vinyl Detective business cards of yesteryear, this one didn't actually state my business. Because that would be all too likely to push up prices.

Not that I didn't have a certain nostalgic affection for those original cards. Since Nevada had been carrying one when she'd first walked into my life.

I left Valerie and her helpmeet with my business card and my twenty pound note, and set off with the empty record sleeve under my arm, heading for the edge of the green and Gail's bakery to rendezvous with Nevada.

And Cass and Desdemona.

And Jasper McClew.

8: PORNOGRAPHIC T-SHIRT

We'd first met Jasper McClew when I'd been hired to look for a record of big band swing music made during the Second World War. It was what they called a Victory Disc, manufactured purely for the use of the armed forces.

It had been recorded by a band called the Flare Path Orchestra and one of the musicians in that band, Johnny Thomas, had been convicted of killing a young woman called Gillian Gadon in a scandalous murder case (you would have thought there was enough killing going on during the Second World War without anyone pursuing it as a private initiative, so to speak).

The scandalous case was known as the Silk Stockings Murder. Johnny Thomas had been executed—hanged—for the murder, but had subsequently, very much subsequently, been proved to be innocent of the crime.

This tragedy had taken place in a little coastal village in Kent, called Kingsdown. This is where Jasper McClew had resided when we'd first encountered him, monetising this heartbreaking tale. He'd been conducting a walking tour of the murder scene, and making people pay through the nose for it.

He called himself a local historian. We qualified this somewhat by calling him a ferret-faced local historian.

We'd also called him ET with a beard, because he bore a marked resemblance to that prosthetic critter, with the addition of a straggly fringe of whiskers.

Now I was pleased, if that's the word, to see that he still looked like ET, though he'd grown his facial hair out into the kind of lavish full beard that was currently fashionable.

Or rather, he'd endeavoured to do so. The end result was the most pathetic attempt at a beard I'd seen since Stinky Stanmer had gone down a similar route. Though at least in Stinky's case the fad for beard oil had not yet emerged in its full horror. Which meant in that other encounter we had been spared the sort of obscenely glossy gleam and intense patchouli scent which now emanated from Jasper's facial hair.

I suppose at least it had the merit of being different from his straggly earlier iteration, though with Jasper's tiny child's face it looked more incongruous than ever, as he peered out, lost and blinking within it.

His clothing had definitely improved, though. He'd previously favoured the sort of waxed cotton I'd recently seen worn by Valerie and her spouse when they failed to sell me a complete copy of *Murder in London*. Now Jasper was wearing a baggily well-cut jacket in some kind of moss green cloth and, underneath it, a chunky but trendy-looking sweater in a sort of ivory colour with a faint greenish tinge which went very nicely with the jacket. I couldn't see whether he still favoured ill-fitting jeans (also à la Valerie and squeeze) because he was currently sitting down, little legs out of sight, at a table on the pavement outside Gail's.

Nevada was sitting with him. There was no sign of the Higgins siblings. I wasn't quite sure whether to be thankful or disappointed. "Here he is," said Nevada, smiling in greeting and rising from the table. "What can I get you, darling?"

"You'll never guess," I said. And she nodded cheerfully and promptly went to fetch me a much-needed coffee.

Jasper was holding out his hand to be shaken, though evidently he didn't feel it necessary to stand up to do this. So I shook it standing up while he remained seated, rather as if I was being received by a diminutive monarch. I sat down to equalise things. "What brings you here, Jasper?" I said.

This was the right question, judging by the way his eyes brightened with boyish enthusiasm. "I have a new project," he said. "A rather exciting new project. A podcast. It's something of an odd expression, I know, arising from the conflation of the word 'broadcast' with the now obsolete technology of the Apple iPod—"

"*McClew's Clues*," I said. Anything to shut him up.

"You've heard about it, then?" he said, his little bearded face lighting up.

"I've heard about it," I allowed. "But I haven't actually *heard* it, since there aren't any podcast episodes yet. And the website is still under construction."

Jasper either didn't hear this or managed to blithely and

thoroughly ignore it because he churned on, saying, "It deals with the coldest of cold cases."

"Yes, I know," I said. "I read all that on the website. Which is still under construction."

"As you know," said Jasper, still not hearing or still blithely ignoring, "I have had some considerable experience in solving cold cases, such as the Silk Stockings Murder. Correcting that hideous wartime miscarriage of justice which saw an innocent man hanged."

While I agreed with the hideous miscarriage of justice bit, I wasn't sure how much had been done to correct that. Hanging someone wasn't the sort of thing you could retrospectively correct. And rather less importantly, I wasn't sure how much credit Jasper could take for it.

"As you know, I had intended to write a book about that case," he said. "After all, it was my scoop. But before I could properly put pen to paper—or rather words to a Microsoft Word file—I found myself sidelined in the most outrageously unjust and unfair manner."

What had happened was that the media had discovered there was a pretty young woman involved in the situation, one who provided great optics, travelling around as she did in a gaudily painted hippie van. Her name was Opal Gadon and she had at least as much claim as Jasper to exposing the truth about that "cold case".

Once they found they could make her the focus for reporting on the case, no one had the slightest interest in photographing Jasper's hairy little face, or recording any of the words coming out of it. Bummer for him.

"I don't intend to let that happen again," said Jasper. I was impressed by the quivering bitterness and repressed anger in his voice. "This time I have come to a contractual arrangement with the principal participants involved. A solid and robust contractual arrangement with these participants."

"This is Desdemona and Cass?" I said.

"The Higgins twins. Yes."

"Are they twins?" I said.

"Well, not chronologically," said Jasper.

"How is anybody a twin if not chronologically?" I said.

Jasper shook his head as if impatient with my obtuseness. "Twins are more marketable. They raise the profile of the project. And, as perhaps you've noted, 'the Higgins twins' has a pleasant ring to it. A certain euphony."

"You mean it rhymes, sort of. But not quite."

"I don't expect you to understand the nuances," said Jasper.

"Have you asked them about this?" I said. "Cass and Desdemona? Whether you can refer to them as twins?"

"Not as yet."

"Well you'd better make sure you do," I said. It seemed to me that Desdemona was unhappy enough being Cass's sister without the further burden of also being mendaciously marketed as his twin.

"I will ensure that I do," said Jasper, with maximum snottiness and sarcasm.

"By the way," I said, "where are Cass and Desdemona? Nevada told me they were with you."

"They were indeed, but unfortunately they learned that

they had urgent business in town which has now called them away."

"What were you guys doing here, anyway?" I said. "Did you come for Barnes Fair?"

"No," Jasper chuckled. "That was merely a felicitous and fortuitous coincidence. I mean, bumping into you and your good lady at the aforementioned fair. No, Cassio and Desdemona and I came here to do some field recordings on location at the Olympic Studios. Or rather at the erstwhile site of the Olympic Studios. These were a renowned popular music recording studios used by many of the top recording artists of the day, particularly during the 1960s and 1970s."

"I know about Olympic Studios," I said, hoping to forestall a further avalanche of all-too-familiar facts.

"It was also the location where Loretto Loconsole recorded the soundtrack music for *Murder in London*," said Jasper.

"I knew that, too," I said, continuing my Quixotic quest to get him to shut up.

Luckily, at that moment, Nevada arrived with a coffee for me, a fresh one for herself and even one for Jasper. Any feelings I might have had about the undeserved nature of the last were compensated for by the fact that he was compelled to stop talking while he drank it. Good thinking, Nevada.

During this brief but welcome period of caffeine beverage-imposed silence, I glanced under the table and took note of the rather stylish shoes Jasper was wearing. Real leather and they didn't look cheap. The same for his trousers—although they weren't made of leather, thank all the gods. But they too looked stylish and not cheap.

All in all he'd received an impressive makeover. I suddenly put this together with his anger and bitterness about being supplanted by Opal on his previous "scoop". She had proved a much more attractive visual at the time. And although she still would now, indeed most people would, he was doing everything in his power to make himself look presentable and camera-ready.

"Did Jasper tell you why he wanted to talk to us?" said Nevada.

"No," I said. "I didn't realise that he did. I just thought we were old friends getting reacquainted."

Before the manifest insincerity of this statement could really begin to make itself felt, Jasper set aside his coffee and leaned forward excitedly. "That's right," he said. "That is why I alluded to it being so fortuitous and felicitous meeting you here. The two of you. Because you were both involved in the Great Kentish Heist."

"The what?" I said, although I had an all-too-clear inkling of what he was getting at.

"That is what it's now called, or rather what it will be called when the term gains traction as soon as my book on the subject is published."

"I thought you were concentrating on podcasts these day," said Nevada.

"Well of course it will be a podcast as well," said Jasper, as if this went without saying but he was happy enough to spell it out for Nevada, since she was a bit slow. "But I feel that the Great Kentish Heist merits the in-depth exploration which can only be provided in the form of a full-length book." He focused his bright little eyes on me. "I am referring of course to the daring daylight armed robbery which took place not long ago in Kent. In which you and your fair partner here were involved."

"We weren't involved," I said. "We just ended up on the wrong end of a gun."

And not for the first time, I thought.

"Yes, but you *were* there," said Jasper. "You were actually present when it was taking place. And although of course I was also involved…" I repressed the urge to point out that his "involvement" solely consisted of writing about the event after the fact for a small local newspaper. Indeed, for the online edition of a small local newspaper. "…The two of you…" Jasper waved his hand in a generous, expansive gesture encompassing Nevada and I. "…You were actually there as events unfolded and thus can provide invaluable eyewitness details. Local colour, so to speak."

"So you'd like to interview us for your book?" said Nevada politely.

I knew where this was going, I thought gleefully, and it would end in Jasper being sent an invoice that would cause his tiny eyes to pop out.

"All in good time. All in good time. But, first of all, what I would really like to do is to speak to one of the armed robbers involved."

"And I'm sure you can," I said. "Just so long as they'll agree to receiving a prison visit from you."

Jasper shook his head, teeth parting in his beard in a good-natured smile. "Ah, no. I mean of course, certainly I shall. I shall do exactly that. And indeed I have already made some contact with certain of those individuals. But the one I really want to speak to, the armed robber I am most eager to interview, is the one who got away."

Nevada and I looked at each other. "Princess Seitan?" I said. It was an extraordinary name all right, not least invoking the vegan foodstuff as it did, instead of the dark lord of the underworld. But it was the name she went by.

"Yes."

"I imagine the police would be eager to interview her, too," said Nevada sardonically.

"Yes, but of course I have no intention of sharing my sources with the police." Jasper watched us beadily, grinning. "Or rather, sharing *your* sources."

"Our sources?" I said.

Jasper just sat there and smiled at us, apparently very pleased with himself and his cleverness.

"You think we're in touch with Princess Seitan?" said Nevada.

"I think you *know* how to get in touch with her," said Jasper.

"Well, that's very flattering," said Nevada. "But I'm afraid you're wrong."

Jasper winked at us. I'm pretty sure it was a wink and not just a nervous twitch. "I don't expect you to admit to me that you know how to contact her."

"That's good," said Nevada. "Because we don't."

"She is a fascinating individual," said Jasper.

"She certainly is," said Nevada. "But we still can't hook you up with her."

"No need to admit anything," said Jasper good humouredly. "But if you should happen to find yourself communicating with her, at some point in the future, please tell her I would be very eager to make contact with her myself."

"What makes you think we know how to reach her?" I said. The last time I'd seen the person in question she'd been peering at me with her striking sea-green eyes through a Chinese opera mask and brandishing an AK47 automatic rifle. And then scooting on an electric scooter. Rather rapidly away from me. Which was, I must say, the way I wanted things to remain as far as she was concerned.

Although those green eyes of hers really were striking…

Jasper leaned towards me, the patchouli smell of his beard oil momentarily overwhelming the far more welcome aroma of the coffee. "Because that wasn't the first time you'd had contact with her, was it, at the heist? You'd actually met her before that, hadn't you?"

This was true enough. I remembered the food van, appropriately enough bedecked with skulls, outside a famed music venue in Brixton, where Princess Seitan had served me a rather unforgettable meal. My mouth watered treacherously at the memory.

Also treacherous was the memory of her remarkable eyes.

She certainly wasn't boring, I'll say that for her.

"I think it has the makings of a bestseller," Jasper was

saying. "My book about Princess Seitan and the Great Kentish Heist."

I noticed that Princess Seitan was now the primary focus of the book. Or, rather, that he'd now admitted that she was.

"I fully expect there to be a commitment to film a Netflix series based on it," he said. "Unless, of course, another platform has a more advantageous offer to make to me."

His new confidence was impressive. Although, come to think of it, he'd always had confidence.

What he didn't have was anything solid to follow it up with.

Jasper sat back in his chair and gave both of us the benefit of his most charming smile, which wasn't much of a benefit. But at least his sitting back took the patchouli beard oil out of olfactory range. "And I'd be more than happy to make some kind of financial arrangement with the lady in question," he said. "And there will even be a finder's fee for you."

"Okay," I said. "You've got completely the wrong idea about this. I don't have access to the lady in question, who happens to be very dangerous—"

"And very cool," said Nevada, who was something of a Princess Seitan fan.

"Very dangerous and very cool," I said.

"And rather fit, come to think of it," added Nevada.

"Not as fit as you, darling," I felt obliged to say, and then wrestled the conversation back to the subject at hand. I looked at Jasper. "I have no contact with Princess Seitan, and I have no idea how to make contact with her. However fit and dangerous and cool she may be."

Jasper just grinned at me. "Well, if you should happen to run across her…"

"I won't," I said. "And, Jasper, while it may be all right to mess around in cold cases—and I'm not even saying that it is—it is very much *not* all right for you to mess around in cases that aren't cold. Cases that are very warm."

"That are in fact red hot," said Nevada.

"Right," I said. "Red hot. The police are actively looking for this person."

"Well, naturally they are," said Jasper calmly.

"And anyone with knowledge of her whereabouts would be obliged to go directly to the cops and tell them. Unless they wanted to end up under arrest themselves."

"But sometimes," said Jasper soothingly, "it's possible to reach out to someone and send them a message without knowing their whereabouts. Without having any idea where they actually are."

"However, that's not the situation here," I said.

"However," Jasper said, possibly echoing me with deliberate sarcasm, "if that situation should change, please ask her to get in touch with me." He gave us his business card.

It seemed to be the morning for it.

I remarked on this as Nevada and I walked back to the village green and Barnes Fair, now in full swing, leaving Jasper and his perfumed beard thankfully behind.

"You don't know the half of it," said Nevada. "Or rather, the third of it."

"What do you mean?"

"I gave Jasper my business card, too."

"Why in god's name would you do that?" I said.

"Don't be angry," said Nevada.

"I'm not angry, I'm just baffled. Why would you…? Oh."

She grinned at me. "Got it?" she said.

"You're going to sell him some very stylish clothing at a cutthroat price."

"At a surprisingly affordable price," said Nevada. "But yes, at an enormous markup compared to what I originally paid for it."

"He does seem to be getting some fashion advice from somewhere," I said.

"From shops," said Nevada, who'd evidently extracted this information from him. "Which is fine as far as it goes. But shops are just going to sell you the stuff that they have in stock, obviously. And at full price. Whereas I can offer a bespoke and personalised service involving vintage garments which are unique, stylish and distinctively destined for the individual."

"You don't have to give me the sales pitch," I said. "I'm already on board."

Nevada took my hand.

"I didn't find the record, by the way," I said. "I only got the cover."

"I know. I knew as soon as I saw your face."

We crossed the road, which was a time-consuming business, as it was now buzzing with traffic, and returned to Barnes Fair, which was now crowded with people.

"What happened to Cass and Desdemona?" I said. "Jasper said they had business in town."

Nevada didn't exactly blush. That wasn't something she did. But she did look chagrined, in a sort of prim way. She looked primly chagrined. "Ah," she said. "Well, I suppose they did, in a sense. Or at least Desdemona did, after I spoke to her."

"You spoke to her?"

"Yes, I felt obliged to pass on Chloë's message to her."

"About the hotel where she's staying? In Covent Garden."

"The NoMad. Right. I felt I had to give Desdemona that message…"

"Well, of course you did," I said. "Chloë asked you to."

"Thank you."

"No need to thank me. You couldn't really have done anything else."

"But thank you for being supportive," said Nevada.

"Always my pleasure."

"So, anyway, I told Desdemona where Chloë was staying, and as soon as she heard that, she skedaddled."

"In the general direction of Covent Garden?"

"I assume so. And Cass took off after her."

"To do what?" I recalled Cass's vocal disapproval of his sister's interest in Chloë. "Try and stop her?"

"I assume so. Good luck with that."

I paused and took out my phone. We were still on the fringes of the fair and the noise level was manageable, though I could already hear music from somewhere—live music, big band jazz, and it wasn't bad. Plus the annoying woman could be heard intermittently making her irritating announcements over the public address system. Everything from reporting lost children to requests to move cars because they were lowering the tone of the place.

So this was my last chance to make myself heard on a phone call without shouting. And that would be unprofessional. Of course, I could have made the call while we were still having coffee, but I didn't want Jasper overhearing.

"Who are you calling?" said Nevada.

"Chloë."

"Can I have a word when you're finished?"

I nodded, just as our client answered her phone. I updated her about the frustrating find of the empty sleeve, and the tantalising but equally frustrating possibility that the boot fair couple might actually have the vinyl at home, in a different sleeve. If only they would let me look.

"Did you get their phone number?" said Chloë.

"No," I said. "And before you ask why I didn't push them for it…"

"I wasn't going to ask," said Chloë mildly. "I assume you didn't push them for it because they seemed reluctant and you didn't want to alienate them completely and lose any chance of getting the record."

"Well…" I said, relieved and more than a little impressed. "That's exactly right."

"But I also assume you gave them your number?"

"Yes. Right again."

"Great. Then we'll just have to keep our fingers crossed and wait, and hope they get in touch with you."

"Okay, yes, that's exactly what we'll do. Meanwhile Nevada would like a quick word." I handed the phone over to her.

Nevada took it rather gingerly but gamely plunged ahead. "I just wanted to let you know that I passed on your message to Desdemona," she said. "About where you were staying. No, by sheer coincidence she'd come to visit the studio here in Barnes. The one we told you about. Yes. For their podcast. Yes… I wouldn't be at all surprised. But unfortunately I think Cass is on his way, too. He got wind of where she was heading. Yes. I'm afraid so. Okay, bye." Nevada hung up and looked at me.

"Was she pleased?" I said.

"About Desdemona? Yes. Cass, not so much."

"Well you can't win them all," I said.

"You have to take the rough with the smooth," said Nevada.

"Into every life a little rain must fall," I said.

"Every rose has its thorn."

"She can cross that bridge when she comes to it."

Nevada snorted with laughter and said, "It takes grit to make a pearl."

"Is that a cliché?" I said.

"It is now."

Before we could come up with any more stultifying aphorisms, I decided it was time to track down the live music which had caught my ear. We manoeuvred through the crowd packing the village green over towards the duck pond and the arts centre, and discovered a large transparent plastic tent stationed nearby, full of musicians. This was the source of the big band jazz, and it was surprisingly high-quality stuff. We listened happily for a while, sitting on one of the benches by the pond and then decided to call it a day.

We were wandering past the arts centre, heading for the bridge over Beverley Brook and then homewards, when a voice hailed us.

"Hey! Over here."

We turned to see a familiar tall, lean scarecrow figure beckoning to us. It was our friend and neighbour—well, near friend and near neighbour—Erik Make Loud. Onetime guitarist for a psychedelic band called Valerian. Who, come to think of it, had also recorded at Olympic Studios.

Today, characteristically, Erik was dressed in very skinny black jeans, pink Converse high tops, a black leather jacket, a long—very long—purple silk scarf trailing almost to the ground. And a T-shirt featuring what was apparently the cover art of an album by someone called Jauk, which was vaguely reminiscent of a Roxy Music glamour girl cover except on second glance, indeed first glance, proved to be vividly pornographic. Assuming you considered masturbating with religious objects pornographic.

All in all, an average day's outfit for Erik.

"Come and try this ghost pepper marmalade," said Erik enthusiastically. All in all, a fairly typical opening line. "They have Carolina Reaper as well," he added.

Erik was standing in front of, and pretty much monopolising, a stall run by a pair of young men, rather anxious-looking young men at the moment, who were presumably brothers, since the sign on the stall read *Hermanos Jalapeños*. These uneasy entrepreneurs were selling, or attempting to sell, various sorts of chili comestibles. Mostly in the form of bijou bottles of sauce and jars of jam. But they did indeed also have various spicy marmalades.

Erik insisted on us trying several of these—small disposable wooden spoons were provided for this purpose by the brothers behind the stall. With diminishing enthusiasm, it must be said, as they'd begun to realise that this very skinny and very wealthy local rock star who was happily hoovering up their wares was vanishingly unlikely to actually part with any of his money.

Soon our tongues were on fire, and our consciences too. Unlike Erik, we felt embarrassed to just shamelessly exploit the free sample principle. So finally we bought some jalapeño jam to soothe our sense of scruples and led Erik away from the stall. We felt we had to detach him from the beleaguered capsicum siblings before he went through the rest of their stock. His tongue was apparently fireproof and, combined with his utter shameless enthusiasm for freebies, he could have remained happily sampling all day.

But he was equally happy to now amble along with us between the stalls on the crowded green. He glanced over at me.

"What have you got there, mate?"

"A cover without a record inside," I said.

"Very annoyingly," said Nevada.

Erik reached out for the cover and I surrendered it to him. He could hardly do much harm. Well, possibly crease the ironically immaculate laminated flipback sleeve, but that wouldn't have bothered our client. She wanted what was inside. Or, rather, what wasn't inside.

I took Erik's interest to be just standard baseline nosiness, aggravated by the—rather foolishly unnecessary—protective way I'd been carrying the record cover.

But to my surprise he studied it with a happy little smile of discovery. "I remember this," he said.

"You've actually heard of it?" I said.

"I've more than heard of it." He had now flipped the sleeve over and was reading the credits on the back. "Hey, he's here today, you know."

"Who is?" I said.

Erik looked up at me, his eyes gleaming with the happy awareness of one springing a very satisfactory surprise. "Lanky Lockridge. 'Tenor and soprano saxophone', as it says here. Which is something of an understatement…"

"You know him?" I said.

"That fella can play. Of course I know him. We used him on some of Valerian's tracks."

"And he's here today?" I said, becoming aware that I was rapidly turning into someone whose mission in life was to ask Erik Make Loud short, factual questions.

Judging by the way Erik was grinning at me, he thought so too. "You're listening to him now," he said, jerking his head in the general direction of the duck pond and the big band tent.

I was fighting the urge to ask another short, factual question when Nevada came to the rescue by asking it for me. "He's playing the jazz?"

"Yes. Well, him and about twenty other shortsighted gentlemen of a certain age in bulging cardigans."

"Right now?" said Nevada. "Right here?" She was doing a great job at taking over with the short, factual questions.

"Yup," said Erik. And, "Yup" again.

"And he played on this record?" said Nevada. She didn't seem to share in any of my short, factual question shame.

"There's his name right there." Erik tapped the record cover with his finger. I noticed he was wearing black nail polish. Oh well.

"Along with some other leading lights of the day," said Erik. He suddenly held the cover closer to his face. Despite the crack about shortsighted musicians, he was himself a gentleman of a certain age who was too vain to wear corrective lenses. "Bloody hell, there's Johnny Scott on one track. I didn't know he was on here."

"Do you think he might have a copy of this record?" said Nevada.

Erik lowered the cover and looked at her over the edge of it. "You mean Lanky Lockridge?"

"Yes."

"Well, I imagine he would have *had* one. Many moons ago. Who knows if he'd still have it now. I certainly wouldn't bet on it. But he definitely would have had one at the time. Back in the day. When this was first recorded. Everybody who played on it got a copy. He handed them out, the Italian composer, Loretto Loconsole. Very nice chap. Gave records to all the musicians."

He smiled benignly at us. "I certainly got one."

9: DOUBLE-BREASTED PYJAMAS

Here in the middle of the bustling activity of Barnes Fair, with the cries of children, the annoying blaring of the posh woman on the PA, the chugging of the diesel generator, and the syncopated rising and falling of the big band music, there was nevertheless a distinct and emphatic little pocket of silence as Nevada and I stared at each other, and then stared at Erik, who stared back.

"You played on this record?" I said.

Erik grinned delightedly, a man who'd pulled another rabbit out of his hat. "Who do you think this is?" he said, tapping the cover again with his black-nailed finger. "Vi King? Who the hell did you think that could be?"

In fact, we'd discussed this the previous night, Tinkler and Nevada and I, when we'd been studying pictures of the album cover. All of the credits for the record had been well-known jazz musicians, with the exception of the guitarist, who was indeed credited as one Vi King.

"A blatant pseudonym," Tinkler had said. "A *nom de gig*,

123

if your darling will forgive me the butchering of her beloved French." He'd looked cautiously at Nevada, in case she might punch him. "But that's what they call it. When somebody plays under a fake name."

"I believe you," Nevada had said.

Meanwhile Tinkler had gone online, where he'd found a number of theories about who Vi King might really be. The leading contender, and the one that Tinkler plumped for, was Jimmy Page.

While it was true that Page had indeed been a session guitarist in London in the 1960s—I had an excellent Burt Bacharach record he played on—I had disputed his alleged presence on *Murder in London* because, by the time it was recorded, Page had left session-playing behind and had in fact joined a fairly well-known band called Led Zeppelin.

Tinkler, however, had stuck to his guns.

Now, in the middle of the merry mayhem of Barnes Fair, Erik Make Loud was addressing exactly this question to Nevada. "Who did you think Vi King was?" he said.

"Jimmy Page?" she suggested tentatively.

This was clearly the right answer, or at least the right wrong answer, because Erik roared with laughter. "Page? Don't be daft, gorgeous. He was already in Zeppelin by this time. Well in."

"That's what *he* said," said Nevada proudly, taking my hand.

"What fool told you it was Jimmy Page, then?"

"Well, Tinkler suggested it…"

"Did he, now? Right…" Erik took out his phone and

proceeded to track down Tinkler and give him hell for even suggesting that Jimmy Page could have been involved in playing the guitar solos on *Murder in London*. It was a lengthy and a richly profane conversation—or, more accurately, monologue—with Tinkler on the receiving end of all the jocular abuse.

It persisted while we weaved our way back through the crowd to the north edge of the green again, planning to return across the road to Gail's Bakery where we'd have another coffee, at one of the tables outside if we could grab one, presumably while Erik continued teasing Tinkler.

But he had finished and put his phone away before we got there. Nevertheless, we offered to buy him that coffee.

Because, obviously, we were eager to learn more about his connection with *Murder in London*.

"Very kind, but no thanks," said Erik. "I'm meeting Helene for brunch at Sadie's." He turned decisively away from us as he said this, clearly preparing to depart. But he suddenly froze, standing there motionless for a moment, then turned back to us. It seemed a thought had struck him. "Why don't you join us?"

We enthusiastically accepted, and not just because Sadie's was our favourite local restaurant. We were still determined to pursue this remarkable stroke of luck. For surely that was what it was?

So, once we reached the restaurant, we sat down with Helene, punk rock star of yesteryear and now Erik's long-term girlfriend, and endured a detailed repetition of how dumb Tinkler had been to think Jimmy Page had played on

Murder in London, and then orange juice and champagne and scrambled eggs on muffins. Although the term "endured" could hardly be applied to any of the latter.

"Why didn't you put your real name on the record, doll?" asked Helene.

"I was freelancing. I was moonlighting. I was a blackleg. In other words, I was supposed to be recording with Valerian and not with anyone else. And certainly not on any other record labels." Erik sipped his Buck's Fizz, or mimosa as Sadie's was wont to call this concoction in deference to our American friends. "I only ended up on this session because I had a mate on it."

"Lanky Lockridge?" I suggested.

"Right, like I told you, Lanky had played sax on some Valerian tracks, so I'd got to know him then. And so when he was recording this album for EMI… it was basically a jazz session, and they were all jazz musicians. But on some of the tracks they needed someone who wasn't a jazzer. They needed some young buck who could play scorching acid rock guitar. And for some reason he thought of me." Erik laughed at this, and so did Helene. They were scrutinising the empty sleeve of *Murder in London* fondly, while I kept a paranoid eye on it so it didn't get soaked in champagne and orange juice.

"This was a movie, then?" said Helene.

"Yeah, darling. Movie soundtrack, right," said Erik.

"Have you ever seen the movie?" said Helene.

"Can't say that I have. It was in Italian, wasn't it?"

"Among other languages," said Nevada, who had become

a bit of an expert on *Murder in London* aka *Bikini of Blood* since last night. "Actually I believe it was shot in English, and then dubbed into a multitude of tongues."

"A multitude of tongues," said Erik, giving the phrase the sort of obscene connotation one might have expected from Tinkler. He'd probably been hanging out with him too much.

"But it was originally shot in English," said Nevada. "After all, they filmed it in London."

"Oh, yeah, that's right," said Erik.

"It looks well mad," said Helene, studying the garish cover art. "I'd love to see it."

"We've got a copy," said Nevada, casually. "On Blu-ray." As if this obscure addition to our already fairly enormous film library hadn't only arrived last night.

"Oh, wow, can we see it then?" said Helene.

"Of course, we'll lend it to you."

"Though I suppose we could stream it," said Helene.

"Only very dodgy copies available online," said Nevada knowledgably. She'd been doing her homework. "And of course you only get the extras with the Blu-ray."

"Like the isolated music track," I said.

At this Erik, who had glazed over and been focused on whatever inner landscape a rich, elderly rock and roller who'd taken far too many drugs still possessed, took a sudden and renewed interest in the conversation. "So we could hear my solos," he said.

"Absolutely," said Nevada.

"Great, we'd love to borrow it," said Erik.

"What about the movie itself?" said Helene. "Is it any good?"

"We haven't watched it yet," said Nevada, a trifle diffidently. "We've been very busy."

"Well then, come over and watch it with us," said Erik. "Come and see it in the AV room."

"Oh yeah," said Helene. "We've upgraded the telly and the sound system and it's *astounding*." She stretched out the three syllables of the word and then chuckled. "You won't want to leave."

"We'd love to come and watch it with you," said Nevada, glancing at me to confirm that this was all right with me. And it was more than all right with me. I wanted to see the film and I knew from experience that Erik's AV room, despite the pretentious nomenclature, would more than deliver the goods.

"Okay then, that's great," said Helene. "How about tomorrow night?" she suggested, looking in turn at her other half for confirmation. Erik gave the casual nod of the lord of the manor approving some minor mutilation of a peasant. "Sure," he said.

"Tomorrow's good for us," said Nevada.

"Great, it's a date then," said Helene. She handed the record cover back to Nevada, who gratefully took charge of it. Clearly she'd been as worried about the champagne and orange juice as I was.

"You said you had a copy of this?" said Nevada. "Complete with vinyl in it? Once upon a time?"

"You bet," said Erik. "Good old Loretto gave one to

everybody who played on the session." He tapped the photograph of Loretto Loconsole with a cigarette-stained fingertip. The yellow of his skin contrasted strikingly with the black varnish of his nail. "He was proud of it. And so were we. Sometimes a record turns out good. And this one turned out *brilliantly*."

"I don't suppose there's any chance you still have that copy?" said Nevada.

This occasioned even more laughter than the earlier scorching acid guitar remark. "Darling," said Erik. "I had *cars* in those days that I can't find anymore. I have *houses* I've misplaced." He shook his head. "Sorry, but I've definitely lost that record. Some decades ago."

"But," I said, "Lanky Lockridge would also have had a copy."

Erik nodded. "That's right, mate. But do you really think he'll still have it?"

"Well, at least he won't have been living the rock and roll lifestyle all these years," I said.

This went down well. "Very true, mate, very true. But he'll have been living the jazz lifestyle. And that's not necessarily much better. Not when it comes to carefully preserving your material possessions."

He was right about this. "Still, it's worth a try," I said. "And if you don't mind introducing us to Mr Lockridge…"

"Of course, of course. No problem. We'll grab him as soon as he's finished his gig at the fair. His gig in the plastic tent."

But by the time we finished our lavish and prolonged

brunch and sauntered back to the village green, I was alarmed to note that the big band music had ceased. "Maybe they're just taking a break," said Nevada, walking at my side as Helene and Erik dawdled behind us. They clearly had no sense of urgency about our mission. And it seemed churlish to hurry them when they'd just paid for our meal. But I definitely sensed an opportunity slipping away.

And when we reached the fair, my worst fears were confirmed. The band's tent was empty except for a couple of stragglers who were packing up. And since they were a drummer and an electric bass player, clearly neither of these were Lanky Lockridge.

To his credit, Erik was suitably contrite.

He hurried up to the bass player, who seemed not just to recognise him but to be actively pleased to see him. "Hey, Adolphus, mate," said Erik. "Have we missed Lanky?"

"Oh hello, Erik," said the bass player. He was a chubby pale man who was wearing, as if to deliberately give the lie to Erik's earlier comment about cardigans, a very garish bright red cowboy shirt. "Yeah, he was asking after you, too."

"Shit," said Erik. "When did he leave?"

"Oh, about half an hour ago. We wrapped up ages ago. The gig, that is. I'm only hanging around here because my wife and daughter have got a stall at the fair." He nodded towards the open entrance of the tent. "And as soon as I step out of here they'll expect me to help them. Selling baked goods."

"Oh well," said Erik vaguely.

"Yeah, flogging jam roly-poly to the masses soon palls, as you might imagine."

"Right, yeah. Never mind. Anyway, if you see Lanky, tell him I'm sorry I missed him."

"All right," said Adolphus. "There was someone else here asking after you, too."

"Oh yeah?"

Adolphus grinned at him. "Someone you won't have been so sorry to have missed."

"Who's that then?"

"A very swinging individual," said Adolphus.

Erik looked blank for a moment, then comprehension dawned. "Oh Christ," he said.

"Yeah, that's right. Your friend Simeon. You dodged a bullet there, mate."

"Yeah, well thanks for the warning."

"Well, you're not out of the woods yet," said Adolphus, again nodding to the open entrance. "He's still around here somewhere. So watch your step. It's not safe to go back in the water, so to speak. He said he was going to the *arts centre*, for a *herbal tea*." Adolphus made an effeminate tea-drinking gesture with his little finger extended. "So watch out."

"Right mate, thanks," said Erik. And then he led us out of the tent, defeated. "Sorry about that," he said, putting his hand on my shoulder. "Looks like we've missed Lanky. But I've got his number somewhere, and I'll give it to you."

"That would be brilliant," I said. "Thanks." I couldn't really justify the enormous disappointment I felt, not least since the chance of Lanky Lockridge still having a copy of the record I was looking for, after all these years, was very remote indeed.

Erik's hand, which was still on my shoulder, suddenly tightened convulsively, gripping me so tightly that it was painful. I quickly looked over at him in alarm; my first thought was that he might be having a seizure. With Erik this seemed all too plausible a possibility.

But in fact he was grinning. Ecstatically. "Wait a minute," he said. "Wait just a freaking minute."

"What is it, doll?" said Helene. She sounded a little concerned herself.

"Guess what?" said Erik triumphantly. He turned and looked at me, so apparently the question was directed my way.

"What?" I said.

"Lanky wasn't the only one who was at that session," he said, delighted.

"No, you were, too, doll," said Helene.

"No, not me," said Erik. He was still looking at me, and there was happy mischief in his eyes. "That bloke Adolphus was talking about back there." He nodded towards the tent, where Adolphus the bass player was still hiding from his destiny of selling baked goods.

"The guy you want to avoid at all costs?" I said.

"That's him. Simeon Swithenbank."

"Hang on," I said. "He didn't play on *Murder in London*." There weren't that many musicians on the session, and though I couldn't say I'd memorised all their names, I certainly knew that none of them were called that.

"He didn't play on it," said Erik. "But he was there. At the sessions. He's a journalist. A music journalist. He was just a kid back then, who liked to hang about at recording sessions.

Come on." He made an imperious gesture and marched us all towards the arts centre. "Adolphus said he'd be in there. Drinking mint tea."

"Herbal tea, doll," said Helene.

"Come on," said Erik impatiently.

As it happened, we didn't even have to go inside the arts centre. Because the stylish glass walls spanning the front of the building allowed us to see inside even before we'd started up the steps at the entrance. And at this point Erik succeeded in spotting his prey from a distance. Quite a distance. He immediately led us back out of range, after pointing out a slim, well-dressed elderly man sitting alone at the window sipping, yes, a tea of some kind.

"That's him," said Erik with a whisper, a massively unnecessary whisper given that the person in question was indoors and we were outside, and a considerable distance away. "Simeon Swithenbank, known as Swinging Swithenbank. With considerable irony." Erik leaned towards us confidingly. "He lives with his sister. You know the type."

"I'm not entirely sure I do," I said.

Erik sighed and explained. "Middle-aged man? Well, elderly man now I suppose…" he seemed reluctant to concede the point since, if Simeon Swithenbank had been just a kid in the days of *Murder in London*, he must be somewhat younger than Erik. Nevertheless, the chance to heap abuse on him was apparently too good to forego. "So… elderly man? Living with his sister? You must know the type. Or at least get the picture. You get the picture, don't you, doll?"

"Yeah, I do," said Helene. "But then I've met him, haven't I?"

"Yeah, he interviewed you about the Blue Tits, didn't he? Anyway, lives with his sister. Elderly gentleman. Living with his sister. Sexless loser. Male spinster." He seemed pleased with this litany, and led it to a circular conclusion. "Lives with his sister. They're a pair of old maids. He never even had the gumption to be gay. Good writer, mind you. Could have been one of the leading music journos of his time. But the music papers wanted him to write about pop music and he wouldn't do that. Can't say I blame him. But he didn't much want to write about rock or prog or blues or soul either. He was a jazz purist. So he never came to anything."

"The fate of the jazz purist," I said.

"But he wrote a piece about the Blue Tits," said Helene. "So he must like punk music, too."

Erik suddenly looked furtive.

"What's up, babe?" said Helene.

"Well, to tell the truth, hon. He did that piece as a favour for me. I think he always quite fancied me, you know. Not that he'd ever have done anything about it."

"Didn't even have the gumption to be gay," I said.

"Right," Erik said.

"Sexless loser," said Nevada.

"You got it. But a bloody good writer. Did a very nice piece about recording the album."

"*Murder in London*?" I said.

"Yes, he wrote a brilliant piece about us recording it. For the *Melody Maker*. Or was it *New Musical Express*? Couldn't mention me in it, of course. Because I was there incognito. But it was a complete rave."

I suddenly wondered if this had been the rave review described by Chloë, which had got the record company so enthused about the project.

"He kept talking about this book he was writing," said Helene. "When he was interviewing me. It was more like I was interviewing him at times. He wanted to tell me all about it. Said he was working on this book…"

Erik laughed. "He certainly is. He was working on it back then, too."

"Not the same book?"

"Very much the same book. About the music scene then. The jazz scene then. And I imagine he's still writing it about the jazz scene now. It must be about a million pages long. But he's never going to finish it. He can't commit to finishing it. He can't commit to anything. Same as with the sex thing. Speaking of sex…"

He looked at Helene, grinning. And she smiled back at him, a rather cheeky smile. "What say we go home and smoke some hash and have a bubble bath, baby doll?"

"Sounds like a plan, daddy doll. Definitely sounds like a plan."

"I'll call Bong Cha and get her to put the suds in now." As he took out his phone he frowned at me. "Don't forget to bring over the movie tomorrow."

"We won't," said Nevada.

Erik completed his instructions to Bong Cha and, as he put his phone away, we began to say our goodbyes. But suddenly he turned around and saw something. The happy expression on his face, no doubt anticipating hashish and carnal frolics in a foaming tub, vanished instantly to be replaced by a hunted look. "Oh, shit," he said.

We all turned around to look where he was looking.

The elderly man we'd last seen sitting safely behind a sheet of glass, sipping tea, was now striding towards us at a determined clip, with an ironic expression on his face. If I hadn't known better, I would have said he knew we were talking about him.

Despite the warm summer weather he was wearing a tightly buttoned white shirt under a three-piece suit—although it took a moment to realise this. One's first shocked impression was that he was walking around in his pyjamas. This was because the suit was made of a dark brown material with a thick white vertical stripe, highly suggestive of gentlemen's nightwear.

But no, it was definitely a suit, double breasted and rather archaic looking, Edwardian perhaps. His sharply pointed and gleaming black patent leather boots were echoed by a gleaming bow tie, which also seemed to be made of black leather. Was such a thing possible?

But if the leather bow tie seemed suggestive of a racy fetishism, the rest of the man's appearance belied that. Partly it was the flower in his buttonhole, a rather large white lily with wilting green leaves. And then there was his face. Despite a large nose and floridly thick lips, he had a gentle, tentative look. His pale eyes were set wide apart and peered out timidly through spectacles with heavy wooden frames. Yes, wooden.

His hair was shoulder-length but thin, and of a strange nicotine-yellow colour.

Altogether he looked like a dandy from another age who had found himself stranded in this strange new time and place. But his voice was firm and confident, imperious even, as he hailed us.

"Hello, Erik," he yelled, striding rapidly towards us.

"Uh, hello, Sim," said the profoundly wrongfooted Erik.

"Hello, Helene, how are you?"

"Fine and dandy, Simeon."

"I saw you through the window of the arts centre," said Simeon, his eyes glittering with mischief. "It seems you were too shy to come and say hello, so I thought I'd solve that problem for you. The mountain has come to Mohammed, although I suppose we shouldn't say things like that these days." His head suddenly swivelled, bringing his unsettling gaze to bear on Nevada and myself. "And who are your friends?"

I introduced myself and Nevada, and said, "I understand you were at the recording sessions for *Murder in London*?"

I expected him to ask me to remind him what this had been, or at least to have to think for a moment about it. But instead his response was instantaneous. "Yes, that's right," he said, as if he'd just come from there. He gave me a steady look while I tried to make up my mind if I should ask some questions to sound him out and determine whether he actually knew what I was talking about, or whether he was mistaken or bluffing or, given his interesting dress sense, a trifle demented.

But he solved the problem for me by saying, "Composed, conducted and arranged by Loretto Loconsole, Michael Garrick on piano, Barry Morgan or Jackie Dougan on drums, Coleridge Goode on bass, Lawrence 'Lanky' Lockridge on saxophone and reeds, although Johnny Scott played flute on at least one track I believe." He gave me a thin smile. "A genuinely first-rate line up and a rather wonderful album."

Then his smile widened and he looked at Erik. "Apart from the appalling guitar solos," he said.

Erik yelped with laughter and slapped him on the back.

"Listen, Simeon mate," he said. "My friend here was wondering if you could help him out with something?" Erik indicated me and again Simeon rotated his head to look my way. There was something reptilian in the way he moved. He blinked his eyes slowly at me, doing nothing to lessen the reptilian impression.

"Yes?" he said.

"You seem to recall the session really clearly," I said. A sudden and unnerving possibility had occurred to me. Perhaps something had happened recently to cause our new friend to refresh his memory about *Murder in London*.

And perhaps I wasn't the only one who was looking into what had happened back then…

"Yes," said Simeon Swithenbank. "I happen to have a very good memory, particularly when it comes to music and musicians. Especially when I've written about them. And I wrote about that recording, both at the time—"

"Yeah, brilliant piece, mate," said Erik. "Was it in the *Melody Maker* or the *NME*?"

"*Disc and Music Echo*," said Simeon patiently. "As I was saying, I wrote about it both at the time and subsequently, for my book."

"Your book about British jazz," I said.

He seemed to brighten and become a little less defensive. "Yes, that's right."

"I'd love to read it."

He positively glowed at this, as simply and innocently happy as a child. "Well, it needs a bit of tidying up, you know, before it's actually published, but, as soon as it's out, I'll be happy to notify you."

"So there'll be a section on *Murder in London*?" said Nevada.

"Yes, quite an extensive section," he said.

I wondered just how long this book would be.

"Were you aware of the real murder?" said Nevada. "The real murder that took place in London? And the scandal?"

"Oh yes, poor Loretto."

"And poor Jackie Higgins," I said, half-expecting him to ask who she was. But he just nodded, acknowledging that I had a point.

"Yes, of course. I'll go into all that. In some detail."

Nevada was giving me an excited look, but I felt we were getting away from the real topic here. "I understand that Loretto Loconsole gave copies of the record to everyone at the session."

Simeon blinked at me. "Oh, yes."

"Did that include you?"

"Certainly. We got along very well. Loretto was a most charming man and he very much appreciated the publicity I generated with my article about the recording sessions."

Like a man jumping out of an airplane and hoping his chute would open, I took the plunge. "I don't suppose you still have that record?"

He blinked again, this time with amusement. "Oh, yes."

"You won't be offended if I ask if it's in good condition?"

"Do you mean do I know how to take care of my records?" Simeon Swithenbank smiled steadily at me. "Allow me to put it like this. I have a Linn LP12 with a Naim ARO arm and a Lyra Kleo cartridge, if that puts your mind at ease? Oh, and I put my records faithfully back in the inner sleeves after playing them and store them in an upright position away from sources of heat."

I ignored his irony. Or was it sarcasm? "Sounds like it will be in great shape."

"Yes, even after all these years, I can assure you that it is."

"And I don't suppose you'd be willing to sell it?" I said.

He didn't blink this time but the amusement continued. "Certainly," he said. "I assumed that was going to be the destination of this discussion."

"And you were right," said Nevada.

"So you're happy to sell it?" I said.

He nodded. "Providing the price is right."

"We'll make sure the price is right," said Nevada confidently.

We exchanged contact details, Nevada looking after

this, which was just as well since I felt too light-headed with excitement and victory for any such mundane administrative activity.

We all said our farewells and, as we began to walk away, Simeon Swithenbank suddenly took me by the elbow and held onto me so that we fell back from the others. His head dropped as he addressed me confidentially.

"Erik thinks I'm joking," he said. "But I'm not. Those guitar solos really were appalling."

10: CAKE AND GIALLO

It was around about this time that we began to realise that something was very seriously wrong…

On the surface, all was going swimmingly and things could hardly have been improved. Simeon Swithenbank might have been a bit eccentric, to say the least, but his eccentricity wasn't of the variety that called into question his memory or his honesty.

If he said he had a copy of the record we were after, and it was in great shape, then I believed that he did and it was.

And we'd even begun to discuss a ballpark figure for the sale and it was beginning to look like it might be reasonable, or at least not too extortionate. Which was good, even though it wasn't our own money we were spending.

What's more, he hadn't merely solved our problem of finding the record.

"It looks like he can help us out with the other half of our assignment," said Nevada.

"The other half?" I said.

"I mean with providing Chloë with more information about her grandfather…"

"I know what you mean," I said. "But I don't think our assignment has two halves. We've been hired to find a record. Nothing else."

Nevada smiled one of her most placating smiles. "But Chloë did say she'd be very happy indeed if it so happened that you could do both."

"What she actually said," I said, "was that she wanted me to find the record and also find the true identity of the killer."

"Well, exactly," said Nevada.

"Exactly what?"

"Perhaps Simeon will be able to provide some information which helps with that."

"Perhaps," I said. "Or perhaps it will turn out that the true identity of the killer is Chloë's grandfather after all."

Nevada stopped smiling. "Perhaps it will. I hope not. I like her."

"Me too," I said.

Anyway, any lingering worries I might have had regarding the reliability of Swinging Swithenbank, as Erik called him, were utterly allayed by the phone conversation we had on Saturday night, only a few hours after meeting him. And we didn't even have to ring him; he called us.

"I've just been rereading my account of the *Murder in London* recording sessions," he told me. "And indeed all the furore surrounding the events. Of the real murder in London, as your little friend referred to it. On that houseboat in Rotherhithe. I shall look forward to telling you all about it."

"We'll look forward to hearing all about it," I said. "My little friend and I." And, despite all my reservations, I was telling the truth about that. There was something oddly calming and authoritative about Simeon Swithenbank. If anybody could provide some insights about what had happened in that distant time and place, concerning that tragic, bloody and long-forgotten crime, I believed it was him. He seemed to be a real journalist, with respect for fact and detail.

And he'd actually been present then and there, and had personally known some of the people involved.

Anyway, he gave us his address in Chiswick and we arranged to come and visit him there after the weekend. Then I called Chloë to give her a further update.

"We've met someone who can tell us about the session and who has details about that whole situation," I said, and told her about our new friend in his three-piece pyjama suit. Although I omitted the details of his suit.

"Simeon Swithenbank?" she said. "I remember the name. He wrote an article about the recording. That was why there was so much excitement about *nonno*'s record. It was a fabulous article. So he's still alive and you managed to track him down?"

"It was a piece of luck," I said modestly. And honestly.

"Very well done indeed." She sounded jubilant and her reaction gave me a warm thrill of pleasure.

"One more thing," I said, feeling rather jubilant myself.

"Yes?"

"He says he has a copy of the record. And it's in very good shape."

There was silence on the line, then a few quick words in Italian. They sounded like happy words, though. "That's wonderful, thank you."

"We haven't actually got it yet," I said.

"Nevertheless, very well done indeed."

I told her the ballpark figure we'd worked out for the price and she agreed to it instantly. I hung up, after she'd blown me some kisses down the line, and found Nevada watching me.

"Did she say anything about Desdemona?"

"Nope," I said.

"But she sounded happy?"

"Yes, but that was just because I told her about the record," I said.

Nevada gave me a droll look. She didn't seem entirely convinced.

The grand screening of *Murder in London*, aka *Bikini of Blood*, was to take place at six o'clock the following night at Erik's house. I suppose it was now Erik and Helene's house, since she'd been elevated to the status of permanent live-in girlfriend.

They resided in Barnes in a highly desirable riverfront property just around the corner from the Bull's Head, a well-known gastropub and renowned music venue. Nevada and I could have easily walked there from our own house, but, as fate would have it, that day we were coming from the other direction, Kew, where we'd already been for a walk. Quite a long walk.

We'd taken advantage of the gorgeous weather to enjoy an extended summer afternoon's stroll and we were running a trifle late.

We'd originally planned to go home before heading over to Erik's, so perhaps foolishly we hadn't brought the Blu-ray with us. Which presented a logistical quandary if the gala screening was to go ahead as planned.

"It's all right," said Nevada, as we waited for the westbound District Line at Kew, after working out which platform it came in on and getting to said platform—a task which required either genius level IQ or a long-term acquaintance with the station and its maze-like eccentricities of construction. "Tinkler can pick it up for us."

Tinkler was also invited to the screening, naturally, being a close mate and dope smoking crony of Erik's. And, like our other best friend Agatha, Tinkler had a full set of keys for our place, in case of emergencies.

Or for running useful little errands like this.

Nevada rang Tinkler, got his voicemail, and left a message asking him to stop off at our place on his drive over to Erik's, to let himself in and pick up the Blu-ray. This was accompanied by a detailed description of not only where he could find it, but also where he could find treats for the cats and how many of these he was allowed to dispense.

"The little darlings might as well benefit from a visit by Uncle Tinkler," said Nevada after she'd hung up.

This marathon voicemail was soon acknowledged by text from Tinkler and then followed up a second text as we sat waiting for our next train at Richmond.

Got Bikini of Blood, it read. *Also fed cats. Also bringing cake.*

The addition of cake was classic Tinkler.

We caught the train from Richmond to Barnes station which, despite its name, was still some miles from Erik's abode, and changed there for one to Barnes Bridge, which wasn't. Indeed it was a very short walk, first past Gustav Holst's house with its elegant New Orleans-style lattice balcony, and then that redoubtable hostelry, the Bull's Head. I was tempted to look in here and check who was booked to perform. The late Michael Garrick—who, as noted, was one of the luminaries on the soundtrack to *Murder in London*— had been a regular at the pub's gigs.

Indeed, over the years, many jazz and rock legends had played there, including Erik Make Loud himself, though I was a little reluctant to accord him the legendary designation.

Erik's home was a handsome white edifice. We admired it anew as we rang the bell beside the front door.

For a long moment we stood there, having ample opportunity to read the doormat (*"Not you again!"*) and listen to loud but distant music in the house which alerted us to the fact that at least somebody was at home, although not sufficiently at home to bother answering the bloody door.

Finally this door was flung open and Tinkler peered out at us. He looked rather chastened, which was an unusual expression for Tinkler. "I'm afraid we've eaten all the cake," he said.

"Already?" I said.

"I know, I know. But Erik and Helene got stuck into it…"

"And I suppose you didn't eat any of it yourself," said Nevada, with a decidedly cynical inflection as Tinkler escorted us inside.

"Well maybe a little."

"You will be punished later," said Nevada.

"Fair enough."

Despite the lack of cake, it was an entertaining evening. Erik's screening room, sorry, "audio visual room", really was of high-end home cinema standard—"This gives the Olympic Studios a run for their money," Nevada would whisper at one point during the film. In fact Erik's lair was probably bigger than the small screens at the Olympic.

The image on the new TV was so clear and well-defined that, though it didn't involve any 3D malarkey, it did in fact give the impression of depth and three dimensions, even when showing this crazy old Italian thriller. Which, as Chloë had promised, was a beautiful transfer with razor-sharp images and intensely brilliant colours.

Before the screening officially began, Erik, ever the thoughtful host, offered us a variety of snacks and iced vodka in a staggering array of flavours—"Hmm, what have we got for you tonight? Mango and passionfruit, lemon birthday cake, raspberry crush, spicy tamarind, marshmallow, toffee popcorn… Try the lemon birthday cake. That's Hel's favourite, isn't it, doll?"

"Not since we discovered toffee popcorn vodka, doll," said Helene.

These tempting, not to mention intoxicating, treats were spread out on the battered old silver wooden coffee table which I recognised and found somehow comfortingly familiar; this at least had not been upgraded. The snacks had been prepared for us by Erik's live-in housekeeper, Bong Cha. Bong herself was not present, having sensibly taken the night off, but she'd done us proud. "Try the taramasalata and scotch bonnet pepper on scalded Lithuanian rye bread," urged Erik, evidently a fan of the spicy things in life.

There was, however, no cake. And when Nevada pointed this out there were furtive glances at a chocolate-smeared but otherwise empty plate, accompanied by a gratifyingly shame-faced silence, which Erik curtailed by starting the movie.

In addition to the state-of-the-art television, this room also had an excellent and recently improved sound system, which was just as well, what with the film's soundtrack having to contend with increasingly hysterical laughter from Erik and his paramour. And Tinkler, too, once the movie really got started.

It was clear that Erik and Helene, though oddly not Tinkler, were as high as kites. Which meant at least they were enjoying themselves, and weren't bored.

Not that you were likely to be bored by this movie.

Chloë's account of it had been accurate, as far as it went. And the highpoint of the film was definitely the sequence in which the heroine, under attack on her houseboat and unknowingly dosed with LSD, had to fend off the attackers with the help of her faithful and rather terrifying dog. The film was shot in a dislocated, bravura fashion with extraordinary visuals to convey the heroine's drug-saturated perception. It was astonishing stuff and we all watched, rapt, even Helene and Erik temporarily silenced. No hysterical laughter here.

But no synopsis could do justice to the strange lapses of logic and outrageous plot twists of the rest of the film, which seemed to take no account of plausibility, consistency or indeed basic reality. For example, one of the smugglers in search of the missing cache of LSD was a creepy assassin type in a black raincoat and black hat, wearing black-lensed sunglasses indoors and out, who wielded a sinister vintage handgun…

"Mauser C96 machine pistol," called out Erik immediately when he saw it. Erik was something of a military buff and had no embarrassment about advertising this obsession.

"With the wooden shoulder stock," said Nevada, because as it happened my darling knew a thing or two about weapons.

"And the integral box magazine," said Erik, not be outdone.

"Shut up both of you," said Helene. "I want to watch this movie."

"Yes, it would be terrible if we missed a nuance of the subtle and complex narrative," said Tinkler.

"You shut up, too," said Helene.

But Tinkler was right to mock. Because the Mauser-wielding, black-coated assassin was killed at one point—his throat torn out by the Doberman. Only for him to appear again, apparently alive and well, and then be killed again. This time by the girl on the houseboat, herself presumed dead and drowned, but now revealed to be alive, having escaped from her assailants and swum for miles along the river at night, often underwater apparently, and always nude of course. She proceeded to kill the black-coated assassin with a knife in a fight in the surprisingly well-equipped kitchen—sorry, galley—of her houseboat.

Only for the black-coated assassin to rise again later in the movie to attack and dispatch the houseboat girl's treacherous musician boyfriend at a swinging sixties London discotheque.

I must admit the treacherous musician boyfriend had it coming. But even I winced at his decapitation by a jagged shard of one of the mirrors which spiralled around the dancefloor at the discotheque, providing multiple reflections of the go-go girls doing the twist in their moiré miniskirts and white boots. And also offered a bewildering and surprisingly suspenseful chase scene which Nevada pointed out was stolen from Orson Welles's *Lady from Shanghai*, before Helene hushed her.

At which point the houseboat girl turned up, wrestled his gun away from the assassin—rather too easily, I thought—and shot him dead with it.

Indeed she blew quite a number of holes in him, and in the surrounding groovy discotheque furniture, white feathers flying from a large red sofa in the shape of a pair of giant voluptuous lips. This ballistic carnage prompted Erik to expound about the ammunition used in his beloved Mauser. "The most high-velocity handgun cartridge available before the .357 Magnum," he said, as a glass wall featuring a Warhol-style mural was blown to bits.

"Shut up, doll," said Helene.

However, high-velocity ammunition or not, the bullet-riddled, black-coated assassin appeared yet again, undaunted and very much still alive, at the end of the film, when the sunglasses and black hat and black coat were torn away to reveal that not only was the assassin a woman, but that she didn't have any clothes on. Black coat and black hat notwithstanding. Well, of course. There was a final hand-to-hand fight between her and the equally nude houseboat girl in the studio of a pop art painter.

Both of the women were soon covered with paint of various colours, the red paint indistinguishable from blood—or at least from fake movie blood—when a palette knife was drawn across an exposed and vulnerable white throat, finally killing one of the combatants.

But which one? Both the dead body on the floor and the exultant victor standing over it holding the palette knife were so smeared with paint as to render them unidentifiable.

So who was the survivor?

We only gradually discovered the answer to this after the triumphant combatant showered the paint off herself in a brightly lit, freestanding cylindrical glass shower stall—the painter had a stylish pad—and, as the dazzling colours of paint swirled in psychedelic spirals down the shower drain, our heroine was finally revealed.

The houseboat girl had survived triumphant.

She dressed herself in one of the painter's stained overalls and a rather natty leather jacket, and walked out of the house into a crescent of London houses. "That's Powys Square," said Erik.

"I believe you're right," said Nevada.

As the heroine walked away into the rising sun, we discovered she was being covertly watched by a shadowy figure following her. It was... you guessed it, the black-coated assassin. Back from the dead, yet again.

And then a close up revealed the black-coated assassin's face.

It was the houseboat girl.

Yes, she was simultaneously walking away, heroic and triumphant in paint-stained overalls and leather jacket, and watching herself walk away, sinister and menacing in black coat and black hat.

Go figure...

The baffling ending was enthusiastically embraced by Erik and Helene, though. "What a great fucking movie," said the former. "Let's watch it again," said the latter.

As much as we'd enjoyed the film—and despite its weirdness and resolute refusal to make sense, we had enjoyed it—we'd no desire to experience it again, at least not so soon.

So, Nevada and I excused ourselves, leaving Tinkler loyally ensconced on the sofa with the happy, and very stoned, couple for the second viewing.

We went downstairs, the extremely catchy music of the film's opening credits echoing above us, and let ourselves out of the house. A very pleasant and very short riverside walk took us back to Barnes Bridge station, where we raced up the steps as our train rolled in. We caught it by the skin of our teeth and three minutes later we were back in the familiar wooded paths of Barnes Common, wending our way homewards to our house and cats.

"Well, that was fun," said Nevada, strolling beside me.

"No cake, though," I said.

The next morning we'd hardly got out of bed and fed Fanny and Turk when the doorbell rang. It was Erik and Helene, looking surprisingly none the worse for wear considering that they must have been watching—rewatching in fact—a crazy Italian thriller just a few hours ago while out of their minds on drugs.

We invited them in and made coffee for everyone. Nevada and I were still in our dressing gowns but our guests' decades of the rock and roll lifestyle had exposed them to a lot worse than that, so we didn't feel particularly uncomfortable.

Erik plonked the Blu-ray of *Bikini of Blood* down on our table. "Thanks for that," he said. "Quite a viewing experience."

"How many times did you watch it in the end?" said Nevada.

"Twice, no three times."

"No, doll," said Helene. "Only twice. The third time we found that Korean women's beach volleyball final on the other side."

"Oh yeah. Oh my god, that was almost as much fun as the film."

"Well, it was very good of you to come all the way over

here, first thing, to return it," said Nevada. She decorously sipped her coffee instead of giving it the robust slurp I knew she really wanted to indulge in.

"No problem," said Erik.

"No problem at all," said Helene.

There then ensued a rather odd silence. Helene and Erik were looking at each other. So Nevada and I looked at each other. Silent communication between couples. Ours resulted in Nevada setting her coffee cup aside and saying, "Was there something else?"

"Something else?" said Erik. Rather shiftily, I thought.

"Another reason you came over, besides returning the Blu-ray?"

"Yes." Erik actually seemed relieved and eager to have been called out. "Yes, we wanted to apologise."

"Apologise?"

"About the cake," said Helene.

"That's right," said Erik.

"We wanted to apologise for eating all of it and not leaving any for you," said Helene.

"Tinkler ate most of it," said Erik.

"No, doll, he didn't. Let's be honest here. You and me ate about eighty-seven per cent of the cake. Tinkler at most ate about thirteen, fourteen, fifteen per cent."

"I'd say more like twenty-five," said Erik. "Twenty-five per cent was down to him. But whatever. We're sorry."

"It was very greedy of us," said Helene. "And bang out of order. So we wanted to apologise."

Nevada and I had been looking at each other throughout

this duologue, not sure whether to be touched, baffled or amused. While admittedly it was only good manners to apologise to your friends for having eaten all of the cake, this did seem a little excessive.

"Oh, it's fine," said Nevada breezily.

"No it isn't, it was rotten of us," said Helene.

"Yeah, rotten," said Erik.

"Don't give it another thought," said Nevada.

"Well, that's really very good of you," said Helene.

"Handsome, I call it," said Erik.

"Good manners, you see, doll? They're such nice people."

"Aren't we just?" I said.

Erik, who I could see was growing weary of apologising and being nice—behaviours which weren't necessarily in his home key, so to speak—grinned at me in amusement. It was an okay-let's-cut-the-crap kind of grin.

"And we were wondering…" said Helene.

Nevada glanced at me. *Here it comes*, was what we were both thinking, though what "it" was and why it had to be prefaced with elaborate cake apologies, we had no idea.

"Yeah, we were wondering," said Erik, "if you could give us the, you know, *recipe* for the cake."

Nevada and I were more deeply baffled than ever. "Recipe?" I said.

"Yeah, *recipe*," said Erik, eyebrows wiggling wildly, almost salaciously, as he emphasised the word.

"Not for the whole cake," said Helene quickly.

"Yeah, just for the special ingredient," said Erik.

"The special ingredient?" said Nevada.

"Yeah," said Erik. "We want to know where we can get our hands on the special ingredient."

"Because it was really special," said Helene.

"My word, I'll say," said Erik.

"I mean," said Helene, leaning back in her chair and gesturing expansively with both hands, "I have done a lot of acid in my time, I mean a *lot*…"

"Me too, doll, me too," said Erik, never to be outdone in matters drug-related.

"And I've never…"

"I've never either…"

"Had such *great shit*," said Helene.

"It really was great," said Erik.

"So smooth."

"Right, doll. And intense."

"Right!" said Erik. He gave a sigh and raised his eyes prayerfully towards the ceiling of our little living room. "The acid in that cake was the best."

After a moment when no one said anything, I said, "There was acid in the cake?"

"And we know we ate it all and it was very greedy of us," said Helene.

"So that's why you guys were so high last night," said Nevada.

"We were tripping out of our boxes," said Erik.

"My god, were we?" said Helene. "And that movie, that dog on the houseboat…"

"And don't forget the women's volleyball," said Erik.

"We haven't laughed like that in years."

"But why wasn't Tinkler high as well?" said Nevada. And then, immediately realisation dawned on her. "Because he's immune to hallucinogens."

"That's right," said Erik. "Poor bastard. Good acid is completely wasted on him. He shouldn't have eaten any of that cake. What a waste. We could have had that portion for ourselves…"

"Doll," said Helene.

"I mean we could have saved it for you guys," Erik hastily corrected himself.

"That's right," said Helene.

"So what we're saying," said Erik, "is that we know it was really rotten of us to stuff our faces with the cake and not even share any of it with you, but we're hoping…"

"We're really hoping…" said Helene.

"That you'll either tell us where you got the cake, or at least where you got the special ingredient."

I felt the need at this point to summarise. "You want us to tell you where to get the acid that was in the cake."

"Yes!" said Erik joyfully.

"Why?" I said.

"Look, we know you're pissed off at not getting any of the cake…"

"No, we're not," said Nevada.

"Well, you'd be totally entitled to be," said Helene. "After all, it was your cake."

That led to a brief silence. Then I said, "No it wasn't."

"Yes it was," said Erik, never one to surrender a point

willingly. "That's why it was so rude of us to have eaten it all. And we quite understand you being pissed at us…"

"We're really not," said Nevada. "We're not pissed at you. And it really wasn't our cake."

"It was Tinkler's cake," I said. "Tinkler provided the cake."

Helene and Erik looked at each other. It was their turn to be baffled. "No it wasn't," said Erik.

"He definitely said he'd brought it from your house," said Helene.

"He came over here before he went to your place," said Nevada. "That's true. But that was to pick up the Blu-ray. He didn't bring the cake from here."

"Yes he did," said Erik.

"He definitely said he did," said Helene. "That's why we felt so bad about eating all of it and not leaving any for you. It was your cake."

"Our cake, which was full of LSD," I said.

"Really good LSD," said Erik, grinning nostalgically.

I turned to Nevada but she already had her phone out. "Answer, Tinkler," she snarled. And then, as either the phone or Tinkler obeyed her command, he did. "I'm putting you on speaker, Tinkler."

"Oh good," said Tinkler's voice from the phone. "What a splendid way to start the day. On the speaker phone. On the phone speaker. Do you know what the time is? I was blissfully asleep and dreaming of… well, never mind what I was dreaming of. We don't want to go into that on the phone speaker, or the speaker phone."

"Tinkler," said Nevada patiently, "where did you get that cake you took over to Helene and Erik's last night."

"Where did I get it? Look, I'm really sorry we didn't leave any for you. I know that was disgraceful behaviour…"

"Forget that. *Where did you get it?*"

"From your house."

"You found the cake here when you came over?"

"No," said Tinkler. "It was delivered."

"Delivered," said Nevada. She looked at me. Things were beginning to make sense. But I can't say it was a very welcome sense.

"Yes, it was delivered while I was busy feeding your cats treats as I'd been ordered. They rang the doorbell and handed it over to me. It had a really nice pink box."

"Who is 'they'?" said Nevada. "Who delivered it?"

"Just some courier woman. Some very fit courier woman."

"She just delivered a cake in a pink box."

"A fancy pink box," said Tinkler. "From some fancy cake place."

"Which one?"

"I don't know. Madame Blavatsky's Emporium of Delectable Comestibles. Or something."

"So that was all there was, a cake in a box with a stupid name? No invoice, or…"

"There was a note," said Tinkler.

"A note?" said Nevada.

"From Agatha."

We all fell silent.

"Are you still there?" said Tinkler's voice, rather forlornly, from the phone.

"There was a note from Agatha," said Nevada. "With the cake."

"Yes."

"What did it say?"

"'Hope you like the cake, lots of love, Agatha.' Something like that."

"We've probably still got the note," said Helene.

"Hey," said Tinkler. "Is Helene there?"

"Me, too, mate," said Erik.

"Hello, mate," said Tinkler.

"Hello, mate." The male greeting ritual, mercifully brief, concluded at this point.

"We can probably retrieve the note," said Helene. Rather quicker on the uptake than Erik, she had realised that something was amiss here. "It went in the bin, but Bong Cha probably hasn't emptied the bins yet."

"Yes, please, get the note," said Nevada.

"No, don't bother getting the fucking note," said Tinkler from the phone.

"Why not?" said Nevada fiercely.

"Because it's not a handwritten note or anything. It's just a printed gift message like you get when you order something for a friend from a third party."

"Oh," said Nevada. She turned to me. "Can I get your phone and use it, love?"

"Of course," I said.

She left her own phone on the table where Tinkler's

disembodied voice continued to converse with us and went through to the bedroom to get mine.

"So, Tinkler," I said. "It seems the cake was spiked with acid."

"Yeah, I'd pretty much worked that out," he said. "That would explain why I woke up this morning feeling a little woozy."

"I thought it didn't have any effect on you, mate," said Erik.

"It just feels a bit like I'm coming down with the flu, but then I don't come down with the flu, if you know what I mean," said Tinkler.

"Got you."

"And I only even feel that if it's really strong stuff."

"Oh, this was really strong stuff," said Helene.

"Are you sure it was in the cake?" I said.

Helene and Erik stared at me.

"Well," I said. "Maybe it was in something else you ate that evening?"

"It was in the cake," said Erik stubbornly.

"Don't forget I felt it, too," said Tinkler.

"Maybe it was in something else that you ate? That all of you ate?"

Helene was shaking her head. "No, all we ate was the cake and the canapés Bong Cha made. And you and Nevada had some of those."

"Could it have been in the vodka?" I said.

"I didn't have the vodka," said Tinkler. "I was driving."

"And you're sure you felt something this morning?"

"Yup."

"It was in the cake, mate," said Erik. "Why are you so busy trying to make a case for it not being the cake?"

"Because…" I said, and just then Nevada came back with my phone to her ear.

"No, please don't," she was saying. "There wouldn't be any point. There isn't anything you can do. Well, maybe. But I'd really rather you didn't. It's not your fault. It's absolutely not your fault. How could it be your fault? Please, please, please don't. Well, don't do anything definite. Don't do anything rash. All right. Call me later. All right. You too. Take care."

She hung up and looked at us. "That was Agatha. I should never have called her. It was obvious she didn't have anything to do with sending us the cake. I knew that. I shouldn't have called her."

"You had to check," I said.

"No, I didn't," said Nevada. "Now she's talking about cutting her holiday short and coming back, just because I told her about this. I knew damned well she had nothing to do with it. Some little shit just knew enough about us to use her name."

She put my phone down on the table beside hers. Her blue eyes had that stormy look they acquired when she was angry. In this case, very angry.

"So," said Helene. "Some little shit sent you a cake dosed with acid."

"With really strong acid," said Erik.

"And they made out like it was a present from your friend Agatha."

"That's right," I said.

"And I intercepted it," said Tinkler. "I inadvertently intercepted it."

"And we ate it," said Helene.

Erik was looking at me. To his credit, he looked somewhat concerned. "So it turns out that someone is trying to fuck with you," he said.

"Not just that," I said. "Although that would be bad enough. But someone tried to slip us acid without us knowing about it. And…"

"And?" said Erik.

"And that's exactly what happens in the movie."

11: CAT PEOPLE

We didn't tell Chloë about the acid in the cake incident.

Nevada and I discussed whether we should, but in the end there seemed no point, and nothing to be gained, in doing so. "For a start," said Nevada. "We can't be sure that it has anything to do with this case."

"I hope it does," I said.

Nevada looked at me quizzically for a moment and then her expression cleared. "Because then at least we know why it's happening, what it's got to do with. That's dreadful syntax, but you get what I'm saying."

"Right," I said. "Because if it's not connected to this…" I still hesitated to use words like "case". They made me feel like I should have a bottle of bourbon in the bottom drawer of my desk. And a desk for that matter. "Because if it's not connected to this situation…"

"Then someone is fucking with us for a totally unknown reason," said Nevada. "Which is even worse."

"Which is slightly worse," I said.

"So, to summarise," said Nevada. "We have to make some assumptions here. So let's assume the attempt to dose us with acid is related to us being hired to look for *Murder in London*."

"Okay," I said.

"And we make that assumption not only because of the timing of when it happened but, and this is really the persuasive bit, because there is a similar incident in the film." She looked at me. "Feel free to play devil's advocate."

"Okay then," I said. "Let's be sceptical about this. And, really, how similar is what happened to us to what happened in the film? After all the heroine of the movie wasn't given LSD in a cake." In fact it had been slipped into her cup of tea, by her sleazebag boyfriend.

Nevada shook her head. "There's no way anyone could replicate exactly what happened in the film. For a start, if we wanted to stick to the script it would have to be *you* giving me the LSD."

I grinned at her. "Assuming you're the heroine," I said.

She grinned back at me. "And assuming you're my boyfriend. But I think we can safely assume both of those as givens. In all modesty."

"So what we're saying," I said, "is that this was as close as somebody could get to what happened in the film?"

"Right," said Nevada. "In an imperfect world such as this one."

"And why would they want to do that in the first place?" I said.

"That is the question," said Nevada.

"To frighten us?" I said. "To warn us off? To freak us out?"

"Those are all strong possibilities," said Nevada. "But you're supposed to be playing devil's advocate."

"Oh right, okay," I said. "More scepticism then. So if this attempt to dose us was supposed to replicate what happened in the film, it not only fails to do so in the method of delivery…"

"Cake versus tea."

"Right. It also fails to replicate what happens once the acid is taken, inadvertently, by the girl on the houseboat. In the movie she's subjected to a harrowing attack while she's high. Whereas absolutely nothing like that happened last night…" I stopped because Nevada was staring at me. "What?"

"We didn't get the cake because we weren't here at home," she said.

I saw where she was going with this, and it sent a deep, cold thrill through me.

"So maybe we also didn't get the attack, because we weren't here at home," I said.

"Right," said Nevada.

"Holy shit," I said.

"Right again," said Nevada.

It had now become, for obvious reasons, a matter of some urgency to conclude our business with Chloë as quickly as possible. We couldn't be certain that what had happened recently was connected with her hiring us, but it was just common sense to wrap things up rapidly and see if our situation went back to normal.

Luckily the means of wrapping things up rapidly was to hand…

We phoned Simeon Swithenbank that evening to confirm our appointment with him—and presumably also with his sister, since Erik was so insistent that they lived together—at his house in Chiswick the following day.

I woke up that morning feeling cheerful and almost light-hearted. And as the hour of our meeting grew nearer I could feel a growing sense of relief coming over me.

Because Simeon could not only provide us with a copy of the record for Chloë, but also with what sounded like a useful cache of information about her grandfather. So we could discharge our duties to our client on both fronts.

And have done with her.

It seemed a bit unfair to think of Chloë Loconsole in those terms. I liked her a great deal.

But it appeared she had brought some unwanted and unwelcome complications into our lives, so the sooner she was gone, the better.

We took the train from Barnes to Chiswick, a journey that took all of three minutes, rolling through sunny galleries of greenery on this summer morning, and across Barnes Bridge with a brief glimpse of the glittering river. At Chiswick we got off the train, hesitated while we got our bearings, then went up the staircase and over the railway lines to the platform and the exit on the other side.

To our right was a bus stop with a red E3 double decker just pulling in. But we were heading in the other direction. "My god, this place is beautiful," said Nevada.

Despite it being just across the river from us, we'd never actually used Chiswick railway station before. And although the main street and busy shopping district in Chiswick was very familiar—replete with great charity shops as it was—we'd always approached it from the other direction; Hammersmith. This was a new route to us.

We had turned right out of the station, walked past a small parade of shops and were now strolling down residential streets. Very leafy, very lovely residential streets, shady and quiet and lined with large house equipped with huge gardens. It was these which had occasioned Nevada's comment.

"And there's a lot of money around here, too," I said.

"I'll say."

Apart from the road and the occasional passing or parked car, the place looked like it had been untouched since Victorian times. There were enormous trees swelling up out of the pavement and spreading overhead. Someone clearly hadn't got the memo about having cutting them all down and turning this city into a wasteland devoted solely to providing support for the automobile.

I began to reevaluate Simeon "Swinging" Swithenbank. "If he can afford to live around here…" I said.

"I know," said Nevada. "It hardly matters if he's a sexless male spinster stuck with his sister."

We walked hand in hand down the beautiful, peaceful streets. It was almost like we weren't in London, or at least not in the London of this century. Evidence of money was everywhere, not least in the vast private school lurking nearby. But there were also garages the size of barns, driveways like landing strips, detached buildings as big as farmhouses. All here in the middle of the busy city. And, above all, trees. Beautiful mature trees on both sides of us as we walked along, and bushes and hedges.

Only the occasional bus stop suggested that this was a neighbourhood where ordinary mortals were tolerated.

We went down Burlington Lane, then Staveley Road and then down a side road called Staveley Gardens. The houses here were more modest, which was almost a relief. By more modest, incidentally, I mean they were mostly semi-detached instead of detached and merely large instead of absolutely huge. They were also considerably more modern than the ones near the station.

As we turned a corner we were suddenly aware of intense activity.

My heart gave a lurching, lopsided beat in my chest when I saw the ambulance.

And the police cars.

Nevada and I looked at each other. And we started to run.

As we ran, we were both hoping exactly the same thing; that the presence of the police and ambulance and a growing crowd of gawping onlookers would all turn out to have absolutely nothing to do with the man we'd come here to meet.

But they were right outside his house.

The doors of the ambulance were shut and a paramedic was standing at the back. As we arrived he moved to the front and climbed into the cab. The crowd opened to make way for them and the ambulance pulled away, moving off down the road, gathering speed and switching on its siren.

None of this looked good.

Nevada turned to the nearest of the onlookers, a woman in a pink tracksuit who looked like she'd just returned from a run. She was holding a matching pink water bottle and was talking with a shaven-headed man who was laden with bags of shopping.

"Excuse me," said Nevada, at her most polite and charming, "do you know who that was being taken away in the ambulance?"

The woman turned to the man. "They're the people from 272, aren't they?" She looked at Nevada. "There's an old couple who live there."

"They're not a couple," said the man with the shopping. "They're brother and sister."

"Well, anyway," said the tracksuit woman, "it's the man."

My heart was thudding in my chest. "What about the man?" I said.

"It was the man who was attacked. It's so horrible. He's such a nice old fellow."

"Attacked?" said Nevada.

"Yes," said the woman. "Is it just me, or are these happening all the time now? Attacks like that?"

"It's not you," said the man. "They're happening all the time. You can't turn on the news without hearing about someone being attacked. Do you remember that one at the petrol station? They were beating it off with a broom or something."

"Wait a minute," I said. They looked at me as if surprised that I could speak. "Are you talking about dog attacks?"

"Yes," said the woman. "That's what happened. He was attacked by a dog."

Nevada and I looked at each other.

"Was it his own dog?" I said.

The woman shook her head impatiently. "They don't own a dog."

"That's right," said the man. "Not dog owners. Him or his sister."

"Then whose dog was it?" said Nevada.

The man and woman shook their heads thoughtfully in perfect unison.

"No one seems to know," said the woman.

"Nobody knows where the dog came from," said the man.

"So no one has come forward to claim it," said Nevada.

The woman stared at her in puzzlement, "What do you mean?"

"No one has taken responsibility. No one has admitted to owning the dog."

The man and the woman looked at each other. "There is no dog," said the woman.

I felt a vertiginous sense of unreality about to engulf me. I looked over at Nevada to see if she was experiencing the same, or something similar. Apparently she was, with a side order of angry impatience.

"You said he'd been attacked by a dog," said Nevada. "The man who lived there." She pointed at Simeon Swithenbank's house.

"He was," said the woman, apparently willing to match Nevada in the angry impatience game, and perhaps even raise her bid. "He just went off in the ambulance. With his sister."

"Did the dog get her, too?" said the man. He sounded worried about his neighbours, which I suppose was a good and admirable thing. But I was dealing myself into the game of angry impatience and I just wanted him to shut up.

"Okay," said Nevada, strategically deescalating and smiling her most charming smile again. "It's my fault, I'm just a little confused. Because you're talking about the dog who attacked him…"

"Yes," said the woman, who was apparently still in the game and not willing to buy the sweetness and light Nevada was dishing out, at least not yet.

"But then you said there was no dog." Nevada kept smiling and added a silly-me shrug. "So I guess I'm just being thick…"

"They haven't *found* the dog," said the woman.

"There is no dog in the sense that they haven't found the dog," added the man helpfully. "So when you were asking about the dog's owners coming forward, nobody even knows where the dog has got to, let alone the owners."

"Oh, I see," said Nevada.

"So the dog just… what… ran off?" I said.

"Apparently," said the man.

"Although no one saw it run off," said the woman.

"Was it a Doberman?" I said.

The woman took a shocked step away from me. "Is it your dog?"

"We don't have a dog," said Nevada promptly, and truthfully. "We're cat people."

"Why did you ask if it was a Doberman, then?"

"Someone was having trouble with one," I said.

I didn't explain the person having trouble with one was a character in a movie, filmed nearly sixty years ago. But my answer seemed to satisfy her.

"Well, that's the thing," said the man. "No one knows what breed of dog it was. No one seems to have seen it. Nobody knows where it's come from and nobody knows where it's gone."

We made our way back from Chiswick, reversing the journey we'd undertaken less than an hour earlier. There is a strange phenomenon whereby when you return using a certain route, it seems to take a lot less time than when you came along it in the first place. That was certainly true of our walk back through what had so recently been strikingly beautiful and agreeable streets. It was an unsettlingly quick and altogether strange experience. Because everything now had such very different associations.

At least, as I said, it was brief. Mercifully so. As was our wait for the train. And the train journey itself was again only a few fleeting minutes.

In fact, everything went by so swiftly that it was as if we were being repatriated with magical speed to the real world from some alternate realm of existence. And not a pleasant alternate realm of existence.

We got off at Barnes, Nevada looking at her phone as we crossed the footbridge. "It was a Doberman," she said, viewing a news feed. "Somebody saw it."

"Does it say anything about Simeon?"

"In hospital in critical condition."

It seemed callous to return to discussion of the dog, but I did. "And nobody knows where the Doberman went?"

"That's right."

Which was very odd. Because although the woman in the tracksuit and the man with the shopping had been right, and dog attacks, even fatal ones, were sadly all too common, I'd never heard of one which involved the dog leaving the scene of the crime and successfully evading capture.

And this dog seemed to have vanished into thin air.

We walked homeward through the common. It wasn't even noon yet, but it felt like the day was already over. Well and truly over. And we both felt exhausted and beaten.

So we weren't exactly in the mood for visitors.

The small front garden of our house was largely screened from view by the rich and attractive variety of shrubs Nevada had so assiduously planted over the last few years, including some healthily burgeoning cedar trees. This meant that, as we walked towards our gate, we couldn't see if anyone was sitting on the small but tasteful selection of garden furniture we'd arranged outside the front door.

Therefore it came as a surprise, and in the circumstances not an entirely welcome one, for a voice to hail us as we approached.

"Oh, hello there."

The voice was posh, polite, young.

And fairly familiar...

Any uncertainty about the source of it was instantly dispelled as our visitor rose from his seat and stepped into view, bringing his tall, lanky form to the gate to greet us.

Cass Higgins.

I was a trifle disappointed that he wasn't wearing a hoodie consisting of variegated tartan this time. Today's was boring charcoal grey and just had the Princeton logo on it.

He politely opened the gate for us, as if he was a doorman employed for the purpose. Perhaps we should get one of those, I thought, not entirely rationally, as he shook hands with us.

"Sorry to surprise you," he said.

"Don't worry," I said. I didn't add that it was a day for surprises.

"I just popped by," he said. "And when I rang the doorbell and you weren't at home, I thought I'd take a chance and wait. So I sat on that rather nice garden sofa you have there. I hope you don't mind."

"That's what it's there for," said Nevada.

We all looked at each other for a moment, standing becalmed between the garden gate and the front door, both currently shut. There was a lightning unspoken discussion between myself and Nevada about whether this conversation should continue indoors or whether we should try to get rid of our invited visitor out here. It concluded with us giving in to the inevitable—we'd had a tough morning, but good manners were still good manners—and so I took out my keys and opened the door, and we led Cass in with us.

He was still talking about the sofa. "It's a really nice garden sofa," he said.

"Thank you," said Nevada.

"Did you get it from John Lewis?"

"Yes," said Nevada.

"Beautifully made," said Cass, who seemed to be eager to say nice things to us. Though in fairness, he wasn't coming across as insincere. I found to my surprise that I liked him better than I had on our first encounter. Perhaps because he'd been with his sister then, and her behaviour had been dictating his. He seemed something of a different person now.

Not so much of a different person that I didn't want to just get rid of him, though.

Like I said, tough morning.

He was still going on about the bloody garden sofa as we went into the living room and sat down. "It was very comfortable," he said. "Just sitting there. And very cool and pleasant and relaxing being out there in your garden surrounded by all those beautiful plants."

I could see he was even making inroads with Nevada. She was very proud of her gardening skills. "And your cats came out to inspect me," he added.

"Both of them?" said Nevada.

"Yes, first one. Then the other one came out as the first one went in again, in a sort of changing of the guard. They each took a quick look at me then returned indoors. I'm not sure if that signifies that I passed the inspection or I failed it."

"It probably signifies they wanted someone to feed them," said Nevada, ever the pragmatist.

"Look, Cass," I said, "I don't want to be rude, but…"

"Of course, of course. But why am I here? Of course…" He sat looking at us, his rather large hands clenched, almost prayerfully, between his knees, mouth open to speak. But then it seemed he couldn't say anything, so he just sat there silently.

I'm not sure if I sighed audibly, but sigh I did. "Would you like a coffee?" I said.

"No, no, I don't want to impose," he said quickly. He paused again, mouth open to speak, and this time he did manage to do so. "I don't suppose you've seen Desdemona, have you?"

Nevada and I exchanged a look. "No," said Nevada.

"Not since you guys were here the other night," I said.

"And not since I saw you both with Jasper in Barnes," said Nevada.

"You don't have…" Cass hesitated. "You don't have any clue where she might be?"

"No," I said. "None at all." I didn't feel it was incumbent on us to point out that she had last been seen hightailing it in the direction of Covent Garden and Chloë's hotel.

"Sorry," said Nevada. Apparently neither did she.

And in any case, Cass must have been aware of all that and had in fact apparently set off in pursuit of her at the time. So his having lost track of her was a different and more recent situation.

"And she hasn't been in contact at all, in any fashion?" he said.

"No," said Nevada. "Not in any fashion."

There was silence for a moment, Cass looking at his big hands folded in his lap. And then he looked up at us. It was a look of concern.

"Forgive me for asking," he said, "but are you guys okay? You seem a little stressed out."

There was so much to get annoyed about here—including the avuncular tone, very much that of a media shrink feigning compassion about some poor fool's problems, and the implied superiority this automatically conferred upon him—I couldn't immediately decide on my top pick.

One thing I was sure of, though. I was annoyed.

But Nevada beat me to it. "We've had a hard day," she said curtly.

"Sorry."

"Is that all right, Cassio?"

"Sorry, sorry, sorry."

"It is Cassio, isn't it?" said Nevada with icy politeness.

"It is," I said.

She looked at me.

"Jasper confirmed that," I said. "Or perhaps let it slip. It is a rather embarrassing name."

Nevada grinned at me approvingly and then we both turned to look at Cass, née Cassio.

He held up his hands defensively. "Fair enough, fair

179

enough. I apologise. None of my business. I know, I know. It's just that I was wondering if Desdemona had been adding to your woes. She has a handy knack for doing that."

"We've already told you, we haven't seen her," said Nevada.

"I know."

"Or spoken to her."

"I know."

"Or had any kind of contact with her."

"I know, I know, I know. I'm sorry."

"There's absolutely no reason she'd come around here," said Nevada, "And, in fact, as far as I can determine, it's the last place on earth she would come."

As if recognising the conclusive nature of this peroration, Cass rose to his feet. "Okay," he said. "I'm sorry to have wasted your time." He started for the door.

"You haven't wasted our time," said Nevada, instantly contrite now that our visitor was heading out.

"No, but I've wasted mine," he said ruefully.

"Are you sure you wouldn't like a coffee?" I said, or rather forced myself to say.

He glanced at me, perhaps trying to gauge my sincerity. I hoped he wasn't very good at this. "No, but thank you, thank you very much." He shook hands with us and took his leave.

I felt bad for a few seconds after his departure, and then I began to feel angry. And, apparently so did Nevada.

"Why the hell did he think we were stressed out?" she said.

"You mean he doesn't know us well enough to know

whether we're stressed out, or whether we always look like this?"

"Right. Exactly. How the hell did he know we were looking stressed out? We weren't exactly tearing out our hair or rending our garments, were we?"

"No," I said.

"So how the hell did he presume to know we were looking stressed out?"

"I don't know," I said. "Unless he had some inside information."

Nevada looked at me silently for a moment, then she began to nod. "Like knowing about what we'd just found in Chiswick."

"That would definitely count as inside information."

"And, knowing what had happened, he came here to see what effect it'd had on us, to see how shaken up we were. And to gloat."

"Assuming," I said, "that any of those tenuous suppositions are correct."

"Why else would he have been asking why we were stressed out, and smirking at us like that?"

"In fairness," I said, "he wasn't actually smirking."

"I think he was," said Nevada.

"And also in fairness," I said, "it could just be that we came across as being obviously stressed out."

Nevada took a deep breath as if about to launch into a tirade then slowly let it out. "I was just about to start railing in an obviously stressed out way that I'm obviously not stressed out," she said.

I took her hand. She took my other one, and we sat there on the sofa, four hands locked together, looking into each other's eyes, as Turk strode in and let out a loud, sour howl, as if as to say, *Enough of the sentimental nonsense, I want to be fed.*

So we fed her, and also Fanny who emerged from the woodwork as soon as she heard the sounds of food preparation. This return to mundane domestic routine was probably exactly what we needed at that moment.

What we probably didn't need was the doorbell ringing.

But it did.

Nevada and I looked at each other.

"What are the odds that's Desdemona?" I said.

"To turn us into liars about saying this was the last place on earth she would come," said Nevada.

"Yes."

But it wasn't Desdemona.

It was Chloë.

12: PINT-SIZED POWER DRESSER

Chloë Loconsole could not have presented a more different picture from the first time she'd appeared on our doorstep.

Gone entirely was the teenage Euro backpacker look. To be replaced by what I can perhaps best describe as the young businesswoman of the year look.

The *chic* young businesswoman of the year.

She was wearing a two-piece suit in a very pale shade of cream.

The jacket had wide lapels (I would later be told this was in fact something called a shawl collar) and a single button that was firmly buttoned at the waist. It was just as well it was firmly buttoned at the waist because, as far as I could tell, she was wearing nothing at all under that jacket. She certainly wasn't wearing a bra. The smooth bronze of her skin and the undisguised swell of her breasts, as displayed by the V-shaped opening in the front of the suit were, to be candid, magnificent.

The matching cream trousers were long—well, as long

as they could be on the shortish legs of this pint-sized power dresser—and straight, with perhaps a hint of a flare.

But I hardly noticed these after my poor male mind was blown by that jacket and the silken tanned skin within. Which I suppose was its general intention. After walking into a business meeting dressed like that, I imagine a fair portion of the men—not to mention the women—present would be reduced to basic life functions.

Like remembering to breathe.

The shiny, black, high-heeled, very high-heeled, shoes which completed Chloë's ensemble accounted for a startling increase in height since I had last seen her, when she had been shod in sensible hiking boots. I noticed that these gleaming black shoes had tiny red bows, which made a stylish echo with the small red ribbon in her curly halo of gleaming black hair.

I was glad I noticed this subtle detail; it suggested I was beginning to belatedly recover some of my higher intellectual functions.

Chloë flashed a quick smile at me then another at Nevada, who had appeared at my shoulder.

Nevada immediately made me feel a lot better about my poleaxed response to our visitor by saying without hesitation, "My god, you look fantastic."

"Oh, thank you."

"I'm not just saying that."

Chloë chuckled as we led her inside, her high heels clicking emphatically on the floor of our hallway. "No, I detected your sincerity. Thank you."

"What a superlative suit."

"Thank you again, but these shoes are killing me." She slipped them off and kicked them to one side of the hall with a casualness which suggested either a healthy lack of respect for high-end material belongings, or simply the possession of so much money that she could afford to treat them like that.

"Come inside and put your feet up," said Nevada.

"Thank you. I promise I won't stay long. I've only come for a very brief visit."

"You can stay as long as you like," said Nevada.

"Would you like some coffee?" I said.

Chloë sighed and smiled a devastating smile at me. "I was hoping you would say that."

When I brought the coffee through, Chloë was tucked in an armchair in the lotus position, massaging her bare feet. "Forgive me for rubbing my feet in your living room," she said.

"I'm just relieved that Nevada isn't doing it for you," I said, and both the women laughed.

Chloë unwound her legs from the lotus as she accepted the coffee, giving me a quick smile which faded to be replaced by a tense, worried expression that seemed oddly familiar.

I would only realise later that this was exactly how Desdemona had looked when she had first arrived at our house a few nights ago…

"I meant what I said when I told you I wouldn't stay long," said Chloë.

"And I meant what I said, too," said Nevada. "When I told you to stay as long as you like."

Chloë nodded and took a quick sip of her coffee, still looking very serious indeed. "Thank you, that offer may prove very useful, more useful than you can know."

"By the way," said Nevada, "is that an Italian suit?"

Chloë made a humorously sour face. "No, I'm afraid it's just Ralph Lauren. Hence American-made. I feel tremendously disloyal wearing it." She looked down at her stunning décolletage. "It's well-cut though. And at least the wool is from an Italian mill."

Later on Nevada would quietly inform me, "Three grand for that suit. Without accessories. And never mind the shoes."

"Oh well," I said. "At least she saved some money on underwear."

But right now Chloë set her coffee aside decisively. "I felt I had to come in person to see you both," she said. "Because I have a very big request to make, and I wanted to be able to look the two of you in your eyes when I asked you the question."

"Okay, that hasn't tensed me up at all," I said, and both the women laughed again and Chloë relaxed a little.

"All right," she said. "But you must be willing to say no to me." Her brown eyes were wide open and guileless as she made this statement. A massively disingenuous statement, as far as I was concerned. I doubted very much that many people had ever said no to Ms Loconsole.

"Anyway, the thing is, I only have a couple more nights at my hotel. And when I move out it's my intention to find an Airbnb or something similar to rent." She glanced at us to see if we were following this so far. We were. "I've been actively looking for such a place. Or, rather, to be entirely honest, my *nonna* has been looking for me. She is actually much better at that sort of thing than I am. She really is a wizard with a search engine." She smiled, as if fondly reminiscing. "Raffaella is a very groovy granny. She has taken to the online world like a duck to water. Or maybe I should say, like a spider to a web. She certainly understands social media better than I do. When I get the company up and running she will be in charge of internet publicity."

Her smile faded. "But, at the moment, she is quite concerned about me being in London on my own. She keeps threatening to come here and look after me, as she puts it. Meanwhile, she is looking for an appropriate place for me to rent. But locating a suitable one is proving somewhat problematical." She sighed. "My preference would be to simply remain at the hotel. But things have become rather complicated there. And uncomfortable."

"Uncomfortable?" said Nevada. Like me, she'd concluded that our guest wasn't just talking about the room service.

Chloë sighed again, more profoundly this time. "Yes. It's Cass."

Nevada and I exchanged a quick glance. Which Chloë must have registered because she nodded and said, as if replying to our unspoken question, "Right. He just can't stop himself interfering." She gave us a direct, challenging look. "I mean interfering with myself and Desdemona. As you might have ascertained, we have… a history together."

"And history is repeating itself," said Nevada lightly.

Chloë smiled, apparently relieved that this was all coming

out in the open. "Yes, very wittily put. It is indeed. History is very definitely repeating itself. We had an affair in the past and at one point it seemed it was all over, permanently concluded, but…"

"But it isn't," said Nevada laconically.

"Quite. Quite right. In fact it has commenced again." She smiled, as if she just couldn't help smiling, which made it rather an irresistible smile. "And I am very glad it has." But that smile faded soon enough. "Unfortunately Cass seems unable to accept this fact."

"Why?" said Nevada.

Chloë shrugged, the stylishly cut shoulders of her cream jacket rising and falling. "For all sorts of reasons. Desdemona is his younger sister and she's had some bad experiences in the past so he is incredibly protective of her. Quite legitimately protective of her. And, of course, that isn't necessarily such a bad thing…"

"But in this case…" said Nevada.

"Yes, in this case," said Chloë, "he needs to learn to just let go of her." She drained her coffee and set it aside. "But there are other matters, too."

"Your grandfather," I said.

That luminous brown gaze met mine, level and candid. For some reason it crossed my mind that this woman would be a remarkably convincing liar.

"Yes, my grandpa and his grandmother. Poor Jackie." That seemed to be her standard way of referring to the dead woman. "Desdemona can accept that my *nonno* is innocent…" She shot me a lightning glance, instantly picking up on what I was thinking. "Of course, nothing is proved yet." She shrugged again, the shrug somehow suggesting helplessness this time. Like a child who needed comforting. Despite myself, I felt instantly protective towards her. I didn't feel any less protective when she gave me a soulful look. "And, as I have told you, I am hoping you will be able to help me out with that. Establishing his innocence."

"Okay—" I said.

"Or his guilt," she added emphatically and hastily. And she said it with such force that, for the first time, I actually believed she might be willing to accept this unpalatable possibility.

"Right," I said.

I would have said a great deal more. Since I'd decided now was the time to tell her about Simeon Swithenbank and the dead end we'd hit in that regard.

Because a dog, straight out of *Murder in London*, had savaged him and left him in hospital fighting for his life.

But I didn't get to say any of this, because Chloë held up her hand.

"Please let me finish. I was going to say that Desdemona is at least willing to conceive of my *nonno*'s innocence as a possibility. But not Cassio." She smiled a harsh, humourless smile. Her teeth were perfect. "So for that, and other reasons, he doesn't want his sister to become involved with me. Again. Or ever." She murmured something in Italian which I didn't really need translating because it was so clearly an angry obscenity. "It's an incredible hassle since he found out where I am staying."

Nevada took a deep breath. "I'm sorry," she said. "That's entirely my fault. I told Desdemona about your hotel. And I told her in front of Cass. So he was bound to hear. I should have been more circumspect."

"It was absolutely not your fault," said Chloë firmly. "But it will be great if I could stay somewhere he couldn't find me. Somewhere he wouldn't think of looking. Somewhere Desdemona would be free to visit me at any time…"

She looked at us.

"I couldn't stay here with you, could I?"

Nevada and I exchanged a look. It had been pretty obvious what she was leading up to, but in the event it was still something of a surprise.

Chloë quickly added. "Just until I can find a suitable Airbnb. Just a brief interval of couch surfing."

"Oh, we can do better than a couch for you," said Nevada. I could see she was already thinking what needed to be done to the spare room to render it inhabitable.

"You mustn't let me talk you into doing something you don't want to do," added Chloë.

"If you think that's possible," I said, "you clearly haven't got to know Nevada yet."

Nevada took my hand and said, "And this one is remarkably stubborn, too."

"Are you really sure?" said Chloë. "I can stay here?"

"You said you wanted to look us in the eye," I said. "So look us in the eye."

Both Nevada and I gave her a bug-eyed stare and she burst into laughter. "All right, you've convinced me. Thank you so much. It won't be until a couple of nights from now, and it won't be for long. I promise."

"Don't worry. Stay as long as you want," said Nevada.

"There is one thing you need to know, though," I said.

"That you guys snore?" said Chloë playfully.

"No, thankfully," said Nevada.

"That your cats snore?"

"Again, no."

I felt the need for bluntness now instead of cute cat jokes. "You said you want a place where Cass won't think of looking. Where he won't find you."

"Yes?"

"So you need to know," said Nevada, all seriousness now too, "that Cass was just around here."

"Here?"

"Yes, just before you arrived."

Chloë's sleek brow furrowed momentarily with calculation. "Had he come here looking for me?"

"No, looking for Desdemona," I said.

Chloë's brow smoothed again. "Poor Cass," she said. It almost sounded sincere.

"And naturally we weren't able to help him," said Nevada. "Even if we wanted to."

"So his visit was in vain," said Chloë. She was looking thoughtful. "But it will have had the useful side effect of establishing in his mind that I am not here." She nodded. "Good. That means it is even more safe for me to come and stay here." She smiled at us, all charm and sweetness. "With your permission of course." The sweetness and charm suddenly ebbed away to be replaced by awkward uncertainty. "There is one thing that *you* need to know, though," she said.

"That you snore?" I said.

"No, neither of us do," said Chloë. She gave Nevada and me a steady look, to see if we got it.

"So you may not be alone when you're staying with us?" said Nevada.

Chloë seemed relieved to have this out in the open. "Again, with your permission. If Cass now believes that Desdemona isn't here…"

"Then this is the perfect place for her to be."

"To be with me," said Chloë. She gave us a searching look. "If you guys don't mind…"

"Of course we don't mind," said Nevada.

It took a moment to sink in that we'd said yes, then a very grateful Chloë gave us both a hug.

Now was the time, I thought, to tell her the bad news about Simeon Swithenbank. But, as if on cue, Chloë's phone rang and she glanced at it. "Sorry, I must dash," she said. "This is most important."

We followed her into the hallway where she put her high heels back on with a martyred sigh.

Just before she left, she said one more thing, very casually, as if it was of no significance.

"I know it sounds crazy, but I've got a feeling someone has been following me."

Then she smiled and left.

192

13: TWO DOORS

It's nice when, instead of having to go looking for a record, the record comes looking for you.

It doesn't often happen, but it did happen with *Murder in London*.

And in this case it was more than nice, since with the catastrophe which had befallen Simeon Swithenbank, and the fact that the couple from Barnes Fair—Nevada and I had taken to calling them the Empty Cover Couple—hadn't called me back, and might never call me back, I was completely out of leads.

The morning after Chloë had visited us in her mind-blowing business suit, I was just clearing away the remains of breakfast, ours and the cats', and washing dishes at the sink when the phone rang. I dutifully dried my hands and went to answer it. When I'm actually on a job, as I formally was now, I try and maintain an efficient and businesslike demeanour at all times.

And I was just as glad this was the case, and that I took this particular call…

I'd thought at first it might be Chloë again, in which case I was determined to give her a full update, including the attempted acid dosing and the Doberman attack on the unfortunate Simeon. But it wasn't Chloë.

Instead it was an old frenemy, I don't think that's too strong a term, called Lenny.

He didn't waste time with salutations or enquiries about my health. "I understand you're looking for a record," he said.

"I'm always looking for a record, Lenny. It's an affliction and one I believe you'll be able to identify with." Lenny had spent the last few decades selling secondhand vinyl, mostly at vastly inflated prices, in various premises around London. He currently had a shop in a basement in Ladbroke Grove.

"Specifically," said Lenny, at his most portentous, "I am given to understand that you're looking for a copy of the Lansdowne release of *Murder in London* by Loretto Loconsole."

All at once, and just for once, Lenny had my full attention. "How did you know I was looking for that?"

"A little bird told me."

"Would that little bird happen to have been a blue tit?" I said. I emphatically sensed Lenny's enormous disappointment radiating down the line in the ensuing moment or two of silence. I'd spoiled his fun and his chance to seem powerful and masterful. And I'd also incidentally confirmed my deduction.

Erik Make Loud's girlfriend Helene had once been in an all-girl punk group called the Blue Tits. And before he became exclusively a vinyl retailer, Lenny had dabbled in running a record label. And he'd signed Helene and her band. So the two of them knew each other, and that connection seemed the most likely way Lenny could have heard of my quest.

"So what if it was?" said Lenny sulkily. "Are you still interested in the record?"

"I don't see why I wouldn't be," I said.

"I could easily sell it somewhere else," said Lenny. "In fact, I have a number of cashed-up customers just ready and waiting with their mouths watering to buy this item. In fact, thinking about it now, they really ought to have priority over you. I don't know why I phoned you at all. Well, I'd better be going then…"

Was he really such a temperamental little martinet that he would jeopardise a lucrative record deal just because he'd been disappointed in his attempt to mystify and impress me?

The answer was a definite yes. So I reluctantly but promptly set about mollifying him.

"I only guessed it was Helene because I just spotted that I've got a message from her on my phone," I said to him, lying through my teeth. "And when I saw her name I just happened to remember that you guys knew each other back in the day."

"I signed her band to my Crypt Kix record label," said Lenny. I let him tell me this and other facts which I already knew quite well, until he managed to overcome the damage to his fragile ego. Then we finally got back down to business. "Anyway, I have a copy of this record you're looking for."

"Good," I said.

"Are you interested in buying it?" he said.

"Yes, very interested."

"I have a number of cashed-up customers waiting with their mouths watering, ready to buy this item."

"Yes, I think you did mention that."

"So I couldn't let it go for less than fifteen hundred pounds."

This was an absurd sum, of course. But that was the only kind of sum that Lenny recognised. On the other hand, the rarest titles on Lansdowne, such as *Dusk Fire* by Don Rendell and Ian Carr (with Mike Garrick on piano) could change hands for almost this much. Assuming they were in near-mint condition.

"Is it near-mint?" I asked.

"Of course it is," snapped Lenny.

I did some rapid calculations. This was too much money. But, on the other hand, I could hardly let a perfect copy of this record slip away. Especially when I might spend almost as much, or indeed more, buying partially damaged copies piecemeal to try and collect all of the tracks in a condition which would allow for mastering a new release.

So I took a deep breath and began haggling. Lenny took the usual position that this was his price and it was final and he had no intention of budging. And then he proceeded to budge. By imperceptible degrees. I finally got him down to the ludicrously arbitrary price of £1,130. It was still north of a grand and therefore far more than I'd wanted to spend. But at the same time I'd sensed that the thousand-pound mark was a psychological barrier for Lenny and there was no way he was going to sell it for less. So, whatever happened, we were on the hook for a thousand.

When you looked at it this way—admittedly a lunatic way to look at it—the additional hundred and thirty quid didn't seem quite so bad.

So we agreed the price and I paid right away online, completely clearing out our PayPal balance and having to transfer some funds from our bank account into the bargain. But I wanted to strike while the iron was hot, given that Lenny was such a whimsical, not to mention volatile, little creature.

He agreed to pack the record properly and ship it out to me by a reliable high-speed, high-security courier—which these days could mean a kid with a bicycle and a backpack—and get it to me by tomorrow.

"Who was that?" said Nevada as I hung up the phone. She was coming in through the back door with Fanny at her feet, squeaking happily. My darling was in jeans and the old red-and-black checked long-sleeve shirt she wore for working in the garden. She had a smear of dirt on her brow, as she often did, transferred there by her gardening gloves when she shoved her hair out of her eyes. As always, I thought it looked very fetching, and as always it made me want to kiss her, among other things.

"Lenny Nettleford," I said.

"Lenny of Chablis and beret fame?"

It was true that Lenny did like to drink expensive white wines, and indeed one must grudgingly admit that he even knew a thing or two about them. But no such concessions needed to be made in the matter of his berets, which he wore in a variety of colours, and in none of which he looked less than absurdly silly. "Yes, him," I said. And then proceeded to fill Nevada in on the deal I'd just sealed. "It was more money than I wanted to spend…" I concluded.

"But if we've got the record, we've got it," said Nevada, energetically patting Fanny in happy celebration. Fanny had no idea why we were celebrating, but she was happy, too, purring furiously. "And it'll save us all the fuss and hassle of going on searching."

"That's what I thought," I said.

"And anyway, we'll just bill Chloë for whatever it costs. A girl who's so disdainful of her three-K, two-piece Ralph Lauren can spare the odd thousand or so for a very rare record."

"That's also what I thought," I said. "But it still sticks in my craw having to charge her so much…"

"I know," said Nevada.

"Especially when the money is going to Lenny."

"I know, love," said Nevada. "But never mind. And well done." My garden girl came over and kissed me. "By the way, did he offer to sweep me off to the Greek Islands on a whirlwind holiday of sun, sea, sex and sand? In the case of Lenny, I suspect mostly sand."

It was true that Lenny, despite being married most of the time, had a thing about Nevada and was constantly trying, in his own maladroit and pitiful way, to take her away from me. Usually to the Mediterranean.

"No, for some reason he neglected to do that this time."

"I must be losing my touch," said Nevada.

"Either that or he's losing his," I said. "I suspect the latter."

Just then the phone rang. It was Lenny again. I showed it to Nevada. "Speak of the devil," she said. "Here, let me answer it. Hello, Lenny. I know. We were just talking about you. Yes, we were just talking about that. No, I'm afraid the answer is still a very firm no. That's very sweet of you, but if you do I'll call the police."

The record arrived, as promised, the very next day. First thing in the morning, in fact. Nevada knew what it was, so she eagerly watched me open the package. The cats, who had no idea what it was, also watched with apparent fascination.

As well they might.

Because at least Lenny hadn't scrimped on the packing material and sent this thousand-pound-plus LP in the sort of soft cardboard envelope intended for posting wildlife calendars. Something I'd known other record dealers to do, though admittedly not with an item of quite this value.

What Lenny had done instead was to take the sort of purpose-built cardboard box which was intended to accommodate a dozen LPs and devoted it solely to the protection of this one album. Perhaps not such a silly idea. But what definitely was a silly idea was to completely swathe the outside of the box in brown adhesive tape. Layer after layer of brown adhesive tape.

So much so that it was impossible to find a seam or flap or entry point on the parcel. It had been rendered into a glossy, seamless enigma of a puzzle box.

I took out the scalpel I kept for just such eventualities

and began to probe carefully at the corners of the big, shiny, tape-swathed oblong.

"The problem with all this fucking tape," I said, painstakingly deploying the scalpel, "is that I can't see where to open the box."

"I suppose he thought he'd reinforce it…" said Nevada.

"All he's reinforcing is the chances of sticking this blade into the box in the wrong place and damaging the record," I said, a trifle tetchily, I fear. "Because I can't see what I'm doing."

"Fucking Lenny," said Nevada forcefully, and loyally. And both the cats made small noises as if agreeing with her.

I slipped the scalpel blade into the very edge of the box, only inserting it as shallowly as possible and working it carefully along, so all I cut was cardboard. There was now a seam open in the box. I did the same procedure in parallel and then along the two short edges, and lifted a rectangle of cardboard away, exposing what was inside the box.

What was inside the box was more tape. "Christ," I snarled.

I tried insinuating my fingers and extracting the tape-wrapped mass inside the box, but it wouldn't budge. I forced myself not to lose my temper but rather to pause and take stock. I was sweating and my girlfriend and my cats were watching me.

I wiped my brow and said, "There's more than one way to skin a…"

"Don't say cat," said Nevada.

"To skin an annoying, beret-wearing record dealer."

"That's better," said Nevada.

I went and got the scissors from the kitchen. More normally applied to the task of cutting up premium cuts of meat for our cats, these were razor-sharp and could be equally effectively deployed to the task of freeing a record packed by a twat.

With Nevada helping like a nurse assisting a surgeon in the operating theatre, I was able to slide the cutting edge of the scissors into the hole in the box. And with her forcing up the cardboard surface so it was safely a few millimetres away from the contents of the box, I began to cut. It got rapidly easier as I went along and, in a few seconds, there was a long diagonal cut right across the big face of the box, straight through the shipping label and our address, scrawled in Lenny's inimitably horrid handwriting.

Then it was a simple matter to peel back the two cut sections and the box was entirely open on one of its big sides. With Nevada's help, I wrestled out the contents, which turned out to be a diabolical sandwich consisting of several LP-sized squares of cardboard interleaved with newspapers, free newspapers naturally, since Lenny was a thrifty soul, and all secured with what must have been another half a roll at least of brown adhesive tape. No thrift evident there.

And, finally, at the centre of it all, the record.

Murder in London.

The cover was rather more yellowed with age, and more worn, than the one I'd picked up at Barnes Fair. So maybe I would do a swap, so I'd have a mint cover with a mint copy of the vinyl…

LP and cover were nestling together in a polythene liner

with the LP in the original paper inner sleeve packed outside the cover. This, at least, was the way that a professional should ship a record. If you sent it through the post with the vinyl *inside* the cover, it could bounce around and tear that cover. I'd seen that all too often.

So a few points to Lenny.

A very few points.

I took out the record and stared at the vinyl.

And stared.

And stared.

Instead of looking at the record, Nevada was looking at my face.

"Isn't it the right record?"

"Oh it's the right record, all right," I said quietly, handing it to her as I went to get my phone.

I felt strangely, dangerously tranquil as I dialled Lenny's number. I don't know what I would have done if he hadn't answered. Probably gone straight to Ladbroke Grove to track him down in person in his basement lair and pull him across the counter of his shop by the lapels of his alpaca coat. But luckily—for him as much as me—he did answer, and promptly. "Hello, Lenny," I said.

I was astonished at how calm and normal my voice sounded. Apparently Nevada, who'd by now had a chance to examine the record, was also astonished. Judging by her expression.

"Did you get the record?" said Lenny cheerfully.

"Yes, it just arrived as a matter of fact."

"Good. Well packed, eh?"

I almost gave in to the temptation to give him a lecture about not using so much fucking tape. But there were more important things to talk about. "Lenny," I said, "there's a hole in the record…"

"Of course there is. You'd be in trouble if there wasn't. You couldn't play a record if there wasn't a hole in the centre of it." He gave a little man of the world snigger.

"But this hole is not in the centre," I said. "I mean, not *just* in the centre. There's another hole, Lenny. An additional hole, a hole I can put my finger through." Nevada was demonstrating this right now, putting her finger through it. "Right through the vinyl in the middle of the playing surface."

"Which side?"

I started to lose my temper. "What do you mean, which side? It's a *hole*, Lenny. It goes right through. So it's on both sides. That's what makes it a hole."

Nevada put a hand on my shoulder. I realised that I'd begun shouting. The cats were both staring at me, aghast.

"A manufacturing flaw," said Lenny breezily.

"It's not just a flaw, Lenny. And it didn't happen during manufacturing."

"Then I wonder how it happened," said Lenny. He said it in an innocent voice, in a spirit of pure enquiry.

"It's been damaged by heat," I said.

"Heat?"

"An intense localised source of heat," I said. I was calming down as I was forced to articulate what I thought had happened to the record. The poor little record. "The vinyl is warped around this hole and the microgrooves are melted.

It looks like someone used it as an ashtray and left a cigar burning on it."

"Ashtray…" said Lenny. "Cigar…" It sounded as if some memory was stirring in his greedy little head.

"That's all I can suggest," I said, by way of conversation.

"Ah," said Lenny. It now definitely sounded like he'd remembered something. He cleared his throat but said nothing. There ensued a lengthy pause.

"Sounds like it was overgraded at near-mint," said Lenny, finally.

"You think?"

"I suppose I could offer a partial refund…"

"A partial refund?" At this point Nevada took the phone from me, because I'd begun shouting again.

"Hello, Lenny. Nevada here. I am standing with my finger through the hole in the playing surface. It makes for quite an arresting image. I imagine if I was to post it online, to plaster it all over the socials, with an account of how you sold this to us as 'near-mint' and are now offering a *partial* refund… Yes, that's right. Yes, please do. Thank you. No. No way. Absolutely not."

Nevada hung up, looking pleased with herself. "Lenny is sending a full refund immediately. It should be with us…" she glanced at her phone again, "…right about now. Yes, there we go." She showed me the screen. "Is that the full amount?"

"Yes, he's even refunded postage."

"I should hope so."

"Well done."

Nevada put her phone away. "Thank you."

"What was that bit at the end," I said. "When you were saying absolutely not? Another invitation to a Greek isle?"

"Not this time. This time he was asking if he could have the photo of me with my finger through the hole in the vinyl. 'Purely for his personal use,' as he put it."

"Yuck."

"Indeed."

I picked up the LP with the hole in it. With the two holes in it. "Lenny said we could keep this. Free of charge."

"How generous of him."

I examined the record more closely. "Actually, it might be. There may be one or two tracks on this that we can salvage, the ones furthest from the burn hole. We'll have to check with Chloë's mastering engineer."

Nevada gave me an uncertain look.

"Only if we can't find a better copy," she said.

She obviously felt that it would reflect on our professionalism if we were to hand over a junker like this to our client. And, come to think of it, I agreed with her. "Right," I said.

"And we will find a better copy."

"Right," I said again, a little less convincingly this time.

They say that when one door closes, another door opens.

Which is what happened next.

Or, in this case, two doors.

The first door opened when I got a phone call from Erik Make Loud. "Mate," he said.

"Hello, Erik."

"How's the search for the record going? *Murder in London* by maestro Loretto Loconsole." He briskly pronounced the name with a surprisingly convincing Italian accent. At least, convincing to me. Then I remembered that he'd actually met the man in question, so he'd had the opportunity to hear how he said his own name. All those years ago…

"Not too well, truth be told," I said.

"Helene told me she'd put you onto a possible lead."

"She did, and please say thank you to her."

"But no dice?" said Erik. For all his bluster and drug-addled obfuscation, when the chips were down he was a perceptive fellow.

"Afraid not," I said.

"She told me that Lenny was certain he had a copy."

"He was certain. And, in fact, he did have a copy."

"No good, though?"

I paused and chose my words carefully. I didn't want to get angry all over again. "To describe it as unplayable would be generous."

Erik made some sympathetic tutting noises. "So back to square one, mate?"

"Afraid so," I said.

"Well, maybe not. I realised I'd never got around to giving you Lanky Lockridge's number. You know, the bloke who played sax on *Murder in London*?"

"I remember," I said. In fact it was on my to-do list to chase Erik for this phone number. And it was a considerable relief not to have to do so, since chasing Erik Make Loud for anything was a noticeably unrewarding pastime.

"So here you go. Just texting it to you now."

"Thank you."

"You're very welcome."

"And be sure to thank Helene for me," I said. "It was a good idea to approach Lenny and it's not her fault it didn't pan out."

"No," said Erik. "It was Lenny's fault. Because he's a great big hairy twat."

On that gracious note we said our goodbyes. I duly received the text with Lanky Lockridge's number. I phoned this right away and got his voicemail. I left a message which remained unanswered for several days, during which time I continued to gently pursue the elusive saxophone player.

But before I got through to him, the other door opened.

I received a text message from a number I didn't recognise.

It read: *We met at Barnes Fair. U bought a record cover without a record inside it. R U still interested?*

I almost dropped the phone in my eagerness to text them a reply. I indicated that I definitely was still interested.

There was no response for what seemed like an eternity, but later checking on my phone showed it to be one hour and forty-seven minutes.

And this time the message was: *Had a quick look. Could not find the record. Lots to look through, however. Want to come and look yourself?*

Well, there was only one answer to that.

14: BUMPER STICKER

The Empty Cover Couple lived in Hillingdon, which is a borough on the western outskirts of London. While it wouldn't have been impossible to get there by public transport—Elizabeth Line to West Drayton, then a considerable walk—we opted to drive. And since we didn't possess a car of our own, this meant borrowing a friend's.

And, as usual, we asked Tinkler.

Tinkler had no aversion to driving us around, but he also had no aversion to just lending us his vintage Volvo DAF and himself remaining at home. But in this case he was pursuing neither of these options. Because Agatha was back.

As Nevada had regretfully predicted, hearing about the fake cake order—in which her name had been used, or rather misused—had caused Agatha to prematurely terminate her holiday in the south of France. And she had returned to London. She'd arrived last night and immediately called us up. "I'm so sorry you cut short your vacation," said Nevada.

"Well, you can cut short your apologies," said Agatha.

We briefed her on what had been going on, bringing her right up to date, and she'd promptly volunteered to join us on our jaunt to Hillingdon and the Empty Cover Couple.

So there was no way on earth Tinkler wasn't going to come along, too.

And since there was also no way on earth that Agatha wasn't going to drive the vehicle she was travelling in, Tinkler was relegated to being a passenger in his own car.

Which, frankly, he loved.

We all rendezvoused at our house, Agatha arriving first to drink coffee and make a fuss of the cats and, truth be told, to be made a fuss of herself. By us, since we hadn't seen her for what seemed like months. Tinkler himself arrived late. I'd started to get worried because I didn't want to exhaust the patience of the Empty Cover Couple.

"Is that really what you're calling them?" said Agatha.

"Well, I only know the name of one of them," I said. "The woman. I never did learn what her husband was called."

"And we have to call them something," said Nevada. "Hence Empty Cover Couple."

"Flawless logic," said Agatha. "What's the woman called?"

"Valerie," I said.

"Like the Amy Winehouse song," said Agatha, who began to hum it and then sing it, rather beautifully.

This potentially lovely interlude was interrupted by the doorbell. Tinkler at last. And when he came trotting in, it was obvious why he was late.

THE VINYL DETECTIVE

"Mr Sharply Dressed," said Agatha.

"That's my new name," said Tinkler. "I'm going to have it legally changed."

"Is that a funnel-neck cashmere cardigan?" said Nevada. Tinkler was indeed wearing a rather sleek black cardigan. "Yes."

"And is that a Seasalt Cornwall garment-dyed, pure linen overshirt?"

Tinkler sighed and surveyed the handsome purple shirt. "Yes, you know it is."

"And Iron Heart jeans made of indigo overdyed selvedge denim in a relaxed tapered fit?"

"Yes, yes, you know they are. Because you sold me everything I'm wearing. Except underwear. At an outrageous price."

"At a very reasonable price," said Nevada. "At a startlingly reasonable and highly affordable price, considering what you were getting for your money."

"Yeah, yeah," said Tinkler. "The boilerplate. Or do I mean the terms and conditions?"

"Did she really sell you everything except underwear?" said Agatha.

"Even the shoes. Yes."

"But you are wearing underwear?" said Agatha.

"Yes," said Tinkler. Then suddenly he beamed at her alertly. "Are you?"

"Right, that's enough of that discussion," said Nevada, clapping her hands briskly. She glanced at me. "We want to be hitting the road."

210

I was grateful for this intervention because, as mentioned, I didn't know how patient Valerie and her nameless spouse were going to prove to be. On our brief acquaintance at Barnes Fair, I hadn't formed the impression they were the most easy-going of souls.

As we trooped out of the house, after briefing the cats about the likely hour of our return and carefully locking up behind us, Tinkler said, "Anyway, that's why I'm late. Sorry I'm late, by the way. But it's entirely because of Nevada."

"Me?" said Nevada, all at once a picture of wide-eyed, blue-eyed innocence.

"Yes, because you've sold me so many nice clothes."

"Ah."

"Or do I mean so much nice clothing? Curse the treacherous complexities of language. Anyway, I've got so much nice stuff to wear I couldn't decide what to put on this morning and I changed clothes about seven times."

"And why did you do that?" asked Agatha casually.

"Because of you, of course, don't toy with me," said Tinkler. But he said it happily. "Because I wanted to look nice for you. Because I haven't seen you for *ages*."

"Oh come on," said Agatha. "I haven't been gone that long."

"An eternity," said Tinkler.

"Well, you do look nice," said Agatha.

"Thank you!" said Tinkler.

"All thanks to me," said Nevada.

"Largely thanks to you," said Tinkler. "But mostly thanks to me having the good sense to buy stuff from you."

"That's true," allowed Nevada.

"Anyway, thank you for saying I look nice," said Tinkler.

"Well, it's true," said Agatha.

"Thank you. So… are you wearing underwear?"

"Enough of that," said Nevada.

"Sorry, I just wanted to put my mind at rest," said Tinkler.

"Or at the opposite of rest," said Nevada.

"Or at the opposite, right."

"Where are you parked, Tinkler?" said Agatha, possibly to change the subject.

"Just around here."

We were turning the corner that led into the small side street which ran between our house and the grounds of the Abbey. Sure enough, waiting here was Tinkler's little red car, parked pointing away from us and towards to the main road for a quick getaway. Or, in Tinkler's case, a slow getaway.

As we walked up to it, Agatha said, "What's this, Tinkler?"

"It's my car."

"No, what's this *on* your car?"

"A custom-made bumper sticker which cost me a pretty penny."

Sure enough, there was a new sticker on the bumper of the car. It was a yellow hazard warning diamond shape of the kind which usually read *Baby on Board* in black type and featured a pair of tiny footprints also in black.

Except this one read *Body in Boot*. And featured a skull and crossbones.

Tinkler looked at each of us in turn as we all stared at him silently.

"It's okay," he said. "There isn't really a body in the boot."

"This time," said Nevada.

"Okay," said Tinkler. "So the bumper sticker might be considered a little tasteless." Then he added eagerly, "But not as tasteless as the cocktail cabinet I once had made from a child's coffin."

"No," said Agatha. She had her hands lightly on the steering wheel and her eyes were drifting casually across the road ahead. There wasn't much to see yet in terms of traffic challenges or driving hazards because we were taking a short cut through Richmond Park. Or rather, a long cut. We were taking the scenic route, towards Isleworth. "The bumper sticker is much more tasteless."

"Why?"

Since we were driving at a low speed on a quiet road with nothing but beautiful rolling green scenery on either side of us and the occasional distant—very distant—deer, Agatha allowed herself the luxury of glancing over her shoulder and looking at Nevada and I in the back seat. "Do you want to tell him or shall I?"

Nevada leaned forward so her lips were almost at Tinkler's ear and proceeded to explain carefully, as if to a child or fool, "The bumper sticker is worse because the so-called child's coffin never actually had a child in it, or anyone at all. It was merely the repository for some documents. The boot of this car, on the other hand…"

"I sense that you're waiting for me to say something," said Tinkler.

"The boot of this car actually did have a body in it," I said. Indeed my heart was thudding unpleasantly at the memory.

"And it's no joking matter," said Nevada.

"Ah, but there you see I disagree," said Tinkler airily.

"Really?" said Nevada.

"Yes, really," said Tinkler. He suddenly sounded serious. Which was a very unusual way for Tinkler to sound. And then he twisted around in his seat to look at us, and he looked serious, too. "Okay," he said. "So there *was* a body in the boot. Of my car. And after you got rid of it—did I ever thank you for that, by the way? Disposing of bodies is way outside my skillset, so I'm really glad you guys dealt with it. So thank you."

"You're welcome," I said. I must have said it very bluntly and harshly because Tinkler immediately fell silent. I felt a little bad about being so rude and belligerent to my best friend. But I still had dreams about leaving that body in the woods.

Or, rather, nightmares.

After a moment or two Tinkler resumed, which was an indication of his unusual seriousness and his need to get this out, whatever it was. "Anyway, after it had the body in it, even though it didn't have the body in it anymore, I felt very strange about driving this car. Even being in it. Even having it parked outside my house."

"I can imagine," said Agatha quietly.

"So I thought about getting rid of it, of course," said Tinkler. He had turned forward again so he was facing away from us, looking out at the road ahead. And we couldn't see his face. "But that just seemed like a defeat. And I *like* my car. It wasn't the poor little car's fault that some evil shit had used it to hide a body."

"Poor little car," murmured Agatha in agreement.

Tinkler shrugged. "So I needed some kind of strategy to reclaim the car, so to speak. To change the way I thought about it. Does that make sense?"

"For once, yes," said Nevada lightly. "For once, something you're saying actually makes a lot of sense."

"Thank you." He seemed to appreciate her efforts to put things on a more cheerful footing as much as her avowed agreement. "So I dreamed up that bumper sticker. And, as soon as I thought of it, I started laughing. And I began to feel better. And when I got it printed and stuck it on the car, I laughed some more. I laughed a lot more. And I felt even better. Now every time I see it, it reminds me that there isn't a body in the boot. And when anybody else sees it, it's just a joke. A sick joke, admittedly, but no one looking at it would ever dream there really was a body in there, once. And by putting the whole thing out there in public like that, by telling the truth when nobody knows I'm telling the truth…"

"Except your good friends here," said Agatha.

"Except my good buddies here," said Tinkler. "Right. Having the truth out there in plain sight like that, like a public confession, that makes me feel better, too. It makes me feel a lot better."

He shrugged again. "It helped me get over it. The trauma. And I kind of took repossession of my car and I was able to keep it after all."

"I'm glad you did," said Agatha. "I like driving it."

Tinkler turned back to look at us. His puppy dog eyes were imploring. "Do you understand?"

"Of course we understand," said Nevada. "Why do you think we're going so far out of our way and driving through Isleworth and Heston before joining the M4?"

"Why?" said Tinkler.

"Partly because it's more scenic," I said.

"Partly because it's more scenic," agreed Nevada. "But mostly so we can avoid Chiswick."

"So we can avoid going anywhere near Chiswick," I said.

"Because that's where the dog attack took place," said Agatha.

"Right," said Nevada. "So... unpleasant associations."

"And guilt," I said.

"Guilt?" said Agatha.

"If we hadn't got Simeon involved in this business, he'd still be alive and well," I said.

"He is still alive, though, isn't he?" said Agatha.

"Only just," I said. "By all accounts. And not very well at all."

"And he definitely had a copy of the record?" said Agatha.

"Not just that, but he kept a journal in those days," I said. "And he might have been able to..."

"Tell you who the killer was?" Agatha spoke casually,

and her full attention appeared to be on the road ahead of us, but I doubt if it was.

"Perhaps not quite that," said Nevada. "Maybe give us a…"

"Clue," said Tinkler. "Go on, you can say 'clue'. He's the Vinyl Detective, isn't he?"

"Okay," said Nevada, more than willing to take him up on the challenge, though I rather wished she wouldn't. "Yes, indeed, we were hoping something in his account of the recording sessions and the people and the situation at the time would give us a clue to the identity of the killer."

"Give the Vinyl Detective a clue," said Tinkler, flashing a sardonic look at me from the front of the car; this is why I'd wished Nevada hadn't taken him up on the terminology.

"Give *us* a clue," said Nevada firmly.

"You can't share the clues," said Tinkler. "You're not a detective."

"Of course she can," said Agatha. "And of course she is."

"They can't both be detectives," said Tinkler.

"Why not? Nick and Nora Charles were detectives," said Agatha. "Effectively speaking."

"Who the hell were Nick and Nora Charles?"

"Remember Dashiell Hammett's *The Thin Man*?" said Agatha. "Well that was a Nick and Nora Charles adventure. They were a husband and wife team of sleuths."

"Well, that's a lousy comparison," said Tinkler. "Because these two aren't married, are they?" He jerked a thumb to indicate us in the back seat. "They're just living in sin."

"And sinfully happy," said Nevada, taking my hand.

"Please," said Tinkler. "We don't have any vomit bags in this vehicle."

"You're just sick with envy," said Nevada.

"What envy? Envy for what? Agatha and I could be holding hands, if she wasn't driving."

"Don't count on it, buster."

"Call me buster, I like it," said Tinkler. "But getting back to the man, now tragically hospitalised, with the record and the handy journal with the identity of the killer in it…"

"With potentially some *clues* to the identity of the killer," said Nevada.

"Didn't you say he had a sister?"

"Yes," I said. "They lived together. Erik seemed to think that was a pretty funny domestic arrangement."

"He should talk," said Tinkler. "Look at him and his house keeper. But the point is—"

"There's a point, is there?" said Agatha.

"The point is, the sister wasn't attacked by the dog, was she?"

"No," I said. "She went off in the ambulance with him, but just to…"

"Keep him company," said Nevada.

"So why don't you approach the sister and ask her for the record and the journal?"

"*Tinkler*," said Agatha.

"Don't sound so shocked," said Tinkler. He turned to look at me. "I bet he thought about it."

And indeed I had, though I was a little ashamed to admit it.

Nevada came to the rescue. "Of course we've thought about it." She glanced at me. "But the poor woman has hardly had a chance to come home from the hospital."

"And so we haven't had the heart to approach her," I said.

"*Yet*," said Tinkler cynically.

"Well, we won't have to approach her if we find a copy of the record today," said Nevada.

"You'll still need his journal or whatever it is, to work out who really committed the murder," said Tinkler. "The *Murder in London* murder."

"That's where you're wrong," I said. "If we do get hold of a copy of the record today and it's in good shape then that's the end of this 'case'. We give the record to Chloë—"

"Sell it to her," said Tinkler, correcting me.

"We sell it to her, and then we wash our hands of the whole affair," I said.

"Chloë's too nice to wash your hands of," said Tinkler.

Then all of us in the car fell silent, all for our own individual reasons. Finally, Agatha broke the silence. "There isn't any chance it could just have been a run-of-the-mill dog attack?" she said. "So to speak."

"Not with the dog running off like it did," said Nevada.

"Assuming it did run off," I said.

"What else could it have done?" said Agatha.

"Somebody could have driven it away in a car after the attack," I said.

"Somebody…" said Agatha.

"The same person who drove it there in the first place," said Nevada.

"Admittedly we're just theorising," I said. "But it almost never happens in these cases that the dog isn't found at the scene of the crime."

Agatha nodded. I could tell by the motion of the back of her smooth tanned head. She was keeping her eyes on the road now as we emerged from the park and set out on our very roundabout route to our destination.

Traffic was light and it was a pleasant drive on a lovely summer's day. I would have said a pleasant, casual drive, but there was nothing casual about the way that Agatha drove. She kept us just under the maximum legal speed in all situations, nimbly evading queues and bottlenecks, and somehow always managing to be the first one away from the traffic lights when they changed.

When she wasn't concentrating fully on driving, which was often since, as I say, it wasn't a demanding journey today, she joined in discussion of recent events with us.

More specifically, she joined in discussion of what the hell was going on, and who could be behind it all.

"Okay," said Agatha, "so we have a fifty-year-old murder…"

"Almost sixty years now," said Nevada. "Not wishing to be pedantic."

"No," said Agatha. "It matters. Because…"

"Because who the hell cares about what happened almost sixty years ago?" said Tinkler.

"This is serious," said Nevada irritably.

"No, I am being serious," said Tinkler. "We think someone is interfering with you guys because you're looking for this record, right?"

"Right," I said, "although I'm pretty sure the interference isn't about the record so much…"

"As about you finding something out," said Agatha.

"Finding something out about the murder of Jackie Higgins, right," I said. "Since I've apparently been hired to try and do that while simultaneously looking for the fucking record."

Nevada put a hand on my knee. "Entirely my fault," she said.

"Not entirely," I said. "Most of the blame lies with Chloë Loconsole."

"Because you were so moved by her money," said Tinkler. "I'm sorry, I mean because you were so moved by her *plight* that you couldn't resist taking her case—is it all right if I call it a case now, too? You were so moved by her plight, you just had to help her."

"Something like that," I said.

"Were you moved by her plight because of her big brown eyes?" said Tinkler.

"Something like that," I said.

"She has big brown eyes, does she?" said Agatha.

"She has very nice eyes," said Nevada.

"She's utterly gorgeous," said Tinkler. Adding, as he glanced quickly over at Agatha, "Remembering always that I'm primarily and hopelessly besotted with your good self."

"Remembering always that," said Agatha, smiling.

"You should have seen her the other day, Tinkler," said Nevada. "She was wearing a two-piece suit…"

"Sounds boring."

"And very little else."

"Holy moly. Suddenly not so boring," said Tinkler.

"Nice suit, was it?" said Agatha.

"Ralph Lauren Sawyer wool crêpe tuxedo jacket with silk-satin shawl collar, silk covered buttons and shoulder pads."

"Sounds nice."

"Two grands' worth of nice," said Nevada crisply. "And Seth wool crêpe tuxedo trousers with mulberry silk stripes and silk lining. Yours—or rather, hers—for another grand."

"A thousand pounds," said Tinkler, aghast, "for a pair of *trousers*? This car cost less than that."

"While obviously it's time well spent," I said, "discussing Chloë's clothing…"

"And the hot little body inside it," said Tinkler.

"Steady on, old chap," said Agatha.

"By the way, when he said it's obviously time well spent," said Tinkler, "I think that he was being sarcastic."

"I got that," said Agatha. "Because instead we should be talking about…"

"Who exactly is responsible for trying to slip us LSD in a cake," said Nevada.

"A very delicious cake," added Tinkler.

"And getting Simeon Swithenbank torn apart by a dog," I said. And there was no amusing quip from Tinkler in response to this. Just a moment's silence. Perhaps appropriately enough.

"So do you have any idea who it could be?" said Agatha.

"How about the girl in the three-thousand-pound suit?" I said.

There was a considerably longer silence now in Tinkler's small car as we sped through Heston towards the M4.

"You think *Chloë* is behind this?" said Tinkler.

"She could be," I said.

"But she hired you."

"Think about it," said Nevada.

"But she's the one who wants to clear her grandfather's name."

"What if it can't be cleared?" I said.

"Oh," said Agatha. "I see."

"Do you?" said Tinkler plaintively.

"Yes," said Agatha. "If she's actually convinced of his guilt, but still wants to clear his name…"

"Still wants to clear…" said Tinkler. "You mean hide the fact that he's guilty?"

"Conceal it forever," I said. "Then what does she have to do?"

"She has to make sure that any evidence gets lost," said Tinkler. "Forever."

"Any evidence and any witnesses," said Nevada.

"Holy shit," said Tinkler.

"But to get rid of any evidence and silence any witnesses…" said Nevada.

"She has to find them first," said Agatha. She quickly glanced over her shoulder at me. "Which is where you come in," she said.

"Right," I said.

"Getting you to find anyone who might have definitive knowledge of her grandfather's guilt," said Agatha, thinking it through. "And then permanently silencing them…"

Nevada was nodding. "Like a hunting dog flushing birds out of the undergrowth and, as soon as they're exposed, the hunter shoots them down."

"Holy shit," repeated Tinkler. "Chloë Loconsole— beautiful, bisexual and deadly."

"Assuming it's Chloë," I said.

"I thought that's what you were just assuming."

"Only because Chloë knew about Simeon Swithenbank," I said. "She knew he might have some useful information about her grandfather and the murder. Because I told her."

"You had to tell her," said Nevada. "We're working for her and we have to keep our employer briefed about progress."

"Anyway," I said. "As a result of that, Chloë knew about Simeon. But maybe she wasn't the only one."

"Who else?" said Tinkler. Then he answered his own question. "Erik? And Helene? Because they introduced you to Simeon in the first place…"

"We try not to rule anyone out," said Nevada, "but I think we can safely exclude those two."

"Because they have absolutely no motive," said Agatha.

"That we know about," I said. "After all, Erik did play guitar on the soundtrack sessions for *Murder in London*."

"Do you really think Erik could be involved?" said Tinkler.

"He's just playing devil's advocate," said Nevada fondly.

"And if Erik didn't want us to talk to Simeon," I said, "all he had to do was not tell us about him in the first place. Not even let us know he existed."

"Good point," said Agatha.

"I think a more likely candidate would be someone Chloë told," I said. "In fact, anyone Chloë told."

"And who might that be?" said Agatha.

"Well, she seems to be pretty tight with Desdemona," said Nevada. "No obscene japes, please, Tinkler."

"I wouldn't dream of it."

"Why would Desdemona want to conceal the guilt of the man who killed her grandmother?" said Agatha.

"At this point," I said, "we're not trying to discern motives."

"Discern, eh?" said Tinkler.

"We're just thinking of people Chloë might have told," I said.

"So, Desdemona," said Agatha.

"And her brother Cass," I said.

"But Desdemona and him fight like cat and dog," said Tinkler. "Or do I mean Desdemona and he?"

"True," said Nevada. "But though I don't see Desdemona keeping Cass directly in the loop about everything we do, I could easily imagine her keeping Jasper in the loop. They do seem to have bought into this stupid podcast project of his."

"And if she told Jasper…" said Agatha.

"Jasper could well have told Cass," said Nevada.

"So Cass is a suspect."

"And Jasper himself, too, of course," I said, and everyone laughed.

And I have to admit that I laughed as well.

We wouldn't be laughing for long.

15: FOR SALE

"Yay, *outing*," burbled Tinkler happily, as we raced towards our destination, engine humming and tyres buzzing on the tarmac of the fast lane.

"Who's being outed?" said Agatha. "Not you, finally coming to terms with your sexuality?"

"Oh, I came to terms with that years ago. My problem is getting other people to come to terms with it."

"No details, please," said Agatha. Then she fell silent as she concentrated on changing lanes, filtering to the left and exiting the motorway as we neared Sipson.

We turned off the M4 and took a secondary route northwards toward Stockley Road and then turned onto Cherry Lane. Names like this were flagrantly and cynically misleading as we discovered, passing endless rows of rather grim identical strips of housing, with the only greenery a school playing field on our left. We were now in West Drayton itself, where, after the endless procession of dreary residential streets, our eyes were finally relieved by the leafy expanse of Drayton Hall Park.

Agatha glanced at the satnav and said, "Destination in approximately fifteen minutes."

"What are you going to charge the bewitching Chloë if you do find the record?" asked Tinkler.

"Well, it's currently changing hands for somewhere in the neighbourhood of a thousand," said Nevada casually.

Agatha whistled. "Really? Is it worth a thousand pounds?" she said.

"That's what Lenny was going to charge us, anyway," I said.

"That's what Lenny *did* charge us," said Nevada. "North of a thousand pounds. The bastard. Until he was compelled to refund it. The fucker." Nevada still hadn't forgiven him for selling something more akin to an ashtray than a record. Nor should she.

"And how much will you pay these bozos for it, assuming they've got it?" said Tinkler.

"We've already paid them," said Nevada.

"I gave them twenty quid at Barnes Fair," I said. "As a down payment."

"As a payment in full," said Nevada.

Agatha whistled again, and somewhat more enthusiastically this time. "Twenty pounds for a thousand-pound record…"

"If they've got it…" I said.

"They said they've got it," said Tinkler. "Didn't they?"

"No," I said. "They said they've got a lot of records and that I could come and have a look for it."

"Well, that's not so good," said Tinkler.

"Which is one reason I've invited my friends along," I said.

"So you can help us look," said Nevada.

"Since they've got a lot of records," I said.

"Sneaky," said Agatha.

"Anyway, if they've got it and if it's in good shape," I said, "we'll work something out with them."

"Do they have any idea how much it's worth?" said Agatha. "The Empty Cover Couple?"

"The bozos," said Tinkler.

"Apparently not," said Nevada.

"So you could just give them twenty quid."

"We've *already* given them twenty quid," said Nevada.

"Will you really charge Chloë a thousand pounds for it if you get it for twenty quid?" said Tinkler.

"Look," I said. "If they have the record, and if it's in acceptable shape…"

"You said good shape a minute ago," said Tinkler.

"My standards have dropped since this conversation began," I said, and everyone laughed. "But no one is going to get ripped off. Not Chloë, not these people…"

"The Empty Cover Couple," said Agatha.

"The bozos," said Tinkler, who wouldn't let it go.

"Valerie and her lover boy," said Agatha, humming a tuneful snatch of the Amy Winehouse song.

"Whatever we call them," I said. "If they've got the record and it's worth buying, we'll give them a fair price for it."

"We'll see about that," said Nevada, who was more ruthless in matters of money than myself.

"But note that word 'if'," I said.

"Noted," said Tinkler.

"Until the record is safely in our hands and confirmed to be in good shape," I said, "this is all just so much speculation."

"Right," said Tinkler.

We had now reached the other side of West Drayton, having passed the railway station which we would have made use of if we hadn't enlisted Tinkler's car. And his sparkling banter. We were soon driving along Swan Road, which became The Green and then Mill Road, which carried us across a band of water called the River Colne. Now there was a dense green mass of trees on our right and residential streets to our left. We were heading along something called Thorney Mill Road, which caused Tinkler to chuckle a dirty chuckle when he learned of the designation. "What's so funny about Thorney?" said Agatha.

"Sounds like horny."

"Well, that body of water over there is called Horny Pool."

"Really?"

"No, Thorney, you fool," said Agatha. "Okay, it's just up ahead on our left. Kingfisher Gardens."

We had passed the last of the houses and now there were dense green clumps of hedges and trees on both sides of us. "Doesn't look like there's anything here…" said Nevada worriedly.

"No, over there on the left," said Agatha.

There, in a gap in a hedge was a white farm-style gate, standing open. There was also an estate agent's sign on a pole beside it. We drove through the gate onto a weed-grown gravel drive that wound back and forth, then ran straight for a short stretch, lined with large oak trees on our left, before opening up into a rectangle in front of a large house of greyish brown stone.

"My, what a big house," said Tinkler.

"Did anyone see what that sign by the gate said?" said Nevada.

"For sale," said Agatha.

She switched off the engine and in the ensuing silence, gradually chipped away at by our growing awareness of birdsong, we sat in the car staring at the big house. The big and empty-looking house.

It was a hot summer afternoon with sunlight slanting down on us at intervals as vast broken masses of smoky-dark cloud passed overhead, tantalising us with the dangerous promise of a storm. The whole day had a grey-green feel, mixing sunshine and imminent thunder.

And the house and garden seemed very quiet, with no sign of life.

"You don't think they've sold the place and moved out?" said Tinkler, evidently thinking of the estate agent's sign.

"Since yesterday?" I said.

We opened the doors of the car and got out and stretched our legs. Despite the name Kingfisher Gardens, the only birds I could see were crows. Numerous crows, active and intelligent looking and gleaming black. "Maybe they've just moved *in*," said Agatha.

"If they've just bought this place, then they didn't need your twenty pounds," said Tinkler, looking at me.

Personally, I was looking at the garden. It was a big garden that enclosed three sides of the house. There were tall trees at the far end on each side, forming a screen at the edge of the property, with plentiful crows perched in the high branches, occasionally skimming down to engage in unknown crow activity as they sauntered through the long grass. Some of the sauntering crows wandered onto the driveway and surveyed us boldly.

We had once got to know a crow rather well. His name was Hiram and we'd encountered him both in London and on a visit to Sweden. Those encounters had left me with a healthy respect for the intelligence of the whole corvid family.

Beyond the forward guard of crows, the overgrown lawn was scattered with wild purple flowers sprouting up like weeds. Highly decorative weeds. I noticed Nevada surveying the grounds with the assessing eye of an avid amateur gardener.

"This place is rather magnificent," she said. "The Empty Cover Couple are dark horses." She turned to me. "Did they look rich when you saw them at Barnes Fair?"

"You saw them, too," I said.

"Oh, yes. Albeit briefly."

"And they didn't look particularly rich then," I said. "But they did have a nice vintage car."

"What was that?" said Agatha, suddenly taking an interest in the conversation.

"Something Sunbeam," I said. "Or Sunbeam Something."

"Alpine Sunbeam?"

"That's it," I said.

"Worth much?" said Nevada.

Agatha shrugged. "Twenty or thirty grand if it's in nice shape."

"It was in nice shape," I said.

Agatha looked around. "I don't see it here."

"Garage over yonder," said Tinkler, pointing to a rectangular green wooden outbuilding with white trim set some distance away in the garden but connected to the gravel drive by a narrow sandy dirt track. Narrow, but wide enough for a car. Certainly wide enough for an Alpine Sunbeam worth twenty or thirty grand.

"So there is," said Agatha, looking in the direction Tinkler was pointing. "Detached garage, eh? Further signs of money."

"Would you like to join me on an Alpine trek?" said Tinkler, heading towards the garage.

"All right, Sunbeam," said Agatha, evidently not to be outdone in the feeble pun stakes.

He held out his elbow at a jaunty angle for her to take, like a character in an Oscar Wilde play heading in for dinner at the ball. Surprisingly, she took it, like another character in an Oscar Wilde play.

And so the two of them set off in the direction of the garage, not exactly a romantic couple, but certainly in close companionable proximity, leaving Nevada and me standing on the driveway in front of the big and rather quiet-looking house.

We looked up at the house. The house looked back down at us, its big windows reflecting sunlight, revealing nothing to us except perhaps that they had been recently cleaned, which was a relief, suggesting that the place was occupied or at least not abandoned. Or not abandoned for long, anyway.

"Well, let's see if they're in," said Nevada, moving decisively and trotting up the stone steps to the front door, which was wide and wooden but painted a brick red colour, and perhaps even intended to look like red brick for reasons unknown, and which had a big circular brass button in the centre of it, evidently to summon the dwellers within.

Nevada firmly pushed the bell.

At that moment, before I could follow her up the steps, my phone rang, comically as if it was connected to that brass button and responding to Nevada's touch. I didn't recognise the number calling, but I answered anyway, bracing myself for a scam call, and a recorded one at that.

But a woman's voice greeted me.

This I felt I should recognise; it certainly sounded familiar.

"Hello, remember me?" she said, rather merrily. Whoever she was she sounded middle-aged, or older. And also like she'd had a few drinks. Rather early in the day for that, I thought. But who was I to judge?

"Possibly," I said, still trying to work out who this was.

"I'm Valerie," she said. "I knew you were wondering," she added proudly, as if she believed she'd been rendered psychic by drinking too early in the day. "I'm the lady from Barnes Fair. You remember? You very kindly gave us twenty pounds. For an empty record cover. And I've been feeling bad about it ever since. Desmond keeps saying he'll have a proper look, but he never will, so if you wanted to come and have a look yourself like you said…"

"We're here now," I said patiently.

"Beg pardon?"

"We're outside your house now."

"Jesus," she said. "Really?"

"Yes," I said patiently. "My girlfriend is ringing the doorbell at this moment."

"Really? Jesus. I don't hear anything…"

"Perhaps it's broken," I said. I certainly hadn't heard anything when Nevada pressed it.

"I don't think so," said Valerie, sounding somewhat offended. She was definitely drunk. "Hang on a minute." There was a pause and then she shouted so ferociously that I had to hold the phone away from my ear to prevent damage to my hearing. "*Desmond*," she bellowed. Then she repeated his name several times at a similar volume. Finally she evidently got a reply because she altered her messaging and yelled, "Go and see if someone is at the front door."

I didn't ask why she didn't just go to the front door herself. Perhaps she was too drunk.

"So," she said, resuming our conversation. "You've come to look for the record?"

"That's right," I said, patiently.

"That's a bit of a coincidence," she said.

Not really, I thought, given that you'd invited us here to arrive just about at exactly this moment—I checked the time on my phone. But I didn't say any of this, because there wasn't much point arguing with a drunk.

And I still very much wanted that record, if there was any chance at all she—and Desmond—had it.

So don't antagonise the nice drunk-in-the-afternoon lady.

And speaking of Desmond, he was apparently yet to emerge from his lair deep in the bowels of the house because Nevada was still waiting patiently on the doorstep. She turned and looked at me. "Is that them?" she said.

I nodded.

"Where are they?"

"In there, apparently," I said, pointing towards the house.

"Oh, good," said Nevada, with a certain dry note of irony. Nothing could ever be easy was the subtext.

I made sure that Valerie couldn't hear me and I said, "She's drunk."

"Hurrah," said Nevada.

I hoped that Desmond wasn't also drunk. But judging by the length of time it was taking him to get to the front door of his own house, this was a fairly forlorn hope.

"Who are you talking to?" said Valerie. She sounded a trifle put out that I wasn't giving her my undivided attention.

"My girlfriend."

"The one ringing the doorbell?"

"She's stopped now."

"That's probably why I can't hear it anymore. Not that I could hear it before, either. Where the hell is Desmond?"

Good question, I thought.

"Your girlfriend…" said Valerie.

"Yes?"

"Was she the girl with you at Barnes Fair?"

"Yes."

"She's quite pretty."

"Thank you."

"You're a lucky chap."

"I know."

"Desmond is a lucky chap, too."

"I'm sure he is."

"We're very happy together," she said. She said it somewhat pugnaciously, as if I'd just offensively suggested the opposite.

"I'm sure you are."

"By the way…" she said. She said it with a rising inflection of enquiry but her words just trailed off and were followed by a lengthy pause.

"Yes?"

"What?"

"You were asking me a question."

"Was I?" She really was drunk.

"It sounded like you were about to ask me a question," I said.

"Was I? Oh yes, I was going to ask how you found our address. Very clever of you."

"Not really," I said.

"Oh, yes, it was. Don't be modest now."

"No, really, it wasn't very clever of me. You gave it to me."

"I did what?"

"You gave me your address."

"I did?"

"Yes." I tried not to sigh. At least, not audibly. Just because she was drunk didn't mean she was deaf.

"When?" she said.

"Yesterday," I said.

"I rang you yesterday with our address?"

"You texted me," I said.

"I texted you with our address?" she said. I sensed more inebriated pugnacity brewing. "No I didn't."

"Perhaps it was Desmond," I said, offering an olive branch. They didn't seem like a couple who were big on communication.

"I'll ask him. Here he is. Desmond, did you text the gentlemen who was looking for the record?" There was an inaudible reply. "No, Desmond says he didn't text you," said Valerie. Then, with a note of triumph, "And he says there's no one at the front door."

I looked around me. Crows were standing at various points on the driveway observing me with alert interest. They looked like they could tell me something to my advantage, if only I asked the right question.

There was the sound of birdsong from the trees and a distant, very distant, murmur of traffic. Wind rustled in the leaves.

As I stared at the crows and they stared back at me, it suddenly all fell into place.

I couldn't believe it had taken me so long to see it.

"You don't live in West Drayton, do you?" I said.

"No," said Valerie. "We don't. Did someone text you

saying that we did? Sounds like someone's playing silly buggers." She was amused.

I wasn't amused. I was far from amused.

I was frightened, very frightened indeed.

"It's a trap," I shouted as I switched off the phone and ran to Nevada. She was still at the front door, but now she was turning towards me and stepping away from the house as though it was suddenly contaminated. Tinkler and Agatha had wandered some distance over the lawn full of purple flowers, towards the detached garage. But they'd heard my shout and they too were now turning towards me.

I had reached Nevada. I grabbed her hand.

We ran towards the car.

Tinkler and Agatha came running, too.

"What's happening?" called Tinkler.

Nevada and I were tugging the car doors open.

I replied to Tinkler but I was looking at Nevada. "The Empty Cover Couple just rang me. It's the first time they've been in touch."

"Fuck," said Nevada.

The wind suddenly strengthened, stirring through the tree branches, making shadow shapes on the overgrown lawn.

We all scrambled into the car. Nevada and I in the back, Agatha at the wheel, Tinkler beside her.

"Get us out of here," said Nevada. "Please."

"On it," said Agatha.

We had driven in towards the house along the driveway, which began as a winding shape before turning into a straight lane that terminated in an oblong of gravel, and Agatha had parked the car with its nose pointing towards the front door. To leave again would normally have necessitated some laborious manoeuvring on the small gravel patch before the car was turned around and facing in the right direction for departure.

But it was one of the oddities of Tinkler's vintage Volvo DAF, often remarked upon by Agatha, that because of its "Variomatic" transmission it could move as quickly in reverse as it could going forward.

So Agatha didn't waste any time at all turning the car around. She just threw the car into reverse and, looking keenly back over her shoulder, jammed her foot down on the accelerator.

The little car bucked and bolted backwards, moving like a hare fleeing from a fox.

We shot backwards along the straight section of driveway, accelerating steadily, although Agatha was going to have to slow down when we took the first corner, at the end of the line of oak trees, which led to the curving further stretch of drive.

We were all looking backwards as we zoomed away from the house.

So we all saw the figure who stepped out from behind one of the large oak trees, about halfway down the strip of road.

A tall, lean figure, presumably a man, though for a number of reasons I couldn't be sure of that.

Not least because we couldn't see the face of the person in question, thanks to the sunglasses they were wearing. Not to mention the black hat. And the details of their physique were, of course, hidden by the highly unseasonable black raincoat they were wearing on this summer's afternoon.

Any ambiguity about this being—or at least being intended to evoke—the sinister assassin from the film of *Murder in London* was immediately removed when the figure raised a gun.

"*Get down*," shouted Nevada.

I knew nothing about weapons but Erik Make Loud had helpfully identified the weapon the black raincoat person was holding as a Mauser machine pistol when we'd seen it in the film.

I was less concerned about this detail at the moment than the fact that the gun was firing at us.

Although, as the rear windscreen of the car exploded, I did recall Erik's obliging information about it shooting the most high-velocity handgun cartridge available before the .357 Magnum.

Broken glass showered in on all of us, landing on our heads and getting into our hair because we'd all, as Nevada had suggested, ducked down in the car. In fact, I was huddled low on the backseat with my legs jammed down in the footwell. On the other side of the car, just opposite me, Nevada had done the same.

I couldn't see Agatha or Tinkler, but the fact that at least she must have ducked and was now below the level of the windscreen was indicated by the fact that her steering became slightly erratic at this point.

She was more than entitled to be driving slightly erratically because not only was she steering the car backwards, she was now also steering it blind.

But we didn't slow down.

In fact our speed *increased*.

I calculated that we must have passed the gunman—gunwoman?—by now.

I was tempted to sit up and look back out the front windscreen and, since we were still moving in reverse, watch the black raincoated figure vanish in the distance behind us. I must have made some small move which indicated this intention because Nevada reached across the car and seized me and held me down.

It was just as well that she did, because at the moment when I'd planned to raise my head, the front windscreen exploded.

The figure in black was behind us all right, and still shooting.

More glass rained down on us, and then a second downpour of it, dislodged from where it had originally landed when the car jerked violently to the left.

We had reached the corner and Agatha was steering from memory, taking us around it.

She wasn't steering from memory for long, though, because now I saw her sit up straight. I began to sit up too. "Stay down," said Nevada.

"Everybody else stay down," said Agatha.

She was looking over her shoulder and steering backwards again. There was more gunfire, but it didn't make contact with the car. I took the chance on taking a look—

risking not just a bullet but Nevada's wrath—and saw the black raincoated figure in the distance, standing in the middle of the drive, looking at us disappearing.

They lowered their gun and a second later vanished from view as we twisted around a curve in the driveway, rendering them invisible.

The car twisted along the serpentine curves of the drive at full speed for a few seconds and then burst out of the white wooden farm gate at the entrance.

Here Agatha hit the brakes, spraying gravel on all sides of us, and paused for a split second to look both ways on the main road.

Then she reversed us out at full speed so we were pointing back towards London and home.

And then she put the car into forward gear and put her foot down.

16: AIR STEWARDESS

The drive back to London was uneventful—compared to the infernal events which had immediately preceded it—although extremely windy for us occupants of Tinkler's car, with both the front and rear windscreen blown out. We were very lucky it was the middle of summer instead of the middle of winter, or we would have been well and truly frozen.

Even as it was, we got pretty chilled by the swift passage of air funnelling through the car. Said swift passage caused by our considerable speed.

No one was tempted, however, to ask Agatha to slow down.

We all wanted to get the hell away from West Drayton and home again as fast as possible.

One might have expected the sight of a car missing both its windscreens to have attracted some attention. But we'd pulled over and stopped as soon as we were safely on the far side of the River Colne and used a tool from Tinkler's boot—remarkably, there were some in there—to knock the remaining pieces of glass out of the edges of the windscreen. It was like removing the last scattered teeth from the maw of some big, sad beast.

But the idea was that if we removed it when the car was stationary, it wouldn't work itself loose and blow out on us at unpredictable intervals and on possibly dangerous trajectories while we were in motion.

And a side effect of this complete removal of the remaining glass was that it made the car appear virtually normal—because it turns out that no glass at all looks a lot like intact glass in its proper place, thanks to the transparent nature of the stuff. Unless you were astute enough to spot the lack of reflections on it. Or studied us carefully while sitting beside us and inspecting the car in profile, so to speak.

And there was very little chance of that, at the rate Agatha drove.

So to anyone who saw us, the Volvo looked intact and unremarkable, though its occupants were somewhat strangely and inexplicably windblown.

Agatha dropped Tinkler off at his little house on Putney Hill before taking us home and then driving Tinkler's car to a friend of hers whom she was confident would be able to source replacement front and rear windshields for it, and install them skilfully and promptly.

Her confidence was reassuringly rooted in her having phoned him and confirmed this while we were defanging the poor beast beside the River Colne.

"It'll be in good hands," she'd told Tinkler as we left

him by his front gate. "It'll look as good as new by the time Gavin's finished with it."

"I know it will," said Tinkler. "I trust your judgement. I trust your friend. Any friend of yours is a friend of mine, allowing for my rampant sexual jealousy."

Agatha had kissed him, chastely, on the cheek, then driven us home in turn and dropped us off. And then she took the car to Gavin's somewhere in north London. She'd confided to us that it wasn't just his ability to source esoteric spares and do an admirable job installing them that commended Gavin for this task.

He also wouldn't ask any awkward questions about the previous windscreens having been removed by gunfire.

When the doorbell rang, I was preparing supper and Nevada was working in the back garden.

Both of us were trying in our own way to unwind and recover from the trauma of the events earlier in the day. To reclaim domestic normality.

So someone arriving at the door wasn't necessarily a very welcome development.

I went to the kitchen window and looked out.

Then, reassured, I switched off the gas under the saucepan and put a lid on it; handily, I'd reached the stage in cooking my signature dish—one-pot macaroni and cheese—where it could be left for pretty much any length of time, and it would only taste better.

I went to the front door and opened it. The scent of our

garden swept in on a warm breeze, chiefly the medicinal sweetness of the Meerlo lavender we'd planted on either side of the entrance.

But it was supplemented by the scent of our visitor.

Her perfume was a more complex, musky fragrance than the plants. I couldn't identify any of its components.

But I could tell you that it didn't smell cheap.

Our visitor was a woman who on first glance appeared to be somewhere in youthful and energetic middle age. I would later learn that she was actually in her seventies. One would never guess it by looking at her. She was solidly built and broad shouldered, though some of that was no doubt thanks to tailoring. The same elegant tailoring of her skirt and jacket which reduced any suggestion of being overweight. The jacket and skirt were navy blue, her blouse was white silk and she had a small red silk scarf hanging nattily down in double strands.

The red, white and blue colour scheme were mildly suggestive of an airline stewardess. A first-class airline stewardess. But this impression was instantly dissipated by other details, such as the broad silver bracelet, which on second glance turned out to be an amazingly flat and no doubt amazingly expensive wristwatch.

Although not particularly tall, she gave the impression of height, partly thanks to her high heels but mostly due to the military erectness of her posture. Her hair was pure white, probably too pure to be entirely the result of nature, and trimmed chicly short in an urchin cut which emphasised her high cheekbones and large gleaming brown eyes. Although she had a large chin, none of it was fat. Rather it was suggestive of bulldog tenacity.

The eyes were already a giveaway, but the real hint to her identity was a very familiar backpack, which she was carrying sportingly slung over one shoulder. It wasn't a light backpack and the way she carried it so casually, just her left hand on its strap keeping it steadily in place, was suggestive of surprising physical strength. Her right hand was holding a clutch of shopping bags of assorted bright colours and interesting shapes, all of which had thin string handles and all of which came from the most expensive shops in London.

But, as I say, it was the backpack which prompted me to say, "Chloë's *nonna*?"

"Yes," she said. Her voice was a smoky purr. "And you are the detective?"

"Not really," I said. But nonetheless she leaned forward and kissed me on both cheeks as if we were old, and rather dear, friends. To cover my embarrassment—I was, after all, English—I quickly said, "Here, please let me help you with that."

She offered me the bags of high-end shopping, which in aggregate probably weighed as much as a small feather pillow.

"No," I said. "The backpack."

The droll look on her face as she shrugged it off and handed it to me suggested that the shopping bag feint had been intentional, and for her amusement. Or maybe a test.

The backpack was heavy as hell, but I managed not to flinch as I took it from her. Which was just as well because the elderly woman was lifting it one-handed. "Chloë said she would be staying here?" she said.

"Yes, she mentioned that. But she isn't here right now. And she didn't say when she would be."

"She is on her way tonight," said her *nonna*. "I thought I'd help her and bring her things over for her. I am Raffaella."

"Hello, Raffaella."

"I am her grandmother, but you've already said that."

"Yes."

"And in Italian."

"Yes, don't expect any more from me," I said.

She laughed and I led her inside. There were so many of those shopping bags that she had to pause in the doorway to manoeuvre her way through. The shops represented included Alexander McQueen, Zara, Freddy, Burberry, Smythson, the gloriously named Cyberdog and of course Harrods.

The way she happily dumped this crazily expensive merchandise on the floor reminded me of her granddaughter's casual way with shoes. As soon as she was unencumbered, Raffaella unbuttoned her jacket, slipped it off and hung it up unceremoniously on the Charles and Ray Eames coat rack in the hallway—full marks to her for recognising this for what it was and not mistaking it, as some did, for a colourful piece of modernist sculpture.

Then she turned towards me, sniffed sharply, and said, "You are cooking."

"Just finished, actually. Come on through."

I led her into the kitchen. "Chloë says you make very good coffee," she said.

"That's very kind of you," I said. "Or rather, of Chloë."

"I wasn't saying it to be kind. I was saying it because I was hoping you'd make me some," she said, and laughed.

"Of course," I said. But before I could make any moves in the direction of coffee preparation, she stepped to the cooker and lifted the lid off the saucepan, dodging a puff of trapped steam with the nimble expertise of long experience. She sniffed at the contents, covered it again and looked at me. "Pasta?"

"Yes," I said, fearing what might be coming, from this woman from the land of pasta. "Macaroni and cheese."

"We call it *maccheroni*," she said. For some reason she was staring with thoughtful fixity at the drawers of our kitchen units. All was explained when she suddenly stepped forward and pulled open one drawer, gave a glad little cry—good guess, *nonna*—and drew out a fork from our stash of cutlery. She lifted the lid off the saucepan again, dug in with the fork, extracted a small sample, blew on it, and then ate it daintily off the fork with one hand under her chin to catch any falling fragments. Her face assumed a speculative, almost puzzled expression. Then she nodded and looked at me.

"This isn't bad."

"I'm glad," I said. And I was. In fact I was mightily relieved that the lady from the land of pasta hadn't just taken my saucepan and thrown it through the window.

"What is the cheese? Cheddar?"

"Yes."

She nodded again. "British cheese is a joke," she confided. "If you'll forgive me, British cheese is all just a big joke. Cheddar is the one exception. Cheddar isn't bad. To be more accurate, cheddar can be very good. I'll eat cheddar, sometimes, even in Rome."

"Well you can eat some tonight, in London," I said.

"Thank you," she said. She put the fork neatly into the sink, which won my heart and then, to my surprise, opened the cutlery drawer again, extracted another fork and took another sample from the saucepan.

Additional marks to *nonna* for not double dipping.

This time she nodded vigorously as if confirming a theory and gave me an alert birdlike look, and said, "This is actually good. This is actually very good."

"Thank you," I said. "It's a vintage Cornish cheddar and I use organic milk…"

"What's the pasta?" she said, cutting to the chase.

I showed her the Garofalo packet.

"This is Italian," she said.

"Yes," I said.

"They use proper bronze *formas* to make it."

"That's right," I said.

"So that the *maccheroni* is rough and the sauce sticks to it."

"Yup," I said, for variety's sake.

"No wonder the taste is excellent." She looked at the saucepan carefully as if weighing up a grave decision. Then she smiled at me. "I was thinking of trying another fork. But I don't want to spoil my appetite. You did invite me to supper, did you not?"

"Oh yes," I said. Then, "Well, I hadn't, but I would have done if you'd given me a chance."

"Thank you." She poked the still-warm saucepan with a gentle finger. "What is in the sauce?"

I happily told her how this recipe, gleaned by Nevada from *New Scientist* magazine of all places, didn't require a white sauce because it used the starch from the pasta, and hence could all be cooked in one pot.

"It's a lazy man's macaroni and cheese," I said.

"It's a sensible man's macaroni and cheese," she said. Then she looked alertly around. She'd heard the back door opening before I had. A moment later, Nevada came through in her gardening clothes. "Oh," she said. "I thought I heard someone…"

"Nevada, this is Raffaella, Chloë's *nonna*. Raffaella, this is Nevada."

"*Piaceri*," said Raffaella.

"Excuse me a moment," said Nevada. It was somewhat more than a moment before she returned, considerably dolled up.

"You really didn't need to, darling," said Raffaella. "You are so beautiful anyway, you didn't need to get cleaned up and dressed up just for me."

"I couldn't receive a guest in my gardening garb," said Nevada gamely.

"You have such beauty anyway, such natural beauty, clothes don't matter." She glanced my way. "In any case, men don't care about a woman's clothes. They just care about what's inside."

"Ain't that the truth," said Nevada.

"At least this one can cook, hey?"

"He certainly can. Would you like some wine?"

"Yes please. Red, please." Raffaella had spotted our wine rack and was now looking through it. "This is all French?"

"Yes, mostly from the Rhône."

She shrugged forgivingly. "You're young. You'll learn."

We were just finishing eating when Chloë arrived. She came through the front door and observed the casually dumped, high-end shopping bags with disapproval. But not, apparently, because they'd been casually dumped. "*Nonna*," she scolded. "I told you not to bring my stuff here."

"You had too much to carry," said Raffaella, wiping up the last of the cheese sauce from the mac and cheese from her plate with a piece of bread—she approved of the Poilane sourdough we'd served her, with certain reservations about French baking in general though, naturally.

"I could have managed." Chloë sat down at the table and joined us. Her grandmother looked at her.

"Well, they're here now," she said, drawing a line under the discussion.

"I'm sorry you missed supper," said Nevada.

"I can fix you something," I said.

"No, I've eaten," said Chloë.

"Of course she has," said Raffaella, and the two women exchanged a look which could have meant anything but seemed to speak of a strange subtle undercurrent of hostility. "And I imagine she won't be staying here tonight," she said.

Chloë gave her a sharp look. "As it happens," she said, "I will be spending the night somewhere else."

"Of course you will," said her *nonna*.

"Which is one more reason you shouldn't have brought all my stuff here."

Raffaella shrugged. "One lives in hope," she said cryptically.

"So, if it's all right, I will just take a few things with me, overnight things," said Chloë. "And then I will move in here properly—so to speak—soon." She gave us a smile, a somewhat forced smile. "Providing that's still all right with you guys."

"Of course it's all right with us," said Nevada.

"Good," said Chloë.

There then ensued a somewhat awkward silence. Before I could think of something to say to break it, Raffaella spoke up, as if declaring a truce. "You're lucky you're staying here," she said. She made a gesture with one hand, encompassing our little home.

"I know I am." Chloë looked at me and Nevada. "It's very good of them…"

"No, I mean you're lucky because this one can cook." Raffaella nodded at me. "We had a nice meal. Not like those terrible restaurants you took me to."

"I'm sorry," said Chloë, somewhat dryly.

"It's not your fault," said her *nonna* magnanimously. "They were all reputed to be very good restaurants." She leaned towards us and added confidentially. "But they were terrible."

I was summoned away from this interesting discussion by the ringing of my phone.

It wasn't a number I recognised. Nor did I recognise the voice of the woman when I answered it. It was a rough, throaty voice, but somehow smooth. Like coarse velvet. Perhaps a smoker's voice. "Is that the Vinyl Detective?" she said.

"I'm afraid so," I said and she laughed. It was an appealing laugh, rather dirty and naughty sounding.

"A mutual friend gave me your number," she said.

"And what friend would that be?" I said.

"Well maybe friend is too strong a word. Perhaps acquaintance. Certainly you'd be a lot smarter if he was just your acquaintance."

"Well, I'd hate not to be smart," I said. "Who are we talking about?"

"Jasper McClew."

"Definitely just an acquaintance," I said, my guard instantly going up.

"Very sensible," she said. "He is an odious little toerag, isn't he?"

"I can't fault you there," I said. "But how can I—"

Forestalling my question, as if impatient with anything so obvious, she said, "Jasper the toerag told me about a record you were looking for."

"And what record is that?"

She sighed. "Are we really going to do this?" she said.

"Do what?"

"Play footsy like this. All right, if you want to, so be it. *Murder in London* by Loretto Loconsole. Catalogue number...

hang on a minute…" There was silence for a second and then she came back. "SCX 3596."

At this point I was all attention. Unless she was a very good actor—and I couldn't rule that out—she actually had the record there with her and had just gone to check on the catalogue number. "On the Columbia label," she said. "No wait, the EMI label… Wait, is it both?"

"Yes it is," I said.

"It's fucking confusing."

"Yes it is," I said.

"Anyway, is that the record you're looking for? Because if it's not I'll hang up right now and not waste any more of your valuable time. Or mine."

"Don't do that," I said. "It's definitely the record I'm looking for."

"Jasper indicated, in his weaselly way, that you're looking to buy a copy."

"Did he?" I said. "That was good of him." Which I suppose it was.

"He also said that it was a very rare record and you'd be willing to pay a lot of money for it."

I hesitated. "Are you still there?" she said.

"Yes," I said. "And both of those things are true. Provisionally."

"Provisionally?"

"Well it's indisputably a very rare record," I said. God knew that had been established recently. "But whether I'm willing to pay a lot for it is…"

"Provisional," she said.

"Yes."

"Provisional on what basis?"

"On the basis of what kind of condition the record is in."

"You mean whether or not the vinyl is in good shape," she said.

"Yes."

"Well, I'm no expert," she said. "But I've always tried to take decent care of my vinyl. And it looks pretty good to me. Admittedly, last night when I was preparing a meal I was short of a plate, so I grated the celeriac onto this record instead, but it seems to have cleaned up pretty well…"

"Very funny," I said, and she laughed.

"I'm really not an expert," she said. "But I think it's worth you checking this record out and, if you like what you see, making me an offer on it."

"Why are you selling it?" I said.

"For the money, why else?"

"Why sell it now?"

"It hadn't occurred to me before. I mean, I never realised that it might be worth something. It was worth something to me. I mean, I liked it. I liked the music. But Jasper made me aware that it could actually be worth quite a lot of money."

"Good old Jasper," I said. And she laughed some more. But when she started speaking again, she sounded deadly serious.

"I understand that it could be worth well over a thousand pounds," she said.

"Or well under," I said.

"Over a thousand pounds was the phrase quoted to me," she said stubbornly.

"Well," I said. "It's true I recently paid over a thousand pounds for a copy," I said.

"You've already bought one?" She sounded puzzled.

"I bought it for £1,130 to be exact," I said. Then I told her about the transaction with Lenny. Her reaction was a mixture of horror and laughter. As well it might be.

"It really had a hole in it?" she said.

"Two holes," I said.

"Well, I can guarantee this copy only has one. And whatever you end up paying for it, I can guarantee it will be in vastly superior nick to that one you just described."

"Okay," I said. "I believe you." And I did. "So the next thing to do is for us to arrange an appointment, and an assessment."

"It sounds like seeing the doctor. The Vinyl Doctor."

"Please," I said. "I've only recently come to terms with being a detective."

She chuckled. "So you'll come and have a look at the record and make a decision?"

"Unless you could bring it to me."

"I'd rather you came here," she said.

"All right," I agreed, trying to ignore the faint alarm bells which were ringing in the distance.

"And if you're happy with the record you'll pay me on the spot? At whatever price we agree?"

"Sure," I said.

"In cash?"

"No way," I said. "Some form of electronic transfer. To your bank account or PayPal or whatever you prefer, and we do the exchange."

"No, it's got to be cash."

"Then we're in a bit of a quandary," I said.

"Because you're unwilling to rock up to the home of a complete stranger carrying a thousand pounds in cash?"

"Right," I said.

She laughed and said, "How can you be so untrusting?"

"You might well ask."

"So it looks like this is going to have to go in two stages," she said.

"I come to you and assess the record, then if I think it's okay I come back with the money and then we do the exchange."

"Very good. Ten out of ten. You're pretty quick on the uptake. Have you done this sort of thing before?"

"Not if I could avoid it."

She laughed and said, "Okay. Let me start by giving you my address."

"And your name."

"What? Haven't I said?"

"Not unless I missed it," I said.

"How rude of me. I'm Juno. Juno Brunner."

17: DOUBLE BOOKED

"Juno Brunner?" said Nevada.

"Yes," I said. "It seems that Chloë was right and she's still very much alive."

Chloë and her grandmother had both left now and our little house was quiet. Raffaella had left with dinner inside her and Chloë with at least some wine and cheese, despite her protestations of having eaten already, and her grandmother's firmly held opinions on English cheese. Not to mention French wine.

Plus they'd both had coffee. No contention there, just some approving nods and shared glances of approval from both of them. Which was gratifying.

Raffaella had headed off to her hotel in central London, somewhere called One Aldwych, and a place which she grudgingly conceded to liking, although she didn't approve of the restaurants in the vicinity. And Chloë had headed off to an unspecified destination, but one which her grandmother obviously also didn't approve of.

"Do you reckon she's going to rendezvous with Desdemona?" said Nevada.

"I imagine rendezvous is a polite word for what she's going to do with Desdemona," I said, and Nevada laughed.

"And her *nonna* doesn't approve," she said.

"Old-school Italian granny," I said.

"Who presumably wants loads of babies. Grandbabies, I mean," said Nevada.

"Great grandbabies, actually," I said.

"Right. Good point. Anyway, hence a certain hostility concerning the whole Desdemona thing."

"The whole Desdemona thing," I agreed.

I'd deliberately offered no account of Juno's phone call until the Loconsoles had left, and Nevada and I were on our own. Because after the dog attack on Simeon and the gun ambush on our good selves, it was clear someone was tracking our moves. And I couldn't be sure that Chloë wasn't the source of the information.

Or indeed the source of the mayhem.

So I'd waited until she and her grandmother were safely and definitely gone before I told Nevada about the call. "I knew you were being cagey about something," she said. "And that something was Juno Brunner, eh?"

"Yes."

"Lesbian frogwoman," said Nevada. "Sorry, that just doesn't have quite the same mellifluous ring to it when it's not coming from Tinkler."

"Lesbian frogwoman and potential murderess," I said.

"That doesn't have a mellifluous ring to it coming from anyone," said Nevada. And I agreed.

"And she has a copy of the record we're after."

"Allegedly," I said.

"Well, that's the point," said Nevada, "isn't it? She claims to have it."

"She certainly does. She definitely does."

"And doesn't this all seem a little too good, or a little too coincidental to be true?"

"Not necessarily," I said. "It would make sense that someone who worked on the film would have a copy of the soundtrack album. Erik said that Loretto Loconsole distributed copies to the musicians who played on it. Maybe he did the same with people who helped to shoot the film."

"Maybe," said Nevada. "But I think that perhaps I smell a rat."

"What I smell," I said, "is vinyl. Rare vinyl."

"So you think she really has a copy?"

I remembered the way Juno had paused on the phone while she'd checked the catalogue number. It could have been a performance while she consulted the details online. But, if so, it had been a masterful one. "Yes," I said. "I really do."

Nevada sighed. "Well, I suppose we'll find out soon enough. When do we meet her?"

"Tomorrow," I said, feeling the stirring of the old familiar excitement. I might actually soon have a copy of this record in my hands.

In just a few hours…

* * *

That night we were awakened from deep sleep in the early pre-dawn hours by an unearthly screaming.

"Cat fight," I said.

"Turk," said Nevada.

This was a logical conclusion, both because Turk was the more likely of our two felines to get into a scrap and because Fanny, the only other contender, was right now lying between us on the bed and sleepily squeaking with complaint about the sudden activity that had disturbed her slumber.

Nevada and I lunged from the bed and into the hallway and then the sitting room. I opened the window while Nevada was unlocking the door. In the intersecting illumination of the three small garden spotlights we could see Turk standing frozen in a posture of ritualised feline aggression, staring up at the back wall, on top of which was a surprisingly small black-and-white spotted cat. At the sound of the window opening, the little black-and-white cat jerked around and looked at me.

At the sound of the door opening, it fled, scooting along the wall as far as the garden shed, then leaping off its roof down into the street below.

As Nevada held our back door open, Turk came reluctantly inside, frequently and combatively glancing back the way she'd come. Her tail was swollen to an enormous size, part of a natural defence mechanism to make her look more formidable. We made a fuss over her, complimenting her on the brilliant defence of our small garden, and then put out some cat treats for her as a reward for bravery, the sound of which spilling into the bowl lured Fanny from the bedroom, so we gave her some too. For having the good sense not to get into a fight.

Then we all went back to bed.

It was only the next day that we noticed Turk was limping. At first we weren't sure, but, after some anxious observation, we confirmed it; Turk was definitely favouring her left hind leg and walking with a strange stiff gait.

So naturally we were straight on the phone to the vet as soon as they were open that morning. "We're in luck," said Nevada as she hung up. "They've got a cancellation and can fit us in, in just a few hours." She looked at me with those endless blue eyes. "There's just one problem…"

"In a few hours we're scheduled to meet up with Juno Brunner to examine her copy of *Murder in London*."

"We can postpone."

"I don't think so," I said. "If there's a chance to get hold of this record, my instinct is we have to go for it. Now."

Nevada bit her lip. "Then I'd better get back to the vets and tell them we can't make it."

"No way," I said, glancing at Turk, who was currently sitting curled on a cushion on an armchair, looking perfectly calm and peaceful and contented, despite being the cause of all these complications. Or perhaps perfectly calm and peaceful and contented because she was the cause of all these complications. "We want to make sure that Turk's okay."

"But…"

"So you go to the vet," I said. "And I'll go and meet Juno."

Nevada shook her head briskly. "No, I'm completely

against splitting up. You know that." She smiled at me. "It's contrary to policy," she added. And she was still giving it her best smile.

Any minute now she was going to begin wrapping me around her little finger, so I decided I had to be firm about this. "We need to do both these things," I said. "At the same time."

"I agree. But I think I should be the one who goes to the meet with Juno Brunner. You can escort Turk to the vet."

"Hold on," I said.

"Listen, love." Those big blue eyes were fixed on mine as she went to work on me. "We don't know anything about Ms Juno Brunner."

"We know a bit about her."

Nevada nodded. "I agree. We know she might actually be the one who killed Jackie Higgins."

That shut me up for a moment.

"And look what happened last time we went to meet someone who was allegedly selling us the record," said Nevada.

Again, she wasn't wrong. Tinkler was now driving a rental car while the famed Gavin was installing new windscreens in his Volvo DAF. The old ones having been spoiled by a great deal of gunfire.

As had my nerves.

And our general peace of mind.

"This is very different," I said. "It's a completely different set up."

"If I was the opposition," said Nevada. "And I'd just failed to kill us with one plan, then my next plan would be a completely different set up. Of course it would. You don't use the same approach twice." She kept making sense.

"I need to be the one who goes to Juno," I said.

"Listen, my love. You could be going into danger."

"By the same token, so could you."

"With all love and respect," said Nevada, "if a situation goes south then I'd rather it was me in that situation and not you. I have more of the skillset to deal with it."

She just kept on being right about this. But that didn't mean I was going to agree with her.

"Look," I said. "I'm the one who's dealt with Juno up to now. I'm the only one she's spoken to. I wouldn't exactly say we've built up a robust bond of trust between us, but at least she knows me. And she's expecting me. If we start moving things around, changing the person who's coming to check out the record, I think she could get difficult."

"Do you think I won't be able to tell if the record is the right one?" said Nevada.

"No."

"Do you think I won't be able to tell if it's in decent condition?"

"No." By now Nevada, while not an expert, could certainly tell the difference between a playable piece of vinyl and an absolute junker. "But I do suspect that Juno Brunner is quite a difficult person and I have a feeling that we might only get one shot at this. So I don't want to spook her by making any changes to her arrangement. Especially at the last minute like this."

"Well, now you're spooking me," said Nevada.

"And I really don't think she's dangerous."

Nevada didn't say anything to this. She just gave me a look. It wasn't a great look. We kept on arguing for a while and in the end, to my surprise, I won.

Tinkler turned up an hour later to drive Nevada to the vets. We'd been waiting for him to arrive before we made any attempt to corner Turk and put her in the cat carrier. She'd already sensed that something was up, though, and as soon as Tinkler came in the front door she made a beeline for the cat flap in the back door. Nevada got there first and locked it. "Sorry darling," she said as Turk looked at her and gave an outraged yowl of betrayal. Before this feline renegade could make a break for the front door and the other cat flap, I came through with the cat carrier.

This was one of those cheap brown cardboard ones that folded up. We'd learned from bitter experience that trying to get Turk into the elaborate, expensive, solid plastic-and-metal one we'd bought at some expense was a battle we were unlikely to win. She'd hold ferociously and tenaciously on to either side of the opening and fight like hell while we struggled to force her in.

So we'd adopted the use of this cheap disposable alternative, which was essentially just a cardboard box with holes in it, albeit a sturdy one, which opened at the top.

It was the opening at the top which was the crucial bit. It meant we could just lift Turk into it, then close the flaps on top of her.

Which was what we proceeded to do now, Nevada scooping up Turk in a brisk hug then airlifting her into the cardboard cartoon. I sealed it up as soon as she was inside. Cue more and much louder feline accusations of treachery.

"Relax, Turk," said Tinkler. "You're going to the place where they have the good drugs." He looked at me. "Keep telling her that. It'll eventually win her over."

"I'm not coming to the vet with you guys," I said.

"What? Why not?"

"I'm meeting up with Juno Brunner to examine an allegedly immaculate copy of *Murder in London*."

"Allegedly is right," said Nevada. Dealing with Lenny and his cigar ashtray had clearly left its mark on her. "Assuming it exists at all," she added.

"Hang on," said Tinkler. "Juno Brunner?"

"Yes."

"Lesbian frogwoman?"

"You see?" said Nevada. "It just sounds better coming from him."

"And top murder suspect," said Tinkler.

"And that doesn't sound good coming from anyone," said Nevada, giving me a reproachful look.

"You're seeing her today?" said Tinkler.

"In just over an hour." I checked the time, feeling a tightening of tension inside me.

"Why not postpone?" said Tinkler, as Nevada nodded vigorously.

"If there's a chance of nailing down a copy of this record," I said, "I really don't think we should miss it."

"And I really don't think he should go there alone," said Nevada.

"Where does she live?" said Tinkler.

"On a houseboat."

"Lesbian frogwoman on a houseboat," said Tinkler. "Definitely dangerous."

"Possible murderer on a houseboat," said Nevada. "Definitely dangerous."

Nevertheless, I remained firm and a few minutes later I walked Nevada and Tinkler out to his car—as mentioned, a rental, a rather nice Mini Cooper in British racing green with a white roof—and helped them put Turk in her box on the back seat with the seatbelt around her. Turk shuffled around in the box and found a ventilation hole she could peer out of and give me a reproachful look of her own.

I was in everybody's bad books today.

As they drove off, Nevada was staring out the passenger window, looking at me.

And it wasn't a happy look.

Juno's houseboat was moored at Thames Ditton Marina. Getting there, since I wasn't waterborne, involved catching a train to Surbiton and then walking down St Andrew's Road and The Mall to Portsmouth Road, an increasingly pleasant walk as I neared the river. The marina was opposite a BMW dealership and its entrance looked like that of a downmarket shopping centre.

But once I walked down the dirty stone steps and could smell the Thames, some of the romance of life on the water began to suggest itself to me. The boats were moored in a strip of captive river with grassy banks sloping down to it on each side. At the bottom of the banks, the grass gave way to a narrow concrete walkway just above a shallow slope of angled bricks which went down into the water. Short lengths of docking consisting of wooden planks jutted out between the boats from the concrete.

I walked down the walkway, grass on one side of me, boats on the other, until I came to the one I was looking for. I'd been concerned that I wouldn't be able to recognise it, despite Juno having told me exactly where it would be moored. I wasn't exactly an expert on boat-spotting.

But it turned out to be easy enough to identify.

Because it looked exactly like the houseboat in *Murder in London*.

I only now belatedly realised that the colour scheme of that boat, like this one, was that of the Union Jack or a mod roundel. The precise colours of swinging 1960s London. Red, white and blue.

The boat was on my left as I walked out onto the short length of wooden dock, bobbing gently in the water with foam rubber floats and big empty plastic bottles protecting it from direct contact with the dock, which tapped gently against the boat with the rise and fall of the water.

It was an elegant vessel with a long curved body—or hull, I suppose—painted a rich, dark, gleaming blue with brilliant white trim, and immaculate white decking. It was a colour that must have been diabolically difficult to keep clean, but someone seemed to be managing. The dazzling white decking had brilliant red trim and a large red-and-white structure rose from it. There was a name painted on the side of the boat in gold.

I was rather disquieted to see that this was *Jackie.*

I assume that stepping from the dock onto the boat would no doubt have been an absurdly easy procedure for anyone accustomed to such matters. But for me it took a careful moment or two of planning to make sure I stepped across at the right height. And to time it correctly so that the boat, which drifted regularly in towards the dock, temptingly close and then away again, out to a teasing and somewhat dangerous distance, was near enough to avoid an embarrassing comedy plunge into the rather dirty-looking and no doubt cold grey-green water.

Eventually I made my move and stepped across onto the edge of the houseboat, doing what I thought was a rather neat and subtle job of it. I believed I'd landed softly and undetectably.

But the instant I stepped aboard, deep inside the boat a noise began.

The barking of a dog.

18: HOUSEBOAT

If asked to choose the least welcome sound for me at this point in my life, a dog barking would certainly have been a leading contender.

The barking was followed almost immediately by a woman's voice, relaxed and casual, calling out.

"Come on in."

If you've ever wondered why the stupid girl in the horror movie goes down into the basement all alone when you—and in fact everyone in the audience—is screaming at her not to, I am now in a position to tell you.

And it isn't just because she can't hear you screaming at the screen.

It's because it seems foolish to turn back.

Socially foolish.

In fact, embarrassing.

So, to avoid embarrassment, I made my way across the deck to the door of the housing section, which was ajar, and stepped inside, immediately and rather clumsily moving down a couple of steps as I did so, to avoid falling flat on my face.

Here, in a rectangular room lit by daylight from horizontal windows on either side, a woman and a dog waited for me. The latter, at least, seemed pleased to see me.

And I was in turn pleased to see that, whatever breed he was, he certainly wasn't a Doberman. In fact he looked rather like Snoopy, with his big jutting bottle of a muzzle ending in a tiny black nose. Admittedly Snoopy with a very curly perm. And a blond dye job.

The dog had been lying on a large tartan beanbag but had risen from it in honour of my arrival. His eyes were gleaming and a pink tongue protruded from a mouth which looked for all the world as if it was smiling at me. But then he took a quick sidelong glance at his owner and, seeming to take a cue from her, put his tongue back into his mouth, dropped his welcoming gaze and lay back down on his beanbag, chastened.

"Are you afraid of dogs?" said Juno Brunner.

"Not until recently," I said. "And this one looks all right."

"Then come in."

I came all the way inside.

Juno was sitting beside the dog in a white wicker chair with a tartan cushion that matched his beanbag. She looked surprisingly youthful considering the age she had to be. But presumably a life spent swimming had its benefits.

Her hair was entirely white but rather lustrous, worn in a long pony tail draped over one shoulder and fastened with a triangular ebony clip. Her tall lithe form was clad in a chunky grey sweater and paint-stained skinny jeans which ended halfway down her calf, exposing smooth white skin marked by what at first glance I'd taken to be the delicate blue tracery of veins but on closer inspection proved to be the thin elaborate strands of some kind of tattoo.

I couldn't identify what it was supposed to be. Perhaps it was just an abstract pattern. It ran down both her legs on the outer side, like the seams of stockings. Her feet were shod in worn and grubby espadrilles which had once been a banana-yellow colour but had long since been modified by diesel oil and other stains.

There was music playing. It was so familiar that it took me a moment to identify it. *Scheherazade* by Rimsky Korsakov. It was just at the bit with a big violin solo. But, come to think of it, that describes most of *Scheherazade*. The music stopped abruptly, cut off as if by a knife.

But it wasn't a knife, rather the remote control Juno was holding in one hand. Not just any remote control, though, a slender gold-and-black one, so as not to lower the tone of the place.

Her eyes, an unreadable pale grey, watched me as I stood there.

"Well, come over," she said. "And sit down."

There was a second wicker chair set at an angle to hers. That was the only available seat in the room other than a padded bench that ran along one wall under the window, and which was an unsociable distance away. So I took the chair. But as soon as I sat down in it, I realised it was uncomfortably close. Our knees were almost touching.

Juno didn't seem to notice. I supposed that on a houseboat

you became accustomed to not having a lot of room. She seemed very relaxed, so I relaxed too. It was pleasant in this small room, afloat on the unseen water. The low ceiling made for a cosy feel.

My hostess set the elegant remote control down on a white wicker table with a black glass top which would have also looked quite elegant if there weren't mounds of melted wax and half-burned candles dotted across it. And then she turned to give me her full attention.

Meanwhile I'd been giving my full attention to our surroundings. I'd traced the source of the recent music to a circular Bang & Olufsen speaker, also a gold colour. A Beosound A9, a rather tasty item which I coveted as a piece of furniture, never mind for the sound it could make. But it cost north of three grand.

And one could get a perfectly good Ralph Lauren suit for that.

At the far end of the room, an open doorway led into the next section of the boat where I could glimpse the kitchen, or galley as I suppose I was obliged to call it. A string of white Christmas tree lights had been fixed around and above the doorway, and were switched on and shining decoratively, though it wasn't the season for them.

Besides the wicker furniture, the speaker and the string of lights, the whole place was rather eerie and unsettling, and I abruptly realised why—because it was so familiar.

As far as I could tell, apart from some details of furnishing, the boat looked just the way it had in the film.

As if it had been carefully and lovingly preserved.

Like a shrine.

I met Juno's gaze. There was a hint of some emotion in her eyes. Something sardonic. Amusement? Contempt? She seemed to be waiting for me to say something.

All I could think of was to state the utterly obvious. I gestured at the boat around us. "It looks just like the one they used in the movie."

I seemed to have said the right thing, because it gave her a chance to sniff derisively and say, "That's because it *is* the one they used in the movie."

"Really?"

"For sure. When they needed a houseboat for the picture they decided not to rent one. They bought one outright." She looked around at her little home. "Sometimes they do that for films. It's all about the money. It's an investment. They even buy houses they're going to shoot in, then flip them afterwards. You can make a tidy profit like that. But not in this case. Not after what happened in here. Nobody wanted it. So, once the police had finished with it, it was for sale cheap. Very cheap indeed. And, as it happened, I needed a place to live just then. And what could be better for someone who works on the water? On the water and *under* the water?"

I wondered if she still did scuba diving. There was no sign of any of the relevant gear, but then you wouldn't keep it in your front lounge. Not if you were as tidy as this woman clearly was.

"I'd always wanted to try living on a houseboat," she was saying. "And I'd never see one as nice as this, as cheap as this, again. So it made sense to buy it." She looked at me, presumably for validation. I suppose she got it because she leaned down and caressed the dog. An unconscious, unguarded gesture, as if she was beginning to feel at ease in my presence. "So I put in an offer and they accepted it and I took possession. After it was free of the filth."

For a moment I winced inwardly, thinking she was talking about the gore left on the murder scene. But then it clicked. The word *filth* was a nickname, a slightly archaic one, for the police.

Just to be sure, I said this out loud. "The police?"

I wouldn't have thought memories of the police, and therefore inevitably of Jackie's murder, would have prompted much in the way of good humour, but Juno seemed positively cheered by this line of discussion. "For sure," she said. And she grinned at me, a big wide grin, and I saw that one of her teeth, a canine, had been replaced with a silver one.

It was rather striking.

"I know what you're thinking," she said.

"People keep telling me that," I said.

"Who else?"

"Chloë." She didn't seem to recognise the name. I hesitated, realising that I might be making complications for myself here, but in for a penny, in for a pound. "Chloë Loconsole," I said.

Her face tightened and her mouth closed. Goodbye silver fang.

"His granddaughter?" she said. "Granddaughter of the fucker who killed Jackie?"

"Do you really think he did it?"

She chuckled, a rasping sound. "Of course he did it. He used her, he fucked her and then, when he'd had enough of her, or when things started to get complicated for him, he killed her."

"Why would he do that?" I said.

"Because he was a man. You have heard of male violence? Against women? If you haven't, I can offer you a rich variety of examples."

She had a point there. An unarguable point. "But from what I've heard," I said, "he wasn't like that."

"What do you mean, he wasn't like that? He was a man, right?"

"But not all men are capable of that kind of violence," I said. It was perhaps a futile gesture, but I felt I had to stand up for those of us who weren't total psychopaths.

"Are you kidding?" Juno seemed amused. "Boys will be boys. Killing a woman comes naturally."

"It doesn't come naturally to me," I said. I was starting to get a little angry.

She smiled again, that silver fang glinting. "I'm sure you're a very nice chap."

"Thanks," I said.

"Very gentle and considerate and sensitive." She was watching me with amusement as she delivered this litany. "And that you trim your girlfriend's toenails and cook her a very nice supper."

"Only one of those," I said.

She smiled, shaking her head. "I still say you could kill someone. Providing it was a woman. Any man could."

"Even if that's true," I said, "and any man could…"

"Believe me little darling, they could." I didn't especially like being called little darling, I must admit.

"Even if any man could," I said, "it doesn't mean that a man did, in this case."

"What case?"

"Jackie's case."

She glared at me. "Don't call her that. You don't have the right to talk about her as if you knew her, as if she was a friend of yours."

I'd got into the habit of referring to the dead woman this way because of Chloë. At least I hadn't called her "poor Jackie". I doubt if that would have gone down too well.

"What do you want me to call her? Miss Higgins, stunt coordinator?"

Juno chuckled at that, suddenly recovering her good humour. "Assistant stunt coordinator. I was the stunt coordinator and she was my assistant." She glanced at me. There was something different in her manner now. Almost like shyness. "Would you like a drink?"

I overcame my surprise. I didn't particularly want a drink, under the circumstances, but I thought it would be a good idea to encourage any signs of hospitality in this rather difficult and spiky woman. "Yes please," I said.

She got up and moved towards the door at the rear of the room, the dog immediately rising and following her like her shadow. "What do you want?"

"What have you got?"

"Red wine or red wine."

"Then I'll have red wine please."

She chuckled again and went through into the galley and began opening cupboards, the dog watching her with intelligent interest, tail wagging. A moment later she came back, followed by her canine chaperone, with a bottle and two drinking glasses. The wine was a pinot noir with a brightly coloured label. She set the bottle down on the candle-strewn tabletop and held out the glasses.

"You can have Babar the Elephant or Tintin," she said. "They used to have mustard in them. French mustard of course. Hence the popular French children's characters. Anyway which one do you want?"

"Which Tintin is it?" I didn't bother telling her that he was actually a popular Belgian children's character. Now didn't seem the time for pedantry.

She scrutinised the glass. "The one where he goes to the moon."

"I'll have that one."

"Good choice." She gave me the glass. "It's clean," she said, when she caught me inspecting it.

"I'd expect nothing less," I said.

She laughed. "You have to keep things clean on a boat, or everything goes south very quickly. Very quickly indeed. With amazing rapidity, as it happens."

I thought about the brilliant-white paintwork of the deck and began to realise just how much work she must put in to keep it looking like that. So it wasn't all sitting around and listening to *Scheherazade* with her dog lounging at her side.

I sipped the wine as she watched me closely.

"How is it?" She'd tensed up again. She really was remarkably ready to take offence.

It wasn't bad at all. "Floral and fruity," I said.

Now she really did relax. "That's what I think," she said, and took a deep sip from her own glass. Whether it was the change in her tone of voice, or the act of drinking the wine, but the dog now gave a happy little sound of approval and settled down properly, stretching and spreading himself out on the floor. His tail flicked towards me, as if lazily indicating that he'd accepted me. I wondered if his mistress had also done so, and he'd picked up on it.

"What's the dog's name?"

"Burlap. Like the…"

"Bag?" I suggested

"Like the material."

"Because of the colour?" I said.

She flashed me a quick, appraising look. "Yes."

"What kind of dog is he?"

"A very nice dog."

"I meant what breed?"

"Why? Are you thinking of buying one?" she said.

"No," I said, with a mild feeling of déjà vu. "We're cat people."

She sampled the wine and then, apparently having made me wait the statutory length of time and pissed me about sufficiently, she answered my question. "Cockapoo."

"A cross between a… cocker spaniel and a poodle?"

"You're a sharp one," she said. "For a cat person."

"I must have read about them somewhere. About the breed."

"What did it say?"

"Never have one on a houseboat," I said, and she laughed.

We both sipped our wine in companionable silence for a while. "What were we talking about?" she said, finally, setting her glass aside. Babar looked quite chic against a backdrop of half-burned candle stubs and black glass. "Before our little conversational detour about dog breeding?"

"I'd say Jackie Higgins," I said. "But I'm worried you'll bite my head off if I get her name wrong."

She chuckled her rasping chuckle. "That's all right, Jackie Higgins will do. Little Jackie Higgins. Sounds like someone in a nursery rhyme, doesn't it?" The smile suddenly faded from her face and all at once she looked stricken, her eyes vague and distant. A woman lost in memory. The dog picked up on her mood change instantly and made a worried noise deep in his throat. He climbed off his beanbag and went and rested his chin across her thigh.

That brought her back and she began absent-mindedly stroking the dog's head. She even smiled again. A somewhat sad smile, though. "Yeah, we were talking about Jackie, weren't we? And you were trying to sell me on the idea that Loretto Loconsole didn't do it." She looked at me. "Trying to sell me on the idea that he didn't kill her."

"He had an alibi," I said.

"The idiot at the hotel?"

"The concierge at the hotel, yes."

"An alibi which he could have paid for," she said.

"Maybe."

"The police thought so."

"And we trust the filth?" I said. "Back in 1969?"

"We don't even trust them now," said Juno, and poured us both some more wine, moving carefully so as not to dislodge the dog who was still resting his head on her thigh. As a man who had gone to great lengths not to disturb comfortable cats, I quite understood this. "All right, say for the sake of argument that he didn't do it. Who did?"

I took a deep breath and braced myself. There was no point trying to dodge this one. And I had a feeling that if I did, she'd know instantly I was dissembling, and that it would blow any trust that was developing between us.

"A lot of people think you did," I said.

I was ready for a wide number of reactions, none of them particularly pleasant, and if I'd been asked to pick a winner I would have opted for her throwing her floral and fruity wine in my face. But to my surprise she just nodded mildly. I might as well have been talking about the weather.

"They do, all right," she said. "They certainly do think that." She set her wine glass aside and reached down for the dog, grabbing him with both hands and vigorously caressing him, rubbing his skinny ribcage on either side. He lifted his head from her thigh and rose up slightly off the floor on his hind legs, obviously loving it. For a moment, woman and dog were utterly involved in this simple act of mechanical happiness. Then she looked up at me, grey eyes gazing directly into mine, and said, "I didn't kill her. I couldn't kill her. I loved her."

She looked back down at the dog, rubbing him again.

"Didn't I, darling?" she said. Then Juno Brunner lifted her eyes and looked at me again. "Have some more wine." She filled our glasses again. "Do you want some cheese? I've got some very good Welsh sheep's cheese."

I wondered what Chloë's grandmother's position would be on Welsh sheep's cheese. It hardly bore thinking about.

"No thanks," I said. But then, embarrassingly, my stomach gurgled loudly.

Juno laughed. "Liar." She went back into the galley, followed by her loyal hound, and returned with cheese and crackers, both surprisingly high end. I devoured them gratefully and greedily, washing them down with the wine, which made an ideal accompaniment.

"Bon appétit," said Juno, also eating quite greedily, I was glad to see. She paused to feed one of the crackers to the dog, who crunched on it thoughtfully and politely, as though to make a distinction between his table manners and our lack of them.

"Why don't you ask me?" said Juno suddenly.

"Ask you what?"

"How I can live here, after what happened here."

"I take it you don't believe in ghosts," I said.

"I don't, as it happens. But if Jackie's shade did turn up, I would only be glad to see her." She looked at me to see if I believed her. This was clearly supposed to be a further demonstration that she'd loved Jackie Higgins and couldn't have killed her.

I'd believed her so far. But now I began to wonder if she was laying it on a bit thick…

I decided it was high time to get down to business.

"You won't think it rude of me," I said, "if I…"

"Use the loo?"

Now that she mentioned it, the wine had begun to make that a priority. "Well, that too. But I was going to say…"

"Oh, the record. Right. I'll get that when I show you to the loo."

"Isn't it called the head? On a boat?"

"Very good," she said. "You'll be helping me get this thing up and down locks soon."

"I doubt it," I said.

She chuckled and rose to her feet. The dog got up, too, tail wagging. "Come on, I'll show you the way. Though you could hardly get lost."

We went through the door at the back of this room, through the galley, and into the bedroom, which looked disconcertingly like it had in the film. Though I couldn't remember if in the film there had been an alcove in the wall with a hi-fi system installed in it. Genuinely high-fidelity, too. I don't know why I was surprised to discover that Juno Brunner had a turntable.

After all, she'd said she took good care of her vinyl. Not much point in that if you didn't occasionally play it on something.

The turntable in question was a Thorens TD-125 in a solid plinth of handsome dark wood. There was also an FM tuner, a reel-to-reel tape recorder and a cassette deck. All of them serious kit and high end in their day, which was about fifty years ago. And still now, if you asked me.

"What are you looking at?" said Juno.

The dog, who had accompanied us, also made a small sound of inquiry.

"The turntable. Well, everything. But the turntable in particular."

"Does it meet with your approval?" said Juno. "Does it come up to your high standards?"

"Definitely," I said. "Especially on a boat, where that super-floaty, suspended sub-chassis will come into its own."

"For sure," she said. "Perfect for a life aquatic. And for when things get really choppy I've got my faithful wireless and pre-recorded, open-reel tapes. Plus a little cassette library acquired over the years."

"Sounds good," I said. "I imagine, quite literally."

"Want to hear something? I promise not to try and jump your bones just because we're in my bedroom."

"That offer is simultaneously attractive and disappointing," I said, and she laughed. "But I really need the loo now."

"Right through here."

The toilet was actually a bathroom, a gleaming chamber with mirror-tiled walls that offered me the reflected image of a slightly drunk and discombobulated young record collector. It was a masterpiece of ergonomics, making maximal use of minimal space, packing in a bathtub and shower combo, toilet, sink and even a bidet. There was also a series of alcoves in the wall which were devoted to innumerable bottles of shampoo, and other toiletries and assorted kinds of soap.

But pride of place was given over to the silver mermaid.

19: SILVER MERMAID

Like the one we'd seen in the movie, this was an elegant object, about the size of a cat.

I'm not sure if anyone else measures things in terms of cats, but I do.

Its silver form was sleekly sculpted and had a suggestion of Henry Moore abstraction about it, its smoothly curved surfaces evoking indigenous art. The fins at the bottom of the mermaid's tail were splayed and flattened to provide a stable base on which it rested. This fishy tail took up about two thirds of the height of the figure. The remaining third, the mammalian parts of the mermaid from the waist up— belly button, breasts, nipples, smiling face, stylised froth of hair—were elegantly reminiscent of a cheerfully sexy Picasso drawing.

Terrifically simple but full of character, a few lines and dots adding up to something warm and appealing. It was beautiful in its minimalism and minimalist in its beauty.

The mermaid's little arms were raised up on either side

of her to presumably suggest swimming, although Tinkler had disrespectfully suggested that it looked like she was coming out with her hands up to surrender to the cops.

To me, it looked more like they were raised in some kind of prayer or act of worship.

They also provided the means to open it up, assuming this one did open. Some of the prop mermaids had been hollow and opened up. Others had been solid and didn't.

Like the one used to kill Jackie Higgins.

As demonstrated in the movie, the way you opened the ones that did open was by tugging on the mermaid's little arms, and then her torso popped off, revealing the long hollow in the fish tail.

I used the loo, flushed it, conscientiously washed my hands while looking at my face in the mirror, knowing what I was going to do.

I tugged on the little arms.

The top section of the mermaid came off smoothly and easily.

In *Murder in London*, this decorative *objet*, or one very like it, had contained a valuable cache of LSD.

The lysergic acid, which Tinkler assured me could come in many forms, often liquid or liquid soaked into blotting paper, had been represented in the film by capsules. Bicolour capsules in red and white, or green and white—as Nevada had pointed out, the colours of the Italian flag.

How patriotic.

In this mermaid, there were no capsules of LSD, real or otherwise, in the colours of the Italian flag.

Rather, just a swirling mix of purple-pink crystalline power, which looked like a sand dune in a miniature psychedelic desert. It smelled rather wonderfully of lavender; evidently bath salts.

A tiny triangle of yellow paper jutted out of the miniature sand dune. Like a shark's fin—to mix the simile.

Or perhaps to begin storyboarding a Tim Burton film…

With a sense of violation and very bad guest etiquette—I even, stupidly, glanced over my shoulder to make sure that Juno wasn't suddenly standing behind me watching me in the tiny bathroom, possibly complete with loyal dog at her side—I began to tug on the piece of paper and extract it.

I did so with an oddly intense excitement growing in me.

Somehow I intuitively knew, with absolute certainty, that I'd stumbled on a vital clue.

I dug it out.

The triangle was the corner of a yellow rectangle of card with some words inscribed on it in flowery handwriting in black ink. The words read, "The calming dream trio of lavender, chamomile and neroli oil, sourced from Egyptian orange blossoms, blended to conjure a soothing perfume to tease your senses, while the restorative Epsom salts ease tired muscles."

There was also a price written on it, which I found far from soothing or restorative.

I did consider probing further down to see if anything else was buried in the purple mound, but, when you're in a hole, in a pile of fragrant bath salts, stop digging.

So I just carefully tucked the tag back into the powder and did my best to leave it exactly as I had found it.

Juno Brunner and Burlap the dog were waiting for me in the bedroom. A blanket had been folded back on the bed to reveal that the mattress was resting on a storage unit. One big enough to contain LPs. And this one did. Dozens of them. Possibly several hundred. I didn't really look carefully because all my attention was on the one that Juno had in her hand.

I'd seen the cover of *Murder in London* so many times by now that I'd become somewhat jaded. Actually, only twice in reality come to think of it. But both times it had proved such a disappointment—empty; cigar ashtray—that I no longer grew excited at the sight of it.

What mattered was what was inside.

This seemed like a paraphrase of Chloë's *nonna*'s remarks about women's clothing, I thought, not entirely soberly.

Juno was smiling at me, and so it seemed was the dog.

"Do you want to hear this?" she said, holding up the record and nodding towards the turntable in its wall unit.

"Why not?" I said.

I slipped the record out of the sleeve and examined it carefully.

There were some spindle marks on the labels, which might normally have been indicative of heavy wear and careless handling. But in this case I suspected were just a consequence of living on a boat where you didn't always have a stable floor under you when you were putting your beloved piece of vinyl on the turntable.

And this one clearly was beloved.

The playing surface looked immaculate.

Bingo.

There was no point trying for a poker face, even if I'd been good at that sort of thing, because I wasn't going to try and beat Juno Brunner's price down.

I was ready to pay top money for a top copy of this record.

And it looked like that was what I'd found.

"I'll have listen to it now, if that's all right," I said.

"That is all right," she said.

I hadn't spotted the speakers initially because they were fitted on adjustable brackets on the ceiling. Not ideal from an audiophile point of view. The speakers themselves, however, were a great choice. LS3/5As. The best small speaker anybody could get, the classic BBC design, fashioned to provide absolutely accurate voice rendering and consequently gave wonderful reproduction of musical instruments of all kinds.

We played the entire record, sitting together companionably on the large bed. Juno didn't try to jump my bones. Perhaps because the dog kept us company, lying contently between us, his curly blond flanks rising and falling gently with his breathing. Much more likely because Juno's sexuality didn't lie remotely in my direction.

Far more importantly, the record played beautifully.

Admittedly, there was a loud popping noise at one point which repeated twice more. Juno looked mortified. But when I took the record off the turntable and inspected it more closely I saw what looked like a piece of eminently cleanable crud.

I used a cotton swab dipped in a mixture of vodka and filtered water—luckily Juno had all of these commodities to hand—and cleaned the crud away.

I put the record back on and *voila*, the three loud popping sounds were gone.

Juno was impressed by my trick with the vodka. I told her under ideal conditions we would have used isopropyl alcohol.

When we finished listening, I put the record carefully back in the sleeve and we all trooped back through to the sitting room again and settled down for some good, old-fashioned bargaining.

Juno and her dog were both watching me with keen attention "What do you reckon?" she said.

"Very nice indeed," I said. "How much do you want for it?"

"A thousand pounds."

"If I say okay immediately will you be bitterly disappointed that you didn't ask for more?" I said.

Juno laughed and said, "I don't know. Why don't you try it and we'll see?"

"Okay," I said.

"Okay to a thousand pounds?"

"Yes."

Juno gave a whoop, a surprisingly youthful and girlish whoop, and Burlap rose to his feet and turned around in a brisk enthusiastic little circle, tail waving. And he then sat back down again and proceeded to go to sleep with such alacrity that it rather called into the question the sincerity of that display of enthusiasm.

Juno made sure both our glasses were full of wine while I made sure the record was safely set to one side, and then we clinked them together in a toast.

"How do we manage this?" she said, as she settled back into her wicker chair.

"The payment you mean?" I said.

"Yes, exchange of money and…"

"Vinyl," I said.

"Yes."

"We'll bring a thousand pounds over, in cash, and you can give us the record."

"All right. Who is we?"

"My girlfriend and I."

"Okay. That sounds all right. So, that's it?"

"I guess so," I said.

"You don't have any questions?"

"Oh, I've got plenty of questions," I said.

"Like what?"

"Why do you have this?" I indicated the record.

"Do you mean, where did I get it? They were giving out copies to people who worked on the film."

"No," I said. "I mean, why do you have it? It's music by the man you believe killed your lover."

"Oh," said Juno, making a big show of dawning realisation. "You mean how can I listen to it, given the associations and all that jazz?"

"Yes. And all that jazz."

She breathed in carefully through her nose as though doing a yogic exercise and then she said, "I suppose it's the same reason I live on this houseboat. It reminds me of her. The music reminds me of her. They gave us tapes of the music as each track was recorded, fresh from the studio. We played them on the set when we were shooting the movie. We played them at parties at night, after we'd finished a day's shooting." She looked at me, those grey eyes assessing and sober, despite all the wine she'd put away. "That music makes me think of her. It brings her back. And it brings back better days." She held out her hand for the record and I passed it to her, a little apprehensive about what she might do, it's true.

But it was still her record. We may have struck a deal, but she retained ownership until money changed hands.

Right now, it was only the record changing hands, reluctantly from mine back into hers.

Juno flipped the album over and looked at the photo of Loretto Loconsole on the back. If you'd given me a year and a team of trained psychologists I doubt if I could have told you what the expression on her face meant. She seemed utterly calm and impassive.

Finally, she said, "I can disconnect the music from him. After all, he only wrote it. He doesn't play any of the instruments. So I'm not really listening to *him*."

I didn't argue with her, although I could easily have done so. Looked at from another point of view, every note of music on the record was his work, emanating from the man, from the most elemental depths of him. It didn't seem like a good idea to say any of this, though.

Anyway, just then my phone rang. It was Nevada.

"How's Turk?" I said. Only as the words came out of my mouth did I realise how worried I'd been, at some periphery of my mind. About my foolish scrapper of a cat.

"Oh, she's absolutely fine. She's just strained a muscle. The vet said to give it a day or two and she'll be walking like normal. Running, in fact. Probably in pursuit of that little black-and-white cat. We didn't even need to take her in for a check-up. Not that that stopped the nice vet from giving her an injection of some potion and charging us nearly two hundred quid for it. Never mind that. How are you?"

"Absolutely fine, too."

"You're safe?" said Nevada. "No one's coercing you into saying that? If everything really is all right, say our nickname for Agatha."

"Clean Head."

"Okay." Nevada didn't actually sigh, but there was a moment of relieved silence during which I heard traffic noise in the background.

"Where are you?" I said.

"On my way to join you. Just in case."

"No need for that," I said.

"Too late to turn back now. I'll be with you soon."

"Okay. Where's Turk?"

"Tinkler took her home."

"Okay," I said. "See you soon." I resisted the impulse to blow kisses down the phone at her. With a few drinks in me, it was a surprisingly hard impulse to resist. But it just didn't seem businesslike.

"See you soon," she said. Nevada had no such scruples

about blowing kisses. We hung up and I looked at Juno who was watching me with droll interest.

"Who's Turk?" she said.

"Our cat," I said. "Got into a fight last night, was limping this morning, hence a quick emergency trip to the vets just now, to be told that everything is fine. And that that'll be two hundred pounds, please."

"Ouch, but at least everything is fine."

"My feelings exactly," I said.

"Does he often get into fights? Turk?"

"She," I said. "And, yes, quite often. She does."

"Go girl," said Juno approvingly. She leaned over and patted Burlap. "This fellow here is a natural-born coward. Fortunately he doesn't have any outstanding health issues either. Unless you count possessing the smallest bladder of any dog in England."

Burlap murmured a mild, sleepy reproof at this slander while his owner watched me with an appraising gaze. "So that was your girlfriend?"

"Yes," I said. "The one who has to trim her own toenails."

She chuckled. "Sounded like she needed some reassuring, though. That you were okay. Did you manage to reassure her that you were okay?"

"Yes."

"Good. Was that a safe word that you used? Clean something?"

I was startled. This woman was sharp as a knife, and after half a bottle of wine. "Clean Head," I said. "Yes, sort of a safe word, I guess."

"To tell her everything was okay."

"Yes."

She nodded. "Smart. So why did she need reassuring? Did she think that I might try and sleep with you?"

At least she didn't say jump her bones.

"No," I said. "She thought you might try and kill me."

Juno laughed. "Well, I suppose that's marginally more likely."

20: PRINCESS SEITAN

I said my goodbyes to Juno and Burlap, both of whom seemed a little sad to see me go. Feeling a trifle unsteady out in the fresh air, after all that wine, I took great care stepping off the houseboat and back onto the dock. And then navigating the narrow concrete path between the grassy bank and the water felt a bit like a tightrope walk…

But I managed it okay.

I'd just left the marina and come onto the main road when I saw Nevada, approaching from the direction of the car dealership. She waved and we waited for a gap in the traffic and then hurried towards each other, had a brief but emotional reunion then walked back to the station, pausing at Sainsbury's to buy some cat food (chicken breast with asparagus), and caught the train back home.

"So tell me about Juno Brunner," said Nevada, settling in her seat opposite me as we accelerated towards Clapham Junction.

"For a start, she owns a dog."

Blue eyes widened. "What? Shit…"

"And I was tremendously relieved to discover it wasn't a Doberman."

"I'll bet. Any chance it could have stood in for one?"

"No," I said. "He's a big softie." I realised I'd become quite attached to Burlap on our short acquaintance. Remarkably attached. Considering I was a cat lover.

"And what was his owner like?" Our train was at full speed now. It flashed past some fox cubs frolicking between a bank of wild flowers and a junction box sprayed with graffiti. London in the summer.

"She plied me with red wine," I said.

"Really? How was it?"

"Not up to your standard."

"Of course not. What else to report?"

"She told me she didn't kill Jackie."

Nevada leaned forward at this information, and not just because I'd lowered my voice.

"She got very sore when I called Jackie 'Jackie' by the way."

"Taking the name of her beloved in vain?" said Nevada.

"Something like that."

"What did she expect you to call her?"

"She simmered down after a while," I said.

"Good. Did you believe her when she said she didn't kill her?"

"I'm not sure."

"Good," said Nevada.

"Good?"

"Always pays to be sceptical," she said.

"I completely believed her at first. But then when she went on…"

"The lady doth protest too much?" said Nevada. She leaned back in her seat.

"Something like that," I said. "She was very convincing, but…"

"But?"

"She's living in the houseboat where the murder happened."

"Not the actual houseboat?" said Nevada.

"The very one. She bought it cheap after the film makers were finished with it. And the police."

"So she bought it and did it up?"

"No, she's kept it pretty much exactly as it is in the movie. Inside and out. Maintained it very nicely, but it remains a perfect replica of the way it was in *Murder in London*."

"Or *Bikini of Blood*."

"Or *Bikini of Blood*."

"Jesus…" Nevada paused and considered. "But doesn't that argue for her not having done it? I mean, how could she bear to live there otherwise? Unless she's a total leering psycho."

"She's definitely not a total leering psycho." I almost said it defensively. It seemed I'd become a little bit attached to Burlap's owner, too.

Nevada gave me a mocking look. "That's a relief."

"But what if she did kill Jackie Higgins?" I said. "And she regrets it, every day of her life…"

"And maybe that's why she lives there?" said Nevada. "A continual act of self-torment?"

"Or a continual act of atonement," I said. "She's even got one of the silver mermaids."

"*What?*"

The look on Nevada's face suddenly made me realise what a grotesque thing this was… To possess a replica of the murder weapon used on your beloved, and to have it on permanent display.

In your stylishly appointed bathroom.

Nevada was staring at me. "Why didn't you get the hell out of there when you saw that?"

"In retrospect, I suppose it does seem a little weird," I said.

"A little? Yes it does. It does seem a little weird."

"But, at the time, it just seemed kind of normal. I mean, the whole place looks exactly like it did in the film. So it sort of made sense to decorate it with one of the props. And it's really nice, the silver mermaid. Kind of sweet and cute when you see it up close. Very appealing. It's understandable someone wanting it as an object to display…"

"It's not sweet and cute when you know it's been used to cave in the head of the woman you loved."

"True. But she seems immune to negative associations."

"No one is immune to negative associations."

"Well she certainly seems to have a very high threshold for tolerating them. Because of course she's also got a copy of Loretto Loconsole's music…"

"Speaking of which," said Nevada. "I can't believe it's

taken this long for me to ask you about the fucking record. The entire purpose of your visit."

"You've had a few other things to think about," I said. "And it was fine. The record. It looks fine and it plays perfectly."

"Thank fuck for that," said Nevada.

"I told her we'd pay her a thousand. I didn't even bother to haggle. Sorry."

"That's all right," said Nevada, reaching out and taking my hand. "That's fine. If I'd thought about it, I could have brought the money with me…" She suddenly looked at me. "Should we get the money? Go to the bank and make a cash withdrawal and go back to her? Seal the deal right away?"

I shook my head. "We're almost home now. And I've had enough for one day."

"Fair enough. You've been cooped up in a small space on a houseboat with a potential murderess. On the very houseboat where her girlfriend was killed, with the murder weapon lying around… where was it?"

"In the bathroom. Full of bath salts. It's only a copy of the murder weapon."

"Because it's hollow," said Nevada, immediately grasping the implication. "And the one that killed Jackie was solid. Right. But still… It gives me the creeps. Her living on that houseboat, with that thing in her bathroom, listening to the music written by the guy who supposedly killed her girlfriend. Does she listen to it?"

"Oh yeah," I said. "On a rather good turntable. She seems to like the music a lot."

"The music by the man who is believed to have killed her girlfriend."

"Yes," I said patiently. "It does seem very weird."

"You think?"

"But if we're going to accuse her of weirdness for listening to music by the killer, then our whole argument about *her* being the killer falls apart."

Nevada nodded. It was a reluctant sort of nod. "I suppose so."

"We can only consider her reprehensible either as a ghoul or as the killer. Not both."

"Well then, I vote for killer," said Nevada.

We changed trains at Clapham for Barnes, continuing our discussion about Juno Brunner.

"Why do you vote for her being a killer?" I said.

"To be on the safe side," said Nevada. "For us I mean."

"She made a very convincing case for why she's living on that houseboat. Got it at a rock bottom price." I knew the latter would appeal to my savvy sweetheart. I didn't quite know why I was so anxious to exonerate Juno Brunner, but I was.

"I see. Was it a condition of getting it at a rock bottom price that she kept it exactly as it was in the film?"

"Obviously not," I said. "But she also made a very convincing case for why she's kept it like that."

"As a shrine to the girl she killed."

"To preserve the memories of the good times. Like I say, she convinced me."

"Well, she hasn't convinced me," said Nevada. She peered

303

out the window of the train as we rolled towards Putney and stations west. "You say you were drinking wine with her?"

"Yes. Quite a lot of wine."

"And she always drank from the same bottle as you?"

"Yes."

"What about the glasses? Did she let you choose the glass you used?"

"Yes. It was a Tintin glass."

"Really?" said Nevada. "Which adventure?"

"*Destination Moon.*"

My darling automatically corrected me. "*Objectif Lune.*"

When we got back to our house, Fanny was sitting outside waiting in the front garden. Which was odd because the back garden was her more natural hangout, and she didn't like using the cat flap in the front. She preferred to wait until someone held the door open for her.

Nevada and I looked at each other as we opened the gate and the little feline reprobate came sauntering towards us, tail held high, asking for some attention and approval.

As we were giving it to her, there was a victorious howl and Turk came hurtling towards us, apparently from the other side of the estate.

She slid under the gate, which now being closed presented no kind of barrier to her—she could also have jumped over it—and joined us.

Again, Nevada and I looked at each other.

"Shouldn't she be inside convalescing?" I said.

"Tinkler promised he'd put her safely in the house," said Nevada. "But I guess he couldn't stay and catsit. He had to get to work. And there's no way he could keep her in there, anyway. There's no way anyone could keep her inside if she wanted to go out…"

I watched Turk circling our legs. There was no trace of a limp now. "She looks…"

"Just fine," said Nevada. "I know."

"It must have been the wonder injection," I said.

"The two hundred quid wonder injection," said Nevada, a tad bitterly.

"I wonder what was in it?"

"Probably about one pound's worth of anti-inflammatory," said my cynical sweetheart.

The cats were both staring up at us expectantly. "All right, all right," said Nevada. "We'll feed you. Just let us get inside…"

We opened the door and went through into the kitchen, followed by the cats. Nevada took out a bag of dried food and I opened the cupboard where we kept their bowls.

And just then a voice called out from the living room.

"*Don't shoot. I'm white.*"

It was the voice of a woman.

A young woman, and a rather amused one at that.

Nevada wasn't amused.

She dropped the pack of cat food, surged towards the knife block and drew out our biggest and sharpest knife. She held it with one hand while, with the other, she grabbed a wine bottle from the rack and passed it to me.

She went into the living room, moving fast and I followed her, trying to keep up, and trying to look dangerous and formidable holding a wine bottle. As soon as we entered the room, we froze.

Sitting there on our sofa, looking very relaxed and quite at home was the person I only knew as Princess Seitan.

She was wearing a green-and-white short-sleeve shirt with 1950s graphics of atoms and rocket ships on it. Her blue jeans were 1950s style too, with the cuffs turned up at the bottom. On her feet, she'd apparently been wearing combat boots but she'd thoughtfully taken these off and left them on the floor before settling down on our sofa and putting her feet up on a pile of cushions.

Which allowed us a very good opportunity to inspect her socks, which seemed to be made out of the material usually reserved for sexy fishnet stockings, except this was dark blue instead of black.

And ending in frilly little cuffs above the ankles.

Her hair was utterly different from the last time I'd seen her. A different colour—streaks of gold and chestnut brown and tied in twin pigtails of the kind associated with schoolgirls of yesteryear.

But her eyes were the same deep emerald green.

They were highly amused now as she looked at us standing there brandishing our makeshift weapons.

"Why do you get to have the knife?" she said to Nevada.

"Because I'm the more ruthless one."

Princess Seitan nodded at me. "And he's only allowed to serve the wine?"

"No," I said. "I also make coffee." Nevada and I looked at each other. "I could make some now," I said, and she gave me an almost subliminal nod.

"That would be super," said Princess Seitan lazily from the sofa.

Nevada and I went back into the kitchen, making faces at each other. The cats were still waiting patiently for their snacks, so we put out their food. But only after Nevada had replaced the knife in the knife block and I'd put the wine bottle back in its proper place in the rack.

Then Nevada went back to join our guest. The cats finished their snacks and scooted while I started the preparations on the coffee and followed as quickly as I could.

The women seemed sociable enough, sitting in a companionable silence in the living room.

"I see you guys have got some new tech," said the recumbent Princess Seitan. "At least it looks new."

"You mean the doorbell cam?" said Nevada.

"Looks like the latest model," said Princess Seitan with a note of professional approval.

"It is," said Nevada, trying not to sound too proud. "We decided it was worth investing in a little home security."

"Highly sensible."

"Especially when, once upon a time, someone tried to send us to prison for a very, very long sentence by planting drugs in our house."

Princess Seitan made disapproving tutting noises and held up her hands in a gesture of wide-eyed innocence. "Nothing to do with me," she said.

Nevada smiled indulgently. "Although you might perhaps know the person who did it."

"I might perhaps," said Princess Seitan. "Do I still get a coffee?"

"Absolutely," I said. I went and finished making it. It was the good stuff, so it took a little longer but Nevada gave me a look of approval when finally I brought it through and handed out mugs. This was a special guest.

A guest of honour, you might say.

Princess Seitan having settled herself, apparently permanently, on the sofa left us to make do with the armchairs facing her. It occurred to me that this choice of seating arrangement allowed the Princess to keep an eye on what—if anything—was going on in our back garden.

It also meant, if you wanted to be paranoid about it, that Nevada and I *wouldn't* be able to see what was going on in the garden. Paranoia had begun to seem like a healthy reaction lately, so, as I served the coffee, I made sure I took a good look through the window.

All I saw in the garden was one of our cats now snoozing in the shade of a Japanese maple and the other one busily chewing on some grass which she would no doubt throw up later. No doubt indoors, on the floor.

Princess Seitan accepted her mug of coffee with apparent pleasure and settled back luxuriously on the sofa to enjoy it, carefully arranging the cushions around her. "I guess you're wondering why I dropped by?"

"I guess we are," said Nevada.

"Well, I don't know how much you dudes know about the

dark web," said Princess Seitan. "Also known, to its friends, as the darknet."

"Just the basics," said Nevada.

"Well *basically* you can buy anything you want there, providing you know where to find it and you have the money."

"Assuming someone is selling," said Nevada.

"Someone usually is," said Princess Seitan. "And I've had occasion to use the dark web myself in the past for various reasons. For instance, on that little caper where I first met you guys."

"I remember it well," I said.

"We both do," said Nevada.

Princess Seitan nodded as if graciously accepting our compliments. "My so-called employers were making use of it as a resource. So they found me and hired me via the good old, sinister old darknet. Hired me to help them with their various and sundry jobs." She smiled a contented little smile. "Didn't turn out so well for my employers, but it turned out pretty okay for me."

"Because you ended up with the entire proceeds of the robbery," said Nevada. "For example."

Princess Seitan's amusement seemed to grow. "For example, yes. Looking after that money was my job. And a job I did remarkably well, though I say it myself. It's hardly my fault if those other fools got themselves caught and ended up in prison, where all that lovely loot wouldn't do them any good. Or at least it won't do them as much good as it's doing me." She took another sip from her mug. "This is nice coffee."

"I'm glad you like it," I said.

"Anyhoo… I'm semi-retired now." She wriggled her toes in their cute little blue fishnet socks and watched them with evident amusement for a moment or two. Maybe this was how she liked to spend her semi-retirement. Then she took another sip of the coffee and favoured us with her full attention, wriggling toes having apparently lost their fascination. "But I still like to keep tabs on things," she said. "And recently I've been keeping an eye on the dark web more than usual because it seems that someone has been sniffing around looking for me…"

"Jasper McClew," I said.

She gave me the full benefit of those sea-green eyes. "Good for you. Full marks. That's right, it's your little friend Jasper."

"He's little," said Nevada. "But he's not our friend."

"Smart of you, probably."

"And I take it you don't want to talk to him?" said Nevada. "He's working on a book about the heist. Or a podcast. Or both. I've lost track."

"Both," I said.

Princess Seitan gave us a curious look. "Do you dudes really think I should talk to little Jasper? Or that I would want to?"

"No," I said. "But I'm assuming Nevada is asking because he's promised us a finder's fee if you agree."

"You're assuming right, my love," said Nevada.

Princess Seitan smiled and shook her head. "Fair enough. But that's one finder's fee you won't be collecting."

"Fair enough," agreed Nevada.

"Glad we've cleared that up. So, it seems that Jasper has been in contact with my accomplices in the heist, my considerably less successful accomplices who are now behind bars. And one of them told him how they hired me on the dark web. So Jasper was trying to use the same method to get in touch. Naturally he didn't succeed. All he succeeded in doing was getting me to take an interest in him, and keep an eye on him. Online, you understand. And while I was keeping tabs on Jasper, I found out something. Something that would be very useful for you dudes to be made aware of. For your continued wellbeing. If you know what I mean."

"Thank you," said Nevada with schoolgirl politeness.

"Yes, thank you," I said. "But, without wishing in any way to discourage you and your commendable concern for our continued wellbeing, why are you being so good to us?"

Princess Seitan looked wistful. "I felt a bit bad about leaving you guys in the lurch in that duck shed in Nutalich. It was pretty obvious that at least one of those idiots was likely to start shooting. The whole situation was going to shit, and professionalism had gone out the window." She shook her head.

"Except in my own case, natch," she added complacently. "I got the hell out of Dodge, the way a professional should. But I left behind an obvious shit show. And I left you guys in the middle of it."

"It wasn't entirely a bad experience," said Nevada. "Stinky Stanmer ended up under sedation."

Princess Seitan smiled. "He is an obnoxious little creep,

isn't he? Anyway, consider this visit my way of making things right between us for that."

"We'll be delighted to consider it in such a light," said Nevada.

Princess Seitan looked at me and grinned a mischievous little grin. "Plus it was a little naughty of me dosing you like that, at that rave in Brixton." She turned to Nevada. "He doesn't dance very well," she said, as if reluctantly imparting a minor but unwelcome piece of bad news.

"That's okay," said Nevada. "There's a lot of other things that he does very well indeed."

"I hardly wish to interrupt this torrent of praise," I said. "But what is the information which is vital to our wellbeing?"

Princess Seitan seemed to appreciate the return to business. "Okay," she said. "So it turns out that I wasn't the only one keeping tabs on Jasper. Some other party was doing exactly the same. And I was intrigued. Especially when I discovered that this same party was on the darknet, doing hiring for some rather weird and nefarious jobs, with a very specific profile."

"What sort of profile?" I said.

"Well for a start, they wanted to specify the weapon to be used…"

"A Mauser machine pistol," I said.

"Yes, very good. Again full marks for you. And not just that, but they wanted to hire someone with a dog. An attack dog."

"And did they happen to specify the breed of the dog?" I said.

Her eyes green narrowed but her smile widened. "Yes,

they did indeed. Would you care to hazard a guess as to what kind of pooch they required?"

"It isn't a guess," I said. "They wanted a Doberman."

"If you hadn't already exhausted your full marks quota, I'd give you some more now. So I suppose I'll just have to give you a special commendation."

"Did they also specify a black raincoat and a black hat and dark glasses?" said Nevada. "For the person with the Mauser?"

Princess Seitan shrugged. "I imagine small details like that could have been hammered out once they found someone with the right gun."

"How did you know any of this related to us?" I said.

"The same party who was tracking Jasper, and doing all this recruiting, was tracking you."

This information gave me a very unpleasant feeling.

"And you don't know who this 'party' is?"

Princess Seitan shook her head vigorously, causing her pigtails to whip back and forth. "I've tried to find out," she said. "My, how I've tried. But this is as much as I could discover. I trust it's useful?"

"More than useful," said Nevada.

"You might have saved our lives," I said. "Or someone else's life."

"Always happy to help," said Princess Seitan cheerfully. She lifted her hand beside her head, palm towards us, with three fingers extended straight up and her thumb holding the little finger down. Nevada immediately snorted with amusement.

"What's so funny?" I said.

"Girl scout salute," said Princess Seitan.

Princess Seitan said goodbye and left us, but only after scrupulously washing up her own coffee mug. This was very good manners, but also, as Nevada pointed out, made sure she didn't leave any of her DNA on it.

As soon as the Princess was gone, Nevada reviewed our video doorbell footage. This provided some amusement. All we saw of our visitor was when she first stepped through the front gate. She was wearing a Halloween mask which depicted a smiling cartoon cat, with curvaceous lips and long eyelashes, which suggested she was very definitely a female smiling cartoon cat.

The happy girl cat gave us a cheerful wave and then the screen went blank, so we didn't see how she managed to unlock our very thoroughly locked front door.

"The rest of the cam footage has been wiped," said Nevada. "That girl really knows her stuff." There was a definite note of admiration in her voice.

"She doesn't want us to see her face?" I said. "Why? We were looking at her face all the time she was here and she didn't seem to mind." Then I got it. "We were looking at it but we weren't recording it."

"Except in our memories," said Nevada. "Our fond little memories. I imagine if we'd try to take her picture we would have got quite a vociferous reaction." She suddenly snapped her fingers. "Wait a minute. We might have outwitted her…"

I knew what she was thinking. Our new security measures also included a nanny cam, which we called the kitty cam, since we really only used it for keeping an eye on the cats. It was installed in a high position overlooking the living room. As Nevada played the footage for the approximate time of our guest's arrival we saw the room grow dim and then grow dark.

"She drew the curtains," said Nevada musingly. "Why would she do that?"

Then suddenly the cartoon cat's mask appeared, in dramatic close up, right in front of the camera. It was glowing despite the room being shrouded in darkness. More specifically, its eyes, ears, grinning mouth and tufts of hair were glowing. In trippy colours. "Black light paint," I said.

"And she's shining an ultraviolet light on herself."

"Just for our benefit," I said. "And to let us know that she knew exactly where the kitty cam was."

"But how did she know it was a *kitty* cam?" said Nevada.

"She didn't. She just chose that mask because it was us she was visiting and she knows we like cats."

"Mischievous girl," said Nevada.

More mischief ensued as the lights in the living room were switched on. But all the camera showed us now was the inside of the mask which had been propped in front of it, blocking everything else from view. Stamped inside the mask were the words "*Free when you buy two super-size Zest bars*."

"What's Zest?" I said. "Chocolate?"

Nevada shook her head, consulting her phone. "Soap. The mask is a vintage soap freebie from the 1970s."

Then the image of the mask vanished and the screen went blank. There was no more footage from the kitty cam.

"As I think I might have said before," said Nevada, "that girl really does know her stuff."

21: NOT IMPOSSIBLE

I think it's pardonable that I was very wary when, not long after our exotic guest's departure, I got a phone call from a number I didn't recognise.

Another one.

So I said a cautious hello and waited for the other party to start talking.

"This is Lawrence Lockridge," announced a somewhat hoarse male voice.

It took me a moment to put this together in my head. Lockridge. Lanky Lockridge. Who knew that his first name was Lawrence? But just to be on the safe side I said, "Do you happen to play a reed instrument, Lawrence?"

"I play all of them, son. And you can call me Lanky."

"Sorry if I sounded a little guarded," I said. "It's just that I don't recognise this number."

"I'm ringing you back from my landline. You left messages on my mobile but my call plan on that is invidious.

But I won't worry you with my call plan woes. Erik Make Loud put you on to me?"

I had indeed invoked the name of Erik in the sundry messages I'd left for Lanky Lockridge. And it seemed like it had worked. Eventually. "Yes," I said. "He told me that you guys had both played on the *Murder in London* sessions."

"That's right, back in the day. Erik mentioned that you were interested in those."

"You've spoken to him?"

"Yes, son. Just checking you out. I hope you don't mind."

Since I was still checking him out, I could hardly object.

"Erik said you were looking for a copy of the recording. On vinyl."

"Yes," I said quickly. Although Juno's copy was perfect, I wasn't in possession of it yet, and long and bitter experience had taught me not to count my LPs before they were purchased and safely in my hands. So if I could line up another one, it only made sense to do so.

"I understand," I said, "that all the musicians who played on the sessions received a copy."

"I'm sure we did. As a matter of fact Erik reminded me of that. But unfortunately I misplaced my copy several decades ago."

"Oh."

"Yes, sorry about that. And not just for your sake. It was a blinding session. Some great playing. And not just by yours truly. I wish I'd taken better care of it. But it got lost in the shuffle between my first and second divorce."

"Oh, well."

"But Erik said you were also interested in hearing about making the recording. What I can remember about it."

"Yes," I said. "I am."

"As it happens, you're in luck there. Because I haven't misplaced my memories. Not yet."

"Terrific," I said.

"So would you like to sit down for a chat?"

"Definitely."

"Ah, Erik said there's a very good restaurant in Barnes called Sadie's…" He left this statement hanging in the air. It took me a moment to pick up my cue. "Yes, that's right," I said. "Would you like me to buy you lunch there?"

"Ah, that would be very good of you."

It would. But since Nevada and I welcomed any excuse to dine at Sadie's, and since this would be a deductible expense—paid for by Chloë Loconsole—there was no reason for me not to be generous. With Chloë's money.

So we arranged a day and a time. I asked him to confirm by text, and he did, which had the handy bonus of confirming that his mobile number was the same as Lanky Lockridge's. Or, to put it less tortuously, that he was Lanky Lockridge.

Almost definitely.

"So we're going to meet Lanky Lockridge?" said Nevada.

"Apparently. At last."

"Because even though he doesn't have a copy of the record…"

"And Juno Brunner definitely does," I said.

"And Juno Brunner definitely does, we're still going to see Lanky because he might have information about the recording sessions and what had happened around that time."

"Yes."

"In other words, the murder," said Nevada.

"Yes."

"He might know something about it."

"Yes."

"The way Simeon knew something about it," said Nevada.

"It's rather a longer shot than Simeon," I said. "Lanky didn't keep detailed writings about that period."

"But he could still be in danger," said Nevada.

"He could definitely still be in danger," I said. "Which is why only you and I know about this meeting." I'd said nothing about it to Chloë. I felt a bit bad about withholding information from our employer. But not so bad that I wouldn't get over it.

"Are you sure only you and I know?" said Nevada.

"Well, us and Lanky himself."

"Of course."

"And Erik, I guess," I said. "I mean, he doesn't know I've actually arranged a meeting with Lanky, or the details. But he gave me Lanky's phone number in the first place, and he and Lanky are in touch, so Lanky might have told him."

"Starting to get a bit tenuous," said Nevada.

"I agree," I said.

"However," said Nevada. "Tenuous doesn't mean impossible."

"It does not. And if Erik knows we've arranged a meet with Lanky, he might mention it to someone, and that someone could be…"

"Trouble."

"Yes."

"Even more tenuous," said Nevada.

"Yes."

"But not impossible."

"Definitely not."

22: CRUEL ACTIONS

After the close encounter with Princess Seitan, at least our next surprise visitor gave us some breathing space before turning up, waiting until the following morning before they arrived unannounced on our doorstep.

And they very considerately rang the bell instead of breaking in.

I opened the door with a tiny expectation that it might be Princess Seitan again, and a tiny disappointment that it wasn't.

It was Desdemona Higgins. She was considerably more conservatively dressed than the Princess, but that didn't say much. She was wearing a black bomber jacket, bright orange leggings, white socks and white trainers with orange laces.

She didn't look as worried as the first time I'd seen her—which was the last time I'd seen her—but she did look worried.

"I've come to ask you a favour," she said.

"Well come and ask it inside." I led her into the living

room where Nevada was ensconced on the sofa. Consciously or not, I think she was still reclaiming it after its occupation the previous day by Princess Seitan. She looked up in surprise at our latest guest and greeted her politely.

Neither politeness nor surprise quite being sufficient for her to get off the sofa, though.

Desdemona and I sat down in the armchairs after she'd declined coffee.

"I've come to ask for a favour," she said, looking back and forth at the two of us. "It doesn't have to be a favour. I could pay you."

"I doubt that will be necessary," said Nevada, very uncharacteristically. But then she seemed to have mellowed towards Desdemona since her earlier encounters. "What's the favour?"

"I've got to go to my hotel and get my stuff," said Desdemona. "And bring it here, if that's okay?"

I was a little relieved to learn that this was about something so simple.

As it turned out, though, my relief was somewhat premature…

"Sure, that's absolutely fine," said Nevada. "Chloë's already explained that you might be bringing your things. And staying for a while. So go ahead and bring your stuff."

"Well, that's the thing," said Desdemona. "That's the favour. I wonder if you guys could come and get it with me?"

Nevada looked at me. I shrugged. "Sure," I said. I did wonder, however, just how much luggage this young woman had.

"Fine with us," said Nevada.

Desdemona suddenly leaned forward, gazing at us intensely. "It's not that I need help carrying the stuff, or anything like that. I need help *getting* it. Going to the hotel and getting it."

Nevada instantly understood. "You think there might be trouble?"

Desdemona nodded. "Yes. From Cass. He knows that I'm planning to move out, and planning to move in with Chloë. And he doesn't like it."

"It's none of his damned business," said Nevada.

"It's absolutely none of his damned business," agreed Desdemona. "But that doesn't stop him from being my big brother, and it won't stop him from interfering. From trying to interfere. And he's either at the hotel right now, in our room, or he's hanging around outside the hotel, waiting and watching for me to come back. But if you guys are there it will defuse the situation."

"Defuse it how?" I said.

Desdemona smiled. It was rather an appealing smile, with a sudden hint of childish mischief. "Well, if you're there, he won't dare lose his temper. Cass can really lose his rag, and he can even get violent…" Perhaps she saw something in our faces, or at least in my face because she added hastily, "You know, like throwing things and stuff. Just that. Nothing *really* violent. But mostly what he throws is a tantrum. But if you guys come with me he won't dare do anything like that. He won't want to look uncool or impolite. Not in front of strangers."

She gave us a quick worried look.

"No offence, I mean," she said.

"That's okay," said Nevada. "We are virtually strangers."

"So with you two there," said Desdemona, "he'll be the perfect gentleman." The mischievous smile came back. "Even though he'll be seething inside."

From what I'd seen of Cassio, ever eager to be the gent, and the posh gent at that, this sounded like a fairly accurate prognosis.

Nevada apparently thought so too, because she was nodding, "That all sounds fine. Of course we'll accompany you and get your things and make sure Cass is on his best behaviour."

"Like I said, I can pay you."

"Like I said, you don't have to."

"Thank you." Desdemona gave a heartfelt sigh. I hadn't realised that she'd been so concerned about our answer, but clearly she had. She was another one who was good at hiding her feelings. In fact, come to think of it, just about everyone was good at this except me.

"Okay, so I've got a rental car outside. We can go as soon as you guys are ready."

"We're ready now, I think," said Nevada. "Just let me check the cats' bowls…"

We all rose to our feet.

"I didn't want to ask Chloë," said Desdemona. "In fact Chloë has no idea I'm here asking you. I think she thinks the two of us are going to go together, like a united front. To get my stuff. But if she was there…"

"It would set Cass off," said Nevada.

"Right. Like I say, Cass has quite a temper and he can get violent. But the same goes for Chloë." She looked at us, searching our faces to be sure that we understood. "So it's really for the best if she isn't with us. If neither of them are with us."

That was, of course, when the doorbell rang.

And of course it was Cassio.

Though I suppose Chloë would have been nearly as awkward.

He looked at the three of us and said, "All right, Des, what's up? Because obviously something is up."

I was quite impressed with the way Desdemona didn't flinch or try to duck the question. "I'm going to the hotel to get my stuff." She looked at us. "*We* are going to the hotel to get my stuff."

"Why does it take three of you?" said Cass.

"We're just helping Des out," said Nevada.

"And charging her how much?" said Cass, showing his teeth in a mirthless grin.

"As it happens, nothing," said Nevada. "I know, I even surprised myself."

Desdemona sighed. "Cass, they're just helping me out. I just don't want any hassle."

"From me, you mean?"

"Yes, from you."

"When are you going? To the hotel?"

"Now," I said.

Cassio ignored me and looked at his sister. "And where are you going, when you leave the hotel?"

"That's none of your business."

"But wherever you're going, you're going to be with her, aren't you?"

"Yes, of course I am," said Desdemona.

"And you know what happened last time."

"People change, Cass. I've changed, and she's changed."

"That's right," said Cassio. "She's got worse. She's changed for the worse."

"Fuck off."

"Des, you know what happened last time. And you said if you were ever tempted to get back together with her—"

"I know what I said," said Desdemona. "Now fuck off." Then, as an afterthought, "And mind your own fucking business."

Apparently fucking off and minding his own fucking business was more of a mental or spiritual state which didn't actually involve Cass taking his physical leave of us, because he made no move to do so. But Desdemona nevertheless seemed quite content with this arrangement. Presumably since he'd shut up.

So we all filed out of the house in an uneasy group. Desdemona led us to her rental car, parked in the street outside the Abbey. "When did you get this?" said Cass surveying the boringly grey, though very shiny and new, vehicle.

"This morning," said Desdemona.

"I didn't know anything about it."

"You weren't supposed to."

With sibling tensions so obviously simmering, Nevada and I had already decided that we didn't want Desdemona at the wheel, or Cass for that matter. They might think it was a good idea to wrap the car around a tree just to prove a point in their endless bickering, but such a notion didn't much appeal to us.

So during a quick murmured conversation in the kitchen while we'd put out food for the cats, we'd worked out what we were going to do.

"I'll drive," I said, as soon as we got to the car and Desdemona pressed the fob to unlock it. Before any objection could be uttered, I opened the front door and got in on the driver's side. Nevada, as we'd planned, promptly opened the back door and said, "I'll ride in the back with Desdemona."

The notion of this procedure was to separate the Higgins twins—of course they weren't twins, but Jasper's mendacious persiflage was annoyingly infectious—and by having one in the front of the car and the other in the back, we'd prevent any squabbles developing. Or at least prevent them developing beyond the verbal.

Plus, crucially, it thwarted either of them from actually driving and having the chance of wrapping the car around the aforementioned tree. Which would be undesirable for all sort of reasons.

The brother and sister were staring at us, standing outside the car as we sat inside it. After a minute or two of this, Nevada and I were starting to feel a bit silly, if truth be told. But the Higgins siblings caved soon enough, Desdemona first, handing me the fob and getting into the back to join Nevada in a surprising show of obedience.

Cass took a moment longer, making a point of standing

huffily on the pavement before getting into the car beside me and slamming the door. This was rather a wasted gesture because the door had been designed to close smoothly and quietly, dampening any attempts at petulant display.

At least all four of us were now in the car.

"Okay," I said, "so what's the address of the hotel?" I was staring at the satnav feature on the dashboard and desperately trying to work out how to operate the fucker, while trying to appear businesslike and casually in control. I wished Agatha was here.

"You don't need that," said Cass. "It's only just up the road."

"In Putney," said Desdemona.

"I thought you said it was a boutique hotel?" said Nevada.

"It is," said Cass and Desdemona simultaneously and with identical told-you-so inflections. They must have realised how similar they sounded because they both instantly fell sulkily silent.

"There's a boutique hotel in Putney?"

"Just opposite the Arts Theatre," said Cass, curtly but usefully informatively.

We knew the Arts Theatre quite well, Agatha having dragged us there to see a play by her namesake—Agatha Christie—in an amateur production. So I now knew where we were going. I started the car, both relieved and impressed by the instant smooth engine note and we pulled away, much smoothness to be noted here, too, signalled and turned left into Abbey Avenue.

"We may have trouble parking around there," said Nevada.

"It's okay," said Desdemona. "I've got an app where you pay people to park in their driveway. And I've booked a spot near the hotel."

"That's smart," said Nevada admiringly.

"She's only got that app because I told her about it," said Cass sulkily.

As we waited at the traffic lights to turn onto the Upper Richmond Road, Nevada said, "Is it nice? The boutique hotel in Putney?" She was genuinely interested, as was I. We were both astonished that such a thing even existed. And her sincerity must have come across because Cass immediately said, "It's not bad." And Desdemona said, "It's really nice."

No sulky silence ensued this time. Apparently the sibs didn't mind speaking simultaneously so long as they didn't say the same thing.

"So, how much does it cost for two rooms there?" said Nevada.

"One room," said Desdemona.

"The two of you are sharing a room?" I said. I imagined that it would be a non-stop fistfight with both of them in close proximity.

"The three of us," said Cass.

"Three?"

"Jasper, too," said Desdemona.

"You guys are sharing a hotel room with Jasper McClew?" said Nevada.

"He said the budget wouldn't extend to separate rooms," said Cass.

"The podcast budget?" said Nevada.

"Right."

"*McClew's Clues*," I said.

"Right."

The lights changed to green and we turned right onto the Upper Richmond Road and headed towards Putney.

"What's it like sharing a hotel room with Jasper?" said Nevada. Again, the note of sincere interest in her voice removed any taint of small talk.

"It's fine," said Cass cheerfully.

"It's all right," said Desdemona less cheerfully.

"Does he snore?" said Nevada.

"Not that we've noticed."

"Does he take loads of laxatives?" I said, and in the back seat Nevada snorted with amusement. On our first meeting Jasper had indeed dosed himself with intestinal encouragement, and had made us wait until this took effect and he'd had to flee to the bathroom for his noisome fulfilment.

Cass and Desdemona exchanged a look. Something not so easy to do with one in the front of the car and the other in the back. I got the impression that my laxative remark came as a surprise to them, but one that retrospectively made sense. "He *does* spend a lot of time in the loo," said Desdemona.

The notion of a bijou luxury boutique hotel nestling in the heart of Putney—or rather, lining one of the boulevards in the traffic-haunted commercial wasteland approaching Putney—was a little implausible, to say the least. So I was as sceptical as Nevada.

But it would have been an oddly pointless thing to lie about and, sure enough, a minute or two after we drove past the Putney Leisure Centre, the Thai restaurant, the sushi and noodle place, and the bubble tea bar, there it was. On our left, a discreet grey marble and smoked-glass façade located between a vape shop and the little organic bakers where we regularly purchased our sliced loaf of Putney sourdough (good, if a tad salty).

We drove past the hotel, turned right into the side street which housed the post office depot, where I'd been to collect shipments of vinyl on more than occasion, and then down Ulva Road, a favourite of local graffiti artists for obvious reasons, and finally into Ravenna Road. This was where Desdemona had booked a driveway for us to park in. We left the car there and walked back across the main road to the hotel, which was only moments away. Handy parking spot. So kudos to Desdemona, though I was sure it wasn't cheap.

But then this was the girl who'd rented a car to collect her luggage.

And been willing to pay for our help, although it hadn't come to that.

At the glass-and-marble hotel entrance both Desdemona and Cass took out their swipe cards but Cass beat her to it and swiped us in. He seemed determined to be as much in charge of the situation as he could manage, which was proving to be not so very much.

Inside, the small lobby was carpeted—more grey—and cool and quiet with just a whisper of air conditioning. There was a recessed hollow behind a stylish slab of tan wood which was notionally the reception desk, but it was unattended and the place was altogether deserted. Apparently hotel staff had largely been abandoned here in favour of automation like the swipe cards.

Which would prove to be just as well, considering what was about to happen.

We walked across the lobby, which took us about two seconds because it was a very small lobby, to the far wall, which consisted of more grey marble. And the lift which, just for variety, had mirrored doors where we were able to look at ourselves—a rather glum bunch, I have to say, while we waited for it to respond to Cass's swipe card. Then we all crowded inside. It was only just big enough for the four of us. This was a bijou hotel, all right. We stared over each other's shoulders at our own reflections in the walls of the lift, which were also mirrored.

We rose silently for a few seconds to the top floor, which wasn't very far up. Three floors. As I say, bijou. But when the lift door opened, the corridor looked surprisingly long, with two doors on either side of the grey carpeted space and another one at the far end.

We walked along to the one at the far end, Cass authoritatively taking the lead.

He strode up to the door and knocked briskly on it, paused for a moment while he looked at the rest of us, as if to check if we had any questions, and then rapped again. He gave it a few seconds and then said, "Looks like Jasper's gone out."

I was probably not alone in being relieved about this.

Cass swiped his card and the door clicked open.

He led us inside.

"This will only take a second," said Desdemona.

"Since when did it only take you a few seconds to pack?" asked Cass, rather snidely.

"Since I pre-packed everything first thing this morning," said Desdemona.

Game, set and match.

We were standing in a very small, square lounge dominated by a white-leather, two-seater sofa and two matching armchairs. Nevada and I sat down on the sofa while the siblings did their thing, whatever that proved to be, ready to intervene if and when necessary. This hotel room, taken as a whole, was surprisingly large, when you took account of the two bedrooms leading off it, and the bathroom.

One of the bedrooms was a twin-bed affair. We saw this as Desdemona opened the door and went in to get her stuff. Evidently the siblings' quarters. While she did this, Cass gave a fed-up sounding sigh and said, "I'll just use the loo. Back in a moment." He went to one of the other doors and opened it.

For a moment, he just stood in the open doorway and then he made an odd sound deep in his throat, as if reacting to some kind of appalling social gaffe.

It was such an odd sound that it had us immediately up on our feet.

We went over and stood behind Cass, who was blocking the open doorway of the bathroom. He was silent and unmoving, both of which were unusual for Cass. Nevada put her hand on his shoulder and moved him gently aside. He stirred as if waking, then he moved like a cooperative, dutiful child and stood away from the door.

Now we could see into the bathroom.

The light had come on automatically when the door opened, flooding this place, with its white tiled walls, mirrors and chrome, with a brilliantly intense illumination.

Rather too brilliantly intense given what we were looking at.

The first thing we saw was bad enough, given its associations.

The floor of the bathroom was black marble, or fake marble. But whatever it was, the black surface made the silver mermaid lying on it stand out emphatically. It was on the floor just inside the entrance and it insistently drew the eye. It was the first thing you saw when you opened the door.

But it wasn't the last.

As far as I could tell, the mermaid was the same one I'd seen on Juno Brunner's houseboat. Or of course it could be one of the other identical replicas made for the movie. I might have been able to work out if it was Juno's if I'd tried to pull on the mermaid's arms and open it.

I wasn't about do that.

I didn't know if Cass had seen the movie or whether he knew enough about the details of Jackie Higgins's murder to understand the implications of the silver mermaid's presence here. But if not, there was plenty more to clue him in.

Because Jasper McClew was lying on the bathroom floor, in front of the shower stall on a large white bath mat.

His small body fitted quite comfortably on it, especially

given that he was curled in a foetal position. There was very little blood on the mat, just a few red dabs on the white fabric.

It seemed to have come from his head. His hair was matted with blood.

Then I realised why there was so little blood, because I saw the towels, white towels bundled and thrown on the floor in the corner. There was quite a lot of blood on those.

Someone had been doing some mopping up.

Nevada must have thought the same thing because she stepped back out of the bathroom and moved quickly to the door that led to the corridor. I stepped out of the bathroom, too, moving past Cass who was standing there, calm and expressionless as if waiting in a queue.

As I moved out of the bathroom, he went in. He seemed remarkably calm, after his initial reaction, but I didn't have time to think about that now.

I went across the lounge and joined Nevada, who was crouching by the door to the corridor, looking at the grey carpet.

Not entirely grey.

When you inspected it carefully, just inside the door, there were traces of a dark smear that someone had done a pretty good but not perfect job of cleaning up.

Presumably blood is easier to remove when it's fresh.

Nevada and I stood up and looked at each other.

"This is where he was hit," I said.

"Someone got him when he opened the door," said Nevada.

Just then Desdemona emerged from her bedroom with

two large suitcases. "Right," she said cheerfully. "I'm ready to rock." She looked at us, then at Cass, who came striding out of the bathroom.

"He's still breathing," he said.

"What do you mean?" said Desdemona.

Cass ignored her. I imagine he'd had a lifetime of experience doing this. He was taking out his phone. "I'm calling for an ambulance now," he said.

"What's going on?" said Desdemona, staring at us. She dropped her suitcases—they were heavy enough to thud despite the carpet—and hurried to the bathroom. Cass stepped aside to let her in, and did nothing to warn her. Both rather cruel actions in my view, and I should have and would have done something to stop her…

But my brain was only just catching up with what had happened in here, and beginning to process it.

Nevada was a little quicker off the mark.

She went into the bathroom, moving swiftly, and dragged Desdemona back out.

Desdemona had the palest of skin and I would have bet that it couldn't get any whiter. But I would have lost my bet. Her face was now a terrible drained white, a striking contrast with her turquoise eyes which gaped, huge and intense and staring blindly around as if trying to find something to look at which would comfort her after what she'd just seen.

She was breathing like she'd run a marathon.

Nevada wrapped her arms around Desdemona and hugged her in an intense, strangely businesslike embrace. She looked at me over Desdemona's shoulder as she hugged her and at the same time she spoke to Cass, who was busy on his phone. "Can you call the police, too?" she said. "After the ambulance?"

Cass looked up at her. He seemed oddly in his element, handling this crisis, quiet and efficient. I guess he was in charge at last and on some level he was enjoying it. "Yes," he said. "You lot had better clear out of here. There's no point all of us having to deal with the police and all the rest of it."

He didn't have to ask us twice. I went and got Desdemona's suitcases. They were terrifically heavy but I was so pumped with adrenaline they might as well have been empty.

I carried them, and Nevada led Desdemona by the hand as we left the room.

We looked back at Cass.

"Thank you," I said.

"Thank you, Cass," said Nevada.

Desdemona said nothing.

"That's all right," said Cass, as if he'd given us a light for a cigarette.

"Don't touch anything in there," said Nevada, nodding towards the bathroom.

"Of course I won't," said Cass, disgustedly.

"Touch anything you like," I said. "Just don't touch the mermaid." I realised now that the mermaid hadn't any blood on it. At least, none that I'd seen. Why did that remind me of something?

Of course, the murder on the houseboat. They'd wiped that one clean, too, when they'd killed Jackie Higgins.

Cass's grandmother, I remembered with a shock.

"Right," said Cass distractedly. "You lot had better be gone before the emergency services get here."

As the door swung shut behind us he said, "I hope they won't take long."

When we got back to our place I made coffee for Desdemona.

If I was a proper detective, I would have given her a whisky, or at the very least a double brandy. But the thinking about the effect of alcohol on people who'd experienced profound shock had moved on a little since the golden age of detection. Anyway, she seemed grateful for the coffee. Or at least grateful for the gesture of it. She didn't drink much of it, but I wasn't offended.

After a few minutes, she went into the guest room where we'd put her suitcases and closed the door. Presumably to have a lie down.

I certainly would have, in her place.

And Nevada and I were grateful. Because it gave us a chance to talk.

"Notice anything about Cass's reaction?" said Nevada.

"Surprisingly calm," I said. "Suspiciously calm."

"Right."

"Except when he first opened the bathroom door."

"Good point," said Nevada. "But, still, it was almost like he was expecting this."

"Expecting it, but not quite ready for what it looked like when he actually saw it."

"Exactly," said Nevada. She was grinning at me. It was the grin of the crossword addict who was about to add the final word to the puzzle, with a flourish.

"On the other hand, darling," I said gently, "Cass is a control freak. And maybe he was just really happy and calm because he was in his element, back in control of the situation."

Nevada's smile faded, then she nodded in slow agreement. "That would make sense, especially when he'd just been feeling so out of control with Desdemona leaving the nest. Or do I mean flying the coop?"

"Either will do," I said.

"So, where does that leave us?"

"With a silver mermaid," I said.

"Just like the one on your friend's houseboat," said Nevada.

"I wouldn't say we were friends," I said. "She does have a very nice dog, though."

"The question is, does she have a silver mermaid, anymore?"

"Only one way to find out," I said.

"This time I'm coming with you," said Nevada. "Nice dog or no nice dog."

23: HANDOVER

We phoned Juno Brunner, resisting the urge to ask her bluntly if she'd tried to kill Jasper by bludgeoning him with her own silver mermaid, and instead arranged to come over the next day to visit her on her houseboat and buy the record from her.

The following morning, we left Desdemona sleeping late in the spare room and went to the bank in Putney, one of the few remaining bricks-and-mortar banks in this or any part of town, and drew out a thousand pounds in crisp twenty-pound notes. The people at the bank very kindly threw in a free envelope.

Then we caught the train to Clapham Junction, Nevada carrying the money and me carrying a sturdy cardboard box to put the record in. It was one I had recycled from a Dusty Groove shipment. That fine shop in Chicago had the best boxes for transporting LPs undamaged.

If Tinkler had been with me we could have discussed the finer points of safely packing vinyl. But since Nevada was with me, we discussed who might be going around trying to kill people.

People including ourselves.

"So, do we really think Juno is behind all this?" I said.

"Well, let's see what we've got on the scoreboard," said Nevada.

"We have a scoreboard now?"

"It's an imaginary one, but none the less useful. Let's see what we've got on Juno, starting with the attempt on Jasper's life."

"Whoever did it, do we really think they were trying to kill him?" I said.

"Oh yes," said Nevada. "Or at least they wanted to give him a hell of a beating and didn't care whether he died or not. Which amounts to much the same thing."

"How is he, by the way?"

"Last I heard from Cass, serious but stable."

"Is that better or worse than Simeon Swithenbank?" The dog-ravaged Simeon had moved away from the forefront of my mind lately, but the attack on Jasper, and his subsequent hospitalisation, had brought all that vividly back.

"About the same, compared to how Simeon is now. Which is slowly on the mend. Poor bastard."

"Poor bastards," I said, making it plural.

Nevada nodded, looking out the window at the landscape racing by as we hurtled from Clapham Junction toward Surbiton. "Simeon is tougher than he looks."

"Let's hope Jasper is, too. But the question is, could Juno have done it to him?"

"She ticks a lot of the boxes," said Nevada. "We know she knew Jasper…"

"She said he was the one who put her on to us. To sell us the record." I involuntarily checked I still had the empty cardboard box safely and Nevada did the same with the rather more important envelope containing a thousand pounds sterling. "Jasper did her a good turn," I said. "He put her on to a nice little earner. So why would she hit him on the head with her silver mermaid?"

"Turn it around," said Nevada. "She'd already made contact with us, and you'd approved purchase of the record. So what further use did she have for Jasper?"

"Very cynical."

"I try."

"But why would she want to eliminate him in the first place?"

"Part of the general policy of discouraging people looking into the original murder," said Nevada.

"The supposition being that Juno is the original murderer?"

"That's the supposition, all right."

As soon as we set foot on the houseboat, Burlap began to bark. Nevada gave me a sardonic sidelong look. "That must have been encouraging when you came here before."

"I almost turned back," I said.

"But you didn't," said Nevada. "That was brave. And foolhardy."

"I agree with one of those," I said.

We entered the living room of the houseboat and found Juno and Burlap waiting for us, sitting in the same places and looking much the same as before—although Juno was rather more smartly dressed, in a black rollneck sweater and a navy blue jacket with military-style brass buttons and epaulettes. And a pair of jeans without paint stains. She was still wearing the grubby espadrilles, though.

Burlap rose up excitedly at the sight of me, or rather at the sight of us, and rushed over to greet Nevada by sticking his nose in her groin. Nevada didn't mind. She even gave his blond perm a pat.

"Straight to the crotch," said Juno, rising to her feet. "Sorry about that. I'd make some off-colour joke about him taking after his mistress, but…"

Now, while the women were bonding over inappropriate dog behaviour, seemed an ideal time for me to set into motion the plan we'd made on the train on the way here.

It wasn't a very sophisticated plan. "Do you mind if I use the loo?" I said.

"No, of course," said Juno. "You know the way." And then, to Nevada, "Sit down."

I went down the length of the boat to the bathroom. The mermaid was still there.

As far as I could see it was the same mermaid.

But, as people kept telling us, there were duplicates.

I tugged the top of this one to see if it opened. It did. And it was still full of deliciously fragrant purple bath salts. And it still had the corner of the little piece of yellow cardboard sticking up like a shark's fin, with its lyrical description of the salts and its insane price tag. Just as I'd left it.

As far as I could tell, it was exactly the same mermaid as the one I'd seen before, untouched. I suppose it was theoretically possible that someone could have replaced it with an identical copy, and added the right contents and made it look just the same.

But if you had two mermaids, why even bother doing that?

I went back to join the women, and Burlap.

Juno looked up at me as I came in. She'd opened a bottle of wine and set out three glasses. None of them featuring cartoon characters.

"You're a good couple," she said.

"Why, thank you," I said, wondering what the hell they could have discussed in my brief absence for Juno to have come to this definitive conclusion. Both wicker chairs were occupied, and also the dog's beanbag, so I sat down on the padded bench under one of the windows.

"You complement each other nicely," said Juno. "Because you…" she was looking at me. "You are, if you will forgive me, a little on the soft side."

"I will forgive you," I said.

She looked at Nevada. "Whereas this one is as hard as nails."

"When I need to be," said Nevada.

"Don't take it the wrong way, darling," said Juno, pouring wine. "In my books it's a good thing. In fact it's high praise. Women need to be hard as nails, sometimes, if they're going to survive. They need to have that capacity. I certainly did."

"Still do," said Nevada.

Juno seemed pleased. "Yes, you're right. I suppose I still do." She handed the wine to us. It was another pinot noir, but this time the bottle had an elephant on the label.

As we sipped the wine, quite without warning, Nevada turned to me and said, "How was the mermaid?"

"Still there," I said, as casually as I could, having been thus blindsided.

"And it's the same one?"

"As far as I can tell," I said.

"There was a whole bunch of them," said Juno, apparently savouring her wine. Her total lack of surprise at our discussion indicated that Nevada must already have said something to her, which threw me considerably. "And people loved those mermaids. A pair of them were pinched while we were still filming. I remember the prop master throwing a paddy about it, and everyone looking innocent. And then when we finished shooting, everybody was madly grabbing them. For souvenirs. That always happens when a film wraps. But those…" she gestured in the general direction of the bathroom, and the mermaid. "They proved especially popular." She smiled her silver-toothed smile. "I imagine they would have been popular anyway, but because of the murder…" She let the implication hang in the air.

"So what you're saying," I said, "is that there was a ghoulish appetite which fuelled people's desire to grab one of them."

"Well, I didn't actually say that they were ghoulish." Juno paused and took a sip of her wine. "But I imagine I might well have got around to it."

I turned to Nevada. "Anyway," I said, "the one here has the same bath salts in it as last time. They look untouched."

Juno's eyes narrowed. "You are a nosy little Vinyl Detective, aren't you? What else did you discover?"

"That you don't need the thousand quid for the record. Anybody who can afford bath salts with a price tag like that doesn't need any supplementary income."

Juno laughed. "Well, they are very good bath salts."

The dog whined affably as if in intelligent agreement and Juno poured us all some more wine. I was looking at Nevada for answers.

"You told Juno why I went into the bathroom?"

"I wanted to see how she reacted," said Nevada.

"And how did she react?"

"Apparently I passed with flying colours," said Juno. "Especially now you've come back and confirmed the mermaid is still there. And filled with expensive bath products."

"Very expensive," I said.

"Juno knew something was up," said Nevada. "As soon as you went to the loo. So I decided to come clean, and at the same time see how she reacted."

"So that's what she did," said Juno. She clinked glasses with Nevada and then with me. "You've got a keeper here," said Juno. "She's a cut-the-shit kind of girl. I like that."

"And she cut the shit by asking if you tried to kill Jasper?"

347

"Yes. Poor Jasper. Christ."

"Have you ever met him?" said Nevada.

"Not in person. But still… And you think someone is going around attacking people in ways that are reminiscent of the movie?"

"Yes."

"How come? I mean, why would anyone do that?"

"We think they're trying to either scare us off, or put us out of action," I said.

"They're not having much luck," said Nevada.

Juno smiled at her. "I can see that. Anybody coming up against you will have to watch it. You're tough and you've got a mean streak." She looked at me. "Which is good for you. Because you're not tough enough or mean enough."

I said, "When you say things like that it hurts my feelings." And both the women laughed.

Nevada's phone rang. She glanced at it and said, "Sorry, I'd better take this." She went out onto the deck of the houseboat. Burlap looked up at her departure and made a disappointed sound.

"She'll be back in a moment, boy," said Juno.

And indeed Nevada was back in a moment, switching off her phone and sitting down again. "Sorry about that," she said.

"No problem," said Juno. "I wanted to ask. Why haven't I read about it? In the news. Jasper being attacked."

"Man hit on the head with an ornamental mermaid?" said Nevada. "It's not really such a sexy headline."

"But…" said Juno, then she stopped herself as if realising something.

"Right," said Nevada. "But it would be if people knew about the connection with Jackie's killing. Then it would make for a very sexy headline. But nobody knows about that. That's a very old, cold case, and no one has made the connection with it. The person who would have made the connection, and would have had a hell of a good time exploiting the renewed publicity, is the very chap who got bashed on the skull. Jasper McClew."

Nevada shook her head regretfully. "It's a pity. He's missing out on the publicity value of his own story."

"My god, you're a cold one," said Juno.

"Not really," said Nevada.

"Not really? This guy is in hospital, circling the drain."

"Not anymore," said Nevada. "I've just heard that he's recovered consciousness and he's been talking. Surprisingly hard little head he's got. It seems he's in better shape than the chap called Simeon, who was attacked by the Doberman."

"Just like in the movie," said Juno.

"Yes," I said. I turned to Nevada. "Jasper woke up?"

"Yup." She held up her phone. "That was Desdemona. She just spoke to Cass, who spoke to him."

"Does Jasper remember anything about the attack?"

"Yes, he does. His memory is admirably sharp and intact."

I could sense the way this was going. "But not of any use to us?"

"Not of much use to us or anyone else. He remembers opening the door of the hotel room when someone knocked on it. And there was someone standing there in a black raincoat, with a black hat and dark glasses."

"Just like in the movie," said Juno again.

"Yes. And they came at him, and that's the last thing Jasper remembers. Not surprisingly."

We concluded our deal for *Murder in London*. Juno watched me with amusement as I checked the vinyl again—was it likely to have changed since I was last here? But I needed to be sure. And it was fine. So Nevada handed over the envelope and Juno counted the money onto the black glass of the tabletop. I noticed that the melted wax and candle stubs had been cleaned off it. Perhaps in anticipation and in honour of this ritual.

"I hate these plastic banknotes," said Juno.

Burlap murmured in agreement.

When we got home, we found that our domestic arrangement had undergone a surprise change.

Chloë was waiting for us in our sitting room, but Desdemona was gone.

"I hope you don't mind me being here while you weren't at home," said Chloë.

"At least you didn't install yourself on the sofa," said Nevada. True, Chloë was politely perched in an armchair.

"Desdemona let me in," she said.

"Where is Desdemona?" said Nevada.

"She had to go out," said Chloë. "She had to go out because of something I told her." She looked at us. "My *nonna* is coming over today."

"I see," said Nevada.

"Do you?"

"Not really, no."

"My *nonna* has invited herself over here." She gave me an amused look. "She's hoping you will cook her a meal."

"No problem," I said.

"She really has taken a shine to you."

"Too bad," said Nevada. "He's already taken."

Chloë chuckled, then grew solemn. "But that's only one reason she's coming here. That's her excuse. The real reason is that she's got wind of the fact that Desdemona and I are going to be staying here. Together."

"And she disapproves?" said Nevada.

"Very much so. If Desdemona was here, along with my grandmother, there would be quite a scene. Quite an unpleasant scene… What's so funny?"

Nevada and I exchanged a glance. She let me explain. "It's just that Desdemona said almost exactly the same thing about you and Cass. When she went to pick up your luggage."

After a brief pause, Chloë said, "Well, she's quite right. If I'd been there I might have punched him. The thing about Cass is…"

We never did get to find out what the thing about Cass was, because just then the doorbell rang and Chloë's *nonna* Raffaella arrived. She bustled in, holding a bottle of wine wrapped in impressive-looking blue paper. Chloë and she embraced and kissed, and then Raffaella kissed Nevada and myself, and thrust the wine at Nevada. "I've brought some wine. My contribution," she said. "It isn't from the Rhône, I'm afraid."

As apologies went, that one was monumentally insincere. Because the wine was something called Stefano Amerighi Syrah. It was, of course, Italian. And it would prove to be superb. But right now Raffaella was sniffing dramatically. "Something smells nice," she said.

"Doesn't it?" said Chloë. "That's what I was thinking all the time I've been here."

This morning before we'd left to get the record from Juno, I had done the prep work for lunch, so it would be quick and easy when we got back. The fragrance haunting the house was lingering from these earlier efforts. Now Raffaella went into the kitchen, searching for the source of it. She lifted the lid off the frying pan, holding it at a careful angle so the condensation didn't spill everywhere—something I always forgot to do.

She peered in at the sliced green crescents. "*Zucchini*," she said promptly.

"*Zucchini*, right. We'd say courgette."

"And garlic, and…?"

"Turmeric. Fresh turmeric. Diced and gently fried."

She replaced the lid on the frying pan as I turned on a low heat under it and got the chestnut mushrooms and a side of salmon out of the fridge. Raffaella watched with keen attention as I put the salmon in the air fryer, the super-budget air fryer Nevada had tracked down for us. She read the logo on the side. "Gino D'Acampo," she said triumphantly. "Italian."

"So it must be good," I said.

"It must."

While the salmon was cooking—a speedy fifteen

minutes—I went to grate the zest off an organic lemon, but Raffaella took the grater and the lemon out of my hands. "I will do that," she announced. And she proceeded to do so with fearsome efficiency.

Meanwhile I used a slotted spoon to take the fried garlic, turmeric and courgette, sorry *zucchini*, out of the oil in the big frying pan and transferred them to a mixing bowl and ground some black pepper over. By now, Raffaella had grated the lemon zest into a perfect yellow pyramid. It seemed a shame to disturb it, but I did, adding it to the mixing bowl.

"What next?" said Raffaella. She had taken off her expensive-looking jacket to avoid getting stains on it, but that just exposed her expensive-looking blouse to the same risk.

"Next I slice the mushrooms."

"How thick?"

"About finger width…" I said, holding my hand to indicate the size.

Before I said anymore, she got to work, the knife chopping down swiftly and meticulously, while I blitzed the mixture in the bowl with a hand blender. I'd hardly finished doing this when she sliced the last mushroom.

"And now?" said Raffaella.

"Now you can go next door and relax while I put everything on the plates," I said.

She shrugged and went out. Nevada came in with a glass of wine for me and I finished preparing the meal. With the voices of the three women, three very interesting women, rising and falling musically and happily in the next room, I felt an enormous sense of peace and contentment.

It was also helped that no one was trying to kill me at the moment.

The final touch of the meal, the *piece de resistance*, involved dipping the sliced mushrooms in the reserved oil in the big fry pan, the fragrant oil which was golden from the turmeric and infused with flavours of that and the garlic.

I added the sliced and dipped mushrooms to the plates. Nevada, with her finely honed sixth sense appeared at this moment and helped me carry them through, to gratifying cries from our guests.

As we proceeded to eat, Raffaella was vocal in her praise. "The mushrooms are the best part," she said. "They are wonderful."

"They are, *nonna*," agreed Chloë.

"I eat them with my fingers," said Raffaella, proceeding to do so. She nodded at her granddaughter. "She's ashamed of me."

"I've given up being ashamed of you," said Chloë.

When she'd finished devouring the mushrooms—she wasn't merely being polite when she said they were the best part—Raffaella turned to Chloë and said, "Why don't you go out with *him*?"

She took my hand and addressed me confidingly. "She likes girls but she likes geeky boys, too."

"*Nonna*!"

"What's the problem? It's true, you do. You like geeky boys. Why don't you go out with this one? He's nice—he's much nicer than *la strega pazza*." She thoughtfully translated for myself and Nevada. "The crazy witch."

It was pretty obvious that the crazy witch was Desdemona. I began to realise that Chloë had been wise to suggest that Ms Higgins make herself scarce this afternoon.

"And he's intelligent," continued Raffaella, still gripping my hand. "And he can cook." She turned and gave Chloë a triumphant look. "Can the witch cook?"

Chloë sighed. "*Nonna*. Besides everything else, he's in love with Nevada."

"Well, of course he is," said Raffaella. "Who wouldn't be? Of course he is. Look at her." Nevada sat there modestly while everyone looked at her. "She's so beautiful," said Raffaella. "*Bella ragazza*. Look at those eyes." She turned to Chloë, suddenly struck with inspiration. "Why don't you go out with *her*? *La bella ragazza*, instead of *la strega pazza*."

Chloë laughed. "Because she's in love with him."

Raffaella studied Nevada and myself, as though weighing up this statement. "I suppose so," she said, reluctantly.

"And I'm in love with Desdemona," said Chloë.

"Love," said Raffaella contemptuously. "You should think more about cooking. You should be more concerned about your stomach and less concerned about your *fica*."

"*Nonna!*"

(It was pretty obvious from context, but later I asked Nevada what *fica* meant. "Cunt," she said.)

After lunch, Raffaella insisted on washing the dishes and Nevada insisted on drying. Which left me alone in the sitting room with Chloë and gave me the opportunity to do something which was long overdue.

"By the way," I said to her, "what with one thing and another, I hadn't got around to giving you this…"

I took out the Dusty Groove box. She shot me a wide-eyed, startled look, then opened it. Her hands were actually trembling as she took out the copy of *Murder in London*. She slid the vinyl out of the sleeve, took a quick look at it, registered that it was immaculate, then put it back.

Then she kissed me. It was right smack on the mouth and I could taste the wine on her breath as she held her lips to mine.

Of course, that was when Nevada and Raffaella walked in.

"I told you," said Raffaella. "She likes the geeky boys."

24: LANKY

We'd all had enough wine, or at least Nevada and I had, considering we'd started the day drinking with Juno on her houseboat, so we celebrated Chloë's acquisition of the record with nothing stronger than coffee and dessert.

As we ate, we talked about what Chloë should do once she had the reissue of *Murder in London* ready. Nevada and I had been discussing this, and we had some ideas.

"We think you should do an album launch at Olympic Studios in Barnes," said Nevada. "Where the album was originally recorded."

"Of course, the studios themselves are long gone..." I said.

"But we can use the restaurant there," said Chloë. She got the idea immediately, and she liked it. "You guys can organise it for me?"

"Absolutely," said Nevada, happily calculating a further fee.

We elaborated our plans for a while, then Raffaella left

to go back to her hotel and Chloë declared that she'd take the copy of *Murder in London* directly to her mastering engineer, who was based at Abbey Road. This was a very reassuring place for him to be based.

And it was smart of Chloë to take the record there immediately, so it would be safe, or at least as safe as possible, and he could start using it to create a new release of the album.

The only thing that we weren't entirely happy about was Chloë taking the record there unescorted.

She scoffed at our concerns. "I'll be fine," she said. "What's going to happen to me?"

"We don't know," said Nevada. "That's why we want to come with you."

In the end, we compromised by insisting that Agatha should drive her to her destination. Luckily, Agatha was available and amenable to a paying job. A generously paying job, courtesy of Chloë, who hadn't even blinked when Nevada had handed her the bill for obtaining the record— the thousand pounds we'd given to Juno plus our own substantial fee. And she'd paid up immediately.

As Chloë drove off with Agatha, the copy of *Murder in London* in its Dusty Groove box securely belted in its own back seat, like a coddled child, I said, "Thank Christ that's over."

"Not quite," said Nevada. "Our mission is not quite complete."

"How is it not?"

"We got Chloë her record…"

"End of story," I said.

"Not quite," repeated Nevada. "We also promised to help her try and prove the innocence of her grandfather."

"Try is the operative word there," I said. "And we did. Try. And we didn't succeed." Possibly because he wasn't innocent, I thought.

"We're not finished trying," said Nevada.

"Look, love," I said. "I know that would bring us an additional payday, but…"

"I wasn't thinking about the money," said Nevada, and I believed her. "I was thinking about Chloë. And Raffaella. They've had this thing hanging over them for decades. In Chloë's case, all of her life."

"What if he did it?" I said.

Nevada shrugged. "Maybe he did. And if he did, we'll just have to tell them that."

"Wouldn't it be better just to leave things as they stand?" I said.

"As things stand, we still have a card left to play," said Nevada.

"And what card is that?"

"We're meeting with Lanky Lockridge to see what he remembers."

"I wouldn't count on too much from that," I said.

"All I'm counting on is a nice lunch at Sadie's," said Nevada.

"Good," I said.

We were sitting together on the sofa as we talked. Lying together, actually, and now Nevada insinuated her head under my chin, rather in the manner of Fanny, our cat, and lay across my chest. The house was peaceful and silent. So silent that I found myself rather missing the noisy energy of our two Italian visitors.

I even rather missed Desdemona Higgins.

Nevada seemed to pick up on this, too. "Isn't it quiet when the kids leave home?" she said.

It wasn't quiet for long. The phone rang and it was Tinkler. "Is this the lesbian friendly B&B?" he said.

"How the hell did you know?" I said.

"Agatha told me. Chloë told her. Apparently they had a long convivial chat during their drive to St John's Wood together. Beautiful lesbians staying in your spare room. I hope you put up a commemorative plaque."

I was at the kitchen sink, washing the cats' water bowl, when I happened to glance out the window. The first thing I saw, entering from stage right, so to speak, was Chloë. She paused outside our front gate, making no move to enter. Instead she was staring in the other direction. Stage left. Enter Desdemona, hurrying towards her. Both women were grinning widely. And wildly.

Chloë opened her arms and Desdemona literally ran towards her.

And jumped on her.

It was a nimble jump and Chloë caught her with equal adroitness. Desdemona wrapped her legs tightly around Chloë's waist and her arms around her shoulders. Chloë for her part had her arms around Desdemona, hugging her fiercely. They were both still grinning like fools.

Thus they stood there tottering, intertwined.

As a picture of simple bliss it was hard to beat.

I dried the cats' bowl, left the sink and went to tell Nevada that it looked like our houseguests had arrived.

After our earlier lavish lunch we only had a light supper that evening and everybody went to bed early. It was obvious that Chloë and Desdemona wanted to spend some time getting reacquainted and, after working out the bathroom rota with us, they shyly retired to their room. Nevada and I, joined by the cats, did some reading and chatting in bed.

I woke up in the middle of the night, Nevada and at least one cat asleep beside me, and made a fairly urgent visit to the bathroom. On the way back I heard sounds coming from the spare room.

Delighted laughter.

When we walked into Sadie's at the appointed hour, Lanky Lockridge looked like he'd been having second thoughts about spending an indeterminate length of time talking to a stranger, even if it involved a free lunch.

But then he saw Nevada and he brightened up.

We joined him at the table and ordered food and drinks. Lanky wasn't all that Lanky, at least not anymore. He was quite a big man, smartly dressed in a red-, white- and blue-checked Ben Sherman shirt and a brown tweed jacket whose red lining, visible when he reached in his pocket to take out his glasses, matched the shirt rather nicely.

He put the glasses on and studied us with watery but alert pale blue eyes as we made small talk. He had sparse grey hair and his nose was rather large, with the broken veins which indicated heavy drinking. A bad habit that we weren't about to discourage, at least not today.

Any worries about it being difficult to draw Lanky out concerning his work on *Murder in London* proved groundless. After we got a glass of wine in him, he proved hard to shut up.

But if he was garrulous, he was usefully so. And recalling his memories of working with Loretto Loconsole seemed to bring him pleasure.

"Loretto was a blinding piano player, you know," said Lanky. "Sort of in the Horace Silver tradition. They had some top jazz piano men in Italy, believe it or not."

"Romano Mussolini," I said.

Lanky blinked at me in surprise. "That's right," he said. "That's exactly right."

"Mussolini?" said Nevada. "Surely no relation…"

"His son," I said.

Lanky was nodding vigorously. "That's right, Il Duce's son. Top jazz piano player. Nice bloke, too. No one's responsible for their parents, are they?"

"I suppose not," said Nevada.

"Any road, Loretto Loconsole was a great piano man, too, and he could have played on the *Murder in London* sessions. But in those days there were all sorts of problems about foreigners playing in England. Musicians' Union rules. You know about that?"

"Vaguely," I said.

"Loretto was here solely as a composer and arranger, not playing an instrument, which meant there was no hassle with the unions. That's why Michael Garrick got the gig on piano, by the way. Well, that and the fact that Mike was a brilliant musician and a genius. Anyway, as I said, Loretto couldn't play piano himself because of union rules but he was more than happy with Mike's contribution."

"It sounds like you liked Loretto," said Nevada.

"Lovely bloke," he said.

"What do you know about the murder?" I said.

"The girl who was killed? The girl he was seeing?"

"That's right," I said.

"Well, just what I read in the papers, really. There was a big fuss about it at the time."

"Was he upset?"

"Who, Loretto? Of course he was upset. Christ, who wouldn't be? And then the record company got cold feet about putting out the record. And it was such a great record, and we'd all put in so much hard work on it. Ah, well," he sighed, toying with his wine glass, rotating its stem. "You win some and you lose some." He looked at us. "In the end they never even released the bloody thing."

"I know," I said. "That's why it's so rare."

"Yeah, sorry I couldn't help you out with a copy. Like I said, mine is long gone."

"We found one," said Nevada.

"Really?" Lanky seemed genuinely pleased for us. "That's great news. Erik said you were planning to use it to master a reissue."

Tinkler must have told Erik that. Still, it was no secret. "That's right," I said.

"Because the master tapes have gone missing," said Lanky.

"That's right," said Nevada. "But a vinyl original can be even better than a master tape," she asserted authoritatively, "if the tape's in poor condition and the vinyl is immaculate."

Lanky was impressed. "Your missus knows about these things," he said, looking at me.

"She certainly does," I said. She certainly does now, I thought.

"Well, when the reissue comes out, maybe I can get a copy?"

"Of course," I said.

"We'll send you one gratis," said Nevada.

"Thank you. Very kind of you. I should really try and find copies of all my recordings with Loretto."

My thoughts had begun to drift away from Lanky and his reminiscences. It had seemed clear to me that he wasn't going to offer anything especially useful, and lunch was winding down to a pleasant enough but dull conclusion.

But this remark suddenly caught my attention.

"You recorded with Loretto Loconsole again?" I said. "After *Murder in London*?"

Perhaps Lanky had sensed my drifting attention because he seemed pleased to have reawakened my interest. "Oh, sure," he said airily. "Loretto really loved my playing. Even brought me over to Italy to record. I did a bunch of sessions with him there. He flew me to Rome, all above board, got all the proper permissions and everything. Can you imagine? Hiring me instead of local talent. And I played with his missus, too."

"Sorry?" I said. "Whose missus?"

"Loretto's."

"You mean Raffaella?" said Nevada.

"You've heard of her?"

"We've met her," said Nevada.

"Lovely lass. If you see her again, say hello for me, will you?"

"Yes," said Nevada.

"And you said you played for her?" I said.

"Played *with* her. With."

"She's a musician?"

"A singer, son. Not a jazz singer. Pop. One of the biggest girl pop singers in Italy in her day. I think she did Eurovision once. Didn't win, though. Pity. She was a great little singer. Wrote her own stuff, too. Just basic chords you know, on a guitar, and then Loretto would orchestrate them. And she would write the lyrics. Anyway, I played on a session for one of her songs. It was fabulous."

"What was the song called?" said Nevada.

Lanky shrugged. "I can't remember, sorry. And it would have been in Italian anyway."

"Don't worry," I said. "We'll track it down." I reflected that it should be easy enough to find. It would be the song by Raffaella Loconsole with Lanky Lockridge on saxophone.

We finished dessert and the wine and called for the bill. As we said our goodbyes and Lanky snuck a kiss—on the cheek—with Nevada, she said, "It's a relief to know you don't think he did it."

Lanky looked at us blankly. "Sorry, say what?"

"It's a relief to know that you don't think Loretto killed Jackie Higgins."

"Who says I don't think he did it?"

All around us people continued eating and drinking. Cutlery rang on plates and there was laughter and conversation and the quiet commotion of music on the restaurant's sound system. As we stood by our table, however, we were in a tense little zone of silence. Lanky was staring at us.

"I liked Loretto," he said. "Don't get me wrong. And I loved working with him. And it was all none of my business. I don't know whether he did it or didn't. Not for sure. He had his alibi and he got off, so good for him."

I said, "So why would you even think he did it?"

"Because that murder weapon, you know the silver mermaid? I saw him with it. That's why. He had it in his hotel room. A few days before the crime took place."

25: LITTLE BEATNIK

We got home to find our houseguests were heading out. "We'll be back late," said Chloë, kissing me and Nevada.

"Don't wait up," added Desdemona, and she kissed us too, having apparently been infected by these continental customs.

"The note will explain everything," added Chloë as they disappeared.

The note explained that Chloë's grandmother was on her way over and that consequently Chloë and Desdemona had scarpered until the coast was clear. Sure enough, Raffaella arrived shortly.

"I was eating a meal in a restaurant," she announced, hanging up her jacket, "and it was so terrible that I got up and walked out. I paid, but I got up and walked out. I just left it there. My plate with my so-called meal on it. I told them they should be ashamed of themselves. But I left a tip. A pretty big tip. Because it's not the waiter's fault. It's the kitchen's fault. It's the chef's fault. I told them to tell the chef what I thought of his cooking."

She removed her high-heel shoes and set them carefully to one side of the hall, displaying a somewhat different philosophy to her granddaughter in this matter. "So there I was, in the middle of London. Angry and still also hungry. I thought, where can I be sure of getting a good meal? And I thought, that boy can cook. Why don't I go see that nice boy who can cook with his beautiful girlfriend and his nice cats?"

She smiled at Nevada and myself, and indeed one of the cats, Fanny, who had wandered through from the sitting room to scrutinise Raffaella's shoes. "Okay," said our guest. "What are we going to eat?"

Nevada and I had of course only recently returned from our late lunch at Sadie's. But, luckily, I'd already laid the groundwork for an evening meal, expecting to have our lodgers to feed. Raffaella followed me through to the kitchen and started asking questions. "What's this?"

"Diced red onion marinating in lemon juice."

"Why?" She found a spoon and took a small sample from the bowl.

"It takes the heat and intensity out of the onion and makes it almost sweet. The recipe calls for a mild, sweet onion. But I can't get those anywhere."

"In Italy you can get sweet onions," she said, adding grudgingly, "but this is also a good method."

"It's handy because it uses the juice from the lemon that was left over yesterday."

"The one that we grated the zest off?"

"The one that you grated the zest off," I said. "That's

the whole point of today's meal. It uses everything left over from yesterday. The rest of the butterbeans…"

"Those beans weren't bad."

"And the rest of the salmon."

"The salmon was excellent. From the Italian air fryer." I didn't disillusion Raffaella by telling her that the Italian air fryer was probably made in China. Instead, I got the remains of the salmon out of the fridge along with the various other ingredients for the salad.

Then I spooned the marinated onion out of the bowl, leaving behind some rather pretty pink lemon juice.

"You should use this for something," said Raffaella, inspecting it.

"I know." I picked up the bowl and headed for the sink.

"What are you doing? Don't throw it away."

I felt enormously guilty. A child caught doing something forbidden and possibly shameful. "But I can't think of anything to do with it."

"Put it in the refrigerator! Save it. Until you think of something."

"I do," I said. "I have." I stared at the bowl of lemon juice, dyed pink by the red onion. "I've put it in the fridge for a few days while I try to think of some use for it. But I end up throwing it away, because I can't think of anything to do with it."

Raffaella carefully placed a saucer on top of the bowl and put it into the fridge. "I'll think of something," she said.

As we sat down to the meal—Nevada and I both took just token helpings, but Raffaella acquitted herself well—we mentioned our meeting with Lanky Lockridge. "He told us he played with you," I said.

"You say he's a saxophonist?"

"That's right. Lanky Lockridge."

"Isn't it terrible?" Raffaella was adding a supplementary drizzle of Sicilian olive oil to her salmon salad. "I don't remember. I'm sure he was very nice. And if Loretto chose him, he must be a very good musician."

"He is," I said.

"We didn't know you were a singer," said Nevada.

Raffaella corrected her. "I was a singer-songwriter. A little beatnik with a guitar playing in coffee bars when Loretto met me. I was going to be a folk singer." She chuckled. "He had other plans for me."

After we'd eaten, Raffaella thanked me for the meal. "So much better than the rubbish in that restaurant. Now I won't impose any further on your hospitality."

"You don't have to go," said Nevada.

"Enjoy your time alone together," said Raffaella. "You won't get much of it with Chloë and the witch staying here." She put on her shoes and jacket, and then turned and wagged a finger at us. "Tell them they can't avoid me forever."

After she was gone, I had a search online for some of her songs. I couldn't immediately find the one Lanky played on, but there were hundreds of others. We played a few.

"Her voice is amazing." Nevada frowned in concentration. "I wish I had enough Italian to know what she was singing about."

Chloë and Desdemona were still out when we went to bed.

We listened for their return, lying together in the darkness. "It's a bit like waiting for the cat flap," said Nevada.

It was.

Eventually, we heard our two wayward visitors return. Lights went on and off. Doors opened and closed. The toilet flushed. Then all was quiet and I drifted off into confused anxiety dreams about what to do with pink lemon juice.

The next morning, we had a surprise phone call from Juno Brunner.

"I'm in the neighbourhood," she said.

"Our neighbourhood?"

"What other one?" she said. "Any chance of meeting up?"

"Sure," I said, although I was far from sure. What was this about?

"Is there a good pub near you?"

"Albert's," I said, and described the location of our little local gastropub, on the other side of the railroad tracks.

"When will they be open?"

I checked the time. "Now," I said.

"Any chance of meeting soon, then?" she said.

"I guess so," I said. "Is it important?"

"Is anything?" said Juno, and rang off.

When Nevada and I arrived at Albert's, Juno was already there. She was wearing the same military-style blue jacket we'd seen her in last time and was sitting at a corner table with Burlap on the floor at her feet with a water bowl in easy reach. "This is a nice place," said Juno as she rose to greet us. "Dog-friendly. Is that why you chose it?"

"It's a lucky bonus," I said.

"And it's a lucky bonus that this guy's here," said Nevada, bending down to greet Burlap. Like me, she'd become rather fond of the dog.

"He's travelling everywhere with me," said Juno, "until we find a new place to live."

Nevada and I exchanged an astonished glance. "You're getting rid of the houseboat?" said Nevada.

The silver fang gleamed in Juno's smile. "Someone got rid of it for me. They firebombed it."

26: THANK DOG

The horror we felt at Juno's announcement was sharpened by an intense sense of guilt.

I knew Nevada was sharing exactly my sensations because she said, "This is our fault."

"Why?" said Juno with a wry little smile. "Did you plant the bomb?"

"No, but we brought the bomber into your life."

"How do you figure that?"

"It was because you were dealing with us that you were targeted," I said. After what had happened to Simeon and Jasper—and very nearly happened to us—there was no doubt in my mind about this.

The silver fang gleamed. "You forget that I came to you. I approached you to sell the record."

"But still…" said Nevada.

"But still nothing," said Juno. "Some fucker is responsible for what happened, but that fucker is not sitting at this table." Burlap gave a little whine. "Or under it," added Juno.

"What did happen?" said Nevada. "Exactly?"

Juno reached under the table to caress Burlap. "I had to take the pooch for a walk. He demanded it in the middle of the night. Sometimes he does that. Weak bladder. So I got out of bed and got dressed, and we went for our little walk. It's nice and quiet at that time. About three in the morning." She gave us an ironic look. "At least it was quiet until the explosion. It lit up the sky. You could see the flames reflected on the underside of the clouds."

"Holy fuck," said Nevada.

"Anyway, that's the only reason I wasn't on the boat when it blew up. That both of us weren't on the boat when it blew up. And sank."

"I am so sorry," I said.

"We both are," said Nevada.

Juno shrugged. "Like I said, it's not your fault."

"We brought this on you," said Nevada.

"Cut that shit," snarled Juno. She was genuinely angry. "This is not on you two. And thanks to you guys, I still had this in my pocket." She took out the envelope we'd got from the bank when we'd withdrawn the thousand pounds. "And it still had the money in it. So at least I have a bank roll for starting a new life."

"Will insurance cover your houseboat?"

"Probably," said Juno. "Eventually. Being an insurance company, they're always looking for a loophole to wriggle through to avoid paying people. But I'm not telling you anything you don't already know." She smiled a rather vicious smile. "Things got very interesting when they found out the fire had begun with the battery on an e-scooter in the stern of the boat."

"So, is there any possibility it could have been an accident?" I said.

"No."

"Why?" said Nevada.

"Because I've never owned an e-scooter."

We all sat quietly and mused on that for a while. Burlap interrupted the silence by noisily lapping at his bowl. Then Nevada said, "Someone converted the battery on a scooter into an explosive device."

"Looks like it," said Juno. "And added some accelerant for good measure. And when the fire hit the fuel tanks, that was that."

"So they planted the scooter on your boat," I said.

Juno nodded. "Presumably with some kind of timer. Luckily, Burlap woke me up before it went off. Maybe he heard something when they planted it."

"Doesn't he bark if anyone sets foot on the boat?" said Nevada.

"He does if he's awake. But he'd been sleeping beside me, and he's a sound sleeper. But maybe that's what woke him up."

"They planted it as a convenient explanation for the fire," I said.

"A very convenient explanation," said Juno. "The coroner would have discovered the tragic cause. A foolish woman had bought a scooter with a cheap Chinese battery. Who knows, maybe I could have been the poster child for

375

a safety campaign. Tighter regulations on lethal batteries, please."

"But you weren't on board, thank god," said Nevada.

"Thank dog," I said.

"Yes," Juno patted the dog. "Bless him and his weak little doggy bladder."

"Where are you staying now?" said Nevada.

"With an old friend who lives in Barnes. Which is why I'm in your part of town. Her husband's dead so she has plenty of room and doesn't mind putting me up. She's an illustrator. You might have heard of her. Coral Thorn."

"No, sorry," I said.

"She does children's books, used to be quite famous. Like you guys, she's a cat person. But, fortunately Burlap gets along with Atkins, her puss. So we can stay there as long as it takes to sort out a place of our own."

"Another houseboat?" said Nevada.

"I think so." Juno looked at us. "In a way, it's good to lose everything," she said cheerfully. "You know, to let go of the past. Perhaps it's just as well. Clean sweep. Fresh start…"

I realised, moved and embarrassed, that tears were freely flowing down her face.

Burlap got up from the floor and put his chin on her knee.

As we walked back home, we saw a car parked in the little side street between our house and the Abbey. It was not unusual to see a car parked here. What was unusual was the car itself.

It was sleek, it was purple, and it had a Bentley badge prominently displayed on the back of it, so even I had no problem identifying it as a very expensive luxury item.

"My god," said Nevada, "I wonder if Prince is coming to visit."

"If only he was still alive," I said. I would discover I had much more to lament in a moment, because as we walked past the car we were able to see who was inside.

In the front seat were two hulking gentlemen with very shaved heads and very full beards. The beards were dyed in interesting patterns and the hulking bulk of the men was not least due to them having been, once upon a time, in the Swedish special forces. Their names were both Rod, or actually Röd with an umlaut. Röd Strömming and Röd Sill, to be exact.

"Oh, Christ," said Nevada. Then she smiled and waved at them, and they smiled and waved back.

Strange as it may seem, given our initial reaction, the smiling and waving was all sincere enough.

The two Röds were not our problem, and we were not theirs.

The problem for all of us was sitting waiting on our garden sofa outside our front door.

Stinky Stanmer.

He was wearing a bright red cardigan with what I now knew was called a shawl neck and mustard-coloured trousers. Which meant he was visible from quite a distance. "Nice cardigan," I said to Nevada, not entirely ironically.

"Peter Christian," said Nevada. "Their label has some

lovely rabbits on it. Or are they hares? And their knitwear is excellent. Superb range of colours."

"Oh Christ," I said. "You didn't…"

"Sorry," said Nevada.

"Oh well, I hope he paid you through the nose for your fashion advice."

"He most certainly did," said Nevada, somewhat affronted that I might imagine any other scenario.

"Hey bruv," shouted Stinky, who unfortunately had now spotted us.

"Hello, Stinky," said Nevada and I, with an identical note of resignation in our greetings.

"Surprise visit," he said.

"Not such a surprise," I said. "We saw your bodyguards."

"Aren't you going to bring them in and let us give them coffee?" said Nevada, partly because she was always courteous to the hired help, and partly because their attendance would dilute the dread presence of Stinky.

"No," said Stinky. "They'd better stay in the vehicle and make sure it's safe. Around here, someone's likely to pinch it. Did you see my new whip?"

"No, but then we haven't visited your bondage dungeon," said Nevada.

"Ha, ha, nice one. No, 'whip' means…"

"Car, yes," said Nevada. "Excuse me." She gave me a quick look that involved switching her gaze from me to Stinky and back again. I got the gist of it, which was a request for me to try and get rid of our visitor without actually letting him onto the premises, if at all possible. "I'll let you boys chat." She let herself into the house and shut the door firmly behind her.

If Stinky perceived the insult, he didn't let on. He sat back down on our garden sofa and I sat opposite him in one of the garden chairs, wishing we hadn't positioned them quite so close to each other. "Ha, ha." Stinky repeated his false laugh, smiling broadly. "Natchez is dench, isn't she? I mean, she is jokes. I mean, that line about bondage dungeons. You know what, maybe she's right, maybe I should have one..." He paused thoughtfully.

"Natchez?" I said.

Stinky jerked his thumb at the house into which Nevada had so sensibly disappeared. "Natchez."

"Nevada."

"What do you mean?"

"Her name is Nevada," I said. "Not Natchez."

"Are you sure?"

"Pretty sure. Look, Stinky, what do you want?"

"Do you like the new whip?"

"Yes, it's a very nice shade of purple."

"It's a Bentley."

"Yes, I can read."

"It's the Bentley Bentayga hybrid with the extended wheelbase."

"I'm very pleased for you."

"Do you know how much it cost?"

"Look, Stinky..." But there was no way on earth I could derail the boast which was coming my way.

"£189,000," he said, with satisfaction.

"What do you want?" I said.

Stinky shunted along the sofa so he was sitting nearer to me. I resisted the urge to move my chair a similar distance away. He glanced over his shoulder—at the house behind him—then turned back to me and lowered his voice conspiratorially. "It's just as well Natch—Nevada went inside. It gives us a chance to chat properly, privately. About this nang situation."

I had no idea what nang meant, but judging by Stinky's demeanour, he was impressed. "What nang situation?"

Stinky edged even further along the sofa and therefore even closer to me, and leaned forward to compound the situation. I could smell his cologne. It smelled expensive. I wondered if he paid people to advise him on toiletries, the way my beloved advised him on clothes. "All these girls you've got staying with you."

It was an unpleasant sensation to have Stinky know anything about what was going on in my life, and this felt particularly queasy. Nevertheless, I declined to give anything away. "What girls?" I said.

"Chloë and what's her name, Desilu?"

"Desdemona," I said, involuntarily.

"Right. Both of them first-class hotties. Absolutely peng." Then he added piously. "And intelligent, too."

"You've spoken to them?"

"At our meeting."

"You had a meeting with Chloë and Desdemona?"

"Well," said Stinky. "With Chloë. Desdemona tagged along. My word, those two are well into each other." He grinned at me. "But I suspect they're quite adventurous."

"Do you indeed?"

"And let's not forget Natch—Nevada."

"Yes, let's not forget her.

"It must be getting a bit same old, same old with her after all these years."

"*Stinky…*"

"But now's the chance to freshen things up. You've got these three gals under your roof. And they're hella nang galdem. Now, I know you haven't had much experience sexually, so I thought I'd provide you with some tips and advice. I know what you're thinking…"

Stinky definitely did not know what I was thinking at this point. If he had he would have risen smartly from the sofa without delay and fled to the car where his two very large bodyguards were waiting and joined them without pause.

"You're thinking, why is Stinky being so good to me?" said Stinky. "What's the catch? But there is no catch. This is no-strings-attached advice. I just offer it out of the goodness of my heart. Though I wouldn't mind a few pics if you get a chance to take them. So… the thing to do is get Natch, I mean Nevada, involved with one of the girls, Chloë or Desdemona, doesn't matter who's first, see what Nevada thinks. See who she prefers. Get her involved. Solicit her opinion and respect it. Make it a group effort. It will be eventually anyway, if you get lucky. So get Nevada paired off with one of them and then ease your way into a threeway. I know what you're thinking. You want to go for a fourway. Who wouldn't? These three shorties under your roof, of course your mind would tend to go there and involve all of them. But, and I know this will come as a surprise, I'm going to recommend that you steer clear of a fourway. At least at first. Fourways can be tricky. You see, they can all too easily turn into two twoways. A double twoway. And what's the point of that? You end up just having sex with someone while someone else is having sex with someone else, but you all just don't have enough room on the bed. It can end up like having normal sex. It can end up like being in a *couple*. You can find yourself ending up being in a *couple*."

He looked at me to make sure I appreciated the full horror of this situation.

Now it was my turn to lean close to Stinky. Very close indeed. And it startled him. Indeed he moved briskly back down the length of the sofa, to recover his personal space.

"Stinky," I said, "why were you having a meeting with Chloë?"

"Oh. Well, it was about *Murder in London*. What a top album. What brilliant music."

"I see," I said. "So you've heard of Loretto Loconsole's score for *Murder in London*."

"I haven't just heard *of* it. I've heard it. Listened quite closely, a number of times. Like I say, brilliant music. And what a crime that it's so obscure." He smiled at me. "But it won't be obscure for long, if I have anything to say about it."

"Stinky," I said. "Have you been monitoring my activities online?" I had, of course, been reaching out to people looking for a copy of the album. And if someone was sufficiently organised, and sufficiently nosy, they could have easily detected this.

"No," said Stinky. He seemed shocked. "Of course not."

"Really?" I said.

"Really," said Stinky, his bulging eyes gleaming with sincerity. "My personal assistant does all that."

I sighed. I could hear music playing inside the house, quite loudly. I assumed Nevada was playing it in an attempt to banish evil spirits, so to speak. I looked at the evil spirit sitting on the sofa opposite me and I wished I was inside the house, listening with Nevada.

Then I realised how easy that could be. I rose to my feet and said, "Well, Stinky, if you're quite finished giving me advice about threeways and fourways…"

"A threeway is definitely the way to go, at least initially."

"Then I won't occupy any more of your valuable time," I said.

"Oh don't worry about that, mate," said Stinky, impervious to irony. "There was just one more thing."

I repressed the urge to sigh again. "And what would that be?"

"I wanted to invite you and Natch—Nevada to the album launch."

"The album launch?"

"For the reissue of *Murder in London*. At Olympic Studios in Barnes."

I looked at Stinky and he looked at me, his eyes apparently searching my face for a reaction. If he was waiting for me to appear upset, or enraged, he was out of luck. I didn't manifest either emotion. Simply because I couldn't make up my mind which one to go for.

Both seemed equally applicable.

"I am organising the album launch for the reissue of *Murder in London* at the Olympic Studios," I said. It was a long sentence, and long before I finished uttering it, I knew it was pointless.

"No," said Stinky. "I mean, yes, you *were* organising it. But once I offered my services to Chloë, with my radio and television connections…"

"I see," I said. "Well, bye now Stinky."

"Good to see you, mate," he said perkily. Then he nodded towards the house, from which the loud music was ringing. "What is that?"

"I have no idea," I said. Which wasn't true. It was Songhoy Blues, from their album *Résistance*. Discovered by Tinkler, it was fantastic African rock by a band in exile from war-torn Mali, on a rather nice piece of vinyl pressed by Optimal in Germany.

But I wasn't going to tell Stinky any of this. He'd already stolen enough from me for one day.

"It's good," he said.

"Yes, it is," I said. "Goodbye Stinky."

I opened the door and went inside. Nevada was waiting for me. We looked at each other for a moment and then some sixth sense prompted me to open the door again. Stinky was still standing there, pointing his phone in our direction. When he saw me, he pocketed it sheepishly and slunk off.

I shut the door once more.

"What was that about?" said Nevada.

"We were being Shazamed."

27: BOOK ENDS

After hearing about Juno losing everything—except I suppose the most important things—and having to sit through Stinky's Dionysian DIY tips, I felt frankly numb. But the day wasn't finished with me yet.

At least I was spared breaking the bad news about the album launch to Nevada. "Chloë rang," she said when I embarked on my account. "While you were outside, talking to Stinky. She told me everything. We shouldn't blame her."

"I don't blame her," I said.

"She didn't really have any choice. Stinky, loathsome celebrity that he is, can garner much more publicity than we ever could. So we shouldn't blame her."

"I don't blame her," I said. "I blame Stinky."

"Me too," said Nevada. "Chloë was very upset when she found out about our history with Stinky. She's going to apologise in person when she sees us."

"She doesn't have to."

"That's what I said," said Nevada.

"At least we've been invited to attend the launch," I said.

"Chloë said we'd be the guests of honour."

"With Stinky involved, I very much doubt that," I said. At which point there was the rather unwelcome sound of the doorbell. I took a deep breath and went to answer it.

"If that's Stinky come back," said Nevada in a matter-of-fact way, "and he doesn't have his bodyguards with him—and if it's all right with you—I will torture him until he confesses."

"Confesses what?"

Nevada shrugged. "I don't care. I'm easy."

I opened the door and, perhaps fortunately, it wasn't Stinky.

It was Agatha. And she was holding a maroon box with the logo of the high-end Konditor bakery on it. She smiled at us, a rather cheeky smile. "I thought if someone took my name in vain and sent you a dodgy cake, the least I could do is bring you a non-dodgy cake, which really is a gift from me." She handed Nevada the box.

"Thank you," I said.

"You have no idea how glad we are to see you," said Nevada. She'd opened the lid of the box and was peering inside.

"Are you addressing me or the cake?" said Agatha.

"Both," said Nevada.

"Well, just so you know, you're addressing the Double Chocolate Curly Whirly."

"It looks it," said Nevada. "My god."

She went into the kitchen with the cake as I led Agatha into the living room and we sat down.

"Did you know someone around here has a Bentley?" said Agatha. "They were pulling away as I arrived. A brand-new purple Bentley."

"Yes," I said. "It's the Bentayga hybrid with the extended wheel base."

Agatha gave me a look which was in equal measure impressed and suspicious. "Why do you suddenly know so much about cars?"

"Whips, please."

"What?"

"That particular dench whip belongs to one Stinky Stanmer."

"Oh Christ…"

"And I'm not jokes," I said.

"Did he brag to you about it?" said Agatha. "In antiquated roadman slang?" She was no longer impressed or suspicious, but definitely sympathetic.

"About the extended wheel base in particular. Oh, and the fact that it cost £189,000."

"That's not bad," said Agatha. "If it came fully equipped."

"Well, it certainly came fully equipped with his matching bodyguards."

"Those poor Swedish guys? Are they still stuck working for Stinky?"

Nevada came back in with slices of cake on plates. "Yes," she said. "But no more talk of Stinky Stanmer."

"Okay," said Agatha as we tucked in.

"We have bigger fish to fry," said Nevada. "Bigger and considerably more dangerous."

As we ate the cake, we got down to business.

"So this is where we are," said Nevada. "We've got the record."

"I know," said Agatha. "I drove it to Abbey Road."

"But we haven't solved the mystery," said Nevada. "And we are coming around to the view that we may simply have to accept it might never be solved."

"Though," I said, "there's always the grim but simple solution that Loretto Loconsole really was the killer."

"Anyway," said Nevada. "The assumption is that we'll never know. So basically we've decided to give up."

"We just want it to be over," I said.

"That's not like you guys," said Agatha.

"But it turns out that even though we might want it all to be over," I said, "we're not running the show."

Agatha finished her cake and set the plate aside. "What do you mean?"

We told her the story of what had happened to Juno's houseboat, and had nearly happened to Juno. And Burlap.

"This has to end," I said.

"Which is why we're so glad you're here," said Nevada.

"What can I do to help?" said Agatha.

"We need to strategise," I said.

"We need to make some command decisions," said Nevada.

"Sounds serious," said Agatha.

"It absolutely is," I said. "And if we don't make the right decisions, someone is going to get killed. Too many people have already come too close."

Agatha was nodding. "And we think all this violence is because someone doesn't want you to find out what really happened to Jackie Higgins?"

"So it seems."

"So it will only end when you stop looking," said Agatha. She licked some stray chocolate off her fingers. "And when whoever is behind this *knows* that you've stopped looking."

"And believes it," says Agatha.

"So how do you go about doing that? Convincing them?"

"Okay," I said. "So everything we tell Chloë seems to end up leaking to the bad guys…"

"So you're going to tell Chloë you're abandoning the investigation?" said Agatha.

"Exactly that," I said. "Although to give her some kind of closure, we're going to offer our best stab at a solution."

"And that is?" said Agatha.

"That her grandfather actually did it," said Nevada.

"She won't like that," said Agatha. "How sure are you that it's true?"

"A lot more sure since we had lunch with a saxophone player called Lanky Lockridge." We told Agatha how he'd seen Loretto Loconsole with the murder weapon, just before the killing took place.

"Not definitive…" said Nevada.

"But damning," said Agatha. "Poor Chloë. Her world's going to fall apart when you tell her."

"Which is why we want to be sure," I said.

"Sure?" said Agatha.

"As sure as we can be," I said. "We at least owe it to Chloë to confirm with Lanky that there could be no mistake, before we cave the ceiling in on her."

"And make sure it wasn't just the wine talking," said Nevada.

So I got my phone and called Lanky. To my enormous relief, he answered right away; I just wanted to get this over with. After our initial greetings and some fulsome thanks from him for his free lunch, I got down to business.

"Look, Lanky," I said, "are you absolutely certain Loretto Loconsole had one of the silver mermaids?"

"No," said Lanky, categorically.

I stared at Nevada and Agatha in astonishment, and relief.

"What?" I said.

"He had *two* of the mermaids," said Lanky.

"Two?"

"I remember he said he was going to use them as book ends."

And I remembered what Juno had said about a pair of them going missing and the prop master having a fit. My heart sank. I didn't know quite what to make of this new piece of information. But having two potential murder weapons didn't seem to make Loretto any less of a suspect.

"Okay, thank you, Lanky," I said. "That's great." Although it wasn't really great.

"No problem," said Lanky.

Just before I rung off, a thought occurred to me. "Oh, by the way, while I've got you…"

"Yes?" said Lanky.

"I've looked high and low for that Raffaella Loconsole song, the one you played sax on," I said. "And I just can't find it."

Lanky laughed. "That's because it doesn't have my name on it. Not my proper name. I've got some kind of Italian pseudonym. I was Luigi something."

"Oh," I said. "That would explain it." But something was nagging at me. A discrepancy here somewhere. "But I thought you said all your Italian recordings were legit and above board?"

"They certainly were."

"Then why the pseudonym?" I said.

"Because I didn't record it in Italy," said Lanky patiently. "I recorded it here in London."

"Say that again."

"I recorded that song in London."

"With Raffaella Loconsole?"

"Yes." More patience from Mr Lockridge. "It was her song."

"Why the Italian name for you?"

"Because she wasn't supposed to be recording here. Union rules. She was flying under the radar, so to speak. So we recorded it in London but we had to pretend it was recorded in Rome. So all of us invented Italian names for ourselves."

"All of you?"

"All of the lads from the *Murder in London* sessions. Except Erik, because we didn't need a guitarist on that song."

"So Erik didn't know about it?"

"I don't know why he would. He wasn't there."

"But Loretto Loconsole was there?"

"Of course he was. It was his missus. And he was the arranger. And, come to think of it, he played the piano on it, since we were pretending it was recorded in Rome anyway." Lanky chuckled. "So he was the only one who didn't have to invent an Italian name. We pissed ourselves laughing, making those up…"

"How long was she here?"

"Raffaella? In London?"

"Yes."

"I don't know. A few days. At the end of the *Murder in London* sessions."

In other words, when Jackie Higgins was killed.

28: MOST LIKELY SUSPECT

I said goodbye to Lanky Lockridge and hung up the phone. Nevada and Agatha were looking at me. They knew something was up.

"What is it?" said Nevada, gazing into my face.

"Let me ask you a question," I said.

"All right," said Nevada.

"Let me ask both of you a question."

"Okay," said Agatha.

"If a married man is having an affair with an unmarried woman, and that woman is murdered, who's the prime suspect?"

"The married man of course," said Agatha promptly.

"Not necessarily," I said.

"Oh, I see," said Agatha. "A *married* man. Then I suppose his wife could be the prime suspect."

"Right," I said. "She would at least tie for first place in the most-likely-suspect sweepstakes."

"But in this case the wife was in Rome at the time of the

killing," said Agatha. She looked at Nevada. "That's what you told me, isn't it?"

"Yes," said Nevada. But she wasn't looking at Agatha. She was looking at me.

"That's what we told you," I said. "And that's what we were told."

"By Chloë," said Nevada.

"And I'm sure she believes it," I said. "Because nobody even knew Raffaella was in the country at the time of the murder."

"Was she?" said Nevada.

"She was in London. Doing a covert recording session with Lanky Lockridge, among others."

"Holy shit," said Nevada.

"But nobody knew about it," I said. "Certainly the police never knew about it. Or the newspapers. There was never a whisper about Loretto's wife being on the scene."

"Raffaella…" said Nevada, putting it together in her head.

"Excuse me for a second," I said. I went to my laptop and did a quick search for a song by Raffaella Loconsole with sax played by someone called Luigi. I didn't need the last name. I found it immediately.

"What are you looking for?" said Agatha.

"This," I said. I pressed a key and a clip of a song began to play. A song ostensibly recorded in Rome, but actually recorded in London, in 1969.

"Is this it?" said Nevada.

"Yes," I said. The evidence, I realised, in a murder case.

The doorbell rang and we all looked at each other. I went to answer it. I opened the door and Chloë was standing there, looking up at me with an urgent appeal in her eyes, biting her lower lip.

"I'm so sorry," she said, hugging me.

For a vertiginous instant I thought she was apologising for something else entirely, but then I realised she was talking about Stinky Stanmer. "I had no idea he was your…"

"Nemesis," I said, gently disengaging myself from her embrace and leading her into the house. We walked into the living room where Nevada and Agatha were both on their feet, looking at us rather tensely.

"Agatha," exclaimed Chloë happily. I'd forgotten that they'd met. They exchanged a kiss and I had the fleeting thought that it was a pity Tinkler wasn't here to see that.

"Well, I'd better be making myself scarce," said Agatha, glancing at me and Nevada.

"Must you go?" said Chloë.

"Work," said Agatha. "Sorry. Take care, Chloë." Then, to us, "Bye guys. Good luck." Then she was gone.

Chloë turned to us with a quizzical look, but then she heard what was playing on the computer and gave a glad little cry. "*Nonna*'s song," she said. She perched on the sofa beside the laptop, nodding in time to the music and then began to sing along. She looked at us. "It's a very clever song," she said. "It is built on a double meaning. It is called 'Immerso' and it's about a girl who's in too deep. You know, like out of her depth in water? *Immerso nell'acqua*. But she is also *immerso nell'amore*, out of her depth in love."

Perhaps the icy jolt that went through me showed on my face.

Because Chloë tapped the laptop keyboard and switched off the song. She looked at me and then at Nevada. "What's wrong?" she said. "Why did Agatha leave so quickly?"

Nevada and I sat down. "When I was looking for your grandfather's record," I said, "I met a sax player called Lanky Lockridge. He played on the soundtrack for *Murder in London* and your grandfather liked his work so much they became regular collaborators. He even flew him over to Rome to record."

I looked at Chloë. "But he also played on that song by your grandmother." I hesitated. It's not easy knowing you're going to pull someone's world apart. "And he said he didn't go to Rome for that. Because it was recorded in England. For contractual reasons, they pretended it was an Italian record, but they did it right here in London."

I saw Chloë relax, which was heartbreaking in its own way. "So they broke the law?" she said.

"They broke the Musicians' Union rules."

"Is that so bad? Why are you looking so serious?"

"That's not the important thing. The important thing is it means your grandmother was here."

"She was here?" said Chloë.

"When the killing happened."

She looked from me to Nevada and back again. "No," she said.

She'd set out to clear the name of the grandparent she loved. And she'd succeeded.

But only by implicating the other grandparent she loved.

"No," said Chloë again. "She's an elderly woman. People have been attacked, physically attacked…"

"You said she's really good at using the internet."

"She is. So what?"

"Apparently, she's really good on the darknet, too," I said.

"Someone has been hiring people," said Nevada. "People with guns, people with dogs…"

"*No*," said Chloë.

The doorbell rang again. I went to answer it. Raffaella was standing there.

Raffaella was laden with bags from an Italian delicatessen and she was preoccupied with manoeuvring these through the door as I let her in. Which was just as well, because I didn't want her to get a good look at my face. I also didn't know what to say to her, but she was keeping up a continual monologue so she didn't notice.

"You are always cooking for me," she said. "It's nice, but it's not fair. So this time I thought I would provide lunch. I could cook for you, but this is quicker. I just brought you some nice things. I brought you a lot of nice things. I hope you like them."

She took the bags into the kitchen and then came into the living room. Nevada and Chloë and I were all standing up, looking at her as she came in.

Raffaella looked at us and stopped dead.

There was a long silence in the room. Then she shrugged and sat down on the sofa.

"So, you know," she said.

There was the sound of the cat flap and Turk came wandering in, perhaps drawn by the tense silence. Cats can sense these things. She walked across the room, the very quiet and very still room, and then jumped up to sit, of all places, on the sofa beside Raffaella.

I repressed the urge to grab Turk and take her away.

Raffaella was still looking at us. She searched our faces. "You know," she said again.

"We do now," said Nevada.

Certainly any doubt we might have had was banished by Raffaella's reaction.

The rest of us sat down.

Turk pawed at Raffaella and Raffaella absent-mindedly chucked her under the chin. "So, you're a detective after all," she said. "Well done. I'm sick of pretending anyway." She looked directly at me, those brown eyes, so reminiscent of her granddaughter's, gazing into mine. "How did you find out?"

"The song," I said. "The one about the girl who's in too deep."

Raffaella smiled. She seemed genuinely pleased. "Yes. 'Immerso'. That was a good song, one of my best, written fast. In just a few hours, sitting up late at night in my hotel room in London." She looked at Chloë. "I came to London as a surprise for your *nonno*." She turned to me. "Because I suspected what he was up to. He was never such a faithful man. So I decided to take him by surprise. I flew in under an assumed name, with a false passport. It was all much easier in those days. No computers. And I had done it before, to avoid the union regulations when I had recorded in London. And I recorded this time. Just the one song."

She scratched Turk under the chin and Turk luxuriated in the attention, purring ferociously. Her simple animal unawareness of what was going on was sort of heartbreaking, too. "I wrote that song as a warning," said Raffaella, "to Loretto. But he wouldn't heed the warning. You know what he told me instead? After the recording, he told me he was leaving me for this girl, this whore, the girl in the water."

She caressed our cat, smiling. "They had an arrangement. For when they wanted to meet at the houseboat. He'd told me all about it when I demanded to know. By that time he didn't care what he told me, he was so crazy about her. He would leave a message for her, a postcard. No writing on it. Just a postcard in an envelope, her name and address typed on it with a typewriter. I had a typewriter. I could buy a postcard. I left a message for her. And I went to meet her that night."

Turk rolled over and offered her furry underbelly to Raffaella. Raffaella smiled fondly and began to stroke it. "Loretto had shown me those silver mermaids he had obtained. I liked those mermaids. They were very pretty. They were also very heavy. I took one with me. I just meant to hit her with it. Teach her a lesson. Maybe make her look a little less pretty. But…" She shrugged again. "Once I started hitting her, I just didn't feel like stopping."

Turk suddenly caught Raffaella's hands in her paws and they played for a moment, a mock struggle.

"I took the other mermaid back to Rome with me," said Raffaella. "I liked it. Also, a reminder for Loretto if he decided to stray again."

"He knew that you'd done it?" said Chloë.

"Of course he knew."

Chloë gave a little shudder. I thought she was going to break down and cry, but she didn't. Raffaella shook her head, apparently in disgust at this reaction.

Turk had grown tired of the sparring game she was playing with Raffaella and now she hopped down off the sofa and wandered out of the room.

"Do you think he should have told the police?" said Raffaella, glaring at Chloë. "If he'd told the police they would have taken me away, and we would never have had our baby. If I had been put in prison, your father would never have been born. And you would never have existed. Think about that."

Grandmother and granddaughter stared at each other. Chloë didn't look like she wanted to cry anymore. She looked savagely angry.

As much to break this intolerable tension as because I wanted to know, I said, "You brought it back with you this time? The other mermaid?"

Raffaella seemed to welcome the question. She nodded. "I thought it might be useful. I didn't know exactly what I was going to do with it. But I knew I wanted to frighten people off, if they started looking into what really happened in 1969."

"Why did you have to do all this?" said Chloë. "All these things you've done now? It's not like what you did all those years ago. To Jackie…"

"To the whore."

"That was terrible. But least I can understand it."

"Of course you can. Who couldn't?"

"You were hurt, you were angry… But all this. All this you've done now. So many years later. It's all in cold blood."

"What did you expect me to do?" said Raffaella. "Did you expect me to sit by? Like your *nonno* expected me to sit by when he ran off with that swimmer girl? You know, he was actually talking about leaving me for her? Well that was never going to happen. I didn't sit by then and I didn't sit by now."

"Oh, *nonna*," said Chloë.

"What are you complaining about?" Raffaella pointed at me. "When I met him and saw he was a nice boy I left him alone. What more do you want? I could have killed the witch. Do you know that? I could have had the witch killed. At any time. And I didn't." She stared angrily at Chloë. "What more do you want?"

I have quite a few bad memories of this time, but perhaps the worst is the look on Chloë's face at that moment.

29: PHONE CALL

Raffaella was arrested and remanded in custody. In other words, she was put in prison for a relatively short time while she waited to be put in prison for a relatively long time. She was an Italian national but all the crimes had taken place on British soil, so she would be tried here.

Meanwhile Chloë threw herself into her task of reissuing *Murder in London*.

There was a blaze of publicity around the project now, which virtually guaranteed the record would be a success.

Not that we needed another copy, but Nevada and I did finally visit the Empty Cover Couple—Valerie and Desmond—and had a look through their records. I didn't find anything of interest, but on the plus side nobody tried to shoot at us.

And then there was Chloë's album launch, of course. It took place on a crisp autumn evening and Nevada and I had a pleasant walk from our house to the Olympic Studios in Barnes. The place had a festive atmosphere, with music blasting from within. And there was quite a crowd outside, waiting to get in. Among them was Cass, who hurried over to us. He seemed quite excited. "Did you know that Stinky Stanmer is going to be here tonight? In person?"

We said we did know that.

"And Stinky curated the music," said Cass. "I mean the music we're listening to now, while we're waiting. Isn't it amazing? Listen to that…"

It was amazing. And rather familiar. It was the Songhoy Blues, from their album *Résistance*. The track was called 'Sahara' and it featured Iggy Pop. It was definitely a highlight, I reflected philosophically.

"Where does he find this stuff?" said Cass, shaking his head in wonder and admiration.

Just then a purple Bentley glided up. A purple Bentley Bentayga. It came to a stop some distance from us, where the crowd on the pavement was thickest. One of the Röds got out of the front—I think it was Röd Strömming—and then opened the back door.

When you open the doors on a Bentley at night there's a little courtesy light that comes on. It casts a brilliant circle on the ground, with a black shadow capital "B" at the centre of it.

A classy touch.

Stinky stepped out of the Bentley into the adoring crowd, one of the Röds at his side. The other one drove the hybrid Bentley away to a nearby side street where they could plug it into a charger.

Once Stinky was safely inside, we followed. The album

launch was actually pretty good fun. Tracks from *Murder in London* were played by a group of crack musicians, including Lanky Lockridge and Erik Make Loud, who replicated their original solos from the album. They were obviously taking great pleasure in the performance, and so was Chloë, and in fact so were Nevada and I.

When we walked home afterwards we did notice some police activity nearby, but we didn't think anything of it, until the next day when we found out what had happened.

Stinky had on one occasion, not so long ago, left his bodyguards behind and experienced some considerable unpleasantness as a result. This took place at what Jasper McClew called the Great Kentish Heist. Ever since then, Stinky insisted that both Röds accompany him to any public event. That is what they'd done at the album launch the night before.

Which meant Stinky's purple Bentley Bentayga had been left unattended.

And someone had managed to overcome its sophisticated security measures with surprising ease, and drive off with it, never to be seen again.

The only clue was left hanging on the electric charging point.

A Halloween mask of a cartoon cat face which had originally been given away with two bars of soap.

Speaking of Jasper McClew, he never did manage to make contact with Princess Seitan, so his Great Kentish Heist project had to be put on the back burner. Jasper himself recovered from his beating swiftly and apparently completely. It would have been a great pity if he hadn't, because his *Murder in London* podcast proved to be a triumph. Which was gratifying, because it fed into the success of Chloë's reissued album.

Chloë herself had become involved in the podcast, as had Juno Brunner.

When Chloë learned of the destruction of Juno's houseboat—the bomb planted by people working for her grandmother—Chloë offered to pay for it. When Desdemona learned of the situation, *she* offered to pay for it. This was no idle proposal, since as a result of the podcast Desdemona now had considerable money of her own.

But neither of them had to pay for it, because the insurance came through.

Juno bought a new houseboat and made no attempt to replicate the old one. She did, however replicate her sound system. She hired me to replace the vintage hi-fi components and find replacements for her drowned record collection, all paid for out of the insurance money. And quite generously, it must be said.

But the upshot of all the offers to pay for a new houseboat meant that Juno became friends with Desdemona and Chloë. The granddaughter of the woman she'd loved, and the granddaughter of the woman who'd killed her.

* * *

When Chloë and Desdemona got married that October, the brides were given away by Juno and Nevada.

Cass and I were the best men. Tinkler provided comic relief and held onto Burlap, who was a little too eager to join the ceremony.

Chloë's grandmother sent flowers from prison.

That wasn't all; she also sent a message.

One day Chloë and Desdemona came to visit us. While I was in the kitchen preparing coffee, Chloë came out to join me. "My *nonna* wants to talk to you," she said.

I looked at her, seriously surprised.

"I have no idea what she wants to talk about," said Chloë. "She refused to tell me. But if you are willing to speak to her, I can arrange a phone call." She gave me a searching look. "You are under absolutely no obligation to speak with her. And I won't be in any way offended if you refuse. I will completely understand."

"No, it's okay," I said. "I'll speak to her."

"I really mean it. You can say no and I won't be offended."

"I believe you," I said. "Go ahead and arrange the phone call."

"Okay," she said. And then she looked like she instantly regretted having made the offer.

Which I understood, because I instantly regretted accepting it.

But having agreed, I didn't feel I could back out. That didn't stop my regret escalating as the day and the hour of the call grew nearer.

The way it worked is that Raffaella would call me, presumably from prison, at a prearranged time. And if I didn't pick up the call, that was that. We'd have missed the window and would have to laboriously arrange another one.

Or not.

So it would have been the easiest thing in the world not to pick up the phone when it rang, promptly and punctually.

I picked it up.

Running through my mind there were images of a burning houseboat, of a frail but brave Simeon Swithenbank finally emerging from hospital having undergone life-changing trauma, both physical and mental. Of Jasper lying bludgeoned and apparently lifeless on a bathroom floor. Of a cake, intended for us, full of acid. Of a blasted windscreen and a maniac with a gun…

And, of course, ground zero.

Jackie Higgins dead in the bed where she'd been waiting for her lover, her life beaten from her.

This was who I was about to speak to.

The woman behind all of that.

The call connected and Raffaella's voice came on, firm and cheerful and to the point.

"You know that pink lemon juice from your recipe?" she said. "I've thought of a very good way of using it up."

ACKNOWLEDGEMENTS AND NOTES

Thank you to the usual suspects—Nick Landau and Vivian Cheung at Titan for supporting the Vinyl Detective. Stevie Finegan and John Berlyne at Zeno for having my back. George Sandison and Rufus Purdy for editing at Titan. Miranda Jewess, Guy Adams and Ben Aaronovitch, who were all instrumental in getting the series off the ground. And Martin Stiff for consistently great cover designs.

Particular thanks this time around to Dicky Howett and Matt West for providing photo reference of the period movie camera for the cover art.

To Ken Kessler, who offered expert advice on the hi-fi on Juno's houseboat.

To Sarah Brimer for knowing more about my books than I do, and for providing Italian translation even though she's German!

Special additional thanks and full marks to Rufus Purdy for knowing that Amy Winehouse's 'Valerie' was a cover version of the Zutons' original.

And very special thanks to Ann Karas for her invaluable help, reading and commenting on early drafts.

ABOUT THE AUTHOR

Andrew Cartmel is a novelist and playwright. He is the author of the Vinyl Detective series, which was hailed as "marvellously inventive and endlessly fascinating" by *Publishers Weekly*, as well as the Paperback Sleuth series, which features many of the same characters. His work for television includes a legendary stint as script editor on *Doctor Who*. He has also written plays for the London Fringe and toured as a stand-up comedian. He lives in London with too much vinyl and just enough cats. You can find Andrew on Twitter/X at @andrewcartmel and listen to his weekly radio show, Vinyl Detective Radio, via Medway Pride or Reclaimed Radio.

THE PAPERBACK SLEUTH: ASHRAM ASSASSIN

Andrew Cartmel

"An intriguing mystery with an amoral protagonist. Who knew the world of paperback books could be so deadly?"

Ben Aaronovitch, author of the Rivers of London series

"Andrew Cartmel introduces a new kind of heroine, entirely immoral, somewhat venal and slightly foxed."

David Quantick, Emmy award-winning producer of *VEEP*

When a set of rare, impossible-to-find yoga books are stolen from a West London ashram, its leaders turn to Cordelia Stanmer, the Paperback Sleuth, to recover them—a set-up that's a little awkward as they've previously barred her from yoga classes for selling marijuana to their students. But what begins as a hunt for missing paperbacks soon becomes a murder investigation as those involved with the ashram can't seem to stop dropping down dead—murdered with a whisky bottle to the head or a poisoned curry. Can Cordelia work out who the killer is and bring them to justice before they bring an end to her sleuthing for good?

THE VINYL DETECTIVE: NOISE FLOOR

Andrew Cartmel

"Get ready for glow sticks, raves and murder at 150 beats per minute."
Ben Aaronovitch, author of the Rivers of London series

The Vinyl Detective enters the fraught and frenzied realm of electronic dance music.

Lambert Ramkin aka Imperium Dart, techno trickster and ambient music wizard of the 1990s, has gone walkabout, disappearing from his palatial home in Kent. This isn't the first time he's pulled a vanishing act, but he's never been gone so long before and his wife—wives, actually; it's complicated—are worried and hire the Vinyl Detective to find the old rascal.

But does Lambert, a man known for his love of outlandish and elaborate pranks, really want to be found? And are the increasingly strange scenarios that the Vinyl Detective and his friends keep finding themselves in due to his trickery or something far more sinister?

For more fantastic fiction, author events,
exclusive excerpts, competitions, limited editions and more

VISIT OUR WEBSITE
titanbooks.com

LIKE US ON FACEBOOK
facebook.com/titanbooks

FOLLOW US ON TWITTER AND INSTAGRAM
@TitanBooks

EMAIL US
readerfeedback@titanemail.com